I0710587

BERKELEY BRED

Mercer

GREY**HUFFINGTON**

Copyright 2024 © Grey Huffington
All rights reserved.

The content of this book must not be reproduced, duplicated or shared in any manner without written permission/consent of the author except for the use of brief quotations or samples in a book review, blog, podcast, or social media post without harmful or infringement intent.

In other words, if you're looking for inspiration, don't draw it from this book or any book that you read in the Grey Huffington realm. I employ you to dig into your brain and find something suitable to write and for your audience to read. My creativity is precious and duplication (of any manner) is inconsiderate, repulsive, highly offensive, and dead-ass wrong. Please move around.

In the event that this work of fiction contains similarities to real locations, people, events, or situations, it is unintentional unless otherwise expressed by the author.

instagram.com/greyhuffington

LET'S GET SOCIAL

Instagram:

Grey Huffington
(Cover reveals, releases, etc)
Instagram.com/greyhuffington

HuffingtonHQ
(News, updates, etc —headed by Team Huffington)
Instagram.com/huffingtonhq

TikTok:

Grey Huffington
*(Vlogs, updates, promotional images/videos, etc — headed
by Team Huffington)*
TikTok.com/@greyhuffington.com

Pinterest:

Grey Huffington
(*Inspiration, quotes, snippets, visuals, boards, lifestyle, etc
—headed by Team Huffington*)
https://pin.it/695pEOV9m

TRIGGER WARNING

PLEASE READ THIS SECTION!

Seeing this note means the book you are about to read could contain triggering situations or actions. This book is subject to one or more of the triggers listed below.

Please note that this a universal trigger warning page that is included in Grey Huffington books and is not specified for any particular set of characters, book, couple, etc.

This book does not contain all the warnings listed. It is simply a way to warn you that this particular book contains things/a thing that may be triggering for some.

This is my way of recognizing the reality and life experiences of my Romance friends and making sure I

properly prepare you for what is to unfold within the
pages of this book.

violence
sexual assault
drug addiction
suicide
homicide
miscarriage/child loss
child abuse
emotional abuse
mental illness
infidelity
infertility
cancer
criminal activity

CONTENTS

To the women who are still waiting on
their person, this one is for you.

May he be brave
May he be strong
May he be bold
May he be kind
May he be gentle
May he be consuming in the best ways
May his heart be big and pure
May his intentions be good
May his home be your safe haven
May his world be adventurous
May his eyes be your undoing
May his dick be the perfect place to land

G

BERKELEY BRED

Mercer

GREY**HUFFINGTON**

PROLOGUE

WARNING: IF **INFIDELITY** IS **TRIGGERING**, PLEASE **DO NOT START THIS BOOK**.

Hole so big that not even Mother Earth, herself,
can fill it
Not even the biggest bandage
The largest white gauze
The cleanest surgical packing
Or softest cloth
Hole in my chest so goddamn big for every wrong
reason

Angled slightly, I tilted my chin downward for a more snug grip on the chin rest beneath it. My slight discomfort was the easiest to blame for the bow hair no longer brushing against the strings of my violin and the harmonious sounds were no longer striking the air—gently.

And the words? I asked myself, needing to know the reasoning behind their discontinuation.

Discomfort. I stood by that. Though it was beyond the physical and deeply rooted in the mental and emotional state I found myself in on days like today, discomfort was still the source of my agony.

New territory, new feelings, and new desires haunted my soul like a devil after God's most faithful servant. If, for a second, I stopped to evaluate all the things, I'd be caught. For the first time in the last two years, I desperately wanted to be captured, but my hesitancy was a result of being held hostage by the fear of what's next.

Because that thought alone scared me, I decided each day to continue frolicking in the familiar spaces that knew my face, knew my heart, and knew my head. It wasn't safe here, for either of them, but it was home.

Feeling as though my positioning was better, I laid the bow against the violin. The strings and hairs collided again, producing a melodic sound that forced me to close my eyes and open my heart as the words of my newest piece came to me.

Hole in my chest so goddamn big for every wrong

reason

As I lay here bleeding
From the heart
I'm wondering how it's still beating
How I'm still breathing
How my head is still ringing
How my eyes are still seeing
How my body is still feeling
You

Momentarily, I stopped to pen more words on the paper in front of me, afraid they'd all disappear if I didn't. From experience, I knew that waiting to write wasn't in my best interest. I'd lost too many lines to keep count when embracing that method.

I'm wondering if I'll ever be free
Or will there ever be a time, again, when you'll
notice me?
Because this hole so big in my fucking chest
I don't know that I'll survive here much longer
This...
This big hole in my chest has me wondering
Is this my life now
Or am I already dead?

Unsure of the last line, I erased it from the paper I was jotting on. The residue of the dark pink end piece scattered across the paper as the back of my hand pushed them around until they fell off. I lifted the sheet and dusted the remainder before sitting it down again to continue what I'd started. The finish line was a few syllables away.

> *Is this my life now*
> *Or have I died yet?*

I rephrased. The finality of the poem felt surreal.

For two days, I'd tried my hardest to complete the piece but failed. My mind and heart hadn't agreed on many words, not until now. Freeing myself from the shame and guilt of my failed marriage just hours before was possibly the reason for the sudden overflow of creativity. It didn't matter whether it was factual or not. My gratitude for the flexibility my mind had just exercised would remain the same either way.

Though the poem was complete, my heart was still aching and my head was still spinning. I slid the hairs of the bow across the strings once more, this time refusing to interrupt the connection until the healing I yearned for was upon me. The depths of me were filled to their capacity with the euphony produced with each passing second.

The darkness covered me. *Comforted* me. *Caressed* me. Wrapped me like a warm blanket in a space that once kept my blood warm and my heart thumping without fail. But over the last two years, there has been a shift. The chill that slipped into the home we'd built, I imagined, would only last a month or possibly two.

Years later, the chill had grown into something more devastating. It manufactured a draft in our home that left it cold, uninviting, and with an echoing silence that made speaking, feeling, or thinking dreadful tasks. At some point, I stopped floating on clouds and began drowning in the icy, freezing rain they produced.

Oh, Phillip. My chest tightened. How beautiful he was in the beginning. Our marriage aged beautifully for three years before havoc had it in a chokehold. For two years, I'd been fighting to redeem the happiness we once felt, but to no avail. The love our connection was built on had been lost in translation many times, leaving every issue we faced unresolved.

Our closet was spilling with skeletons. Skeletons that I hadn't placed there but was left to unpack on my own. It was too much work for one person. It was intended for two. Alone, I wasn't an army. I was hardly a factor. I'd barely put a dent in the pile. However, with Phillip's help, we could clear it out and kiss it goodbye. That was far too much to ask.

A therapist, marriage counselor, God, a community rooting for us, and each other would be the perfect team. Several times, I'd acquired most of the members, but there were a few I couldn't get on board—one being the man who was once the love of my life. The other being the family of attorneys that condoned his infidelity and foolish ways.

It was because of their lengthy history in divorce court that I had yet to file. Without a doubt, I'd lose everything I'd worked so hard to gain over the last six years due to the simple fact that he was my husband when my rise to stardom took place. It was heartbreaking to even consider.

Making my peace with the fact that my marriage was over had been a year-long process that had proved unsuccessful on so many lonely nights. But tonight, the progress I'd been hunting finally appeared in my line of vision. Like my happiness and full possession of my heart, I was after it.

Until I had my feeling, I strung my violin. And finally, when I met the eye of the storm within me, my arm fell to my waist. My lungs released the breath I'd been holding. My heart released the love I still harbored. My head released the idea that our marriage stood a chance. My guilt was released with the understanding that I'd lost in love and it wasn't at all my fault.

The lack of ability to produce children with Phillip had sent him running for the hills. At the beginning of our disconnection, there was distance and nothing more. As the days turned into months, the distance transformed into something darker, something scarier, something forbidden when you vow to have and hold one another.

After a year, there were dark marks on visible parts of his body. Perfume that didn't belong to me stained his clothes. Panties that were a size too small hid within the folds of his laundry. Money, copious amounts, began disappearing. And as of lately, his absences synced with the depletion of funds in our joint account.

Tapping the screen of my phone revealed the consistency of his ignorance. It was after eight. The call I'd placed six hours ago had yet to be returned. Tilting my head slightly toward the left, I closed my eyes. The digestion wasn't at all easy, but it was necessary. Acceptance was the word of the week for me. By the time it was over, I was destined for evidential freedom.

Not the kind that still left room for apology or rekindling. I'd waited far too long for Phillip to approach me with a solution to our issues. The wait was over now. There was nothing he could say or do to repair things inside me that he'd broken. The gradual acceptance over the past year made this moment a bit less invasive, but my heart was still hurting from the procedure that I was unprepared for and didn't predict the day I said *I do*.

Dwelling wasn't my ministry, not on calls that weren't answered or returned, at least. I'd gotten acclimated to his lack of concern during his stints of absence. I connected the Bluetooth speaker to my cell with a few swipes and taps. Sounds of wind chimes, ocean water, and the flute drowned the sounds around me, including my thoughts that threatened me with a pillow full of tears.

Those days, for me, had ended. There would be no more crying, especially not over a man who didn't see me. Didn't understand my value. Couldn't discipline himself enough to stop inflicting pain on me. Refused to right his wrongs and free me from the cage he'd locked me in. Those days, they didn't exist in my world anymore.

Slowly, I twirled my body to the music while progressing toward the bathroom. Everything hurt so bad, but everything felt so good. With each step, I shed a bit more of the thick skin I'd produced as a coping mechanism for the way my love life was shaping. The tough survivor I'd been forced to become wasn't part of my DNA. I didn't belong in the pit that Phillip had placed me in. If I allowed his actions to continue contouring my future, I'd be unrecognizable by the end of the year. I couldn't fathom it.

My fragility was never supposed to be in jeopardy. My softness was never supposed to be up for sale. My vulnerability, *my sensitivity* were not tailored for the auctioning block they'd been on for two years. Reclaiming it all was my new destiny.

Coming to terms with the fact that Phillip wasn't part of the journey and the fact that it was a solo mission once left me weary. Things had changed. I was ready to change with them.

Cold tile fondled my heart, proving that warmth within me still existed. I tiptoed toward the oversized garden tub, leaving my slippers at the door of the bathroom. The stone tub was gorgeous, a place custom-designed for the lovemaking of two people who were in love indefinitely.

In the three years it had sat in the center of the bathroom, Phillip had only been inside once after pulling a muscle. It was far too painful for him to stand in the shower, so he settled for the bathtub, forbidding me to join him.

Crazily, I'd married a gentle creature. Still, in all his mess, he treated me well. It was the marriage that he treated so horribly. The respect he once had for our union evaporated. He was with me just as he was with anyone else he encountered and that was the issue.

In an ideal world, I was not equal to anyone else he'd ever met. I was supposed to be different. I was supposed to be held to a higher degree.

I twisted the knobs on the tub to start the water. Natural bath salts and a matching bubble bath solution followed. Suds crusted the top of the water, covering it completely. The aroma etched away at the heaviness of my head and heart. I felt lighter as the seconds elapsed.

Retrieving the herbal combination to roll it inside of the rose paper was easier with the kit I'd purchased on a whim. It had been a Godsend. Mugwort, calendula, chakra, lavender, and skullcap mixed beautifully to make the perfect, stress-reducing blend that burned well. With a tap of my finger on the small wheel that produced a small amount of water, I sealed the rose-covered concoction.

I sat the kit that included everything from a manual roller to a lighter beside the tub. The robe I wore slid down my skin, summoning small, fine bumps all over. I stepped into the water as it continued to run. My back leaned against the cushioned pad, eliminating the anxiety of pressing it against a cold surface.

Total relief was near. I could feel it in the depths of me. The joint that dangled from my lips perked up at the flickering of fire on the very tip. Smoke clouded my vision as I pulled deeply, ready to feel the effects. This was the only time that instant gratification rewarded me. I accepted it without fail, basking in all its glory.

My lids fluttered slowly, in no hurry to reopen each time they closed. The euphoria I had intentions of searching for found me instead. The blemishes in my world were masked one by one, becoming distant blurs by the fourth pull.

Though I loved Phillip, I loved myself so much deeper. And when the smoke cleared, it would be the only love that mattered. The only love that would remain standing. The only love that would weather the storm. The only love that would survive the fire.

After my herbs had burned to a crispy nub, I occupied my finger with the exfoliating glove that was made of recycled goods. I drenched the textured fabric with the soap I'd created in the center of my kitchen.

A fresh bar grazed my palms every six months. I had the math down to a science. By the sixth month, the final bar was unraveled and sat on the edge of the tub or in the shower where most of them formed to the shape of our hands and got smaller by the day.

My body was a forbidden rest area for non-beneficial bacteria. I scrubbed my skin clean until I was confident there was none left. Or, at least, it's what I made myself believe. Otherwise, I'd be wrinkled and gray when I finally finished sanitizing my body.

I drained the tub of water as I exited. The plush towel waiting for me was wrapped around my body to shield out the cold air. The rug beneath me soaked up the water from my ankles and feet. I patted the excess with the end of the oversized towel and rushed toward the slippers I'd left at the door.

Inside my bedroom, I located the honeysuckle body butter and relieved my legs of their duty. I sat on the soft fabric of the chair that paired well with the vanity I'd thrifted almost four years ago. Limb by limb, I slathered the butter across my skin. My body heat made the application as smooth as the result.

The idea of burying myself in clothes was repulsive. Without a trace of a thread, I trekked toward the bathroom for the final time. I stood in the mirror, finally recognizing my reflection, as I stuffed my toothbrush in my mouth. The minty toothpaste I'd learned the recipe for left my teeth white and my breath fresh for hours on end.

My skincare routine occupied fifteen minutes of my time. After emptying my bladder, the sheets were my final stop. I pulled the thick, soft sheets back and slid between them. I pulled them up toward my chin and rested my head on the satin pillow beneath me.

The throbbing I'd ignored from the most sensitive region of my frame intensified, forcing me to part my legs slightly to relieve the pressure. Shifting my position, I tried my hardest to find comfort. It evaded me without mercy.

"Ugh." I sighed.

Sleeping with a broken heart was no longer a poem in

my rolodex. It was my reality and had been for the last two years. Tonight, however, I refused to lose a wink. Choosing to focus on the contracting muscles between my legs, I parted them wider and altered my position until my back was against the coolness of my pillow.

The low bun I wore proved to be problematic with the new alterations. Sliding slightly until it hung from the bottom of the pillow, I readjusted myself. My comfort was slightly sacrificed, but the change was bearable.

My middle and index fingers sparked a trail of small, fine bumps along my skin as they glided up my legs and toward my centerpiece. Hairless lips greeted the tips. The second introduction involved silky smooth pink flesh that was sensitive to the touch. Finally, my clitoris welcomed my fingertips by plumping itself, swelling almost twice its size to display its arousal so there would be no mistake about its intentions.

"Um."

I shivered. If it weren't me who was touching my pussy over the last six months, then it wouldn't have known human touch. Phillip's mishandling of my heart had revoked his privileges. Not once had he complained, which told me everything I needed to know. He simply began extending his time away from home, feeling justi-fied enough not to explain himself or check in during his extensive stays elsewhere.

I twirled my fingers in a circle, repeating the same movement over and over. The secretion made the explo-ration of my sensitivity pleasurable. My lids sealed, locking in a blurred version of Phillip dangling over my body as he crossed my threshold.

"Ahhhh." The low groan that followed referenced the lover I once knew in Phillip.

He was a man who understood the assignment in the bedroom. Though he wasn't as gifted with the same tool as the three men I'd been involved with before embarking on a relationship with him, it mattered none. Phillip lacked nothing but length. His skills compensated me for it every time.

It was the hardest pill to swallow the first few months after identifying what was happening to us. His infidelity left me in shambles. The thought of him making love to anyone the way he made love to me when he was in love with me made me sick to my stomach.

There was nothing completely over the top when it came to our bedroom adventures. However, I was left satisfied time and time again. Phillip didn't rest until my pussy was spitting up the thick creaminess that lubricated his dick each time he slid into me.

Whatever it took to get me to my peak several times in one session, Phillip was willing to try. That's where his gift rested, *in his willingness*. For the first four years of our relationship, I'd enjoyed every second of it. Since the third year of our marriage, I haven't experienced that side of Phillip.

My intuition said that it was reserved for someone else. The pain of it all had finally dissolved. I refused to dabble in it any more than I already had. The time had come. Moving on with my life, even if we still shared the same space and the same bed, was my focus.

"Ummm."

I initiated my thumb, inviting it to join the flight fight. The two fingers that once rested on my clitoris pierced the small hole that brought me more joy than most of the things life offered. Ruffled sheets were a result of squirming. Gapped lips were the result of instant gratification. I turned both fingers upward and rubbed the ridges of the spot that was the sure way to my constellation.

"Uhhhh. Sh—Uhhhh."

My back arched. My face contorted. My muscles tightened. I had absolutely no control of my limbs as I chased the peak of the mountain that I visited as often as my heart would allow. Everything around me grew shallow as my depths widened to receive more of what I was offering. My fingers responded by climbing further into my cave, covering more ground and touching familiar territory.

"Ehhh. Uhhh. Oh. Uhhh. Shiii—"

I bounced from the bed as the first wave hit. The second wave commanded my silence. The third and final wave locked my limbs and sent me crashing into the bed one last time.

Just like that, I remained until the tingling subsided, the contracting of my pussy ceased, and the stars that had aligned behind my lids disappeared. Slowly, I turned on my right side and curled in a ball. Sleep stormed me as if it had a reservation.

Mercer · Vallei

Sunrise was the most unappreciated alarm clock known to nature. As it rose, intending to peak later, I did the same. My naked frame stretched upward, reaching for all that God wanted me to have before starting my day.

"Thank you."

They were always the first words to come to mind when I opened my eyes, whether verbalized or internalized. My feet made their home in the slippers beside my bed. I grabbed my phone and headed to the place that knew my fresh morning face best.

After handling my morning routine, I was back in my bedroom, staring at the calendar on the wall. I marked a brown dot beside the number twenty. When I flipped the pages up to review the prior month, I counted the brown dots I'd marked throughout the four weeks.

January was his most unruly month. Ten days in total, he'd stayed away from home. However, his consecutive stint is what left my jaw on the floor. Eight days. A week and one day. He'd rested his head on a pillow other than the one designated for him. This month was shaping up to be more of the same.

Valentine's Day hadn't brought Phillip home. It was February 20th. He was six days into his stay, wherever it must've been. The chocolates and roses he'd left on the counter for me remained, withered and catching dust.

A small chuckle evaded my chest. My head slid from side to side.

Sometimes, you have to laugh to keep from cry—

I stopped myself mid-thought. With furrowed brows, I posed a rhetorical question.

Who's about to cry, Vallei?

I didn't wait for an answer because one wasn't required. The tears had dried. My ducts would no longer produce them for a man who obviously cared nothing about their existence. The words of a very familiar, very true poem I'd written weeks prior as an option for my upcoming album began replaying, looping in my thoughts.

It was one of the few that I remembered every word from immediately after writing it. Others, it took a few weeks, sometimes months, to log into my brain for permanent residency. This one, however, proved different.

My mother called me
She cried for me

My mother is aware of any and everything
She called to tell me she saw me in her dreams
And she cried
She cried
She cried
Feeling the pain from miles away
Feeling the pain of me
In her sleep as she lay

It was me that replayed and replayed
She called to tell me that I'm every bit of her
It was obvious to see
I'd hurt the hell out of myself before I let anyone
else continue to hurt me
And she was right
Right she was
There's no amount of dick
No amount of love
That can corrupt or reconsider what I mean to
myself
Or to the world
I wasn't put here to settle & die
Whimper & cry
Take lie after lie
Shrivel & fry
Even my mother knows that I was meant for more
Far more
And that fact,
I won't ignore
So, mother
Wipe your eyes
Though I'm no good at them,
I'm no longer fearful of goodbyes

The silence option on my phone had been released automatically. As a world-renowned poet, busy work began for me promptly at eight. It ended around the twelve o'clock hour, when I completely shut down and tapped into my art. Some mornings were quiet, with no meetings, emails to answer immediately, or calls to take.

When in my creative bubble, my assistant could filter the important tasks from the ones she could handle herself. She left me with as little to handle as possible, freeing me to create leisurely for months to meet my album's deadlines.

As if she'd heard my heart from miles south, my mother's name lit the screen. I swiped right, accepting the call without hesitation. Her voice was stitched with weariness.

"Vallei, good morning."

"Good morning, Mom," I articulated.

The coolness of my sheets rested beneath me as I took a seat on the edge of the bed, somehow remembering I was bare. The robe that clung to the back of the chair that sat in front of my vanity summoned my attention momentarily. At the sound of my mother's voice, I was drawn in again.

"How are you feeling this morning?"

"I'm fine," I cautioned, refusing to pile my problems on her plate.

"But are you really? You can talk about it if you want. I don't mind. I have all morning, sweetie."

Admittedly, I replied, "I don't. I've given this marriage enough mornings of mine. I'm tired. I refuse to keep putting on this sad show. It's time to wrap it up. I feel like now, more than ever, that is possible."

"Because it is. The moment you're ready, you'll know."

"That moment has come, Mom. I want a divorce."

"Vallei." She gasped, knowing exactly what that meant for me.

"I know it's not an option right now, but I will be making strides to be free from this marriage within the next two years. I can't go on like this."

"I know, baby. I just want you to be careful. He has the best team of divorce lawyers in the state of Huffington and the neighboring states on his team. They're not just good, Vallei. They're impeccable. It doesn't matter what's fair; it matters that they win.

"You've worked so hard for everything you've accomplished. Do not give it up so easily. Now that your emotions have been eliminated from the equation, your mind can have its way. That's most important: acting with your head, not your heart. This way, even if he wins, it won't be much."

"I know. I've waited so long to get here. Now that I am, I am ready for what's next. The idea of sleeping beside him whenever he decides to come home feels so beneath me. It's repulsive."

"Yes, you're ready, Vallei," she alluded. The asseveration had come from a much different place than the rest of her declarations. "I hear it in your spirit."

"Good, maybe you can rest your worries now."

"When God sends you the man he created for you, to love and cherish you without having to be told to. Someone who listens to your heart and can accommodate its girth. You're a lover, Vallei. I know it because I am your mother, and you are me, every bit of me. The misuse of your heart is unfair. But God will send you love, baby. You just wait."

"I know," I averred. "I'd like to go now."

"Alright. I'll call you tomorrow sometime, okay?"

"Yes. That's fine."

"I love you, Vallei. Remember, baby, a man's foolish ways are not a measurement of your love or what you deserve. There's only one man who has the power to measure any part of your life at any point. His name is Jesus. Find peace knowing that Phillip has lost the best thing that he could've ever wished upon a star for. You are more than this situation. You are more than the pain you feel right now. You are loved. You are appreciated. You are worthy. You are healed. I declare it for you, Vallei."

"Thanks. I love you, too."

The call ended with my heart twice its size. My mother was flawless without fail. She breathed life into me from the moment she knew of my conception. Thirty-four years later, she was still part of the reason my lungs still had air.

My cheeks threatened me with a good time, rising slightly to reveal the smile that hid itself in plain sight every day. The genuine one that I hardly got a glimpse of. The one I missed as much as I missed myself.

Fine bumps lined my skin as the robe slid onto my body. I opted for nudity underneath, deciding to embrace the wind that made its way up my legs to have a taste of my sweet juices. As I tied the strings in front, my doorbell rang. Simultaneously, my phone sounded behind me.

Ding dong.

With my phone against my cheek and Mal's call answered, I exited my bedroom in pursuit of the stairs.

"Hey."

"What's up, babe? Did that nigga come home or no?" She addressed Phillip's absence instantly, wasting no time punching me in the gut.

"No. But I'm not worried about Phillip anymore. May he remain where he is. I'd rather his absence than his presence at this point."

I descended the stairs, trying my hardest to peep through the glass cut-out in the door to see who was standing on my porch. I wasn't expecting visitors.

"See, that's what I'm talking about. But still, you're better than me. Those locks would no longer fit his key when he made it back. The block feature on my phone would be activated. And silent treatment, chile, that would be my first and middle name."

"I won't give Phillip or this marriage the energy I could be putting into something beautiful. I'd rather profit from my pain than let it put me behind bars. At this point, those are the only two options. And the last one would only give him more to use against me in divorce court."

"Which is when?"

"I haven't figured that out yet, but I will. Until then, I'm here and I'm playing my part, Mal. It's the only way that any of this works out in my favor."

"I know, babe. Just say the word and I can have my cousins beat his ass for you."

"Mal, I don't wish any harm on Phillip—no one, for the matter. It's never that serious for me."

"That's why you have me. I wish that nigga harm, poverty, and a slow, painful death."

Chucking with a shake of my head, I landed on the first floor. The bell sounded again as I did.

"Is that your doorbell? Who is at your door?"

"I don't know. I'll have to open it to see," I reminded her.

Privy to the fact that I'm a loner and visitations are prohibited, the presence of a stranger piqued her curiosity.

"Well, answer the FaceTime. I—"

I stretched the door slightly, only displaying a few inches of my frame. My DDD-cup breasts were loose. For presentation, they required taming. At the moment, I was not interested in caging them behind the padding of a bra.

No one stood before me. Confusion reshaped the features of my face.

"That's strange," I whispered, shutting the door.

"What's strange?" Mal was loud and evidently concerned.

"I guess maybe I took too long to come to the door."

I started for the kitchen. A morning smoothie sounded rather delightful.

"They're gone?"

"Apparen—"

The wiggling of the door handle startled me. I turned, realizing I hadn't locked it behind me. Panic-stricken, I stilled.

"Vallei!" Mal screamed.

"Yes?" Low mumbling was all I could muster as I trained my eyes on the door, locking them until I noticed a lanky figure entering my home.

"Hello?" I asked the person standing feet away.

"Hello!" Mal remained on the phone, yelling for me. "Vallei. Oh, fuck this. I'm calling Jay. Hold on. Him and his boys about to be on the way."

I thought my heart would leap from my chest. My worst nightmare had quickly become my soul's yearning. Scenes of a man with a perfectly sculpted face and the most precious wood between his generous thighs hemming me up and dicking me down the way that my body needed after breaking and entering my home flashed before my eyes.

Take me, my brain begged.

I swallowed the lump of shame that dried my throat. A simple blink released me from the restraints the idea captured me with. My center ached, not quite dismissing the pleasure my imagination provided or the places it wandered.

"Can I help you?"

Dark skin, the blackest I'd ever witnessed, made it hard to recognize anything other than his white teeth and the eyes that gazed in my direction.

"Can you help who?"

"Mal, I have to go."

"Don't hang up this phone! Who is that?"

"It's fine," I assured her. "I'm okay."

I wasn't sure that I was, but I felt okay. The stirring of my heart and my pussy told me that there was no need to freight. The stranger in my home meant no harm. Even his eyes said so. His posture, too. I softened, relaxing my shoulders as I ended the call.

"Will you say something, or are you just going to stand at the door staring at me?"

"Hello."

The bass of his voice nearly caused me to lose my hearing entirely. If I only ever heard it for the rest of my existence, I wouldn't complain. It was deep. It was sultry. It was commanding. And it was sexy.

My God. I could feel my temperature rise. Suddenly, the cool robe felt like it was on fire. I needed it off at once.

"I'd say sorry for entering your home, but I am not," he disclosed.

Gasping, I turned, fully facing the audacious being at the other end of my home. Like a bee en route to nectar, I glided across the floor until I was only a few feet away, inhaling the woodsy notes of his musky cologne.

"Who are you, and what's your purpose for being here, in my home?"

He stood so close to the door that if he moved a few inches, he'd be on the porch again. That was far too much for my pussy to handle. Even the sight of him was enough for her. She'd been neglected far too long to be cut short of an imaginary victory. When my fingers greeted her as the night ended, we'd remember fond moments like the one we were facing.

Instead of addressing the question at hand, he began surveying the foyer that I'd spent a full eight months designing before finalizing with my contractor. It was my personal definition of grand. From the small twinkle in his eyes, he, too, admired the detail. Four large arches followed one another, all the same in color, opening the space while making it feel larger.

"I love what you've done to the place."

He stepped forward, forcing me backward. My neck ached from the deep curve required to see those dark eyes and follow those dark lips that serenaded every fiber of my being. Hands behind his back, he stepped around me, seemingly more intrigued with the spaces combined to make the home I dreamt of than answering my questions.

Because I didn't have the heart to demand anything more of him than he was willing to release at the moment, I followed behind him as if *I* was the stranger in *my* home. He knew his way around. It was evident in his comfort as he made his way from one room to the other.

"You've been here before?" I asked, tightening the robe on my body.

Suddenly, he paused, turning in my direction. His eyes fought to remain on my face. It was a battle he was losing by the second. I folded my arms on my chest, advocating for his victory, though I didn't mind witnessing his defeat.

"Have you?"

"Yes," he confirmed, tilting his head slightly to brush through his facial hair with his fingers.

"Mercer."

Long, slim fingers dangled in the air, waiting for mine. Tantalized by the long, thick veins that protruded from his arms, snaking down and tripling in number as his hand began, I experienced temporary immobility.

"You are?"

"Va—Fleur," I rushed out, taking his hand in mine.

The softness of his hands made me question his occupation and history. I was immediately jealous, feeling as though God had been unfair in his distribution when it came to this man. He lacked nothing physical. Perfection existed. He stood in front of me.

"Fleur, you're a liar."

His statement followed the retraction of his hand as he stepped away again, leaving me to catch up like a sick puppy in search of its owner.

"Excuse me?"

"I asked for your name, the one your mother gave you, not one you've made up."

"Vallei," I disclosed, "Fleur is my middle name. Novelles is my last name. Is there anything else you need to know?"

"Yes, in fact."

"Before I share any more information with you, I need to know why you're here, walking through my home as if it belongs to you."

"It once did."

Taken aback, I sealed my lips and contemplated the words that would come after his. I didn't have any.

"I owned this home years ago, before I went away and decided to sell it. The person I sold it to happened to sell it to you." He examined the guest bathroom.

"Still, that doesn't tell me why you're here."

If he was requesting I sell, then it was not an option. Not yet, at least. I wasn't prepared. I had a world of things going on. Uprooting suddenly wasn't something I could stomach. My art, my album, would suffer greatly.

"Something that belongs to me is here, Vallei."

"I-I'm not sure wh—"

"One million, seventy-six thousand dollars."

"I, uh," I stuttered, unsure what I was attempting to say.

"It's right back there," he said, pointing toward the backdoor.

"In the backyard?" Words found me.

"Yes."

"I had no idea."

"That's the way it was meant to be."

"Right." I nodded, agreeing to the revelation as it hit me.

The brain cells I thought I had seemed to have taken a hike and left me hanging.

"I'm not here for permission to retrieve my funds. This visit is just a courtesy visit, letting you know what is about to happen. At any point, I don't mind tying your pretty ass to a chair and feeding you myself until I get what I came for. That's not what I want to do, but I will in a heartbeat if you attempt to call the authorities or anyone who should interfere with this process. Unless you want it to be their last visit to your home, please don't call them."

"I, uh."

"Do you understand? Rope results in nasty burns on the skin that I simply don't want you to experience. But if you insist on being defiant, I will make sure you feel every—"

Please. Tie me down. Gag me. Fuck m—

"No need to explain. I'm sure you get the point, right, Pretty?"

Well-poised as threats fell from his lips, he continued through my home as he waited for a response.

"I—"

"Yes," he encouraged, stopping again. "The answer is yes."

He depleted the space between us, placing a finger under my chin to lift my face.

"Yes?" His brows scattered, aiming for his hairline as he asked.

Nodding as best as I could, I swallowed the saliva that pooled underneath my tongue.

"Yes."

"Good." With a tilt of his head, he nodded, releasing me from his hold. "There's a team of two. We'll get started and be out of your hair in a day, two at most."

"Out-outside? A team?"

"Yes. I can't quite remember exactly where I buried the four safes. I'll need to search the entire yard."

"I—okay."

"What is it that's on your mind?" His curiosity made his eyes glisten. His ears perked, prepared to listen to whatever came from my mouth.

"I was... I was just going to ask if you could keep a portion of the soil overturned for planting next month."

"A garden?"

"Yes. Please."

"Would you like it sectioned off? Rocks laid? Beds made? What do you want, Vallei?"

"Just the ground—"

"You're an awful liar." He scoffed. "A garden, that's not all, and neither is overturning the soil."

"Beds would be nice. Six of them, three on each side, closest to the center with a cleared trail for me to tend to the herbs I will be growing."

"And—"

"That is more than enough."

"Let me decide what's enough, Vallei. What else?"

"A small, *really* small creative space. I've been meaning to contact the contractor to have it bui—"

"I'll be out back. Should I need you, is it okay to use the door here?"

He pointed toward the back door.

"Yes."

"Alright. When time permits, supply inspiration for the space you have in mind. They'll need an additional day to make that happen."

"Only a day?"

"They're on my dime. They'll work until I say stop. A

day is enough. While one assists me, the other will begin your projects."

He headed toward the front door as he spoke, putting distance between us again.

"Thank you!" I yelled after him.

Silence followed the slamming of my front door. Lost for words, I stood in the hallway, gasping for the air he'd snatched from my lungs.

Who the hell is this man? I craved answers more than my next meal.

My ringing phone saved me from the rabbit hole I was ready to climb in.

"Mal," I answered.

"Vallei. Don't ever in your life hang up on me like that. Are you okay? Are you hurt? Who was that at your door? I'm over here going crazy."

"Someone I need to know so much more about," I rushed out.

"Huh?"

"Nothing."

"Don't worry. Jay is about to be on his way."

"Mal, please, unless Jay is ready to leave this earth, please tell him to stay home. I'm fine. I'm fine. Really, I'm fine."

I wasn't sure if I was trying to convince her or myself. Either way, the repetition soothed the ache his absence contributed to.

"Okay, you're scaring me, friend. Who was at your door?"

"His name is Mercer."

Mercer · Vallei

As if I didn't own the home I was walking around, I tiptoed, afraid to make too much noise or announce my presence. Though I was alone inside, I was surrounded by an overwhelming presence that confined me with little to no effort.

Tasks as simple as grabbing a bottle of water from the fridge felt intrusive. Somehow, this had become his home again. I was merely a guest.

The sound of movement at the backdoor halted mine. I stilled like a cube of ice as I waited for the beautiful creature to show his face. Anticipation had me by the neck.

"Pretty, where you at, baby girl?"

Baby girl. I melted. As a thirty-four-year-old, I found it offensive to be called anything remotely close to childish pet names. The moment the words left Mercer's mouth, it assured me that it wasn't what I was being called, but it was who was calling the name.

"My name is Vallei," I reminded him as he rounded the corner.

"Your name is whatever I want it to be, Pretty. Can I use your bathro—"

"You're quite contradicting. You're unsure if you want to be a meanie or a gentleman."

"I'm always a gentleman. Well—"

"Yes," I managed, refusing to allow him to spin an even more complex web for me to navigate.

Whatever was on his head, I had no desire to hear. It didn't matter that it could've been completely innocent. There was nothing innocent about the veins that lined his arms and hands. In my opinion, anything that exited his mouth was geared toward my downfall.

"Thank you."

His lips lined the top and bottom rows of teeth. They were absolute perfection, the reflection of the man they'd been created specifically for.

God, how inconsiderate?

I uncapped the water and tipped the bottle so the liquid could demolish the fire burning in my throat. There was little hope for the rest of my body. My best chance was smoldering, which would still leave my skin sweaty and wet to the touch.

Waiting until he returned felt too much like torture, so I took the back stairwell that led me to my bedroom eventually. It was the longer route, but it was preferred. It wasn't until I settled that I noticed my cell phone was no longer in my hand. I'd left it downstairs.

The boyfriend denim and oversized shirt I wore did little to cover me. I still felt completely exposed as I took the same staircase downstairs minutes later. The mirror at the edge of the staircase did little to comfort the nudity that plagued me. Externally, I was clothed. But internally, I wore nothing.

I made it to the kitchen safely and without encountering my special guest. My cell was exactly where I'd left it. Mercer's voice booming through my home had neutral-ized my brain activity, causing temporary memory loss and confusion.

The large window just above the sink made it impos-sible to deny temptation. On the tips of my toes, I peered into the backyard to see the progress that had been made. My eyes never grazed the land. They stopped mid-air, fixated on the pair that gawked through the window, penetrating my flesh and commanding my attention.

Tearing away must've been the hardest thing I'd done all day. My chest caved as I completed the task. A palm pressed against it, attempting to keep my raging heart inside.

Be still. I requested. It was denied.

Pull yourself together, Pret—Vallei.

His words stuck to me like glue.

"Damn you, Phillip." I grunted, knowing that he was the reason behind my thirst.

Being overlooked and undervalued for two years affected parts of me that longed for attention. Not just any kind, but a pleasant kind. The beneficial kind that let me know the untouched parts of me were still function-ing. Even if it was a simple smile or a crippling gaze from a man that could wrap his veiny hands around my neck any night.

Who? my thoughts rang out.

Lifted brows brought a smile to my face.

This is actually happening. I acknowledged the new thought process as I made a beeline for my bedroom, promising to retire there until the man in my backyard left for the night. My feet didn't stop tapping against the floor until I was beside my tub, mentally calculating the amount of cold and hot water I needed to obtain the desired temperature.

As the water filled the tub, I peeled the clothes from my body, one article at a time, until there were no more. I stepped in, wrapping my ponytail until my length was concealed within the makeshift bun. The sleek coating on the stone made it easy to slide until my bottom was flush against the coolness, and my center was underneath the faucet.

The pressure from the water forced my cheeks together as my muscles tightened. My head fell backward due to the immense pleasure soaring through me.

"Uhhhhhh," I moaned.

My tolerance hardly existed. I scooted back slightly, giving my girl the break she was crying for. If not, she'd be spitting up within seconds. I caught my breath before scooting up again, this time lowering the water pressure.

It rained down on me, still pushing me closer to my peak. Realizing its swiftness was inevitable, I sank my teeth into the flesh inside my mouth. My blood quenched my thirst as I began to tingle all over.

"Yeeeeeeees. Yes. Yes." lowly, I groaned.

I pushed against the edge of the tub. Bolts of gratification shook my core, running through me every two to three seconds. I could visibly see the vaginal contractions that sucked the skin of my pussy in and then spit them right back out. My body jerked forward, then backward, repeating the same movement several times before settling.

Bathing wasn't on my list of things to do this evening, yet I was pulling a towel across my skin. I rinsed the soap as my body continued to come down from the high it had reached. I could still feel the tingling of my center and the ringing of my head.

My eyes grew heavier. My heart grew lighter. My body grew tired. I dried every inch of me and reapplied a thick layer of butter. The clothes I'd worn were exchanged for an even bigger shirt that had been thrifted years ago, along with a pair of sweats that were a few sizes too big. The only thing holding them up was the strings that I tied as tight as possible.

Exhaustion wore me down swiftly. Fighting it was nearly impossible. I had little to no strength. My energy had diminished tremendously. Taking the stairs even felt like too much work.

The idea of leaving a stranger to roam my home freely led me down to the first floor where I rested my body on the custom cushions of my couch. It was the very place I waited for Phillip on nights when he refused to come home. I sunk right into the softness. It contoured to my frame, acclimated with the weight of my body from prior encounters.

The promises I'd made to retire in my bedroom were incredibly naive. Creativity was intangible at the moment. Maybe when I was alone again, the words would come to me. Right now, I had nothing for the notepad patiently waiting for me to be inspired.

Emails I'd avoided over the last few hours were the first on my list of priorities. Sleepy eyes blurred the letters on the small phone screen. I peered toward the staircase that led to my laptop. The likelihood of me retrieving it was slim. Instead of forcing myself off the couch, I grabbed the blanket sprawled across the end of it and covered my body.

Using a small pillow, I provided the support my neck needed and stretched my limbs until I found comfort. The calmness was medicine for my soul. The silence that had been agonizingly loud and confronting since the first time my husband stayed away from home was soothing for once. Like a light, I was out.

Mercer · Vallei

Warmth tickled the fine hairs on my face, causing a stir. Gradually, I opened my eyes. My natural lashes shielded my vision. By the darkness that surrounded me, I understood that nightfall was upon me. A tiny beam of light shined down on me from the lamp on the table beside my head. I hadn't powered it on. The sunlight had served as my source before closing my eyes.

The creaminess of the bottom notes tickled my nose. The cologne that I was progressively obsessing over had so many characteristics. I was intrigued by each as they continued to expose themselves. My nostrils flared, savoring the bitterness that followed the softer notes.

Discernment was etched in my DNA. A feeler, beyond almost anything else, I had the ability to determine a person's level of threat to my life within the first few minutes of meeting them. Though I knew the words he'd spoken so calmly earlier were probably true, I also understood that this stranger was no threat.

Phillip. My intrusive thoughts burdened me.

He's not. I finalized, knowing that he wasn't a threat to my life. He was a direct threat to my heart.

"Wake up, Pretty."

"Hm?" I fought for cognizance. I was failing miserably.

At the realization of our proximity, my eyes widened. Mercer was mere inches from my face... from my lips. Visions of him leaning forward, taking them into his mouth, forced my eyes shut again. I rubbed my temple, attempting to process everything and nothing simultaneously.

"I'm leaving for the day. I'll return around noon tomorrow."

"Okay." I managed to get out.

"The guys will be here by eight, tending to your projects before we continue. Is that alright with you?"

"I don't feel like I have an opinion here," admittedly, I responded.

I tucked my hand underneath my face as a yawn nearly split it in half. The fact that I was still tired after such an extensive nap was baffling.

"You are sleep-deprived," he noted aloud.

"Mercer, right?"

"Yes."

"Did you find what you came for?"

Changing the subject felt strategic. Having him analyze me as his eyes combed over my body, a few inches away from me, was far too overwhelming.

"Parts of it."

I slid my head up and down my hand, showcasing the pleasant feeling I received, knowing that his possessions were still hiding underneath the soil, waiting for him to retrieve them.

"Good."

"Come lock the door behind me."

"I will."

"I'm not leaving until you get up, Vallei."

The way he said my name as he'd known me—all of me—my entire adulthood was problematic. It rolled from his tongue so effortlessly and with so much confidence.

"I will."

"I know, and not later. Right now."

"You have so many demands for a man I don't know." I huffed, tossing the cover back and sitting up.

"You follow them well."

His response left me speechless. My eyes rushed to find his orbs in the darkness. He wavered none. His gaze emphasized his statement.

"For a woman I don't know."

Because I had nothing, absolutely nothing, swirling in my brain that would contradict his observation, I remained silent and focused on standing without busting my face on the table behind him. His words left me fuzzy.

His presence left me dizzy. His presence altered my equilibrium. He was utterly intoxicating.

"Goodnight, Mercer. Noon."

To confirm I'd paid close attention, I reiterated the information he'd just given me. Silently, he nodded, making his way to the door where I stood with it wide open. The quicker he cleared out, the quicker I could begin to sober up and digest everything that happened from the moment he pushed the doorbell.

He exited in a flash, filling the void in my world with regret. My mouth watered with words as I watched him walk toward the truck that was waiting with the engine running. I felt my jaw widen with apprehension, but I mustered the strength to keep quiet.

Stay a little longer? I wanted to ask.

Have a mushroom latte?

Pointless conversation?

The possibilities of the next few hours were endless. I waited impatiently for him to turn back so that I could muster the liquid courage to propose anything other than ending his visit. He never did. His long legs rounded the truck, disappearing instantly. Defeat lingered while I locked the door behind him, honoring his request.

I wasted little time grabbing my phone and heading for my bedroom where my violin and notepad were waiting. The buzzing alerted me of a new message. I unlocked the screen at the sight of my mother's name.

God is working in your favor, she'd sent.

Her declaration stopped me in my tracks. Midway up the stairs, I pressed my back against the wall and looked back at the door I'd just locked. So many thoughts rushed me at once. Mal's perfect timing rescued me from the dungeon they'd almost confined me to.

"Yes, Mal?"

"Don't do me like that. I'm just calling to make sure you're still alive."

"Yes. I'm still alive." I chuckled.

My best friend meant well. Her heart was golden. She was my spirit animal until it came to the people she loved. For them, she transformed into an entirely different person. Her pure soul and good intentions quickly transformed into a tainted soul and ill intentions. There was no in-between with Mal.

"Good, now tell me about this Mercer. What did he want, and why did it require him to stay as long as he is staying? Your text said you'd call me when he left. You haven't called yet, so I'm assuming he hasn—"

"He's gone now. For about three minutes."

"Oh, good. So, who is he, and what did he want?"

"The million dollars he buried in my backyard before he sold the home to the couple that sold it to me."

Silence coated the line. I removed the phone from my ear to see if the timer was still running. It was.

"Mal?"

"I'm sorry." She scoffed. "Is this a joke or something? Should I expect camera crews to come out of the closet of my hotel room?"

She was out of the city for work. Though she hated the trips, she loved the money. Her boss trusted her more than most of his employees, so he was forever putting her on a private flight to represent their company.

"No. I'm serious, Mal, but that stays between us."

"When I agree to things like that, please note that it does not include Mea."

"Well, I know that much."

Irish twins, the two were only seven months apart and were born in the same year. They were practically the same age. Mal, being the youngest, was born prematurely. Their mother had just reached the seven-month mark when she entered the world. The two were often mistaken for identical twins because they looked just alike and were so close in age. Their personalities matched, which was as rare as their birth stories.

"Tell me more!"

"Somehow, someway, I think I've found the love of my life," I joked. "This man is gorgeous, Mal. I've never considered a male beautiful under any circumstance. But this man... this man is the exception, love."

"You're joking, but I can also feel the truth behind your humor. I don't doubt that you have because that husband is not it. Was never it. Had potential, yes. But he's proved that he wasn't it all along, time and time again."

"I know." Sighing, I agreed.

"Listen, my best advice is to never let anyone get in the way of finding your forever love. Not even your husband."

I burst into a fit of laughter. My chest caved and expanded continuously.

"See, you hear that?" She giggled. "I haven't heard you laugh, like genuinely laugh, in so long, girlfriend. So, there's something there. I don't care how minor it may be."

I released a heavy breath. "He's beautiful, Mal."

"I believe you. You're every bit of me, and I know you need this time to process things, so I'll let you go. I love you, kid."

"I love you."

We ended the call. I pressed my phone against my chest where my heart was galloping. My head rested on the wall behind me. Still, I'd made no progress. The top of the stairs was still anticipating my arrival. So was my bedroom. So was my violin.

The weight of my body tripled. A journey I managed each day felt a bit harder this time, but I made it anyway. Inside my bedroom, the strings of my violin scraped the tips of my fingers. I wondered how something so callous could create something so precious. I sat in my chair and placed it near my chest, determined to play until I found the answers.

In the meantime, words came to me. I accepted them gladly, allowing my mind to bend and fold as it saw fit.

Wilderness

I'm in the wilderness
Untamable
Unmanageable

Uninterested in being sought after
My tresses run wild
Piled on top of my head
My face burns each time I pick up my pace,
battling with the raging winds
I rise on my own accord
The chirping of the birds play like lullabies
My background singers
The ways of the world no longer rest on my
shoulders
I'm more connected than ever with my beholder
Nothing has ever felt like this before
The storms are welcomed, because they are
followed by the brightest sun
And it keeps returning
My only indication that another day has begun
I'm finally free from captivity
Not you or anyone else will be awarded the right
to capture me

Mercer · Vallei

My eyes darted around the room. The sound of heavy machinery woke me from my slumber. I felt around the bed for my phone. Seeing the sun in its resting place was not good news. It most likely meant I'd overslept, and that was as close to impossible as Phillip turning our marriage around and us living happily ever after. It simply never happened.

11:28 am. The numbers on my screen made me nauseous. I flipped the covers back and stood on my feet. My once-tamed hair was scattered on my head. A wine glass sat on the vanity on its side, just inches away from the edge.

One good look around my bedroom and I was reminded of the night I'd had. My emotions were on the sleeve of my shirt, completely exposed and completely validating my existence. Last night, I'd penned two poems, both with equal representation of the tug-of-war I was having in my heart.

I picked up the notebook from the small bench in front of my bed, curious about the words I'd scribbled before my head hit the pillow and my violin was laid to rest.

Bigger

My love was so much bigger than us
Between us two, there wasn't enough room
I had to find somewhere else to pour it all
So, I found my way to the sea
It clashed with the waves
Buried itself in the sand
Danced with the reefs
That's...
That's what healed me

. . .

The words still made sense, even after sobering. With a nod, I placed the notebook back where I'd gotten it, satisfied with the short piece.

I'll return around noon tomorrow. His words looped in my brain like a Sade track as I polished my face with tone-balancing serum. It was the third step in the skincare routine that I was rushing through. Next was moisturizer and natural rosehip oil.

11:38 am. I peeped at the time, making sure that I didn't miss the deadline.

There was something about the mystery man that said, *punctuality is my sport.* I did not doubt he'd be ringing my doorbell when the clock struck twelve.

I brushed my teeth immediately after tending to the skin on my face. A quick bird bath followed. By the time my hair was in a high bun with my baby hairs shaping my face, noon was upon me. I headed down the stairs, prepared to wait in the living room for the doorbell to sound so that we wouldn't have a repeat of yesterday.

It was clear that Mercer wasn't a very patient man. He wanted what he wanted when he wanted it. And from the looks of things, there would be hell to pay if he didn't receive them.

The boldness of his cologne brushed the tip of my nose long before I reached the first floor. My eyes roamed the open space, searching for the figure I knew was present.

Maybe it's from last night.

Can't be.

The potency was evidence.

He's here.

I panicked, rushing down. I rounded the corner of the staircase to find him right underneath, removing his sneakers one after the other. Crinkled brows and flared nostrils reflected my internal processing levels. I didn't understand anything, especially not him.

"You're already here," I announced.

"It's 12:02, Vallei."

"I'm aware of that bu—"

"You didn't advise me to remove my shoes upon entering your home yesterday."

He changed the subject, showing little interest in whatever was about to come from my mouth.

"How'd you get in this time?" I forced out, regardless, hoping for a response.

He twisted his head toward the right, staring straight at the back door.

"Oh." Dumbfounded, I watched him as he watched me.

"You should be more careful, Pretty. Here."

He leaned down, grabbing two containers from the console in front of him.

"I'm not hungry, yet. Thanks."

"You're going to eat, Vallei. It's part of the reason your body is fighting itself. You're pissing it off. Don't piss me off, too."

"Are you always this grumpy?"

"Grumpy?" He tittered, those teeth peeking from

underneath his lips just enough to send me into cardiac arrest.

"Yes."

"Having someone treat their body nicely is me being grumpy?"

"Kind of."

"It's not. You look like a smart girl. You know better."

You know better. Smart girl. I took from his reply what I wanted and discarded the rest.

"Your jacket?" I questioned, needing him to cover his arms once and for all. They were such a distraction.

"Your point has been made."

It was then that I realized why he was smiling a bit harder. He wanted me to treat my body well, and I'd indicated I expected the same from him. Truthfully, though, I didn't give a damn. I just needed the veins in his arms to quit feeding my fantasy of the same one, slightly smaller, running along his dick.

"The table."

His long body pushed through my home, stopping at the dining table where he placed both containers, along with the mug that was steaming hot. He pulled out a chair for me, though I was capable of doing so myself. I sat down. He remained standing, removing the top from the cup so that he could blow cool air on top to reduce the temperature.

"You don't strike me for the coffee type," he confessed, sipping from what I assumed was tea before setting it down in front of me.

Did he jus—wait.

Mercer matched my gaze, daring me to confront his audacity. I chose not to.

"What gave me away? The thrifted wardrobe?"

Finding humor in my rebuttal, he shook his head. "Nah."

"The oversized clothes?"

"No."

"The home decor?"

"Nah."

"The garden idea? The creative studio idea? The—"

"You, Pretty. You gave yourself away."

"How?"

"It's nothing I can explain. Just drink up. It's an alternative to coffee, made with mushrooms."

"I assumed it was tea."

"It isn't, but I did put a tin of tea on your counter. Drink it before bedtime, and you'll sleep like a baby."

I sniggered, finding it hard to believe the words coming from his mouth.

"I've never lied, and I didn't start with that advice."

Sitting, finally, he lifted the lid on the plate in front of him. I was persuaded to do the same after witnessing what was beneath it.

Turkey bacon. Turkey sausage. Buttered grits. Garlic toast. And the cheesiest eggs.

I wasted little time digging in with the utensils he provided, desperate for a bite of the eggs that looked as good as they tasted. I nodded, praising the dish without words. My mouth was busy accepting another fork full to say anything.

Silently, we both fed our growing bellies. I managed to get almost every compartment clean. The grits were cooked to perfection, not too thick and not too runny. There was a perfect balance of water, butter, and sugar.

Though I could feel Mercer's eyes on me, my hunger never wavered. It wasn't until I had almost cleared the plate that I realized how much I had been avoiding meals and dismissing the idea of food. It was a coping mechanism of some kind. The empty plate in front of me helped me realize it wasn't the healthiest.

Mercer was up on his feet with our plates in his hand, leaving me lonely at the dining room table I'd shared with my husband many nights. The stranger's presence made me wonder what life would be like if it was him sitting across from me each night at dinner instead.

Longing for his handsome face in my line of vision, I waited impatiently for his return. He trashed both plates and took his precious time getting back to his seat. Unfortunately, he didn't sit. He stood beside it, draining the water from the bottle he'd taken from the fridge.

"You'll have to share the information f-for the restaurant that provided this morning's meal," I said, clearing my throat.

His pensive gaze felt slightly intrusive, like he could hear the thoughts surrounding him circling my head.

"You're looking at the provider, Pretty."

He tossed the empty bottle in the trash from where he stood. His accuracy and aim proved that he'd once put those legs to good use. He knew his way around the basketball court. I'd bet my last dollar on it.

In total disbelief, I squinted, trying to figure out if he was being honest or humoring himself.

"You?"

"Yeah. Fix ya face. It can't be that hard to believe."

He is far too good to be true. I winced, realizing how much I'd settled with the man who demanded I adopt his last name. I'd stood firm on my decision to keep my own, and I was quite happy that I had. *There has to be a catch.*

He started for the backdoor. The newfound hunger I immediately experienced as I watched him walk away left me no choice but to spark a new conversation.

"The inspiration!" I yelled after him, raising my voice to the point that it was no longer recognizable.

I had never felt such a strain in my throat, mainly because yelling of any kind was personally prohibited. I didn't live a loud life. My existence wasn't loud. My aura wasn't loud. My art wasn't loud. My thoughts and my heart were the loudest parts of me. I loved loudly. There was no other way to, in my opinion. It was both rewarding and risky.

Either way, I'd never stop. It felt better than waking up to the sun's glow each and every morning. I'd rather die a tragic death than to never love or be loved again. Love was my life's source, and until my time on Earth came to an end, I wanted to love and love again.

"Fo-for the studio."

My words stopped him in his tracks. His eyes were on me in a flash.

"What about it?"

"I-I have it."

"Where is it?"

I dug my hand in my pocket to retrieve my phone. After unlocking it, I opened the gallery and turned the phone around so he could see the small collage I'd created, consisting of four images.

His fingers grazed mine in his attempt to slide my phone from my fingers. All the stars aligned. Each and every one of them sat right above my head, setting my body ablaze. A complete disaster inside out, I clung to the piece of matter like I did the last breath I'd just taken.

"You gone let this motherfucker go or what, Pretty?"

"Uh... ye-yes. Of course."

He succeeded. I watched him tap the boxed arrow and tap the green message icon. One after the other, he entered numbers before sending a message. The chiming phone in his pocket was confirmation that he'd done exactly what I thought he had.

"Got it. I'm outside if you need me."

I need you, I screamed inside.

Vallei. While secretly chastising myself, I watched him walk away again. This time, I didn't open my mouth until the door closed behind him. I wasn't sure when or how my phone had gotten back in my hand, but I held it close to my heart as I leaned my head on the wall.

Gather yourself, I warned. The fever I'd developed for a man I knew nothing about was frightening, but it was as natural as my next breath of air. Fighting it felt most foreign. It required far more energy.

I dialed one of the four numbers stored in the back of

my brain. Mal answered after the third ring. Her somber tone concerned me.

"Hey."

"What's the matter?"

I couldn't fathom a more fitting question.

"Besides the fact that I'm tired and ready to hop on the first thing smoking back to Berkeley, nothing. What's up, baby?"

Sighing, I massaged my temple with my index finger and thumb.

"He fed me this morning." I groaned. "And brought tea over because he could somehow tell that I was deprived. Along with the food that tasted like it was from a five-star breakfast bar, he brought homemade mushroom brew, an alternative to coffee.

"Mal, who is this man? Seriously. How has he heard my body say things that I haven't voiced? How is he so in sync with me? I just... I am so confused right now. And I feel so guilty for being all up in my chest, but what other choice do I really have? Honestly."

"I love you a million times over, Vallei. You know this, right?"

"Yes."

"So, know that this is coming from a place of love when I say it."

"Okay."

I braced for impact, knowing that Mal would always give it to me straight. She meant absolutely no harm and usually didn't cause any. Still, I knew that the storm was coming.

"Do you think Phillip is wondering how you will feel when he's sliding into something hot and ready? When his face is in the pussy of the woman that he's head over heels for? I know you probably don't want to hear it, but that is the only reason that man is shitting on you the way that he is. Phillip is in love, and it is not with you, friend."

Her words would've stopped my heart's race six months ago. However, I knew that they were all accurate. I'd known for a year, but the last six months were concrete proof. There were women before whoever it was he was seeing now, but none made him completely disrespect our union without a care in the world until he opened the legs of his current partner.

Dropping my head, I tilted my feet outward, watching as my soles slowly became more visible. "I know."

It wasn't easy to admit, but Mal knew as well as I did. Whether I admitted it or not, it would remain true.

"So, stop beating yourself up. You've been the better person for far too long. I would've been sliding down a new dick the day I discovered my pussy wasn't the only one my husband was swimming in. He wouldn't be able to touch me."

"He hasn't in six months."

She pushed out a long, hard breath. "How can you even hear right now? Or see?"

"What do you mean?"

"No dick for six months and you live with a man would have me losing my vision and mobility." She sniggered. "I'd have to move on out."

"I've considered it, Mal. I have, but this is my dream home. I worked so hard to get it to this point. I love everything about it but the person I share it with."

"And we both know it won't be yours if you decide to di—"

"Exactly. I feel so trapped."

"Because, you are, Vallei. Your feelings are valid."

"Why he doesn't divorce me and go ahead and live his life however he sees fit, I have no idea."

"Because he will lose the ability to retain all the shit you've accumulated during your marriage. A judge isn't going to want to hear shit he has to say then. But if it's you that wants to end the marriage, he'll go in looking like a sick puppy and lie like he helped you build everything brick by brick so that it works in his favor."

"He didn't, though."

"Oh, I know. He's in a family full of attorneys. That nigga, though, he's almost the definition of a corporate bomb. He couldn't pass the bar, so he's stuck playing dress up every day, going into the office like he has any real business to handle.

"I think they only have him on payroll because they feel sorry for his ass. That's another reason he isn't going to file. He doesn't want his family to feel like he's failed yet another thing in life."

"They're aware of his infidelity."

"They don't know you are. That's the only reason no one has nipped it in the bud or gotten on his ass."

"Penelope has," I informed her, referring to his only sister.

"She doesn't count. I don't know how she even got into that family. She's nothing like them."

"The differences are striking."

"I love her. She's everything they're not."

"Me, too."

"But back to the man in your home."

"Oh God. He needs to leave already."

"I know you well enough to know you didn't mean a word that just came from your mouth."

"Who's side are you on?"

"Yours, which is why I want you to give yourself grace, Vallei."

"I feel like I owe him something. He's been so generous. He's building my garden and a creative studio out back."

"Maybe some head. Or make him some coochie soup full of your natural juices and a pinch of ejaculation."

"I think I'm going to hang up now."

"Do not hang up on me." Mal burst into a fit of laughter.

I could only shake my head as she got herself together.

"No, but seriously, he is generous. Food is the answer, whether it be from parts of your body that haven't been touched in months or something from your fridge."

"That's simple enough."

"He'll be hungry by nightfall. Prepare a meal and feed him. Feed the men that are on his team as well."

"I will. Thank you."

"No problem, Vallei."

"Get some rest and tell them you're ready to come home."

"I'll be back in a week. I'm going to sleep early tonight, and I'm going to make it my business to get out of this hotel room this weekend. Just because I'm in a different city doesn't mean I can have a little fun. I'd love a good lemon drop and some Jazz."

"Sounds delightful, babe."

"It will be."

"Drinks on me," I volunteered, pulling the phone from my ear to send one hundred dollars from my digital wallet.

"Vallei. I can buy my o—"

"It doesn't matter. Just accept the payment and drink up."

"Thanks."

"You are welcome. I have some writing to do. Talk to you later?"

"Yes, of course. I love you, babe."

"I love you, too."

Feeling a few pounds lighter, I stood tall and headed for my fridge. I removed the turkey wings from the freezer to begin their thawing process. I decided to pair them with garlic potatoes and mixed vegetables.

Up the stairs I went with my pen and pad on my mind. By the end of the day, my violin would be begging to be released from my possession. I had so much to say, so many words to write, so many feelings to express, so many sounds to create.

Photoshop

I photoshopped a heart on your chest
I just wanted to see a heartless man at his
very best
The beat red organ that would've made you whole
The conquering of what you didn't have to give
became my life's goal
Thought that I could love you enough for me too
Ended up looking like a fucking fool
With not even my whole heart, anymore, to use
So, I pieced mine back together
I used Photoshop, too
Pasted it back onto my chest
I just wanted to be reminded of myself at my
very best

My fingers didn't stop until the words emptied from my heart. It wasn't until then that I pulled my instrument into my arms and cradled it like a baby, waiting for the notes to etch themselves across my mind.

Five hours later and my chin was sore, the words stopped flowing, my stomach was growling, and the doorbell was ringing. Two hours prior, I'd placed an order from the market for delivery. If ever there was a reason to stay home, I embraced it. I wasn't built for socializing. My batteries always deplete swiftly. Home is where I love to be.

I tiptoed down the stairs one after the other. Darkness was beginning to coat the sky. By the time I reached the bottom of the staircase, the door stood wide open, and the groceries were being brought inside. Because I preferred tipping in cash, I pushed forward despite the audacity of the man in my home.

To my surprise, the face on the other side of the door was a very familiar one. I'd recognize Ursula out of any lineup. Her long, fabricated blonde hair and color-changing eyes that she purchased from the beauty supply store every month or so. The contacts seemed to be a signature look that she felt validated the blonde hair she chose to destroy her natural texture to continuously obtain. Though a beautiful girl, her soul was tainted and it was the number one reason I harbored no hard feelings. That and the fact that she never owed me her loyalty; my husband did.

"Vall—"

"Ursula," I addressed with a nod.

The awkwardness brewing came to a screeching halt at the realization that she was looking beyond me and in Mercer's direction.

"Goodnight," I rushed out, preparing to close the door. The draft was cutting through the sleeves of my shirt.

"Wait."

A palm pressed against my door, stopping it from closing.

"Can we... maybe talk?"

The odds of the very first woman I'd discovered my

husband was having an affair with delivering my groceries was almost as unbelievable as her attempting to talk to me. Neither she nor Phillip knew that I saw right through their illegitimate friendship. Her presence wasn't noticeable until Phillip and I's troubles began to blossom.

I didn't have any concrete evidence, but my heart growing heavy every time I was in the same room as the two of them was enough. The lingering touches, glares, laughs, and hugs were all the evidence I needed. My gut instinct had never stirred me wrong. Ursula's need to chat was the smoking gun.

"Actually, we can't, Ursula. I need to get started on dinner."

"He loves you, Vallei. He really does. And his guilt wouldn't let us go on any longer than the year th—" she whispered.

"Ursula, it was not his guilt. It was his penis. He's sticking it elsewhere. That's why he broke things off with you. It had absolutely nothing to do with me. You don't owe me an explanation. Be well. Take care of yourself. Goodbye." I matched her tone before shutting the door closed.

I expected to find Mercer near, but he was out of sight by the time I locked up and headed down the hallway. I found him in the kitchen, removing groceries from the reusable bags I chose at checkout when placing an order. The less wasteful I was in life, the better I felt about my contributions to the world.

Mercer's frame seemed twice as big as mine, yet he

was still fairly slim, with muscles protruding everywhere. I was almost positive he was in the gym regularly.

"Have you ever heard of boundaries?" Leaning against the frame of the kitchen entrance, I asked.

"When I feel that some have been given, I'll respect them."

He was sharp with his words, cutting just along the surface so the verbal assault wasn't skin deep, but you could still feel every second of the sting it caused. And he only ever said as many were necessary. Nothing more. Nothing less.

Because he'd spoken freely and truly, I had nothing contradictory to say.

"Leave everything on the counter," I demanded. "And please, refrain from opening my front door."

"Noted."

With a nod, he stepped away from the food he'd taken from the bags.

"In approximately two hours, will you still be here? Or will you be near, at least?" Nervous chuckling exited me.

I didn't ignore that it was getting late in the evening. In two hours, this man might've had somewhere to be. Assuming he'd be enjoying the fruits of my labor wasn't it.

"Where do I need to be?"

His words stole the oxygen from my lungs, sucking it right up my chest and through my mouth. I swallowed to relieve my throat of the dryness.

"I-I, uh—"

"Where do you want me?"

The gap between us closed. He was close, too close. So close that I could feel the heat from his skin against mine.

"Here." I gasped, trying to control the irregularities happening in my body at once.

"Then, I'll be here."

I gathered myself as he stepped off, toward the hallway that led to the backdoor.

"Dinner will be ready in a little under two hours. Please maintain an appetite."

"Anything, Pretty."

Anything? What does that mean? I asked myself, unable to tear my eyes from him until he disappeared outside.

I cleaned my hands for the task ahead. The instrumentals playlist I preferred began playing on the small speaker next to the stove at my request. Beige, brown, and cream colored the apron I wore faithfully in the kitchen.

My hips swayed from one side to the other as the music began to enter my system. Thirst plagued me, causing me to search the cabinet for my favorite tea cup. Something warm and spicy would do the trick. The new gold tin on the counter caught my attention.

I was immediately reminded that Mercer had mentioned providing tea for my overly exhausted body. To his dismay, I knew it was just another one of the many concoctions that would require my body's rest but not disable my thoughts. They were the reason I couldn't sleep peacefully at night.

Throwing caution to the wind, I prepared the bags and hot water. Multitasking, I began cleaning the turkey wings as I did so. The water they'd cook in for the first hour was put on the stove as well. Their final thirty minutes would be spent in an oven, covered with aluminum foil to infuse the turkey broth it had made with the initial water supplied.

Because I preferred a more intense flavor, I dipped two bags into the fresh water and allowed the strings to dangle on the other side of the cup. With each second, the ingredients combined. Honey was the last to be added and would require stirring.

Once the water had browned to my liking, I removed the bags and placed them inside a plastic bag. The fridge was the next stop to discourage any bacteria growth. The leftovers would be used for a second cup tonight or a cup tomorrow.

"Mmmmm."

The first sip was always heavenly. The sweetness of the honey, in collaboration with the earthiness of the plants, was the closest thing I'd get to the sacred place while on earth. I could taste the lavender, chamomile, and peppermint. They were only a few of the many flavors but stood out amongst the rest. I blew lightly on the rim of the cup to cool before each sip.

Fresh onions made me tear up slightly as I finished cutting them. I dumped them into the water and started on the bell peppers. There were three different colors that all added a unique flavor to dishes. After I'd cut half of each, I tossed them in the pot as well.

My water was beginning to boil as I finished combining all the ingredients. I left the kitchen with half a cup of tea and a hopeful smile. The taste of turkey wings, garlic potatoes, and green beans made my mouth water. I'd changed the dishes several times before finalizing the simple yet fulfilling combination.

I rested my bones, laying across the couch and sitting my glass on the table with a coaster underneath. A yawn nearly disconnected the top portion of my face from the bottom as I unlocked my cellphone to begin listening to the reference track I'd recorded for a piece I'd yet to complete because I lacked the inspiration.

Somehow, I was reminded of the poem and encouraged to finish it. Speaking freely about being loved properly and handled with so much care proved to be difficult when your marriage was falling apart.

I tapped the triangle on the screen. My vocals began shortly after the violin had its way with the silence. My heart, my soul was lulled to the safe space my creativity had long ago founded for me. It welcomed me with precious melodies.

Mercer · Vallei

"Vallei!" A strange yet vaguely familiar tenor beckoned for my attention.

"Vallei."

Softer. Slower. Closer. Heavier.

Long fingers tickled the exposed skin of my hand, stirring me from my slumber. The smell of charred turkey meat froze my limbs and enlarged my eyes. My heart raced as I fought for mobility.

The food. My brain reacted to the abundant smell of smoke in my home. However, I couldn't move.

"Th-the food." I breathed.

"It's off the stove."

"God, I'm sorry."

An apology felt most natural at the moment. I'd promised a man a dinner that wouldn't come to fruition because my body, heart, head, and soul were all tired. They were fighting for the rest they'd deserved over the last two years since walking out of that doctor's office after being told that the few eggs I produced per year weren't viable and pregnancy would be as difficult as surviving a fall off a cliff.

"For what?" Mercer's words touched me right where I was beginning to heal.

"Dinner. It's ruined. I can go out and grab something to feed you al—"

"That's not why I'm here, Pretty," he informed me.

His dark eyes glistened, even in the low light that surrounded us. Night had fallen. My eyes roamed his body, landing on the towel draped across his shoulder. It wasn't until then that I noticed the wooden spoon in his hand.

"Then what are yoouuuu—mmmm."

He stuffed the spoon in my mouth mid-conversation, not giving me the option to reject his unspoken request. I wouldn't protest his ability to render me speechless because, once again, he had. With a firm nod, I approved whatever it was on the spoon. I was almost certain it hadn't been anything of mine because the one dish I'd put on the stove smelled like it had burned to a crisp.

"Yeah?" he asked, somehow becoming more handsome as his ears perked in waiting.

The validation he sought was heartening. A man with more confidence than the average being could bear was kneeling in front of me, asking for my approval on a dish.

He hadn't asked for my approval to enter my home, dig through my backyard, open my door, bring in my groceries, unpack my groceries, or stand at my stove cooking. Yet, here he was, with a swelled chest and patient eyes, waiting for my response.

"Yes," I assured him with another node.

Stillness captured the moment. Both lost in the gaze we shared, I confided in silence. Mercer did the same. For what could've been hours, we remained. Eye to eye.

And then, suddenly, his hand was still no more. It was around my neck, and his lips were on top of mine. I breathed into his mouth, which he opened for me diligently, in no rush to welcome me into his world.

Slowly, I introduced myself, sure to touch everything my tongue came in contact with. Becoming acclimated with every detail of him was my quest now. Nothing, absolutely nothing, would deter me.

"The turkey meat was able to be salvaged. Give me ten minutes, and dinner will be served."

He lured me from my dream with his words. His lips were still miles away, and mine were still dry from the nap I'd taken. I observed him place the spoon in his mouth and remove everything I hadn't from it.

"You love the kitchen." The rasp made my voice unrecognizable. A cup of water would've been grand, but I didn't have one near.

"So much that I'm building my own."

"Yeah?"

"*The M.* Downtown. Opening in a few months."

"A chef?"

"Yes, Pretty. I am."

"Explains a lot. How long have I been out?"

"Not long enough, apparently. I won't hold you from your bed too long. I just want to feed you, and then I'll be on my way."

It isn't food I hunger for. Neither is it water that'll truly quench my thirst. I thought.

"I'm in no rush for bed." Admittedly, I wasn't. The nap had been much needed. Now, I felt fine.

"Disobeying me makes that statement rather contradicting."

He was up on his feet and headed toward the kitchen in a flash as I tried to figure out the meaning behind his statement. The empty glass of tea that I picked up, prepared to follow behind him like a sick puppy, was exactly what made everything make more sense.

"The tea," I mumbled.

"The tea."

How he'd heard me, I was unsure, but he had. My cheeks flushed with embarrassment.

"I didn't expect it to actually work."

"I warned you, Pretty. I wouldn't tell you anything that was untrue."

The contents on the stove were colorful and smelled divine. The seasonings began to overpower the smell of smoke the closer I got to the selection. The gravy made from small bits of turkey meat sat on the small fire, still boiling, in the middle of the stovetop. The fifth burner was a Godsend.

A whiff of unpleasant smokiness guided my head toward the pot in the sink, soaking in soapy water. Warm, slim fingers pressed against my jaw and chin as my head was angled in another direction. I sighed, wishing I'd been able to pay it forward, but that idea had gone into the dumps. Now, here Mercer was again, feeding me mentally, physically, and emotionally.

"Don't worry yourself with shit that doesn't matter," he urged, protesting the sadness that crept into my spirit.

He peered downward, examining every inch of my face. I was almost certain he'd counted every tiny freckle and blemish I'd been trying to get rid of. I was unclothed, mentally. With those anguished eyes, he ripped the fabrics that kept me shielded. But he, too, had exposed himself. I saw through it.

Who hurt you? I wondered, but the words never escaped me.

"Go get washed up so we can eat, and I can get out of your hair."

He broke eye contact, possibly aware of my revelation.

"Uh, yeah. Sure."

Slowly, I slid from his grasp, wishing upstairs was where I'd find more of him. But I wouldn't. There was more of Phillip. Though no visible traces, because he spent most of his time in the guest bedroom, there were memories of what once was. Now, not even a toothbrush of his rested on our shared bathroom sink.

Anchors clung to my feet. One by one, I placed a foot in front of the other, finding the task slightly harder each time. In minutes, I completed a journey that should've taken mere seconds. Nevertheless, I entered my bedroom and went to the bathroom immediately.

It wasn't the sink that held my interest. The toilet seat met the roundness of my bottom as I sat down, clutching my head in my hands and releasing hard, unsteady breaths one at a time. Something was happening inside me, and I'd be foolish not to address it. With closed eyes and an open heart, I talked to the Man who knew best.

"God, I don't find this funny at all. Please tell me if you're playing tricks on my heart."

My phone vibrated on cue. I was reluctant to answer my mother's call but didn't want to keep her waiting.

"Hello."

The brightness of the bathroom finally began to attack me. Going from a dimly lit space to one full of flooding lights was painful. I shielded my eyes with my hand to filter the light slightly.

"Headed to bed, and you were on my mind. Had to call and check in."

"Thanks, Mom."

"You're alright?"

"Yes. I'm okay." I was. Although, simultaneously, I wasn't.

"Good. Good. I'm off to bed then." She yawned. "Goodnight."

"Goodnight."

Before ending the call, I heard my name being called.

"Vallei," my mom said.

"Yes?"

"God makes no mistake. Remember that," she emphasized.

"I will."

"I can sense that something is bothering you, but I won't press. I know you'll tell me when you're ready. Until then, know that it's already worked out."

It didn't matter the time of day or where I was in the world; my mother's gut always led her to my line when she felt my spirit was unsettled. She was always right. Tonight, something was bothering me, but explaining wasn't in the cards. Another day, maybe. Not this one, though.

"I know. Get some sleep and don't worry too much about me, Mom. I'm fine."

"Alright. I love you. Goodnight."

"I love you, too."

Without haste, I stood and didn't stop walking until the mat in front of the sink touched the bottom of my cushioned feet. Once, and then again, I cleansed my hand with the apple-scented soap in the dispenser.

I returned to the dining room minutes later to find the square-shaped plates from my cabinet decorated with colorful helpings that would've made my stomach growl any other time. To be frank, I was famished. I hadn't eaten anything but the breakfast Mercer had provided. It was bedtime, and we were just sitting down at the dinner table. My stomach might've been empty, but somehow, I felt full to the brim.

It was possibly due to the man dressed in a black top and denim to match that filled me completely. Maybe it was the sly smile on his handsome face. Maybe it was the way his jeans bulged in the front, validating the energy that he exuded. Maybe it was the perfect teeth that hid behind his perfect lips. Maybe it was the attention to detail he paid. Maybe it was the attention in general because it had been far too long since I felt like any way aimed in my direction.

Mercer made himself comfortable in the chair meant for the head of the house. He sat at the end, making a statement that his mouth hadn't. Didn't need to, either. His aura said everything that needed to be said. His actions fell in line.

I melted in the seat a few inches away. My temperature elevated to new heights. Frightening ones that had me tingling from head to toe. Nothing around me mattered. Not even the food that had been prepared when our eyes locked again.

My mouth clacked before closing and then opening

again. Whatever I was trying to say had evaded my thoughts. I couldn't form a word, let alone a sentence. Feeling defeated, my chest caved, and my eyelids sealed together.

"Pretty," he serenaded me, awakening every part of me.

He was no longer inches away. He was upon me. I opened my eyes to find him standing over me. With a finger, he tilted my chin upward, forcing me to look up at him.

"Are you not hungry?" he questioned.

My vaginal walls contracted. My mouth flooded with saliva. My chest ached. My eyes stung from the tiny prickling. My face contorted from the emotional turmoil I faced.

Honesty sat at the tip of my tongue. I'd never been a good liar. It wasn't a characteristic I'd admire if I were able to. I wore my honesty like a badge of honor.

"I haven't worked up much of an appetite," I murmured, feeling the muscles in my face tighten along with my chest.

"I have."

The heat from his fingers was quickly replaced with chilliness. I forced my eyes open after closing them again and quickly regretted it. The illusion I assumed I was wrapped in was a reality that I was faced with upon hearing the buckle of Mercer's pants loosen. He stalked the hardwood floor with conflict written across his features.

"Food isn't my source of supply."

He rounded the table. The slow stride was evidence he wasn't in a rush. When he was ready, he made it back to me.

"It's you."

Right in front of me, he stopped, loosening the button of his jeans.

"Boundaries. Tell me, just say the fucking word when I cross one."

Suddenly, he was giving rules that weren't required. Whatever he wanted of me at the moment would be my pleasure.

His boldness was the solution to my reservations. What he was presenting was nothing short of everything I wanted. I just didn't have the guts to admit it. Mercer was nothing like me. He was sure of himself, sure of his desires, and seemingly treated himself to them as he pleased. I had no objections.

"Domino."

"Hmm?" The single word was baffling. I didn't understand its purpose.

"If I cross a boundary or at any point, if you feel uncomfortable, that's what will bring us back to a safer place... a safer space."

"I do-don't understand."

"You will."

"Domino?"

"Duals as my last name and possibly the only word to steer my mind back to the place it belongs. Understood?"

His warning was clear and though I should've taken heed, I didn't. I was intrigued, wanting to push him to the point of no return. Not to yell a safe word or manage our safe return but to test my limits and his. My nipples perked at the sound of his voice demanding an answer.

Upon noticing it, his arm extended as his fingers clamped together, squeezing the right one until I yelped in what felt more pleasurable than painful. Instantly, I secreted.

"Uhhhhh," I moaned, just above a whisper.

My eyes pursued his lanky frame as my legs parted without permission. The newness of the heights I'd reached in such a short span of time had my head spinning. Mercer's hand around my neck brought me to as our eyes locked.

Leaning down, he revealed his wet tongue before shoving it into my mouth. I sucked it dry of the saliva he'd produced. Simultaneously, my hands developed minds of their own, roaming his frame until I reached the bulge in his jeans.

Winning the lottery couldn't have felt any better than stumbling upon his massiveness. I pushed his pants downward until I was able to free his hammer. Though still in his briefs, there was room for freedom. I stuck my hand through the slit, ready to reveal my prize. However, the swift tap on my wrist halted all movement.

The contractions from my center intensified as the stinging subsided. And at that moment, I discovered my appreciation for pleasurable pain. It was significant and enticing at once. Mercer wasted little time pulling away.

With a tilted head, he wiped away remnants of me from his lips. There were other parts of me I wanted to introduce his lips to. They'd leave a mess for him to clean as well. And if he didn't clean well enough, I had no problem assisting.

"Stand up, Pretty."

Obliging, I stood on my feet, stretching my body to its full potential.

"Undress," he demanded, sitting in the chair he once occupied.

His curling fingering beckoned me. I moved closer, not stopping until he displayed his full palm. My thighs touched his leg. My knee was almost as close to his briefs as I had been seconds earlier.

I removed my shirt first, with his assistance. My bra was next. The sheer cups left little to the imagination, not even the heart-shaped nipple rings that glistened in the dimly lit space. The nod of approval I received made my stomach cave.

He revealed the black lace of my panties after sliding my bottoms down my legs. My lips peeked from the sides, but the fabric was hardly enough to cover my meatiness. It was a problem I'd learned to accept when shopping for the panties I preferred. The ones that made me feel sexy because I had no one telling me that I was on a regular basis anymore.

He rubbed the parts of my skin the panties exposed. I shuddered, catching his eyes again. The sly smirk returned.

With total control and commendable poise, Mercer synched my panties until they crumbled in the fold between my legs. With his right hand, he entered my mouth and removed it almost instantly. He then breached my entrance.

"Oh God."

"Shhhhh. Shhhh." He silenced me, standing from the chair.

His lips caressed mine again. His tongue entered my mouth. His fingers turned upward, brushing against the spot that would send me howling if he pressured it enough. Like that, we stood, exploring each other.

"Mercer." I groaned as his strokes intensified.

"Mmm hm?"

"It feels so good."

My knees shook as my body weakened. I loosened my grip on his lips and leveled my feet with the ground, sure my balance was about to waver.

"It's supposed to."

I wrapped my hands around his biceps, holding on tightly as my body grinded against his fingers involuntarily until all movement ceased. Lines crinkled my forehead.

"Wh—"

"When I need your help, I'll ask," Mercer told me.

His hand was around my neck within a few seconds. This time, he held it tighter. His lips rested against mine. I opened my mouth to accept him, but he declined the invitation as his fingers began caressing my sensitivity again.

"Cum for me," he whispered into my mouth, still withholding his tongue and refusing to swap spit.

His words unleashed the pent-up frustrations,

aligning all the stars in my orbit that had gone astray. I closed my eyes as my knees buckled and my legs weakened.

"I'm cummmmmm—mmmm. Uhhhhhh. Mer, please."

"Look at me," he commanded.

I managed, but quickly after we matched gazes, the intensity forced my eyes shut. My body locked and then loosened as my faucet began to flow. I soaked the panties still attached to my body as well as his hand, up to his wrist.

"Fuck." He grunted, pulling me from whatever universe he'd shipped me off to.

Remorseful of the mess I'd made, I conjured a weak apology. It was all I could muster.

"Sorry."

"Sorry?" Mercer growled. "Don't ever fix your lips to apologize for making a mess. That's what that pussy is made for."

A gasp hiked my chest. Mercer removing his fingers from my flesh while my muscles continued to contract was the disconnection that I wasn't quite ready for. Gaining my composure felt impossible as he removed my panties and wiped my legs with the shirt he'd removed from his body.

Immobility plagued me as I watched him move so effortlessly, so confidently. And before I could protest, I was up in his arms, dangling from his shoulder as he headed up the stairs I'd taken thousands of times.

However, there wasn't a time I could recall that came remotely close to this one.

His internal navigation led him straight to the bed I'd slept alone in too many times to count over the last six months. My body pounced from the forcefulness. Mercer's lips hung as he hovered, taking me in as he adventured. One kiss after the other, he made a trail down my body until he reached my center.

"Pretty face. Pretty body. Pretty heart. Pretty titties. Pretty pussy. Just Pretty. But I'm not interested in the pretty parts of you right now, Vallei. I am in search of your depths. The filthy, downright disgusting parts. Can you tap into them, or should I go fishing until I find them?"

Spreading my legs, I waited to give him the answer to his question. I hadn't been penetrated in far too long. He had no business winning parts of me that he was about to be rewarded with, but he'd picked the right house at the right time.

The universe had put us in one another's path. It would be against everything I believed to disrupt or try to obstruct the connection that it had made. Too lost and too inquisitive, I didn't want to. It felt easier, better to accept what had been sitting right in front of me. Obliging was the most natural, self-assertive thing I'd done since I left the doctor's office two years ago. Until now, everything had felt foreign.

He got the message. There was no need to explain. His thumb grazed my clit, swelling it immediately. He stared down at my nakedness. Though I was fully exposed, I felt the safest I'd ever been. The most appreci-ated. The most desired. The most seen. The most heard. The most admired. *Ever.*

"What do you want from me right now?"

"Rig—uhhh, now?" Massaging my clit and questioning me was hardly fair.

"Hm?" His brow lifted. Simultaneously, his hand stopped moving.

"Mercer, please."

"Anything, Pretty."

"Put it inside of me," I begged.

He fell to his knees, cupping my clit with his tongue.

"Meeeeeeeerrrrcer! What are yo—Mercer."

"I'm not ready, Vallei," he admitted, referring to my request. "I'm not sorry for denial, so I won't be apologizing."

He filled his mouth with my pussy, letting me know it was the end of the conversation. He was a master at meddling. It was noted. He cared to know my desires and tiptoed toward them, slowly, at his own pace, intensifying my yearning and making it feel utterly outstanding to receive them.

Confining his mouth to my bottom set of lips, I closed the gap between my legs slightly, giving him little room to move. His tongue rotated, circling my pebbled nub over and over. Mercer was no rookie. He knew exactly what he was doing.

He'd had practice. He'd studied. And he'd mastered the science of pleasuring a woman. The student's course he'd studied was one lucky girl. But I was the masterclass. Mercer had no time to study the pop quiz that faced him. Somehow, he was passing with flying colors.

"Merc—wait. Hold on."

I felt everything at once. His tongue against my clit. The fingers he'd stuffed inside of me and the thumb that entered my asshole. I rose from the bed, needing to see what was happening below. Still, as I watched him, I didn't understand.

"I will strap you to this fucking bed if you run, Pretty," he warned, still having his serving of me. "Just feel, baby. Give your body permission to just feel."

Finding comfort in his warning, I relaxed against the sheets, believing with everything in me that he'd tie me to the beg and sex me into oblivion.

"There you go, Pretty."

"Uhhhh," I bellowed. "It's happenin' so fast. Mercer."

I tapped his arm, begging him to remove himself from between my legs. Waves crashed against the very core of me, threatening to drown him completely.

"It's happening!"

He remained, refusing to free himself of my flesh. And as I'd warned, it happened. My toes locked to the point of pain. My entire body stiffened. My abdomen became one large swirl as tingling started at my toes and punched me dead in the gut. I caved, but not before releasing a fierce flow of ejaculation that watered Mercer's beard and neck.

He rose from the floor with that familiar smirk on his face. Labored breathing made it hard to speak. I kept quiet, closing my eyes with promises to never give my body to a stranger again.

He's just too good to be true. I reasoned, squeezing my eyes together. It wasn't until I felt his manhood part me like the Red Sea that I opened them. My arms stretched, hands in search of something to hold. I gripped his wrists and prepared to be breached.

"Mmmmm."

Our bodies relaxed against one another, etching the moment in our hearts forever. One by one, he freed himself of my grasp. Mercer's palms flattened just above mine as he pushed my hands upward, stretching my body completely.

"I-it fee—ls sooo good."

Transfixed on his chiseled lips and well-groomed goatee, I opened my mouth to invite him inside so that I could feast on whatever was left of me on the tip of his tongue. Hesitantly, Mercer lowered his face to meet mine. Before letting me have my way with him, he whispered against them.

"Ya internals feel more like home with each stroke, Pretty."

Entangled in his web, I wondered if I'd ever escape. The words that came from his mouth slapped me across my chest, causing irreparable damage. Damage that I would never bother fixing anyway.

From the shakiness of his voice, it was apparent he was trying to keep it together. Instead of dwelling, he continued to stroke me long and gently as if I'd break in two otherwise. I savored every second of his performance.

"Merrrr-Mercer."

His girth was impressive, and so was his ability to hit all the right spots, avoiding slamming against my cervix and drawing discomfort, although he had the reach. Mercer knew things that most men couldn't comprehend or didn't care to discover about the woman's sexual organ. Though it was their playground, they refused to study the intricacies or instructions for proper use. Mercer, however, he held the manual.

"Remember that name, Pretty."

The sound of our connection became louder and louder as he dug into me. My pussy was rejoicing, elated to have company. My fingers had strung her like a guitar far too many times.

"Mercer!" I moaned against his lips.

"It'll be the last and most important."

Our fingers interlocked as he continued digging into my personal garden, feeding my soul along his journey. Just as I began to mount again, he ejected himself from my sleekness.

"Mercer, please."

Silently, he ushered my body toward the front of the bed, where he positioned me on my hands and knees. I clenched my muscles, understanding the degree of insanity necessary to accept Mercer from behind. Hung like a horse, he put every man I'd ever shared a night of passion with to shame.

"Mercer," I whined, clenching the pillow.

"Shut up, Vallei." The low rasp of his voice was like

honey on my tongue. I soaked it up, understanding that he meant no harm.

His anticipated entry was seamless. I craved every inch that he shortened me as we both reacquainted. Finally, his balls grazed the bottom of my cheeks. Everything around me began spinning. I was filled to the brim, stuffed with big, black dick that would leave a lasting impression on my center and my head.

"Safe word?" Mercer asked, noting the time it took to adjust.

I shook my head from side to side, assuring him I was alright. My confirmation was his ticket to oblivion. He gripped my waist, anchoring himself on the memory foam mattress, before drilling into my sloppiness.

"Mercer," I called out.

"Fuck."

His hand looped around, finding my centerpiece and rubbing it as he stroked. I assumed this would be the end of me. The gratification was overwhelming. I lost total control of every inch of my body as it began floating, instantly intoxicated from the new height he'd taken on.

"Mercer."

"Pretty." He whimpered, wrapping his hand around my hair and then pulling me upward until my back was against his chest. With the same hand, he wrapped my neck. The one below continued to fondle my lady parts as the other explored me again. Clutching my breasts and then releasing them. Squeezing my neck before releasing it. Pulling my head backward by my hair.

"Mercer!"

"Shut up and cum on this dick," he advised, aware of the announcement I was ready to make.

Satisfied with the grip on my breast, his hand stayed put as the other worked overtime to get me to that special place.

"Mercccc—"

I splintered. It felt like my body split in two and handed Mercer my G-spot. Everything around me blackened. Suddenly, I was faint. Mercer held onto me as the quaking began. I twitched relentlessly, releasing inhibitions as my body succumbed to another long-overdue orgasm that was not self-induced.

I tried falling forward, but Mercer refused. He held onto me, stroking me through my mess, silently promising that the grass was greener on his side of the garden. I believed every unspoken word he sewed into me.

"Shit."

"Oh God."

Vulnerable to my core, I was stripped of everything I had. Mercer could see right through me to my core that had developed a notable heartbeat for him. The rhythm was unlike anything I'd ever felt or heard before. It was special, just like the man that created it.

My contracting center proved to be the end of him. The nature of my body and the attempt to extract his semen from his sack was successful. Mercer's lips met my ear as he squeezed my left nipple, inducing pain.

"Where the fuck you want it?" he questioned, breathless.

"Wherever you want it," I advised before my body was shoved forward onto the bed.

Mercer navigated my limbs until my back was against the pillows so that I could see everything that was happening. I expected him to stuff my face with the veiny tool in his hand, but he stroked it with his fingers instead.

Utterly obsessed, I didn't bat an eye as I watched him pleasure himself. It was something I'd done on many occasions. Hadn't he drained me of everything I had, I would've joined him, but there was nothing left for me.

Within seconds, the tip lay against my baldness as semen scattered all over my stomach and chest.

"Fuck."

Without warning, Mercer plunged back inside of me, stroking me with more force than he had before. Staring straight into my eyes as our bodies synced once more. And just unexpectedly, he removed himself. His manhood rested on my center again. This time, oozing a second load of semen that rendered me speechless. He'd cum twice.

With pleasure, I tiptoed toward the bathroom to grab a wet rag. I returned with it in my hand, but it didn't last very long. Mercer wiped me down after retrieving the warm towel. It wasn't until I was clean that he proceeded to clean himself. He volunteered to put the rag away, but I insisted on doing so myself. I had to empty my bladder. There was no need for us both to take the same trip.

"I've got it. I promise."

"I can take it back," he hissed.

That voice of his, it would be the end of me. I was convinced.

"I have to tinkle," I revealed, making my point more valid.

Reluctantly, he handed it over. I relieved myself with haste, ready to get back to the man waiting for me in bed. Unfortunately, I returned to a much different man than I'd left. His body was cold and rigid to the touch.

Silently, I found slight comfort beside him. I rested my head on the pillow, wondering what had changed in the last few minutes I'd been gone. Minutes passed without a word exchanged. Limbs remained on the opposite side of the bed, never crossing over and never wrapping around my body.

I turned to face the side of Mercer's head.

"Domino." I sighed, beckoning for his attention.

He faced me, finally. His aggrieved eyes stared back at me with so much uncertainty within them. His gratitude for the life jacket I'd tossed him was apparent.

Wherever he'd gone was no place for him. I wanted him back now and not later. The attention I sought was instantly granted as his eyes shifted in my direction. Worry lines crossed my forehead as I presented the question that had been at the tip of my tongue for the last two minutes.

"Where did you go?"

A kiss on the lips silenced me.

"Somewhere I didn't want to be," he admitted.

"If you could be anywhere in the world right now," I probed. "Where would it be?"

Mercer lifted from the sheets. Carefully, I stalked his every move. Not many were made. He settled between my legs, pressing a thumb against my clit.

"Is she sore?"

"A little," I confessed.

"Then, it's best I made her feel better."

The words slipped from his mouth as he slipped inside of me.

"Meeeeerrrcer."

"You asked, Pretty."

Not comprehending, I petitioned for an explanation. "Hmmm?"

"Right here. Right here is where I want to be."

Mercer · Vallei

It wasn't morning that had awakened me. It was Mercer's hand over my mouth as he gutted me. Gently, he tapped against the spot that would surely send me to a higher place, above all else.

"Mmmmmm. Yeeeessss."

It didn't matter the pace or the intensity. His stroke was pure perfection. Because my center was tender, he made a conscious effort not to inflict any pain. I thanked him in creaminess that made our connection sound like the stirring of milky mashed potatoes, like the ones we'd decided against eating in order to explore one another all night.

We hadn't slept much. The wee hours led to little conversation and lots of acclimating with one another. Silence was our sacred space where we both discovered more than words could ever divulge. And when I finally closed my eyes, I could still feel his on me, right where they needed to be.

He slid into me and reeled back with ease. My girl parts were tender, but they weren't tired. For Mercer, I'd work them to the bone. He was that damn good, and I was that damn obsessed.

"Mercerrrrr."

"Bite," he instructed, sticking a finger in my mouth.

I'd learned rather quickly that he had a fetish for dominance and loved giving orders—in the bedroom and outside of it. Falling in line came naturally. My submissiveness hadn't been nourished in far too long. He was scratching the very itch I'd developed long before I understood the dynamic.

His command milked my center. I lowered my top row of teeth until I felt his skin. I followed through and lifted the bottom row upward. Together, they sandwiched his index and middle fingers.

"Fuck." He breathed into my neck as he closed the small gap.

His teeth sunk into my skin. I was almost certain he would draw blood. However, the pain hardly amounted to pleasure.

"Oh God."

As if I'd missed the point where my body had begun

rising toward my peak, I was incredibly surprised when I arrived.

"Yesssss. Yessss."

I pushed into Mercer, riding the waves that crashed along my shore. The gut-turning orgasm slammed against my core, crippling me. I deepened the bite on Mercer's finger. He sunk his teeth deeper into my neck.

"Urghhhhh."

The howl emptied me of the bit I'd had left after such a glorious night. My body tingled as my limbs loosened, and my eyes rolled backward.

"Goddamn, Pretty," he murmured, ejecting himself from my womb.

He flipped the cover back, exposing our naked bodies. Memorized, I remained still as he released his seeds on my left cheek.

"Urgh! Fuck."

I fully expected him to fall back onto the pillow to finish our slumber, but witnessing him climb out of bed with his wood still in his hand told a story of its own. He grabbed the towel we'd tossed on the floor hours ago and cleaned himself up. I wasted little time cleaning his semen from my skin once the towel was passed to me.

Both up on our feet, I watched him search for his clothing. One by one, he discovered a new article. With each that he covered his skin with, he pierced another part of my heart.

Stay. I wanted to ask of him, but I knew it would be far too much.

I'd already broken every rule in the book for

Mercer. Strangely, I wouldn't hesitate to do so again if the opportunity presented itself. Phillip had his fun, never missing a day or week to do something utterly foul.

With that in mind, the guilt I would've felt probably should've felt, didn't exist. Mainly because Mercer wasn't vengeance for me. He was a breath of fresh air, oxygen to my lungs, and a defibrillator for my heart.

By the time we made it downstairs, he was able to complete his wardrobe. His pending absence was breaking me down with each step I took. Together, we put away last night's meal. It was untouched, yet we were both full.

When he cracked the front door, there was a pain in my chest that required a hand. I rubbed across the top ever so gently, praying it would subside. His sudden change in direction was just the medicine I needed to halt the achiness I felt.

Wide steps landed him in front of me faster than I'd anticipated. He didn't stop when he entered my personal space. He didn't stop until we were eye to eye, cheek to cheek, nose to nose, lip to lip. Mercer parted mine and entered with his tongue.

"Mmmm." His moan was so beautiful. So was he.

He feels like mine. I whimpered internally. He did. In every way, he felt like he belonged to me. I, too, wanted to belong to him in spite of my circumstances. He felt too right, too rich against my lips.

He kissed me deeply and softly, gripping my butt and pulling me closer to him. When he pulled back, I was too dizzy to stand on my own. I used the railing of the stair-well to keep me upright.

"Will I see you again?" I breathed out heavily and unsteadily.

His head shook from one side to the other, shattering my heart into a trillion pieces that would be impossible to mend.

"There's no room for me and conflict here," he said, touching my chest. "Or here." He touched my head.

"I can exp—"

"I'm not interested in an explanation. When these two are aligned, you know where you can find me."

"I-I don't know, Mercer." I cringed, feeling as though I was pleading my case.

"You're a smart girl, Pretty. You can figure it out. Your studio will be finished tonight. I wish you well, Vallei. Last night was everything we both needed."

"Then why—"

"Shhhhhh."

He placed a finger on my lip to silence me.

"Whenever they're aligned," he emphasized.

Nodding, I confirmed my understanding.

"Goodbye."

"It's not goodbye, Pretty. I'll see you later."

My ears stung, a sign that tears were near. Before he saw my face wet with the pain of our nonexistence, I needed him out of my home and out of my head. Because the ladder was too much to handle, I settled for the more doable task.

I opened the door, allowing the cold to enter. The silk

robe I wore did little to stop the wind from hardening my nipples and causing fine bumps to rise all over my body. Mercer proceeded without a word to spare. When he was finally out of the door, I shut it behind him and pressed my back against it.

The tears I'd fought in his presence had evaporated. The pain of his absence had been replaced with the future victory of his return. He'd come back to me. I knew he would. And when he did, the time would be right. For now, I'd just have to wait.

I returned to my bedroom, ears still ringing from the words Mercer had spoken. How he knew my internal struggle so well had me wondering how much of the weight of my marriage was visible on my shoulders.

The second my head rested on my pillow, my phone began vibrating. I rolled over and grabbed it from the nightstand where Mercer had placed it on the charger.

It's in the details. I remembered my mother describing love, the good parts, and the bad.

To my dismay, a wedding ring appeared on the screen. Phillip had decided to return my call two days later. By now, the urge to talk had dissipated. I didn't even want to hear his voice. I let the phone ring out as I curled into a ball underneath the cover, inhaling the lingering fragrance that coated Mercer's skin until sleep rendered me unconscious.

NOTE.

Between the covers of this book is **my** art piece —
beautifully paired words structured for **my** creative
satisfaction and later consumed by others for enjoyment.

It's **leisure for you**, it's **life for me**.
This is just a book to most. **It's art for me**.
My art. I've had *my* time. Have **yours**.

happy reading

Mercer

GREY**HUFFINGTON**

ONE

Mercer

Four weeks later...

"And your medicine, have you gotten more comfortable with the idea of it? Or your condition at all?"

"The condition, not even a little. The diagnosis wasn't simply a diagnosis for me. It was much more. And it's still taking time to come to terms with it."

"It's been almost two years."

"I don't give a fuck if it was twenty," I retorted, sitting

97

up and lacing my fingers between one another. "With all due respect."

A nod sufficed. Ainsleigh knew that I meant no harm, but there wasn't a better statement that would suffice.

"Bipolar disorder." I scoffed, shaking my head from one side to the other. "It took away from me what no man can ever replace, and it's threatening my sanity, too." Sucking my teeth, I stared past her round eyes and at the dull art behind her. "Nah, I haven't come to terms with it. I probably never will."

"I understand."

"Then, please refrain from noting time. I know exactly how long it's been. Six-hundred-ninety-two days. Twenty-one hours." I peered at the stopwatch on my wrist before continuing. "Thirty-six seconds."

"Time," Ainsleigh pressed. "Your knowledge of time is rather fascinating. What influenced it?"

"My father."

"He knew time well?"

"He knew numbers well. Time just falls under the category and the thing that satisfies my craving for problem-solving more often than not."

"Problem-solving." She reiterated.

"Numbers," I clarified, needing her to understand it wasn't any problem; it was number problems I preferred.

"Understood."

"How does it feel knowing that a piece of your father is embedded in you forever?"

"Honored."

"We don't talk about your parents much. Why not?"

"Because ain't shit to talk about."

"There is. Your change in tone and projection tells me there is a lot to talk about."

"Not today. Not next week. Not next month. Most likely, not next year."

"Hmph." She nodded, jotting in her pad.

"Your brothers?"

I relaxed against the couch, feeling my racing heart slow to its normal pace.

"Yeah. I have four and a wanna-be."

"And you're the eldest?"

"I'm not. That would be Chemistry, same mother and different fathers."

"The maybe?"

"Lawe... a cousin that is just as much a brother."

"Any sisters? I've never heard you mention any."

"My mother had all boys. There are six women that could have anything within my grasp thanks to Chem."

"Six nieces?" she asked, showing her pearly whites as she smiled.

"Six sisters."

"Ooooh."

"So, as the second eldest, how was it living with four brothers after your parents' deaths?"

"I was the oldest in our home. Chem went to live with his father when our mother's health began to decline. In addition to Pops, I was Dad to them. They quickly became my seeds, although they hadn't come from my nutsack."

"Chem's absence, how'd that make you feel? The responsibility was suddenly on you."

"Chem didn't live with us, but Chem was never too far away."

"Your relationship is—"

"A1."

"What about the brother under you?"

"Malachi?"

"Yes."

I tilted my head, feeling the ache in my chest that I ignored most days when my little brother came to mind. He was an adult, but he was still that little boy I helped nurture into a grown-ass man. I rubbed through the hair on my chin, trying my hardest to convey my feelings toward him, his situation, and what he'd gone through.

"It's okay," Ainsleigh assured me. "That's what we're here for."

"Yeah." I coughed. The nothingness in my throat was suffocating me silently.

I felt my eyeballs begin to burn as a fraudulent smile stretched my face upward. The chuckle that fell from my lips wasn't because anything was funny. It was a way to contain the emotions that quickly overpowered me.

"What about Malachi, Mercer?" she asked again, forcing the first few tears from my eyes.

I swiped them as quickly as they came, daring any more to follow.

"I failed Malachi," I admitted out loud for the first time.

Another chuckle came tumbling out of my body.

"Failed him? Please elaborate."

Pausing, I prepared to divulge information and feelings that I preferred keeping bottled in, but I had realized long ago that it was the reason I felt so ill. *Mentally and emotionally.* Acknowledging my illness led me to a doctor, which led to my diagnosis.

It wasn't until three months ago that I decided to begin therapy and unpack the things that had sat with me much longer than they should've. Letting go was not an advantage of mine. I held onto things. I needed to dissect them. I needed to understand them.

And I desperately needed to prepare myself in the event that I encountered them again. It was a never-ending cycle that had my palms hugging the sides of my head some nights, praying that the thoughts, scenarios, and analytics would disappear. They never did.

"His, uh... His wife, Anna, was murdered. She was so much more to us than his wife. She was a childhood friend we'd grown up with. Since we started growing hair under our arms and shit, she was around. Jus-just a really good person. Just a really good woman. And she was snatched away from us so viciously and so heinously, with my niece just a few feet away. She was only a few months old. It's one of those things that just eat away at you every day, no matter how many days pass. When my brother was going through that, I wasn't there. I wasn't around. I couldn't steer him back. I couldn't retrieve him. For two years, my family didn't even recognize him. His pain was seeping from his pores. The Malachi we knew was no more."

"Two years, you say," she replied, making more notes.

"Yes."

"You say that as if things have changed."

"Because they have."

"With Malachi, correct?"

"Yes."

"What changed?"

"Aeir." I sighed, a more genuine smile appearing on my face.

I cleared my eyes of any signs of tears and was able to rest my back on the sofa again.

"You feel better?" She'd noticed.

"Yes."

"What does Aeir mean to you? I realized the mention of her brought you joy."

"She's a blessing."

"Please elaborate."

"She's been healing us all. Though it still hurts, her presence makes it hurt a lot less. She did for my brother what we'd deemed impossible. She met him exactly where he was and pulled him from under the water that had been drowning him for two years. Despite what anyone may think of her or Malachi, she loves him beyond his faults. And him, he's given his entire heart to her, even parts he thought he'd reserve for Anna until his dying day."

"A blessing," she repeated.

"A blessing."

"The brother after Malachi is—"

"Makai."

"Your relationsh—"

"I don't want to discuss Makai."

The pain returned. I sat up, shaking my head. His absence was too much to bear on a day-to-day basis. He deserved to be free. Knowing he was behind a wall made me sick to my stomach. I eyed the trashcan that was a few inches away. Continuing to talk about Makai would have a nigga spilling his entire breakfast in that little motherfucker.

"The youngest?"

"Milo. The baby boy."

"Milo." She marked in her notepad as she called his name.

"The brains."

"How so?"

"He's a Neuropsychiatrist and the Chief of Medicine in Psychiatry."

"Interesting."

"He studies the brain."

"Has he studied yours?"

"Haven't given him the chance, but he would if I did." I laughed, knowing it to be very true.

"Have you told him about your diagnosis?"

"For what? To break his heart? Worry him? Make a mess of his mind?" I asked with flared nostrils and stern eyes.

"You're defensive when it comes to your brothers," she acknowledged.

"I'm defensive when it comes to anyone I love. Medicine won't cure that."

"I understand." With a nod, she continued, "Mr. Domino, aside from family, who else do you have?"

I sat with the question for seconds before responding. "My partna, Portland. Shiiiiiid, that's about it. 'Bout all I need. I've never felt like I needed a bunch of niggas aro—"

"Mercer," she interjected.

Back on a first-name basis, I noted. That meant I probably didn't want to hear whatever was next.

"What's up?"

"I'm not referring to friends."

"Then what are you referring to?"

"Your love life."

"There isn't one."

"Has there been? At any point?"

"Yes."

"Do you ever see one in the future?"

Vallei. Her pretty face came to mind immediately. I blinked away those pretty cheeks and big, hopeful eyes to focus on the moment. She was distracting; thoughts of her were at least. I hadn't seen her since I left her crib a month ago.

I'd be damned if I wasn't tempted to return. My schedule hadn't permitted it, and she had just as much as me going on in that head of hers. I recognized a lost soul when I encountered one because I was one myself.

"I'm working right now. My business is the love of my life."

"Do you ever see one in the future?" She wasn't letting up.

"You nosey as fuck."

"It's my job. You pay good money for me to get in your business, so don't make me ask you a third time."

"I met someone," I confessed, ready to move on.

"Oh, now, this is good news."

Just as the words left her mouth, the alarm on the table between us buzzed. I stood up, not offering another word.

"Saved by the bell, Mr. Domino. We will pick back up right here next week."

"Yeah. Next week."

I didn't wait for her to free me from her office. I let myself out. The swift walk to the car was a breeze. Late March had brought along the rain. I wasn't complaining, but it was sure to slow my commute downtown. The rest of my day would be spent combing through the drafted menu. I hadn't settled on the thirty dishes I'd offer but was close to it.

My vibrating phone silenced the music before it was able to get a decent start. Jay had only spit a few words when Milo's name popped up on the screen. Without hesitation, I did what felt most natural. It was a reaction that would always be a result of discovering my blood needed me or simply needed to holler at me.

"What's up?"

"Shit. Shit. Grabbing something to eat to take to the lady. Quick question," he replied.

"Yeah?"

"Why is your location disabled around this time every week on Friday? Then, suddenly, it's back on an hour or so later?"

"Because I'm a grown-ass man and don't have to explain my whereabouts to another grown-ass man."

"Oh yeah?" He tittered.

"That's what the fuck I just said, isn't it? And why are you always watching us like you're the FEDs or some shit? Don't you have some patients to examine or talk to or some shit? Are they not giving you enough work?"

"Come onboard, and my days will be filled with tasks because you're a fucking head case if I've never seen one. Checking on you and Malachi is my job. We all know where Makai is at all times."

"I almost hung up this phone in your face."

"Real shit, though. You good? You aight?" he asked.

There was a much deeper meaning to his questions. I understood what he was truly asking. How he knew my head was troubled without me ever telling him, I'd never understand. Milo had a way about himself. He was privy to things that the average person just couldn't comprehend or recognize.

I'm in therapy. Every 168 hours and I'm back in the same building, same office, on the same couch. I rambled inside, but the words stayed lodged in my brain.

"Yeah. I'm good."

My line buzzed. Timing couldn't have been better. Seeing Roulette's name on the screen could only mean one thing—*paper was calling*.

"Roulette trying to get through. I'ma holler at you in a bit, aight?"

"Yeah. Yeah. Hit my line."

I ended the call without another word. It would only fuel whatever worries or thoughts circling Milo's cranium. To relieve him, I clicked over to answer the incoming call on the other end.

"Tell me something good," I demanded, creeping down the highway with my wipers damn near on full blast.

"Sounds like you're pushing through the storm, so I'll make it quick."

"Appreciate it."

"There's a really big event happening tonight. Small, intimate, but major. Some key players in the city will be in attendance. I think it'll be great exposure for The M. Thankfully, the hosts were at my roundtable last night complaining about their hired help not falling through. They're in need of a chef."

"How many people?"

"Sixty-five. All of whom are possible customers in the future."

"Say less."

"I've already set the plan in motion. You should receive an email with more details in the next five minutes. Upcharge. They have the funds. Tack on fees for last-minute booking and whatever else your heart desires." She laughed. "Have fun with their pockets."

"Thanks for looking out."

"Of course."

Since announcing my interest in covering upscale luxury catering opportunities in the city, Roulette has been on my line three to four times a month with new opportunities. Some for her private events and others for those around the city. I was appreciative of them all. It was exposure for The M, which would be opening in a few months.

Jay finally began spitting his shit. But just as Roulette had mentioned, an email cut right through the next track on his last album. *Tremble & Tremble Annual Charity Dinner* headed the subject line of the message.

Reading and fighting the rain was a sure way to end it all, so I refrained from opening the email for the time being and focused on the road. The darkening sky had little to do with the time of day and everything to do with the violent weather that was in progress.

Flashers of drivers who couldn't bear the treachery of the raindrops blinked under the overpasses. Hadn't the Ford F-450 Super Duty Platinum been my vehicle of choice, then it was possible I'd be pulled over, waiting for the rain to let up, too. However, I was confidently pushing the pedal, making my way downtown.

Arrival was delayed slightly, but I shot a quick one up to God for safely getting me to my destination. Slowly, I made my way to the back door, allowing the raindrops to tap against the outer layer of the Nike jacket that blocked the accompanying winds. Within seconds, I'd gained access.

I passed several doors before entering my office. I rounded the mouse to power up the computer. Emails littered the screen, but there was one in particular I was interested in. It was the first on the long list of those I'd either opened or had no plans to open.

Tremble & Tremble Annual Charity Dinner

Greetings, Chef Domino.

Our wish is that this email finds you in great spirits. Tremble & Tremble Annual Charity Dinner is happening tonight, and our plans have taken a huge hit due to the cancellation of our caterer. We were given the green light to contact you via email, but are willing to discuss this matter on a call if it suits you better.

We've had the pleasure of enjoying your meals amongst friends at a private establishment and thought you'd be the perfect fit for the night. Hopefully, you have availability. If not, please send us an invoice for a sum worth our petition for your availability as we are out of options.

Details:
65 attendees
4-course meal

Premium protein options

We're at our desks. Please feel free to send any correspondence to the emails listed. The entire team is waiting to hear from you.

Operations Management at Tremble & Tremble Law Firm

Technology was still my nemesis, but I was learning the ins and outs as each day went on. The most important tasks for my business, however, I could perform at the drop of a hat. Swiftly, I drafted an invoice that would indeed petition for my availability. Though I didn't have any catering contracts to satisfy tonight, they didn't know it and never would.

THEM INVOICE

BILLED TO:
Tremble & Tremble Law Firm
Berkeley, Huffington
Operations Management

Invoice No. 00345
24 March

Item	Quantity	Unit Price	Total
4-Course Meal	65	$250	$16250
Labor	1	$2500	$2500
Expedited Service	1	$2500	$2500
		Subtotal	$21250
		Tax (0%)	$0
		Total	**$21250**

PLEASE FIND ATTACHED:
- The official invoice payment link. All invoices must be satisfied within one hour of receipt to avoid cancellation.
- A contractual agreement that outlines The M's catering policy, duties, and expectations.

Mercer Domino
Owner, The M - Huffington

I hit send and stood to stretch my legs, mentally preparing to complete the tedious task of combing over the menu for the next hour, which was when the deadline for the invoice would be. Just as I returned to my seat, I heard the back door slam shut. Simultaneously, my phone vibrated twice.

"Mercer?" Pop's voice boomed through the hallway.

"In my office!" I yelled, checking the notifications.

An email was amongst the duo. The second made my head bob and brows raise. The twenty-one-thousand-dollar invoice had been satisfied. The hour I planned to spend going over the menu had quickly changed to an hour of preparation. In five hours, I'd need to be en route to the location listed on the email I'd just received.

Mentally, I began putting together a full menu for the night that would require little prep and cooking time. We would be working against the clock, which I hated, personally, but the timing of the booking gave me little choice and even less to consider as part of the four courses.

"Oh, I know that look on your face. What have you done?" Pops groaned, unsure of what but knowing something was up.

"Kept the lights on another day in here," I summed. "You down to do dinner for sixty-five tonight? Four courses? Premium selections?"

"That's my kind of carrying on. What time are we talking?"

"It starts at seven. We should get there around five—at the latest."

"Sounds like a plan to me. I'm going to get Aeir on the line. I'm sure she'll have a fit if we don't include her."

Her jewelry business was the love of her life, but it kept her behind the desk or in the warehouse she'd created after a surge in business. Whenever she was given the chance to escape, she did. The two loyal employees she had on her team made sure everything ran smoothly in her absence. Because they closed their doors at five every evening, she was happy to accompany Pops and me to a few events.

"I think it's the only time I see her frown." I chuckled. "When we forget to hit her line, or she can't make it all together."

"Which is exactly why it's the first thing on my list of to-dos."

Pops was more of the same. Assisting me with the business was the highlight of his days. Feeling useful after everyone had grown up and gotten families of their own gave him a reason to keep fighting the fight of life.

He was at the restaurant faithfully, even if only for a few hours. Each and every day. His key was put to good use. I wouldn't be surprised if the paint were chipping already. He was always finding something to keep him busy and spare me the headache of taking on everything alone.

"I'm heading to the market to holler at Carlos."

"So, you have a menu in mind already?"

"He said premium options. That could only mean a few things: shrimp, lobster, snapper, and lamb. I'm not fucking with steak tonight, pops."

"I don't consider that shit premium, anyway."

"It can be," I reminded him.

"Yeah, whatever."

He wasn't a fan of steak, but he didn't hate it, either. Every now and again, he indulged.

"I'll handle the sides."

"Bet. Send me the list when you do. I can grab everything at once."

"Alright, headed to my desk now. I have the catering options there."

Any catering opportunities we had, the people who brought us on had the responsibility of putting their own menus together based on our array of selections. We had no time to go back and forth about the menu this time. We had to get down to business, prepping and getting ourselves ready for the unexpected twists that usually occurred during on-site catering. Though we prepared well, there were many things out of our control.

"Be here when I get back, old man."

"Where else do I have to go?" He sniggered.

As I exited, bumping into the rain, again, I noticed it had slowed down tremendously. My vibrating phone quickened my pace. I settled in before tapping the screen to find a missed call from Glacier. I wasted no time hitting her back.

Her face appeared seconds after te first ring. She was such a beautiful girl but the pain of my brother's absence was written all over her face. It rested in her eyes and the permanent worry lines that creased her head. As much as she tried, it was hard to keep it together. That's the reason my family and I rallied around her for support and sanity.

"Hi, Mercer. I hope I'm not bothering you. I–"

"Don't insult me, G. What's up? How are my babies?"

"That's why I'm calling. I just wanted to let you

know I'm leaving this evening, just in case you wanted to stop by before I left."

"What happened to tomorrow?"

"I completely forgot I promised my cousin a dinner date. She's been eager to see me and I've been putting it off for some time, now. I hadn't noticed I'd agreed to the weekend I'd be here until this morning. It's fine if you can't. I just wanted to go over the plans for the shower once more so that we don't have to spend weeks texting and emailing."

"Understood. I'm about to drop by the condo now. I'm on my way to the market up that way, anyway. Be expecting me in about twenty-five minutes. I want to run over the menu I have in mind. Kleu has a few ideas in mind as far as the decor. I'll let the women handle that shit."

"Okay. And, of course. We're supposed to get on a call later this week. She showed me a bit of the decor at dinner."

"Have you talked to Milo and Malachi?"

"Yes. Malachi just left. Milo stopped by on his way from Nature's office about an hour ago. They missed each other by a few minutes."

"Pops at the restaurant."

"I'm almost certain Pops has had enough of me for the month. I've driven that man crazy for the last two days with my random requests," she laughed.

"Bet. Bet. I'm on my way."

"Alright, see you in a bit."

I ended the call, pushing the pedal a bit harder, ready to finalize a few details before my evening got hectic. Wouldn't shit move until I'd sent Glacier on her way with enough love to last her over the month that would pass before we saw her again.

Glacier made the trip faithfully to see her grandmother, which we used as an opportunity to see her and her protruding belly. We made sure we rescheduled our dinners to include them. Instead of First Friday, we now had Final Fridays. The last Friday, everyone cleared their schedules to be together. It kept our circle tight and our bond tighter.

Mercer Vallei

"Last round, everybody!" Pops yelled, attempting to lift already ascended spirits in the kitchen. For four hours, we'd been busy at work. The dinner had been in session for two, but we'd arrived much earlier to get a head start on things.

"How are we doing on the caramel?" Standing over Kleu, I questioned as she stirred.

"We'd be doing well if you weren't standing over me talking, risking the particles from your mouth falling into my drizzle," she sassed.

"Who hired you again?"

Between her and Aeir, I wasn't sure whose business it

truly was. Though Kleu was never officially invited because she made it clear that she didn't want to be standing over anyone's stove cooking for anyone other than her man, I always found her standing over the stove. She'd only accompanied us to three events, but the extra set of hands was always needed.

"I hired myself. I also decided on my own rate of pay."

"Hmm. What is that, exactly?"

"Getting out of my face. That is enough compensation for the night."

She meant it, too. Money was never a factor for any of the family when they came to help, but I slid them enough for their troubles. Many occurred during our time in the kitchen.

"That nigga rubbing off on you. He's ignorant, and you're not too far behind him."

"That's my man, and imma stick by him," she claimed, removing the sauce from the heat and setting it aside.

With a shake of the head, I took a second to grasp the beauty of my view. Not only was I in my comfort zone, but I was surrounded by people who wanted to see me win. Cooking, even when it was dope, had always been my specialty.

With Chem's recipe, there wasn't a nigga in Berkely that could whip up a batch better than me. Find one who said he could, and you'd be in the presence of a liar. It was that simple. Though that title felt pretty damn good to hold, it was nothing in comparison to how much weight the one that I had now held.

Chef Domino - *self-taught* food enthusiast and entrepreneur. ***A legit nigga***.

The piss that had me shifting my weight every other second announced itself again, urging me to head to the toilet. I didn't wish it away this time. From the sight in front of me, I knew my people would hold the kitchen down.

Dessert was the ladies' specialty. After perfecting the boneless caramel cookie recipe, I had little worries. Aeir paid close attention to detail and cooked them to perfection every time. They came out of the oven flawless.

Pops rolled our handmade ice cream that topped the cookie once it cooled down enough not to melt his creation. Caramel drizzled the cookie and ice cream after it had also cooled slightly. Last, the caramel crunch was sprinkled on top.

This was an item that I had no doubt would make every cut until we had our final menu for the restaurant. Clients and their guests raved about the treat. I'd had it enough times to know that they weren't just talking out the side of their necks. It was top-notch.

"I need to hit the head."

"These will be out by the time you return," Aeir assured me, tilting her head toward the cookies. "Just waiting for the caramel to thicken a bit."

Everything was made from scratch, down to the dressing we used for our salad. The M would be known for in-house, from-scratch sauces, sides, dressings, syrups, and desserts. That was not up for question. It added a layer of authenticity to the restaurant that others couldn't compete with.

Though my intention wasn't to compete, I understood that others would try. However, having a customer fall in love with something as simple as in-house ketchup or caramel drizzle would sometimes be the deciding factor for their night out or which place they suggested their friends try for dinner.

I stepped into the hallway and was immediately greeted by two people swapping spit. One I recognized. I hadn't seen the other because I hadn't stepped foot outside of the kitchen until now. The team of servers that cost us one hundred and fifty dollars an hour made that possible. Our tab wouldn't run over five hundred for the night.

According to the time and energy they continued to save us, that was mere pennies. I'd pay their invoice without regret each time we worked together. Their team would be training the team of servers that made it through the final round of interviews for The M. There was no question in my mind. Pops had already confirmed, and Aeir was onboard.

"Chef Domino!" Phillip Tremble wiped the smeared lipstick from his mouth as he called out. "The man of the hour. Everyone is raving about the food, man. That's some pretty good shit."

He was a bit too loud and a bit too fucking friendly for my liking, but he was the nigga that cleared the invoice without hesitation, so I tolerated him *tonight*. It was apparent he'd had a few drinks, and the liquor was heavy in his system. His limbs were looser than the first time I'd seen him, and his tie wasn't too far behind.

Though he was born into a family of lawyers, he didn't fit the mold. I didn't need his credentials to be comfortable with my observation. I'd met five men with the same last name, all attorneys, poised, and carried themselves a lot like my family. They said little, made plenty of observations and carried themselves according to the conclusions they'd drawn from those observations.

I remembered each and every one of them from Rouge. Ass filled their laps, and titties nearly covered their entire faces. Nipples sat on their tongues as they enjoyed the flavor of the month according to the calendar that Roulette carefully created at the top of each year. She stuck to it religiously.

With a simple nod, I continued on my way, not interested in chatting. I was hoping dessert was out upon my return so I could send my help on their way and get out of there myself. I imagined it wasn't too much to ask from God because when I returned, He'd already begun working on my plan.

"Everything is out," Aeir announced. "All sixty-five caramel crumble cake cookies."

"And that's a wrap," Pops added. "I've been cleaning as we've been going, so there's only a few dishes to take care of, and we can get out of here after we pack our things."

"I can handle the rest."

"No. I'll do the dishes."

"It's nine, Aeir. You'll get home to your children and your husband. I'll do the rest."

"I'm fine. I—"

"Malachi is already outside waiting. He should be, at least."

"You told him to—"

"Yes. Because I knew you wouldn't go willingly, I told him to come get his wife at nine. If you know Malachi like I knew Malachi, then you know that—"

"He's outside." She sighed.

"Goodnight, Aeir. Check your account in the next thirty minutes."

"It better not be any extra money in there, Mercer. I'm not playing."

Her warning did nothing for either of us. She wouldn't make good on any threats she made. And she knew that I would fall through with funds either way.

"Put it up for my niece and nephew if you don't want it."

I kissed her forehead and snatched the apron from her hand. "Goodnight."

"Goodnight," she replied reluctantly, wrapping her arms around me.

There was something in her spirit that silenced every unwelcome thought in my head, every voice that didn't belong, and every feeling of failure that I'd ever felt. The sadness of life, losing my parents, losing Anna, losing my aunt, and being plagued with a mental illness I despised all dissipated.

It disappeared when Aeir's body collided with mine.

And though she didn't hug any of the other guys, I always found her arms around me as if she just knew, as if she just understood that I needed it without me having to tell her. She was far from a replacement for Anna. We'd never compare either in that light. They both had similarities but were special in their own ways. She was a blessing. Not just for Malachi but for me, too.

Even for a few seconds, this angel scared away my demons. That was a task that not even I could manage. But she did, effortlessly.

I watched her leave, wondering how God had fit so many precious things into one being. When I finally gathered myself and all the demons she left me with, I turned to find Kleu staring at me with her bag on her shoulder. I chuckled. Lawe had something on his hands with this one. She was with all the shit, and I loved that.

At least one of the women in the family was ready for war, coming with her own weapons and body armor. She was known to shield and protect and was marvelous at her job. She'd go to war behind the ones she loved, reminding me of us all.

"I don't sit around and wait for a nigga to tell me what to do and how to move," she hissed, rolling her eyes.

"Yeah. Whatever, Kleu. Catch Aeir so Malachi can make sure you get to your car safely. He knows you're coming out."

"So he knew I was next, too?"

"He did."

"Leave that girl alone," Pops warned.

"Tell 'em again. I'll see y'all next time, but don't call me 'cause I'm not standing over nobody's stove."

"Umm hmmm." I chuckled as she exited.

"He's going to marry her. Watch what I tell you." Pops grunted. "Watch what I tell you."

"I doubt it, Pops, but you could be right."

"Maybe not legally, but he will."

"That sounds right."

His backpack was on his shoulder. He was edging toward the door, understanding I needed the rest of the night to myself to sort out things in my head, zone out a time or two, and get the rest of the work done. The silence was inviting, and I'd accept the invitation every time.

"I'm not going to sit around and wait, either. I know that this is your golden hour."

"Appreciate it, Pops."

"Just don't let your thoughts get ahead of you. What- ever you're thinking about, God has already taken care of it. Rest your head, son."

"I'll try," I promised.

"That's all I ask. I love you."

"One love."

With that, he was out of the door and on his way home. As for me, my night was just getting started. Over the next forty-five minutes, the kitchen would be wiped clean, and any traces that there had been activity within it would be erased. I took a look at the watch on my wrist and began the timer.

9:48:22pm. It would be precisely when my night ended, and I could retire.

10:51:22pm. It would be precisely when I pulled the covers over me, praying that God freed me from the personal hell my thoughts kept me in at night when I lie with my eyes wide shut.

The headphones went over my ears but were low enough to hear everything around me. While my body opted for something chatty with words, my head was longing for the soothing sounds of John Coltrane. Feeling invincible, I got down to business.

Disinfectant, apple-scented dish soap, degreaser, all-purpose cleaner, and fresh water were all I smelled as I scrubbed and wiped every surface we'd touched. The trash bag grew fuller with each passing second. I was partly oblivious to everything around me and everything within me as I journeyed through the zone that I loved to visit most.

Within thirty minutes and eighteen seconds, the kitchen was spotless. Within fifteen minutes, my equipment and supplies needed to be in the back of my truck, ready to head home for the night. The first load consisted of my most prized possessions. I needed them out of the kitchen and in my personal vehicle before anything else.

Leaving them behind or having them stolen would dampen my spirit and leave me unwell for the remainder of the night. Each knife in the set had cost me over three hundred dollars. As many would consider it overspending, I didn't. Each was worth every fucking penny. If they were ever stolen, I'd hunt the thief down, slit him open, and gut him just like the animal he portrayed.

"CHEF!" The voice I'd heard over an hour prior was a little more sluggish and a lot more intoxicated.

I kept pushing, deciding against stopping to chat. In the state he was in, there wasn't shit to talk about anyway. He'd only interfere with the time that I was banking on to be home and in my fucking bed.

"My w... My wife has been going on and on and on about them damn garlic potatoes. Says th-they remind her of a frie-friend. Baby, tell hi—"

"Phillip," a familiar voice called out.

Soft. Tantalizing. Entrancing. I remembered that voice. I remembered the person who owned it. I remembered her face. I remembered her beauty. I remembered her body. I remembered her pussy. How plump it was. How pretty it was. And how motherfucking powerful it was.

How it looked. How it felt. How it tasted. I was floored with the memories that swelled the nothingness in my throat. My eyes slimmed to slits, breathing going astray.

Some shit you never forgot. Some people you never forgot. Some encounters you never forgot. She fit the criteria for it all. She was an unforgettable experience, one that I planned to revisit as soon as I got some shit off my plate and made time. But not even time could change what was presented to me.

"It's okay, honey," she begged.

She'd stopped me in my tracks. I couldn't move

another inch. So, instead, I turned to face the couple, finding Vallei standing beside the man who'd called her his wife. My eyes darted across her face, down her body, and to the ring that hadn't been on her finger the night my dick was inside of her.

Pretty? My heart saddened. My head rang. My chest caved. But it rose almost immediately after. Simultaneously, I felt my phone vibrate in my hand. I lowered my gaze, finding Jas' name on the screen. I silenced the call instantly, caring more about the woman in front of me than the one on the line. My body was a pit of fire. I was burning inside and out.

She was stunning. The chocolate ensemble rested against her chocolate skin, giving the illusion that she was half-naked. For me, she was. I could see right through that pretty ass face of hers. Her mouth hung with surprise. And hadn't it been for me wanting to stick my dick in it, I would've wanted a bug to fly right in that motherfucker.

She reeked of roses, peaches, pears, vanilla, and all the other shit that would stick with me long after she left, smelling pleasant after the fact. Her makeup was light. I could still see her rare, true beauty underneath the minimalistic approach. The strings that hung off her shoulders hardly disguised her artistic persona. She couldn't help herself.

"I want you to meet my wife, Vallei. Chef Domino is responsible for the food you haven't stopped raving about. Chef Domino, Vallei."

I couldn't even bring myself to nod as names were

exchanged. Everything quickly began to make sense. Her conflict wasn't within herself. It was within her marriage. And that was some shit I simply wasn't fucking with. Not a word fell from my mouth as disgust altered my features. With an upturned lip and bunched eyebrows, I scoffed, turning around and heading for my car again, hoping the cameras would greet me because this had to be some kind of joke.

Not my fucking Pretty.

TWO

Valki

My heart and my head were in shambles. Mercer's handsome face, which had been pressed against mine, lay on my chest and rested between my legs, was disgusted. The sight of me, for him, seemed repulsive. At any second, I imagined he would vomit.

The tension between us was so thick I was sure I wouldn't be able to cut it with one of his best knives. My eyes saddened as we peered at one another, unable to say anything, though our silence said everything. Without a single word, I begged for his forgiveness and the chance to explain.

The moment I lost eye contact with him and was given his back, I shed tears inside. The achiness of my chest and the sinking of my brows revealed emotions that my mouth was forbidden to. The same back I'd clawed at round after round stalked the path toward the door.

Come back. I dared to yell out. The words were at the tip of my tongue. *Wait! Please. I can explain.* I could. I could explain Phillip and I, our situation, and how I was trapped in a marriage that served me no longer. *But will he hear me?* I wondered. *Or not be able to see beyond the surface?* My heart wouldn't be able to handle any answer other than yes. *Come back.*

"Come on, Vallei. I need to get ready to close this thing out. It's time for donation announcements. Maybe we can hire him for our renewal? Yeah?"

As the words fell from my husband's lips, Mercer continued in the other direction.

Phillip's drunken tug after a few words left me mortified. I wanted nothing more than to run behind the man who had managed to resuscitate me after diminishing for two consecutive years.

Whatever pain he felt, whatever disappointment he felt was justified, but the idea of him thinking anything but good things about me made me want to fall on my knees in front of him and demand I be forgiven.

"Yeah?" Phillip repeated himself.

"Phillip, our fifth anniversary was two months ago," I informed him, accepting his hand as we headed for the ballroom.

My words halted his stride. I found something in his

eyes that I hadn't seen in some time. *Remorse. Regret. Sympathy.* It was much too late for either of them to affect me as they would've months prior, but they were there, which let me know that he wasn't as much of a monster as he pretended to be. Somewhere in there, he still cared. In his own fucked up way, he cared. At least a little.

"Tw-two months ago," he repeated as if he was having a sudden epiphany.

"It's fine. Let's just go insi—"

"Yeah. Uh. Let's go inside."

Another look in the other direction and I noticed how close Mercer had gotten to the door. If I allowed him to walk out, it would possibly be the last time I'd see him for the night. I refused to let him leave under the impression that I was something, someone that I wasn't or that the night we'd shared meant nothing.

"Phillip, go ahead. I need to use the ladies' room."

"Alright," he replied absentmindedly, still stuck on the fact that he'd forgotten our anniversary. It was a clear sign that his mind was elsewhere and our marriage had gone up in smoke.

"Go ahead. I'll be in here," he said, pointing straight ahead.

With the tail of my dress pinched between my thumb and index finger, I pushed past the kitchen in the direction of the ladies' room. It was also the direction that Mercer had gone in. Before I made it to the door, he reappeared. Slightly damped from the light drizzle outside, he stepped inside, drying his shoes on the mat to reduce the chances of tracking water on the floor.

The lifting of his head and removal of the hoodie that hadn't been hugging his chest when he'd left out locked every limb on my body. I froze in place, transfixed on the man before me. He demanded my attention, every ounce of it.

The epitome of regal, this man felt like a dream. Mercer was nostalgic, reminding me of the men who were uncompromisingly gorgeous in the nineties when the jewelry was minimal, and the sexiness was always at its maximum. He oozed sex appeal. Every move he made made me want to widen my legs a little more and give him free rein over my body, over my heart.

Stuck in place, he returned my gaze. And just like that, for what felt like an eternity, we stood still. His nostrils flared as his beautiful features crumbled on his face.

"I'm sorry," I whispered, tilting my head to express my sincerest apology.

"I don't give a fuck," he barked.

His lack of discretion caused me to look around, wondering if anyone had heard him or if anyone was witnessing our encounter. A snigger from his direction caught my attention. He pushed forward, pushing me in the process. I held my position, not letting him pass me. If I did, I'd lose him, and that wasn't an option. I knew that he was forbidden territory, and so was I, but I'd be lying if I said I gave one little fuck. I didn't.

I once had, but Mercer made me forget my morals,

forget my vows. While I'd stayed true to them, Phillip had done his dirt and done it without a care in the world. I wasn't, at all, attempting to return the gesture. Mercer had fallen on my doorstep. He'd found me. I hadn't gone searching for trouble.

"I'm not the nigga you can creep with. Get that shit out of your thick skull and move the fuck out of my way."

"Let me explain."

Wordlessly, he tried pushing forward. My hands landed on his chest, pushing him in the other direction. Where, I was unsure, but him being anywhere but out of sight would suffice. His silence was deafening.

"Please."

Peering down at me, he stopped moving. I could see his jaws flexing and the veins in his neck protruding. My center melted when his fingers wrapped around my bare arms, pushing me down the hallway. Unsure of where we were headed, I cared none.

Within seconds, I was inside a dark, cool room that increased the small, fine bumps that Mercer had already summoned. My dress was lifted over my ass, and my body was hoisted in the air. My panties were torn, leaving only the band around the bottom of my stomach.

"Uhhhhhhhhhhhh."

My arms rounded his neck, pulling him closer. His teeth threatened to break my skin as they sunk into the first layer. His anger was evident. It was his intention to punish me. I would gladly accept every inch of his weapon. I deserved it for the turmoil I'd caused.

"Meeeeeerr—ummmm. Yeeeeessss."

"Shut up!" he demanded.

I quieted, muffling my pain as he left a burning indention on my shoulder. He'd marked me.

Suddenly, I was on wobbling legs, bent over something that I was unable to see, as Mercer entered me from behind. My body quivered as I was hit with one wave. The second came immediately after. My orgasm followed, leaving me dazed in the dark. Words began flying from my mouth in spite of the command to quiet.

"I'm sorry," I confessed. "I'm sorry."

A swift slap stung my right cheek.

"Ahhh."

Another, in the same spot, made my pussy's contractions intensify.

"Ummmm!"

A third one made me cry out in pain, yet whimper in pleasure. My walls tightened around him.

"Fuck!" I screamed.

Desperate to relieve the ache, I tossed my body backward into his midsection. The sound of our skin smacking left me spineless. This was the sound of pure, mind-boggling sexual satisfaction. Never, in my sixteen years of intimacy, had I ever experienced anything that came close.

From his girth to his skill, Mercer was a menace. He depleted me with each round we'd gone since the first time he'd entered me. And since that moment, I'd been craving more of him. In an attempt to respect my home and my marriage, I avoided reaching out or stopping by the restaurant he'd mentioned opening soon.

But just like the first time, he was placed right in front of me as if he was meant to be in my line of vision more often than not. I couldn't fight the temptation any longer. I couldn't fight my feelings any longer. I wanted to explore the deepest, darkest parts of him. I wanted to claim him as mine and give him the rights to my heart and soul. I felt, with every fiber of my being, that he was worthy of them.

"You keep fucking me like that knowing you got a nigga? A husband? Fuck is you on, Pretty?"

His questions fell on death's door. There was no way he expected me to answer any of them with his dick lodged inside of me, filling me to capacity. He fisted my hair, pulling my head backward until he had access to my neck.

"Enjoy this dick while you can cause it's the last time you'll have the privilege. My head fucked up enough. I don't need you up there playing with my shit."

He released me forcefully, using the same hand to grip my neck. He thrust, making my walls cream continuously. I'd made a mess of us both. I didn't need a light to confirm. The stirring in the dark and the wetness between my thighs was enough evidence.

When he ejected himself, I almost cried for him to re-enter me. I felt hot semen on my cheeks.

"Mercccc—"

As if he'd read my thoughts, he filled me again.

"You're playing a dangerous game, Pretty," he whispered in my ear. "A dangerous fucking game."

"I'm sorry," I cried out, cumming again.

As I began to unravel, he removed himself from my canal again.

"On your fucking knees." He grunted.

Without hesitation, I fell to the floor. Still in the darkness, he gripped my hair and pulled my head backward until the tip of his dick was on my lip. I took him into my mouth. He stroked my face gently and with so much care. Each time he touched the back of my throat, my eyes watered. The tampering with my gag reflex was risky, especially on a full stomach.

"Merr—"

He disregarded my pleas, sliding in and out of my mouth until his body grew rigid. He removed himself, releasing his seeds on my polished skin. And before I could find my way to my feet again, the glimmer of light from the door shined.

"Stay away from me, Pretty. I'm trouble you don't want to get into because you won't ever be able to get out."

He vanished, leaving me with a million feelings compounding, a semen-stained dress, and a face that matched.

Mercer Vallei

The bright light in the restroom etched away at the buzz I'd received from being with Mercer. The guilt I wanted to feel, expected to feel, had yet to show its face. As I waited, I cleaned his semen from my silk dress with a paper towel. I'd cleaned my body with a wet wipe from my clutch I'd found on the floor near the door of what I learned was the janitor's closet after flipping on the light.

Mercer had completely destroyed my mental capacity. I'd forgotten it belonged to me. I'd forgotten where I was, who I was with, and what was happening around me. All I knew was him when he was in my presence. Somehow, I believed it was all I needed to know in those moments.

Satisfied with my cleaning efforts, I tossed the paper towel in the trash and stood underneath the hand dryer. It sensed movement and began almost immediately. As it did, a familiar face entered the private room reserved for at least four women at a time. With three stalls and a small vanity, it was the perfect girls' room.

I'd never been more thankful for the loud, obnoxious sounds of the dryer than at the moment. Raven's uneven ends bounced from one side to the other as she rattled off a greeting I couldn't hear and didn't attempt to understand. I refused to lower my vibrations to the level she expected me to in order to converse.

The fact that I was almost certain she was the woman my husband had fallen in love with might've had something to do with my lack of motivation to respond to whatever she'd said, or maybe it was the man that had left me with cum dripping down my face like the arrogant, confident piece of work he was. I wasn't sure, but it didn't matter much. She didn't matter much. And as time passed, Phillip didn't matter much, either.

"Nice seeing you, though. It's so good to see a familiar face at these events. So full of testosterone, just like the office. My God."

The dryer cycle ended, finally making her words clear and understandable. I restarted it instantly, choosing to hear it instead. A quick nod and forged smile soothed the guilt in her eyes, allowing her to press forward and into a stall. So that the moment wouldn't repeat itself, I ended my restroom visit seconds after she disappeared behind a stall.

Raven was a paralegal who had begun working with my in-laws three months prior to Phillip's unforgivable acts. Prior to her, his infidelity had been in secrecy. After she began working at the office, things changed. And seven months ago, they reached the point of no return.

He spent as much time with her as he did in our home, possibly more if business hours were included. With her, there was no concrete evidence, but the heart knew. I was no fool, and this wasn't my first rodeo. She was my husband's lover. Hadn't I been sure before, seeing them in the same room tonight confirmed it. Every time she cut out, he was behind her. Whenever he went missing, so did she.

My chest collided with Phillips. He was rounding the corner, possibly in search of Raven. His frustration with running into me instead was apparent. He blew steam from his nose, wishing he was chest to chest with his lover, not his wife.

"Are you ready?" He huffed, stepping back to fix the jacket of his suit.

"I am. Are the donations alre—"

"Yes. We're doing things a bit differently this year. I've announced them. They've already been made. However. Something new Dad decided since the dinner itself always lasts for hours. The older they ge-get, the earlier they want to go home."

His words were slow to come, but he managed each and every one of them, confirming that driving wouldn't be much of an issue. The water bottle in his hand proved he was attempting to sober up. Things seemed to be working in his favor.

Even at my age, getting behind the wheel wasn't a habit of mine. The anxiety of it all left me breathless and unable to focus. There were so many moving parts and things to consider as a driver. Personally, I didn't have the capacity.

"Are you okay to drive?"

"It's the only way we're getting home." He barked. "So why ask, Vallei?"

"Because safety matters, Phillip. There are other ways. I know a few."

Carriage was one. Another was having Penelope, his youngest sibling, take us. By the aggravation in his tone, it became apparent that he wasn't in the mood for me. Though barely recognizable, I could sense the shift in his mood. It was the shift that almost always came before a forced disagreement that led to his disappearance.

"Yeah, then why don't you drive, baby?" His tilted head and curious eyes waited for an explanation I didn't have.

"Let's go, shall we?"

With his hand in mine, Phillip led the way through the entry room and down the hallway. We reached the front door within seconds, both piling into his Range Rover shortly after. The rain was beginning to pick up again. Though I wanted to rest, I kept my eyes open as I observed Phillip's handling of the wheel to make sure our lives weren't in danger. His driving was fine. His heart, though, was in a scary, faraway place.

"Listen," he began. "Why is it that every time we're around my family, you're suddenly uptight and uncomfortable? I've never said much about it, but it's getting notably worse each time we're in their presence. What the hell have any of them ever done to you?"

Aid your infidelity. I responded, but the words were trapped inside my throat. I didn't care to indulge in back and forth that Phillip was batting at.

With Mercer's help, I'd ascended past anything he attempted to snip my peace with. My gratification was beyond him at the moment. He held no power.

The man who had left my face stained with semen and my heart in his hand still reigned supreme, though he was no longer around. Phillip's antics were beneath me, literally and figuratively speaking. I was still floating. And not even for my husband would I come down.

"If this is leading where I think it's leading, I don't want to go there, Phillip. I can't go there. I won't go there. I refuse to go there."

"Go where? Here you go with this artsy-ass, poetic-ass response. Baby, speak English."

His surface-level understanding of anything and everything that pertained to me, our love, and our life together had never been so clear, not until the last few months. It was heartbreaking to know that one was so monotone, so depthless in life. It must've been awful. To live a life of black and white where there were so many gray areas, so many colors, and so many possibilities must've been displeasing.

"I don't have the energy you're in search of, Phillip."

"Energy I'm in search of?" He tittered, sucking the skin of his teeth.

Deciding that misery wouldn't make a believer out of me, I sighed as my words began to fall into place. I lowered a hand onto Phillip's, the one he wasn't using to steer the wheel, as I watched the street lights pass us by.

"You don't have to fight me to be free, Phillip. This disagreement you're sparking is only a ploy for you to free yourself from the restraints of our marriage for however long you see fit. Tonight, I feel really good. I won't give you the satisfaction. I can't give you the satisfaction. You didn't provide it, so you can't have it. I'm sorry."

The words left my mouth as the wheels of his truck stopped rolling. Without haste, and as Phillip fought to find the perfect response, I stepped down onto the wet concrete. I wasn't sure I'd ever been so happy to be home.

A nicely rolled herbal blend and the tea from the tin that I'd been using as my saving grace on sleepless nights were the first things on my mind. The last was the tub full of bubbles that smelled like fresh roses. It would be the last line of the poem my day had scribed before I ended it in bed.

My uneventful entrance was met by the smell of vanilla, caramel, and honey. My soul rejoiced, appreciating the warmth I was invited into. Still somewhere in my stratosphere, above all else, I floated through my dwelling with a smile that stretched my cheeks miles apart, lifted my brows where my hairline usually rested, and kept my eyes tight enough to resemble their closing.

I removed my dress as I entered my bedroom. The coat was left downstairs on the rack. My torn panties were discarded in the trashcan as I walked into the bathroom. The heels that once numbed my toes were replaced with soft, fluffy slippers as I entered. The jewelry, the makeup, and the facade that I was leading a perfect marriage all vanished simultaneously, allowing me to crawl into the shell I loved most.

Warm water cascaded from the faucet of my bathtub as I waited close by, rolling herbs into a piece of perfection. The smell of jasmine and lavender from the bubble bath filled the air, reminding me that a cup of tea was in my near future. I contemplated waiting for the cup of luxury, finally settling on the thought that I'd seek its satisfaction only if I couldn't get to bed on my own.

Unlike the rest of my sleepless nights, this one included Mercer, his haughtiness, his dominance, and his dick. It was an unbeatable combination that induced sleep without effort. I believed, with every fiber of my being, that I'd rest like a newborn for hours on end.

The theory had been tested once, and I wished I

could rewind time to return to that very moment. Mercer was in my arms, in my space, in my world, drowning me with his attention, affection, and ability to drain me of the sexual tension I'd experienced, along with everything else my body had to release.

The water was perfect. I shut it off as it hit the fill line I'd etched underneath the faucet. I rested my head against the cushion behind me, placing the burning herbs on my lips. Closing my eyes, I accepted what was to come. My mind began to process words that were newly combined to describe a feeling buried inside.

Meeting was magic

Babe...
Fuck it, I'll call you tsunami for this,
The way you sauntered into my sight...
A beautiful bliss...
Disruptive & uplifting by nature,
I'm highly upset at how the world portrays you,
Deadly, dangerous, a hazard to health,
"Get up... High... On top of something... Protect yourself"
Those are the procedures... the false information.
Yet, I stood there and embraced you,
Despite the allegations.
At that moment, there was a slight delegation...
I took on your world, and you returned the favor.

Right in front of me, you stood, dark like the
night...
handsome as the rising of the sun...
Unlike the rest of them, I was ten toes down...
I didn't buckle... I didn't run...
And what a gorgeous structure that stood in front
of me...
A fresh & clean start is all you seek...
No wonder you were birthed from a body of water
that runs so deep...
Tsunami, true to character...
As a wave... thoughts of your essence rocked me to
sleep....

"My God." I gasped, placing a hand on my chest.

Suddenly, I needed to be freed from the water. Forgetting a word of the piece I'd just created would possibly be the death of me. I smothered the fire by pressing it into the tray until it no longer existed. I used the natural bath soap to cleanse my body, hating that it was necessary to wash his scent from my skin. I could still feel his fingers pressed against me, feeling so damn good. Feeling so damn right.

Mercer. My body begged for him. The longing caused my legs to spread as my back arced. Washing my skin had never been so delightful. Every inch of me grew sensitive.

With my mouth agape, I swiped gently, careful not to

force my eruption. It was a shame what mere thoughts of him could do to me. Do for me.

After unstopping the tub, the water crowded at the awaiting hole, ready for its departure. I departed, taking a towel to my skin and patting it dry. Body cream was the next thing I felt against it.

Not long after, my pen was between my fingers and the empty page of my notebook was filling swiftly. Once the words were scribed, I read them over twelve times until they were stamped on my heart and impossible to forget. A yawn widened my mouth until the corners of my lips threatened to crack.

I climbed in bed with the weight of Mercer's heart weighing my chest down. His thoughts, they plagued me. There was no doubt in my mind that I'd seek him. How soon? I wasn't sure, but it would be better for us both if it were in the very near future.

It wasn't until I spread my legs across the bed, where his body rested a month earlier, that I realized I was alone in my home. Phillip hadn't come inside. He hadn't even gotten out of his truck. He was on his way to his lover's home before my bottom could hit the tub.

Somehow, someway, I was happy for him. It was best he went where he was wanted because tonight I desired something else, someone else. His name was Mercer, and in due time, I'd have him.

THREE

Pops had run through the list of things we needed to get done by the end of our work day before five when he left to meet Milo and Malachi at his crib. All day, he'd been going on and on about getting all the children. Aside from work, they gave him a sense of purpose. His great-grand-children were his core.

He'd waited years and years to have a little one running in and out of his door. My brothers had taken much longer than he'd initially anticipated, but he was still satisfied in his old age. When they started coming, they didn't stop. Aussie started the *Domino Effect*, but then Ledge added to the party twice. Malachi added another. Milo added two more. Makai added two of his own as well.

The pressure to have children wasn't on me anymore. I was the first that Pops began threatening if I didn't give him some greats. When I got knocked, the threats stopped. By the time I was released, Malachi and Ledge had granted his wish already. But though the threats had ended, I was twiddling my thumbs, wondering when the fuck my seed would enter the world.

I wasn't asking for many. One would do it for me. I just needed someone to love unconditionally and to love me unconditionally, in spite of what doctors were telling me and what hand life dealt me in the future. My brothers were the exception, but as a child of a woman who killed herself and his father, I knew that the love of a child was a different type of love.

Though I was upset with my mother for taking her life and my dad's life, I still loved that woman more than anything in this world. That was the type of love I wanted and needed, and there was no better person to receive it from than a child, one who'd made sure you were good in the end, no matter what.

"Did you hear me?" Pops yelled into the phone, bringing me back from wherever I'd gone.

"Yeah. I'm going."

"Alright. I set the schedule for five every day. We'll change it once it stays lighter outside a little longer."

"Yeah. Aight."

He hung up before I had the chance to. It was near

the seven o'clock hour. If the sign hadn't lit by now, there was a malfunction, or something had gone wrong while adjusting the settings. To confirm it was working and report back to Pops, I unglued my ass from the seat and left the cave I'd been hiding inside all day, still fucking with that menu.

I pressed forward through the construction zone that would soon produce an immaculate layout that had been produced by Lawe and his long-lost brother. Admittedly, the two were a power team. My job was measurements. I had a good time compiling numbers and using the tape to confirm my accuracy.

Within a week of getting the keys, the blueprint was ready, and I was astounded. Not much left me dumbfounded, but their three renditions of the blueprint had me on hush for a few hours. I finally decided on the second one, and the rest is history. Construction started a week later.

We were two weeks in now and would be finished in another three and a half. Shit was moving fast, but it still felt like everything was happening in slow motion. I assumed it was because I was in the thick of it all.

Darkness coated the sky. I looked up to find the moon finding its way above the buildings in Downtown Berkeley. The freshness of the air was exactly what I needed after being buried in work all day. I had a few more hours in me, so the quick break was appreciated.

I stepped outside and turned toward the building. Surely, the sign was glowing. My heart swelled a hundred times, the beating of it drumming against my chest. I could feel my lips turn upward as my head went up and then down, bobbing from approval.

This shit really happening, I told myself. *Shit really happening.*

"It's beautiful," the sweetest, most magnetic voice spoke.

My jaws grew rigid as my nostrils widened and teeth scrubbed against each other, the top and bottom row. Against better judgment, I slowly rotated in the direction it had come from, unable to resist it.

Resist her.

Resist her face.

Resist her essence.

Resist her body.

Resist her spirit.

Resist her frequency.

Resist her existence.

Seeing her dressed in a distressed skirt, a top that barely covered her belly, an oversized coat that stopped at her ankles, boots stopping above her thighs, and a fitted cap that was beige and black like the rest of her attire made my dick hard. She pissed me the fuck off.

The audacity to look so damn good every time I saw her, no matter the occasion or the outfit. She could be in rags and resemble riches. She was so damn fine it made my stomach knot.

With a huff, I gathered my bearings and started for the door, needing her out of my line of vision because the things I envisioned doing to her in that little ass skirt were ungodly. She'd recited vows. I hadn't.

But to protect my sanity and guard my heart, I had to dismiss her. She was dangerous and not because she'd done anything. She'd done nothing. The lengths I knew I'd go to for a woman whose last name I didn't even know was the reason she was dangerous.

And the fact that I knew she was worth every piece of love I had to give, I didn't mind burning her marriage down to the fucking ground to win her in the end. She hadn't been promised to me, though. She'd been promised to someone else. I needed to be okay with that, as hard as it was.

"I'm not happy there, Mercer!" she yelled out.

The cracks in her voice mimicked the ones in my heart the night I saw her next to a nigga that wasn't me. All up in my spot. Holding the hand that I deserved to hold. Standing beside the woman that belonged on my arm.

"I don't give a fuck. You're no good for me, Pretty. Get out of here."

As the door opened, a gush of wind in the opposite direction made the hairs on my neck stand. Immediately, the door slammed shut. I could smell her arousal as the wind settled beneath us, and she pressed her back against the metal carvings.

"I'm sorry." She breathed, awakening the parts of me she'd killed nights ago. "You must forgive me."

I wrapped my fingers around her neck, fighting the urge to pull her lips into my mouth and stick my dick so far up her that it would split her heart in two. She looked up at me with those big, wondrous eyes that stared at me in the dark when I was fighting sleep.

"I don't give a fuck." I barked, staring deep into her orbs.

They were the prettiest. She was the prettiest. And I wanted nothing more than her pretty to belong to me. All of it to balance the ugly parts of me. There seemed to be so many, and only a woman as beautiful as her could contain it.

Closing my eyes, I allowed her calm to silence the war in my head. I loosened my grip and stepped back to give her space.

"I'm not good for you, either. Leave." I tilted my head in the direction she'd come from.

Instead of following directions, she stepped into my space, finding the hand that had just fallen by my side, and pulled it up to her neck. One by one, she placed my fingers around it. She never broke eye contact. She never gave my heart the break it screamed desperately for. She never let up. Never let me breathe. Never let me deny her.

"Yell at me. Scream to the top of your lungs. Tell me how upset you are. Tell me how disappointed you are. Tell me that you wished I hadn't come. But please, don't tell me to leave. I can't take that. I want to be here. I *need* to be here."

"Go home, Vallei."

"Tha-that's not my name."

"You let that nigga put a ring on your fucking finger." I gritted, pushing her back against the door again.

"Hadn't I known you existed in the world, I would've waited until I was gray. I'm sorry," she apologized, pissing me off even more because I knew that she was sorry.

"Go home."

I had no right to be all in her mix. Long before I'd crossed her path, she'd vowed to love another for life. That's what she needed to do and leave me the fuck alone.

"Mer—"

"It was nothing, Pretty. Just sex. Just meaningless sex. Just like you found me, I'm sure you can find another nigga to get that pussy wet."

The words were like knives to my chest, but they were the weapons I needed to get her out of my face, out of my head. As my wish was granted, I felt my world as it began to tilt, flipping upside down.

Vallei's feet moved swiftly down the street, one after the other. From the hand that lifted and swiftly fell, I knew she was wiping away tears from her pretty eyes. I closed mine, refusing to follow my heart and using my head instead. I pulled the door open and didn't open my eyes until I was in the safety of my establishment.

At that moment, it dawned on me that Vallei hadn't been walking toward a car. There were too many empty spaces out front. I doubled back, darting out the door, listening for screeching tires or anything that reminded me of a woman in her feelings. There were no signs.

My legs began moving, one in front of the other as I walked down the long stretch in search of Vallei. She'd disappeared.

"Fuck."

Nightfall was upon us. It was far too dark for her to be walking anywhere. I couldn't have that on my conscience. I wouldn't forgive myself.

The sound of the brakes on the city bus struck my attention. As the doors opened, I watched Vallei take the steps one by one, sleeve sliding across her face to wipe away the residue her tears left. With a lowered head, her sadness was quickly masked with a soft smile and wave at the driver before she swiped a card.

Just as the doors began closing, I approached. I began banging my fist against it without a sense of urgency.

Boom.

Boom.

Boom.

The glass rattled under my influence. Air pressure was released as the doors opened again.

"Can I help you, sir?" the driver asked.

Her lip was upturned, and her eyes were bigger than I'd remembered them from seconds ago.

"Don't move this bus until I'm off," I instructed.

"What?" She yelled behind me because I'd already begun down the aisle.

She was so damn commanding. Effortlessly, she demanded all of my attention. When she was in front of me, nothing more mattered. Though seemingly selfless, I was learning that Vallei was selfish. With me. My attention. And my heart that she didn't know well enough to have gained residency.

But women like her didn't need very long. They'd

come into your world like a thief in the night and take parts of you that you couldn't get, and hardly wanted, back. They left lasting impressions. They imprinted on you. They marked their territory without fail.

Though she was practically a stranger, my heart yearned to know more about her. I wanted to know what made her smile. What made her laugh? What made her day? What intrigued her? What she liked to eat. What fragrance she loved on her skin. What method did she prefer, bath or shower? What love songs were her favorite? What movies made her cry so I could put them on when it was that time of the month and she was experiencing hormonal changes that sometimes required a good, dramatic cry?

I spotted her with no trouble. The desire within me wouldn't rest until I was in front of her. Our bodies were only a few inches apart. I peered at her, taking in her natural beauty.

Her artsy nature was intoxicating. There weren't many women that could throw together a fit like the one she was rocking and look so damn good without trying too hard or doing too much. Everything was perfect. From her bushy eyebrows to her saucer-like eyes, pretty little nose, fat cheeks, and plump lips.

I wanted them wrapped around my dick as I fucked her face for the shit she'd had going on in my head over the last month, especially the last few days. She deserved nothing but good dick. She'd made it clear that she was a bad girl, a tamed, sexy ass beast that I wanted access to whenever, wherever, however.

Those sad eyes stared back at me, their wetness like acid on my heart. She blinked them away as she waited for me to say something, anything. I hardly had a word come to mind. Her beauty silenced me.

"Sir, I have a schedule to keep," the driver informed me.

"Get off the bus," I urged.

"I'm not interested in being anywhere I don't belong," Vallei spilled.

"Vallei, get off the bus," I replied, disregarding what she'd said.

"It was meaningless sex. It was just meaningless sex."

"Come on."

I extended my hand for her to take. She never broke eye contact. She remained seated without intentions of uprooting her body.

"I'm going home like you asked, Mercer. I don't wish to play whatever game you're ready to play. You told me to leave. I'm leaving."

She wasn't a fighter. And from the calm in her tone, I knew that she was a woman who meant exactly what she said, which was why she watched every word she spoke because their truth was vital to her character. She had no intentions of getting her ass up.

I leaned downward until we were eye to eye. Nose to nose. Lip to lip. Against hers, I began unleashing the words that were fighting for freedom.

"I don't ask twice, Pretty, and I've asked three times."

"That's not my name." She huffed.

Seconds ago, she didn't want to be called Vallei.

Now, Pretty wasn't her name. She was so fucking confused, warring with herself in her head. I wouldn't join the battle. There was nothing to fight for. What I wanted, I'd have. It was as simple as that. There was no need for any weapons other than the one in the center of my chest and the backup plan between my legs.

With dick inside of her, Vallei was a goner. Any-fuck-ing-thing I said would fly. I could tell by how she fucked me that she hadn't been fucked good in a while, possibly not at all. Either way, her nose was wide open. Admittedly, so was mine. Because the pussy she was in possession of, I'd never had shit like it. The good head on her shoulders was the icing on the cake.

I reached down and gripped her lower half, lifted her from the seat she occupied, and tossed her ass over my shoulder. She yelped in surprise. Because there were doors closer to her seat, near the middle of the bus, I stood in front of those, waiting for them to open. A brisk knock let the driver know I was ready to depart now that the package was secured.

I stepped off as soon as they parted, back into the wind, but not alone. Vallei squirmed in my arms, trying her hardest to free herself. She wouldn't. I was sure. Not until I was ready to let her down would she succeed.

"Let me g—"

"Quiet, Pretty."

"I want to go home," she mumbled, stopping me in my tracks.

We'd reached my building. The dark alleyway beside it felt more promising than being on public display. I wasted no time carrying her stubborn ass through the small patch of grass. My legs didn't stop moving until her feet were on the ground, and her back was against the brick of the building.

Intensely, I glared at her. From head to toe, I studied her like an open-book exam. I wanted to store every little detail in my head for safekeeping, down to the way she looked in the little skirts that covered everything but almost nothing. It had risen, and she was doing absolutely nothing to fix that shit.

I waited for an explanation, to know what she'd meant by what she'd just said or if she meant it at all. The perplexed, painful look in her eyes wasn't making things clear to me. Nothing was clear to her, either. And that's where my frustration rested.

"Say that shit again, Vallei."

"You don't want me here." She gritted, stomping her feet.

The crinkling of her eyebrows made it apparent that her words were painful to recite. They were just as painful to hear because they were untrue. I did want her here, just not under the conditions that she was here. I'd have to return her. Always. That wasn't it for me.

Images of us in bed, her legs wrapped around me as I dug into that juicy shit between her legs, rendered me silent. I pressed my head against her forehead, moving from side to side as I recalled her lips around my dick. Visions of her sliding up and down as I controlled her pace by grabbing ahold of her hips stiffened me.

"Meaningless sex." She sighed, sadness laced in her words. "Is that all you think of me?"

"Vall—"

"No. Mercer. You don't get to treat me this way. You don't get to do that to me. I need to explain myself. I came to explain myself. Nothing is what it seems. Nothing. I came to see you. To talk to you!" she yelled. "I didn't come t—Merrrcerrrr."

That sounded so much better than the other shit she was spilling. Unable to hold out another second, I buried my dick inside of her. She was leaking, making the task easier than it should've been. Like the missing piece of her puzzle, I fit. It was simple math.

"Didn't come for what?" I managed.

My fingers gripped her chin, forcing her to look up at me as I scribbled my name on her walls with the tip of my dick.

"Mercer," she moaned, sounding like the sweetest lullaby. Without a doubt, her pussy was about to put a nigga to bed.

"Didn't come for what, Vallei."

"Tha—ummmmm yes. That's not my—yeeessss—name."

Sinking my teeth in her exposed neck, I relieved the building pressure. Vallei was too good at working the muscles of her pussy. She was showing no mercy.

"Didn't come for what?" I asked a final time, nearly breaking skin.

"Sexxx." She whimpered, loving every bit of pain she felt because it was immediately offset by pleasure.

I was deep in her ocean, gutting her of cream with each stroke. I couldn't even bear the thought of looking down at my dick. I was certain it was covered in her white thickness.

"You're a fucking liar, Vallei."

Intentionally, I called her by her government name. It was becoming apparent it wasn't what she preferred, but I didn't give a fuck. A married woman wasn't my preference either, but she'd left me no choice.

"Mercer." Begging, she gripped me tighter.

"'Cause why the fuck you always got on these fucking skirts and dresses, trying to drive a nigga insane?

"Mercer."

"Why are you constantly provoking me, Pretty? Why the fu—"

Her lips crashed into mine. I could feel the blood from my teeth sinking into the one at the bottom. I delegated the task of cleaning it up myself, giving her a portion of my body's secretion, securing my place in her stream, in her system, in her world. I marked her.

I made her mine at that moment, not giving a damn who the law claimed she belonged to. As far as I was concerned, she belonged to me. Though selfish, she was my possession. And the way her pussy wrapped my dick like a warm blanket, I was hers.

From the top of my head to the bottom of my fucking feet. This woman had me to herself. Hating the reality of it all, I released her lips and moved downward, taking the skin of her neck into my mouth and biting down.

She whimpered in pain, but the strokes that came

one after the other as her back brushed against the brick of the building filled her with copious amounts of pleasure, outweighing the small doses of pain.

From the grip she had around me and my dick, I knew she'd reached her climax. Hungrily, she tongued me down. Her head swayed in each direction, milking me for my saliva and my semen.

"Shit." I grunted, releasing my load before we both stilled in place.

Seconds passed with us as we were. Her words brought us back to reality.

"This is not all I want to be to you. This is not all that I want for us."

"How much can we be, Pretty, when you belong to someone else?"

I removed my dick. Surely enough, it was covered with her love. I stuffed it back inside my pants. My shower quickly came to mind.

"On paper. Only on paper. Mentally, physically, emotionally, I've belonged to no one for the last two years. But since last month, you've held residency in my head, somehow in my heart. I thought that maybe I'd explore it and lead with my feelings instead of logic for once. Logic has gotten me nowhere in life. But if that's too much to ask of you, then I understand. I'm sorry I came."

She pulled her skirt down as she stepped aside.

"Pretty," I started, but nothing else would surface.

"Don't bother, Mercer. You've made it clear to me

where you stand… where we stand. When I walk away, don't come after me this time."

She was asking too much of me. I couldn't promise her a lie.

"Then don't leave. Let me take you home.'

"No. I'm a responsible adult. I can get myself home, Mercer."

"Where's your car?"

"I don't have one. I'll be fine. I need this time. I need to digest what I'm feeling. I need to get over th-this." She struggled. "Get over us."

Don't do that, Pretty.

"Goodbye, Mercer."

I watched her walk away this time. Though I wanted to reach out and snatch her up, bring her inside, feed her, fuck her some more, and then take her to my crib, that shit wasn't happening. It was safer if we both just let this shit go before it got ugly.

I couldn't help myself. Before I could stop it, I was pushing down the sidewalk, headed for the bus stop where she sat. My shoulder pressed against the glass, summoning her attention.

"Mercer."

"Just need to make sure you're safe."

Nothing more needed to be said. I waited there, unmoving, for twelve minutes and fourteen seconds until the bus arrived. Once it did, Vallei didn't give me the satisfaction of looking my way. She got her pretty ass up on that bus and sat down shortly after.

My work day had officially ended. The few hours I had left in me were quickly reduced to minutes after sliding up in Vallei. She released the serotonin within me, making it hard to think about anything but my bed—*and her*.

I began shutting down for the night, preparing to make my departure. Pretty was still heavy on my mind. To appease the yearning I'd developed for her, I sat at my desk and opened the Instagram app, sure I'd find her there. I was new to the platform.

Aeir and Kleu had started a business page and posted pictures of our progress, employee search, and the proposed grand opening month. We weren't yet settled on the date but would finalize it once construction was complete.

I tapped in her name, the only part of it I knew, and found nothing. Disappointed but not discouraged, I headed to conduct an internet search. The words I typed in were simple but produced great results, including an Instagram profile.

Vallei

Berkeley

Writer

Violinist

The final detail I recalled from her home. The sounds could be heard through the house and in the backyard. When I finally entered her bedroom, I saw the instrument near the bed where she seemed to sit and write whatever was in that pretty little notebook that wasn't far from it.

• • •

Fleur Novelles - 6x Platinum, 4x Grammy Award-Winning Poet, Writer, and Violinist

Born Vallei Novelles in Berkeley, Huffington, Novelles has collaborated with some of the biggest names. However, her rise to fame was in solitude. Fleur, her debut album, went platinum within twelve months of its release, setting her path ablaze. Since, she's gone on to work with Grammy-winning talent, securing her name on the etched plates of the awards herself. Best Writer is amongst one of her titles.

Article after article divulged information about the woman I'd just seen board the city bus for a second time.

Humble.

It was one of the many words I'd use to describe her. A Grammy winner without even a car to her name, she was my type of person. She was my type of woman. One who cared little about the money or the notoriety but about the things that truly mattered in life. Love. Experiences. Freedom. Shit, that made the sacrifice worth it in the end.

"She kept her last name."

The words fell from my mouth by accident. There was no mention of changing her last name, though deeper in the articles, marriage was mentioned. I tapped the Instagram icon that led me to her profile.

Her beauty sparked a fire inside of me. I went through her entire feed, studying each picture carefully. And for the first two rows, I hated every one of them. I hated the sadness that rested in her eyes. The exhaustion in her posture. The unhappiness written all over her face.

I'd seen this woman smile, and the one that I'd seen looked nothing like the one displayed in any of the images. She was dying inside, withering away and right in front of the twelve million people who followed her on the platform.

Somehow, no one had noticed. The fourth and final row of images were ones I wasn't interested in. They were more than two years old, a few featuring her husband. The time synced perfectly. She'd truly lost her spark two years ago when I assumed her love light went astray.

Aside from the pain that radiated from her images, they were flawless. Her dark brown skin and white teeth were slowly becoming my weakness. The public, professionally snapped images of her had my heart pumping at an alarming rate. Vallei wasn't just anything. Baby girl was everything.

She had a good head on her shoulders and a monstrous pussy between her legs. Her priorities were in order. Her paper was legit. She was a creator, just as I was, and I wondered if that's why I couldn't get her stubborn ass out of my head.

I wrapped up my stalking session. Shame never met me during the twenty minutes I spent with her on my phone's screen. But eventually, I got my ass to the truck. My destination was set in stone. There was no possible way I'd be going home alone tonight, not with her on my dome.

She'd made it clear that she wanted more from me, more for us. I only prayed she knew what that entailed. Late nights, hotels, and phone calls full of whispers weren't what I had in mind. I wasn't a silent lover. I wasn't a side nigga.

She deserved better than that, and I, for sure, wouldn't accept anything less than being her man. Since her husband couldn't love, honor, cherish, and treat her like he was supposed to, then he'd have to watch me do that shit. And I didn't fail. Not when it came to matters of the heart.

I burned rubber getting out of the parking lot. The back end of my truck slid from one side to the other. The rain was beginning to fall. The ground was damp, making it slippery. I hit the expressway at eighty miles per hour, pushing it until I neared my exit. I slowed, obeying the traffic laws of the quiet neighborhood in The Peaks. It wasn't until my tires pulled into Vallei's driveway that I breathed freely.

Not giving a fuck what I was walking into or who was behind the door that I was on my way up to, I stalked the path that led to it. My index finger pushed the glowing button. I stepped back, removing my pistol from my waist. Tightening my grip, I waited until the locks turned.

Her scent greeted me, assuring me that it was okay to let my guard down, to stand down. Before she was able to open the door fully and get a look at the tool I was holding, I placed it behind my back. Both hands rested along with it as I waited for words to unveil themselves.

FOUR

Maybe it was seconds.

Maybe it was minutes.

Maybe it was hours.

Maybe it was days we stood before one another soundlessly as energy was transferred. Mine to him. His to me. Until finally, he spoke, making it possible for me to breathe again.

"Fix your face."

His audacity was appalling. He had so much nerve. He reeked of confidence. From his widened stance to his relaxed nature, unafraid of the consequences of his actions. Paranoia evaded him.

Not once had he looked around, looked over my shoulders, or behind him. His focus was contained. His focus was apparent. I was the matter at hand, and nothing more mattered at the moment.

"What is it, Mercer?"

Asking him why he was on my doorstep never crossed my mind.

"You're coming with me for the night."

"Not if it's to have more meaningless sex with you, getting my feelings entangled while you remain free of an—"

"I'd bend you over that nigga's couch and fuck you right now if that was the case. Stop playing with me."

He sucked the skin of his teeth, growing frustrated with my response as the words continued to pour out.

"I'm ready to go home."

It wasn't until then that I noticed the gum in his mouth. So smooth, so sexily, he chewed it.

"Why'd you say it?"

It was the one question that needed an answer. It didn't matter how he felt after responding, only that he responded. Taking a stab at my feelings the way he had only to end up at my door wasn't fair to me, neither was it fair to him.

"Liar," I claimed, mimicking his depiction of me every time he called my bluff.

"I am," he admitted, standing ten toes down. With a

nod, he continued, "I apologize for making such deplorable remarks. My intentions weren't good. I needed you to feel what I felt the other night. But that was pointless, knowing exactly how I'd felt every night before and every night after. Nothing changed."

"I'm sorry you had to find out that wa—"

"I've missed you, Pretty."

He cut me off, finally dropping those big, black eyes and shifting his weight. Once it was balanced again, he looked at me, waiting for a response. How he expected me to give him anything after snatching my soul with his truth was beyond me.

My chest caved, sinking inches as I fought to find the silver lining, fought to find a life jacket. I was drowning in my own despair. Unable to give him anything more than a nod, I held my aching chest in my hands.

"And I'm not sleeping without you tonight."

I nodded, again.

"I need to grab a few things."

"You don't need anything more than the clothes on your back, Pretty."

Again, I nodded.

Whatever you say, Mercer. With him leading, I was confident that I wouldn't be led astray. I stepped forward. He didn't step backward. Instead, he allowed our bodies to fuse. His hand brushed against the side of my face. He held my chin, bringing my eyes up so they were in clear view.

"I'm no boy. I'm a grown-ass man. If you're going to

play with me, turn your pretty ass around and walk right back inside. But if you understand that there is no choosing and I'm your only option from this moment forward, then we can ride."

"I understand."

"Good, because you weren't going back in that motherfucker until I made you understand, anyway."

"We need to talk, Mercer," I released, sighing.

"We will. A little, at least."

The smile that tugged my lips resembled the one my lower lips formed at the secret promises he'd made with that statement. I cracked the door to grab my purse. After locking up, I followed Mercer to his enormous truck, finally realizing why he wasn't worried about a thing. The weapon that dangled by his side had a lot to do with it.

Grabbing my hand, he encouraged me to walk a bit faster. The rain was beginning to pour. We reached the passenger side, where he opened the door and tucked his weapon simultaneously.

Within the next second, I was in his arms, being lifted into the truck. How he was able to carry me like a rag doll was beyond me. I wasn't the tiniest. There was plenty meat on my bones. Nevertheless, I enjoyed each second.

He reached over and strapped me in. A caretaker, he left no stone unturned. He reminded me of a father, my father. I secretly prayed that a woman had already given him what I couldn't. My infertility had been the start of an emotional rollercoaster that I didn't want to revisit.

"Have you eaten?"

"Corn chips. I've been afraid you could smell it on my breath this entire time."

Chuckling, he shook his head. "Open up and let me see."

"No."

"Open up, Pretty."

Because I was beginning to realize I wouldn't win fights with Mercer, I bowed out early. Slowly, I opened my mouth. Before it was widened too much, he covered it with his. Our tongues danced and hands roamed. And when he finally pulled away, I was now in possession of the gum he'd been chewing.

"There. That should make it better."

Stunned into silence, I covered my face.

"Get in."

The gum he'd once chewed, I was now chomping on. As chaotic as it should've been for me to accept, I had no trouble doing so. We'd swapped enough spit and enough body fluids.

"I am, woman. Give me a second." He laughed.

His dimpled cheeks were perfect. That smile, too. He knew exactly what he was doing, showing off those beautiful teeth. He shut the door and made his way around. I tried climbing over to open his door, but the seatbelt wouldn't allow it.

When he finally settled into the car, I was happy to be pulling out of the driveway. I hadn't stayed away from home in the last five years, not unless it was a hotel for a performance, awards show, or a birthday with Phillip. I was excited for the impromptu sleepover and so thankful for the man who'd decided to host it.

The Jazz that crooned through the speakers was heavenly. I rested my head against the seat. Contentment allowed me to breathe easy. Like magnets, we couldn't manage much time apart. Skin to skin was quickly becoming my comfort zone.

My elbow brushed against Mercer's arm as I placed it on the armrest where his was. With a collapsed hand, my palm landed against his. He lifted his fingers, spreading them so that mine had room to fit between. He then sealed the connection by making a fist. When he brought the back of my hand to his lips, our eyes met briefly.

God, he's perfect. I sighed, closing my eyes. *He's perfect.*

With sleepy eyes, I sauntered into the slightly modest dwelling with obnoxiously beautiful fixtures. The home was large but didn't feel as cold as most homes in The Peaks. There was a warmth that welcomed me from the second I stepped inside. It was accompanied by five others that were all different sizes, finishes, and addresses.

"This is beautiful." I gasped, staring at the painting that struck my attention.

It was stunning. A woman with the emptiest eyes stared back at me. Tilting my head, I tried reading the signature at the bottom, but the only letter I could make out was the M. The rest was illegible.

"She," Mercer corrected, standing behind me.

"She?"

The thought of a long-lost lover holding residency in his home, so big and so bold, had my brows crinkling and my ears perked. I waited impatiently for a follow-up.

"My mother," he clarified with a chuckle. "Calm down, Pretty."

"I—"

"Was ready to get in your feelings."

"Mercer," I whined, turning around to face him. Again, he'd called me out.

"Don't worry your heart. I'm not sliding my dick in nobody but you. The day I decide otherwise, I won't hesitate to tell you."

"Yo-you would?"

"Because it would be the day that I decided not to ever dig from your garden again."

My heart sank, considering that as a possibility.

"Come on. We smell like each other."

By the hand, he led me through his home. We passed a sitting room, living room, dining area, full room with a bar that ran from one wall to the other, and three bedrooms before we made it to the master suite. The black-on-black aesthetic with hints of wood was every bit of Mercer.

Very grown. Very sexy. Very dark. Very mysterious with as much warmth as there was mystique. It was the perfect balance. He was perfectly balanced.

Mercer wasted little time undressing. I assumed I was taking a bit too long because my clothes were on the floor, and I hadn't removed a single thread. Hand-in-hand, he led me to the shower, where the water was already running and warm to the touch.

"My hair," I whispered, realizing I was in the shower without a headdress to protect it at all. Just as quickly as the thought arose, it subsided. It didn't matter. Nothing mattered.

In my nakedness, I stood underneath the water with Mercer standing behind me. He wrapped me in his arms and pulled me closer. Our skin reunited. From one side to the other, we swayed, bodies and hearts in sync. If we stayed just like this forever, I wouldn't protest. It felt so good. He felt so good. Together, we felt so good.

"I've missed you, too." Breathless, I finally admitted, "So much it scares me. You feel like a total stranger, yet it feels like I've known you my whole life, as if I've waited my whole life to have you. As if I knew you in a past life. As if I wasn't waiting for an introduction but more of a reunion.

"And since the night we spent together, I've been trying to wrap my head around it while also trying to figure out how to get back to you. Everything about you feels so familiar. Everything about you feels so much like home.

"I care to know more than I already know. I care to

feel more than I already feel. I understand the sacrifice I'm making. I just don't want to do it in vain... or alone."

"From this day forward, Pretty, you'll never be alone."

Silence toyed between us before we spoke again.

"You remind me of my father."

"You remind me of the woman in that painting."

"Your mother."

"Yes. Souls this pretty are hard to come by, but I recognized yours the minute I was in your space. She had the same aura."

"Had?"

"She had demons that were just too powerful for her to contain. Beautiful soul, ugly mind. It got the best of her. She lost her battle with mental illness and took my father with her."

My heart ached. Turning around, I pulled him into my chest and wrapped my arms around him, refusing to let him go, even when he tried releasing himself.

"I'm so sorry," I whispered. "I'm sorry."

When he finally melted against me, gripping me as tight as I'd been gripping him, I realized how hard it must've been to surrender. How long he must've held onto the pain he felt. How daunting it must've been to carry that hurt around. How strong he must've been for everyone around him.

"I hope she left you with beautiful memories, Mercer, to remember her by."

I released him, finally staring up into his dark eyes. There was so much mystery behind them. I wanted to know every bit of detail. I'd spend however long it took piecing together his puzzle.

"The ugliest parts, too," he responded, shaking his head from side to side.

Baffled, I begged for clarity. "What is it that you mean, Mercer?"

He hesitated briefly.

"Her disorder."

I quieted, allowing him to finish.

"She left it for me to remember her by."

Things were becoming clearer now. The words he'd spoken nights prior in the closet made a lot more sense.

"Tell me," I pled.

"She was bipolar. One day, she was perfectly normal, and the next, she wasn't. From the moment she was diagnosed, everything began to spiral, leading to my brother having to stay with his pops and then eventually a hospital stay for her that none of us wanted.

"My Pops didn't like seeing her doped up the way she was, so he signed her out and promised never to take her back. We thought we could manage her illness better at home. That was the worst call my father had ever made, but it was because he loved her.

"He loved her to a fault. By the time the medicine wore off, so did the fight in her. I woke up to find them in bed, both covered in their own blood. She'd murdered him and then committed suicide. She left me with her boys and her illness."

My heart shattered by the thousands. Even with the revelation, it made me want Mercer no less. It made me crave him, the healthiest version and the darkest parts, even more.

"I understand if this makes you think twice abo—"

"I can't have children," I rushed out, desperate to quiet him.

"Prett—"

"We're all flawed, Mercer. Nobody's perfect. But somehow, I still find you to be the closest. This means nothing. This makes me want this no less. Your mother, may she rest in peace, as you said, had a beautiful soul.

"Let's focus on that. Some things were out of her control. It doesn't dirty her character or make her a bad person. It made her human. Just like you. Just like me."

A nod was all I received for a few seconds before Mercer spoke again.

"Have you used your studio?" he asked, cupping my face in his hands.

"No," I admitted shamefully. "I haven't created much since the night we shared. I could hardly get a word out before I saw you at the dinner."

"Why not?" He pecked my lips and pulled back to look at me again.

"I've been feeling uninspired. I have had no inspiration for months and months now. And then you came into my world, and the words started to flow again. But only for a little while."

"Yeah? Uninspired, huh?"

As the questions rolled off his tongue, his hands roamed my body. When his fingers grazed the baldness of my skin, my center ached.

I nodded, anticipating what was next while still answering his question.

And then, at once, he stuffed me with two fingers. My chest inflated as I took in more oxygen. I felt full immediately.

Mentally.

Physically.

Emotionally.

I was at capacity.

In his arms.

In his home.

In his shower.

In his head.

And making my way into his heart.

"Mercer."

"Close your mouth, Pretty, and open your legs. *More.*"

His request wasn't impossible. I was on the verge. His lips hugged mine, silencing me momentarily. He pulled back with fire in his eyes. His raging orbs were evidence of his need to please me.

"More," he rasped as the features of his handsome face revealed his thoughts. His desires. His intentions.

The longing that rested within him increased my sensitivity. I could feel every part of me he touched, physically, mentally, emotionally, and spiritually. The tips of his fingers tapped gently on my soul, commanding obedience. Demanding the surrender that was already in motion.

My knees weakened as I closed my eyes, unable to

stomach the sight of him anymore. He was painfully beautiful. He was utterly addictive. He was the epitome of perfect. Under the definition of flawless in the dictionary, he should be.

"Let it go."

His words of encouragement splintered me.

I came.

I burst.

I creamed.

I melted.

I leaked.

I tingled.

I contracted.

I cried.

Like a once lost cub, traumatized by abandonment, I clung to the one I knew would foster my feelings, lick my wombs, and bandage my heart.

"Mercer."

Tears rolled down my cheeks, masked with the dewiness of my cheeks from the water that ran continuously down my body. There were words that needed to be said. I fought to gather them as I tried catching my breath.

"Pretty?"

With my eyes still closed, I braced for impact. Though unsure how he'd react to the words yet to be spoken, they needed to see the light of day. I needed to hear them. He needed to hear them.

"I don't need saving," I murmured against his chest, resting my cheek where it felt welcomed.

"I'm not trying to save you, Pretty."

Silence fell over us as our bodies parted. The separation lasted only a little while before my back was against the shower wall, and my right breast brushed against the roof of Mercer's mouth.

"Ummmm."

"I'm here to fuck you good and make you forget that hurt ever existed," he preached, claiming my walls again.

He left no room for wondering. I was sure of him. Though I wasn't sure what we were doing or how we'd come about, his presence in my life, I was sure I wanted. *Needed.* Didn't want to be without.

"And after I've forgotten?" My lips were against his ear, requesting his leadership. Requesting his presence. Requesting more of him at full capacity.

His strokes were slow, methodic. I couldn't imagine getting tired of feeling him inside of me. I couldn't imagine getting tired of seeing him stroking me. I couldn't imagine getting tired of seeing him strive to unravel me.

"Then I'll be here to remind you who the fuck you are and what you deserve before I introduce you to some shit that you won't ever be able to recover from. Type of shit that makes your chest hurt, and your cheeks burn at the thought. Type of shit that you'll find nowhere else, nowhere but here. Nowhere but home 'cause that shit ain't a place."

"It's a person," I added.

"So, be my person, Pretty. If not now, soon."

His strokes picked up as he buried his face in my chest. My hands surrounded him. I held him close, held him tight.

"Yeeeessss."

"Pussy so *fuckin'* good."

"Ummm."

He didn't miss a beat. Even with my eyes closed, I envisioned his dark meat buried inside of me, over and over again. I envisioned us, our life together. Though it felt so farfetched, it didn't feel impossible. Whatever it took, I'd make sure I made this man mine.

I sunk into the comfortable mattress without a single piece of fabric on my body. Mercer and all his thoughtfulness left me struggling to keep my eyes dry and my heart intact. I was becoming overstimulated with his caretaking but in the purest, harmless way.

As he patted my feet dry, cleaning between each toe in the process, I gnawed on my bottom lip. When he'd finished, standing straight up with his trunk in my face, I felt compelled to display my gratitude. I reached for him, but he was quicker than me, grabbing my hands and leaning down until we were eye to eye.

"We're not keeping score, Pretty. That's not the way it works."

He was insufferable. How he read me like an open book was beyond me.

"I—"

"Okay. That's your only response. Okay."

"Okay."

"You're going to need to put your pussy on ice if you keep this shit up. There are only so many rounds I can give you and remain respectful because it's some downright disrespectful shit I've tried to refrain from doing to you."

"Please stop sparing me," I pled. "I'm not oppos—"

"That shit is reserved for a woman that is all mine, Pretty. When that day comes, I'm going to fuck you until you can't walk straight for a full week. Until the housekeeper is cleaning your vomit from the floor. Until your skin is raw from the ropes that you unsuccessfully try to escape because the pleasure is far too much for your body to handle. Until you're soaking wet. Until you're begging me for mercy."

"Merce—"

"Shut up, Vallei," he requested, calmly but asserting his dominance. "And brace yourself. This shit is warm."

Like a donut, he glazed my body with oil from a warmer that was on the nightstand beside his bed. I wasn't as surprised by his nourished skin anymore. The measures he took to obtain it explained it all.

His long fingers worked the kinks out of my shoulders first. He then moved on to my breasts, giving them a nice, long rub before massaging my arms. Then, my abdomen.

"Lay back, Pretty."

I stretched out of the towel he'd laid behind me, clenching my walls as I felt his breath near my belly button. I closed my eyes and spread my legs slowly, anticipating the moment I'd feel his tongue against my clit. So many seconds passed. There was nothing. Not even massaging. I opened my eyes slowly.

What I saw before me nearly sent me into cardiac arrest. My heart almost leaped from my chest. A hand hovered over my stomach as Mercer whispered things that had fallen upon deaf ears. Though I couldn't hear or understand what he was saying, I knew who he was saying things to, what the one-sided conversation consisted of, and the topic.

He opened his eyes and resumed. When he finally finished, he fished around the bed to find the shirt he'd laid out for me.

"Hands up."

He pulled it over my head and down my body. It swallowed me whole. As it attached itself to my skin, Mercer attached his lips to mine.

"I'm going to whip up something quick so I can feed you before we go to bed."

I nodded, unable to say a single word.

"You good?"

I nodded, again.

"Aight. Take a nap, sleepy head. I'll wake you when the food is ready."

I watched him walk out of the room, but not before grabbing my phone and plugging it into the charger next to his bed. I listened for the door to close. And as soon as it collided with the frame, my chest sunk into my back.

Pulling myself in a ball, I buried my head underneath the cover and wept. The overwhelming, soulful sobbing was much too difficult to contain. The sounds filled the room. I hoped Mercer hadn't heard a peep because I needed every tear that stained his shirt to be set free.

He was as glorious as the rain after too many days of sunshine. He was as gratifying as the summer breeze during the first bike ride of a busy week. He was love. He was light.

And just a few hours in his space, he'd brought along revelations that I wasn't quite fond of—*or the acceptance of them at least.* Yet, simultaneously, I welcomed the idea. The honesty. The truth that weighed my chest down, made my heart heavy.

I've never been truly, utterly cared for... taken care of. I've never been enamored. Adored. Flawed and all. I've never been admired to this degree. I've never been... **prayed for**.

The man I'd chosen to love and cherish for the rest of my life had shitted on me from the day we learned that conception was nearly impossible for us. The stranger who had stumbled on our doorstep a month ago and given my body exactly what it had been yearning for began praying for a remedy moments after learning of my diagnosis.

Primary ovarian insufficiency. It was a term I didn't have to hear another day in my life, and I'd be okay with that.

My ovaries failing me before I reached the age of forty was not in my life's plan, but God always laughed at those, anyway. Or so I've been told. It made so much sense why I'd been made a mockery by marrying Phillip when Mercer was somewhere in the world, waiting for someone to have and hold as his own. *Waiting for me.*

Oh, Mercer. I wept. He was making the decision to leave everything behind so much easier. He was making everything easier, even falling head first for his potential. Our potential. Though it was forbidden to fall for what could be, I had no reservations. Mercer was, undoubtedly, the exception.

My vibrating phone startled me. Slowly, I rolled over, hoping the caller would give up and end their quest for contact before I reached it. Unfortunately, Mal wasn't a quitter. She hung up and called back a second time.

"Hello," I cracked. Disguising the constant tears was more of a task than I'd anticipated.

The sudden need to inhale would surely reveal sniffles and the heaving of my chest. Even the thought of it all filled me with more emotions.

"Your location," she began. "Where are you? Is everything okay? I came by to check on you, but you're not home. What's the matter? Are you crying?"

I nodded as if she could see me.

"Vallei. Talk to me."

"I must've been so foolish to marry him, Mal. I had to have been," I confessed.

"Where are you? I'm on my way? I have the address."

"No. Please. I'm fine. I think."

The tears continued to fall.

"Vallei, I'm on my way. I won't be satisfied until I see you for myself."

"I'm at his home."

"*His* home?" she questioned.

"Yes."

Over the last month, I'd mentioned Mercer more times than the law allowed. Mal had learned to spell his name backward and forward. She was waiting patiently for his new spot to open so she could drag me down there. Unfortunately, I couldn't wait for her or for it to open. I'd made my way down sooner.

"Oh shit."

"He's too much. He's so much. He just keeps revealing things I've been so afraid to face, things I've been too blind to see... things that I've been too fearful to address. And it's making me hurt everywhere while feeling so good at once."

"Awwww, baby. Has that man fucked you to tears?"

"Yessssss," I admitted. "But more than that, he's so gentle with me, so detail-oriented, so understanding, so caring, and so damn fine. Mal, where has this man been my entire adulthood? Why has it taken this long to find me? I'm pissed."

"Timing is everything, babe. Timing is *everything*."

"I have to end my marriage. Staying is no longer an option, even if it means losing a few dollars. They're not worth my sanity. Experiencing something much more beautiful than what I've been previously exposed to is opening my eyes. I have to get out of it, Mal."

"I know and you will. I trust that you will. I also know how hard you've worked to get to where you are, and that man doesn't deserve to eat off your plate for the rest of his life. Don't make an impulsive decision and regret it in the end. Let's be strategic, baby. First, let's find a damn good lawyer and weigh your options."

"One that isn't afraid to fight for my finances to stay intact."

"One that isn't afraid of them like most of them in Berkeley."

"In Huffington."

"True enough."

As our conversation continued, the tears on my skin began to dry. Mal had always been skilled at coaxing me through crisis. Her and my violin were a duo to whom I was forever indebted.

"Call me when you feel better, babe, or when you're done getting your insides dug out." She laughed.

"I don't feel bad. I just feel... things. I can't quite put a finger on it."

"Don't hurt your head trying to."

"Okay. I'll call you tomorrow. He's made it clear that he's not sleeping alone tonight."

"Neither will you, sounds like."

"I'm not upset about that, Mal. In his arms is exactly where I want to be. That man prayed over me."

"Shut up."

"Yes. Somehow, I revealed that I can't have children. I wanted to get that out of the way in case it was a deal breaker for whatever we have in store. After washing my body in the shower, he oiled me down. I opened my eyes to find him hovering over my belly with his eyes closed and his head bowed."

"Oh, Vallei. You're not escaping this man. I'd be in a

ball crying too. Shit! Who is this nigga, and does he have brothers?"

"They're all spoken for, he told me. All four of them."

"I can believe it! Cousins?" She tried again.

"Haven't gotten that far yet, but I will let you know."

"Ummm hmmm. I'll be waiting. I'm ready to quit my job and kick my feet up."

"I'll call you tomorrow." I chuckled, finally feeling lighter again.

"Love you, babes. Get some rest and know that you deserve all the love you're receiving right now. Don't question it."

"I won't."

"Goodnight."

"Goodnight."

I ended the call with a smile, placing the phone against my chest. The aroma of food that I hadn't cooked was becoming my favorite scent. Remembering what I'd been told while also listening to my body, I closed my eyes with the intention of rest.

Buzzzzz.

The unusual sound of the doorbell quickly interrupted my plans. Mercer's bedroom seemed as if it was miles away from the front door. There was no way I'd be able to determine whose presence was behind it.

Deciding to mind my business and lean into the comfort of his bed, I closed my eyes again. My security was the least of my worries. With every fiber in my body, I knew that Mercer would keep me from hurt, harm, and danger if it was at all within his capabilities.

As I began to doze, the door crept open. Fully expecting to see Mercer, I was flabbergasted when Mal rounded the corner with worried eyes and a sly smile. Her hands lifted, welcoming me in for a hug long before she reached me.

"Dinner will be ready soon, Pretty. You're welcome to stay if you'd like, Mallory."

Mercer peeped his head in to announce and then was gone again, leaving a void that Mal's arms quickly filled.

"Wh-what are you doing here?"

I could feel the swelling of my eyes. The fabric of her jacket brushed against my lids, extracting pain. The soreness was a result of constant wiping and rubbing with the shirt, which was now crunchy in the front.

"You thought I was playing, babe? You should know me better by now. When I said I needed to lay eyes on you, I meant I needed to lay eyes on you."

"Thank you. But I told you I'm fine."

"Now that I see that for myself, so am I."

"Will you be staying for dinner?"

"No. I won't interrupt, but I won't front like I'm not tempted. It smells good in there."

"He's king of the kitchen. I'm not mad about it."

"Listen, all I'm going to say is I'll understand if you never leave this man's bed. Not only was he beautiful, but so was this house, and the look in his eyes when I mentioned your name at the door was as if I reignited a spark. Because, for a minute, I thought I was about to take my last breath. I love a man that totes a big gun, honey."

"A big gun is not all that man is toting, so help me God."

Mal doubled over in laughter, but I was serious.

"Seriously."

"I'll take your word for it."

"Please."

"I'm going to get out of here, babe. Get my behind on home. I have three days to prepare for my next trip. I wanted to hang a bit, but I'll catch you before I leave, right?"

"Yes. Promise."

"Goodnight, Vallei. Take care of your heart, love."

"Goodnight. I'll walk you out."

I slid from underneath the warmth of the sheets. Mercer had left a pair of the white slippers that were lined up at his front door by the bedside. I slipped into them and headed out with Mal.

We reached the door and then for each other. Our arms and hands squeezed, making sure we transferred more love between us before parting ways. I watched her get in her car from the window beside the door.

When she was in and pulling out of the long driveway, I tiptoed toward the kitchen, eager to see what was being prepared. To my surprise, I entered the dining room to find plates on the table with food designed for a five-star dining experience, topping them both.

"Is your friend not staying for dinner?"

I whipped my body around slowly, finding Mercer leaning against the frame that led into the kitchen. I had no idea he'd been standing there or how long.

"I just saw her out."

"I would've. I didn't know she'd be leaving so soon."

"She didn't want to interrupt."

"She wasn't," he assured me.

"It would've taken all night to convince her of that, so I didn't begin trying."

"Understandable."

A moment or three passed with us fixated, unmoving. Time seemed to stand still whenever I encountered Mercer. Everything stopped. Nothing progressed but the beats of my heart per minute and my addiction to him.

"Come 'ere."

I sauntered in his direction, stopping when the tips of my house shoes touched the tips of his, forcing him to share his space with me. He'd called me over, so I doubted he cared, and I was sure it was exactly what he had in mind.

"What's with the tears?"

With a thumb, he brushed my left lid.

"Don't worry about it. Let's just continue our night."

"Nothing continues, Pretty, until I fix whatever is fucked up in your world. Nothing."

"Mercer."

"Anything, Pretty. When I said that, I meant that."

"Whatever do you mean by anything, Mercer?"

"Anything you need. Anything you want. Anything to make you feel better. Anything to make you feel good. Anything to keep you smiling. Anything to keep you protected. Anything... So tell me, why the tears? I don't like them."

"I can't explain."

"Yes, you can, Vallei. You're a poet. The words are there. Use them."

Silently, I stared up at him, knowing that he was accurate. And when the words came to me, I began to explain.

"Being here, being with you, opens wounds I didn't know existed. Helps me shed skin that I've been needing to shed. Makes me realize I've probably never been loved properly, cared for properly. And while it hurts so bad, it feels so good. So, these tears were not sad tears. Not all of them, at least."

"Maybe you were loved. You just ain't gone ever be loved like I can love you, so it will make every effort any other nigga has ever put forward feel minuscule. And that's the way it's supposed to be. Because once you let me, for real, won't be a nigga on God's green earth that can out-love you like me. I'd bet my last dime on it."

A nod had to suffice because my lack of air left me speechless.

"Now, can I feed you so you can tell me why the fuck you ain't single and ready for me to lock you down?"

Another nod lifted my head up and down.

"Good."

I was seated at the table he'd prepared by the time he made it to his seat. He'd pulled my chair out and helped scoot it to the table after I'd gotten comfortable. A quick prayer was followed by forks against the plate, stabbing a dish that I didn't quite recognize.

"Give it to me straight."

Mercer wasted little time getting down to business. I didn't mind a bit. I'd been waiting to explain myself, explain my situation.

"The Trembles are the best divorce attorneys in Huffington. Divorcing Phillip will mean agreeing to give him half of my earnings as well as monthly payments until he remarries or decides he doesn't want any more money from me. I doubt it'll ever be the decision."

"Cheaper to keep him."

I nodded. "But my misery is beginning to be too much to contain. I want out. I just can't figure out how."

"You don't have to."

"I—"

"You don't have to."

"Merc... I don't underst—"

"Anything, Pretty."

"I j—"

"I'll figure it out. Just give me some time."

"How?"

"I will figure it out. Don't worry about how. If you want out, then you'll have out. Just have patience."

"And us? In the meantime?"

"There isn't an us, Pretty. Not yet. I know that's not what you want to hear, but I've done my research, baby. I'm not putting that much paper on the line, even if it's not mine. Your net worth is twenty-eight million dollars. **We** can wait. I'll be here when it's all settled."

"Twenty-eight million. Is it?" That was news to me."

"Did you not know?"

"I didn't. I don't worry myself with those numbers. Besides, that feels a bit inaccurate."

With a chuckle, Mercer put his fork down. Feels a bit low, is what you meant, huh?"

"I didn't sa—"

"How much are you protecting, Pretty?"

"I mean, I silently invest in compan—"

"Just answer the question."

"Thirty-six."

Nodding, he picked his fork up and continued eating. After clearing his mouth, he spoke again. "Yeah. Let me figure that out."

"He doesn't know."

"Doesn't know what?"

"How much I truly have."

"He knows enough and submitting documentation to the courts will make him aware."

"That's what I'm afraid of."

"Don't worry. It won't reach that point."

"Yeah?"

"It won't."

My mind was stuck in the place he'd left it when he said we'd need to put a pause on what we'd embarked on. More than anything, that piece of the conversation had my heart aching.

"I don't want to stop seeing you," I confessed. "Not even for a few days."

"I'm not on no creep shit, Pretty. I'm a forty-year-old man. That shit for kids. And I'm no fool, either. With damn near forty million on the line, I have nothing to lose, but you could lose half."

"There has to be another way."

"Going in guns blazing. That's always an option for me and a sure way to get shit done, but I have too much on the line to risk jail time right now. So, back to option one. I'm here when you need me, but it doesn't go beyond that. Understood?"

With a nod, I confirmed. "Understood."

FIVE

Mercer

Watching her heart break before my eyes wasn't on my list of things to do tonight. Neither was telling her to lie low. Shit, neither was finding out she was holding almost forty million. The bus ride hadn't made much sense until she mentioned not caring much about the numbers. Her character was peeking out, and I was loving every bit of what I saw.

Though creeping with Vallei wasn't an option, neither was the impulsive decision to move her pretty ass into my house tonight so that she never had to return to that nigga. She'd busted her ass to get where she was, and I wasn't going to fumble her bag for the hell of it.

"If there was anything in the world you could do right now, what would it be?" I asked, deflecting. The sadness in her eyes was too much for me.

"Lay in your arms."

"You will. But anything else?"

"Divor—"

"You will. Anything tangible? At this very moment?"

"Visit a nursery. Buying new plants always makes me feel better."

I flipped my phone over and began my search for the closest nursery.

"They're all closed," she informed me. "It's late."

"Somebody will open their doors, Pretty. Money talks. Bullshit walks."

I was still knee-deep in my search when her plate was cleared. She sat back, satisfied with her serving. Just as I was about to ask if she needed anything else, I stumbled across a spot. It was nearly two hours away and closing in thirty minutes. I dialed the number listed and waited for an answer while standing to remove the cork on the fresh bottle of wine that had been sitting on ice in the champagne bucket.

"Greenery Nursery, this is Tanter. How can I help you?"

"Tanter, Mercer. I'm interested in visiting within the next two hours, but I see that you close in about thirty minutes."

"Yes. That is correct."

"How much will it cost to stay open until I arrive and my"—I paused, taking a look at Vallei—"fiancée choose a few new plants to make her feel better tonight?"

"I don't thin—"

"How much, Tanter?"

"How about you give me a call on this number when you're twenty minutes out, and I'll meet you back up here. I live just two miles up the road. Is two hundred bucks alright?"

"I was willing to pay whatever. See you in two hours."

"See you then."

I tilted the glass and allowed the wine to trickle until a quarter of it was filled. I did the same for a second glass. Though I preferred something neat that burned my throat on the way down, having a glass of wine every now and then was quite pleasant.

"Two hours away, Mercer?" Vallei kissed her teeth.

"Not quite, but almost. I figured the extra time would be useful."

I handed her the glass of wine. She sipped, immediately. A nod was her sign of approval.

"A poet," I began.

"Yes. I struggled for so long for my voice to be heard. Years and years of trying to get my work out there. It wasn't until I stopped caring and just started creating more and more that things took off. It happened when I wasn't looking, and I've kind of adapted to that mindset since."

"The part you enjoy most?"

"The words and writing for others. It's where the bulk of my income lies. Writing songs for others. I never imagined being on stage or performing with such big names in the industry, but my words have taken me there, and I continue to do so. I've been living a dream for the last four years. I'm not sure I want to wake up."

"Then don't," I advised.

"Have you always wanted to be a chef?"

"I've always cooked. Always been good in the kitchen. My pots were full of illegal substances, but the enjoyment was still there. In the kitchen, I tap into another zone, one that I feel most true to. But being a chef, never really considered it until the last year or so."

"What changed?"

"Freedom. That and spending my free time in the kitchen. Every day, I'm there, trying to keep myself busy and keep my mind occupied. Too much time to think leads to—"

"Um hmm."

She cut me off.

"Much like writing or playing for me."

"I assume."

"Favorite color?"

"Ha." I chuckled, feeling my cheeks rise. "I think it's a little late for favorite colors and favorite movies."

"Never too late. Favorite color, Mercer."

"Black."

"Figures."

"What about you?"

"Beige."

"I can see that."

"Favorite movie."

"I don't have one. You?"

"Me either."

"Birthday?"

"August twenty-second. Yours?"

"June twelfth."

"Six years."

"Six years?" I questioned.

"The age gap. You're six years older than me."

I nodded, agreeing. "Yeah."

"Have you ever been in love?"

"Have I ever been in love?" I asked, leaning back in my chair. "Very close."

"More than once?"

"Once."

"Who was she?"

"It doesn't matter, Pretty. My thoughts are with you now."

"I don't know that I've ever been in love," she admitted with a sigh. "I thought surely I was in love when I got married, but the last thirty or so days have really opened my eyes and have me wondering if that was truly love or if it was simply better than what I'd received until that point so I didn't consider it settling until now."

"Finish your wine, and we'll take the second cup to go. Let's not muddle the moment with thoughts of negativity stemming from a failed relationship. We've had enough of that already."

She tilted the glass, finishing her wine as she'd been

told. There was something about a woman who followed orders so graciously and without question, allowing you to take the lead, not because she didn't have another choice, but because she trusted you, and it felt most natural to allow you to guide her.

"I'm ready."

There was much more to the statement she made as she stood on her feet. When she began reaching for the empty plates, I tapped her hand.

"Get some clothes on. I'll handle the rest."

"This is all I have other than what I came over in. Maybe I should've brought a bag aftera—"

"I wouldn't invite you to my home empty-handed if I wasn't prepared for your stay. Since the first day that I met you, Pretty, I knew you'd be here someday. Check the last drawer in my closet, closest to the window. You'll find a few things. Tags still attached."

She paused, searching for words.

"Go ahead," I told her, tilting my head toward the exit of the dining area.

Instead of leaving, she closed the gap between us. Her hands went around my neck. With those big, brown eyes, she stared up at me with a smile.

"I don't know that I can voluntarily say goodbye."

"I don't know that I can let you, but we'll cross that bridge when we get to it. Tonight, tonight is all that matters. Get dressed, Pretty. I don't want to repeat myself again."

Her eyes widened with joy. Happily, she obliged, leaving me to clean up the small mess we'd made. I made sure the dishes were put away, and the table was wiped down before going out to start the truck. When I returned, Vallei was dressed and downstairs.

"Ready?"

I'd heard the question, but I wasn't sure if I wanted to answer just yet. I was ready prior to seeing her in the leggings and one of my sweaters that was a few sizes too big. She'd put a spin on the wardrobe that I wasn't expecting but was appreciative of. Digging through my closet had worked out in her favor and mine.

"Merc... I feel like I should be calling you something else."

Her cheeks flushed as they rose to meet her eyes. Her crisp white teeth emerged from behind her lips, making way for that pretty ass smile. My mind went astray, imagining my dick between them motherfuckers.

"I agree," I responded, beginning to hate how formal my name sounded rolling off her tongue while I wasn't in her pussy.

"Baby." Slowly, she released.

With a shrug, I nodded.

"Amor," she followed up with.

I nodded again.

"Captain."

Her hand went to her forehead as she saluted. Chuckling, I nodded with lifted brows and a head tilt.

"Cap."

"Come on, Pretty. Let's get you to this nursery before the lady thinks I'm lying about coming."

"Ready, Cap."

I headed into the dining room to grab the wine glasses and bottle. She wasn't far behind me.

"Leave the glasses."

"You trying to face the bottle?"

The bit of wilderness that lingered in her spirit was appeasing. Though she was a well-put-together woman, I could tell there were parts of her that desired unhinged behavior, even in the smallest fractions.

"Is that what it's called?"

"Maybe."

"Well, yes."

"Say less."

Two plants filled my hands, yet the scrolling had yet to halt. Vallei pushed around a small cart that contained four more as well as everything she'd need to keep them alive for the next few months. The joy in her eyes, as we passed a new set with dark pink patterns on the leaves, stopped me in my tracks. She looked up at me from where she had squatted, waiting for approval.

Denying her or something that improved her emotional and mental state wasn't something I could do. So, each time she found something else she loved, I was onboard and eager for the reaction that quickly followed. Letting Pretty loose in the nursery was like giving a sugary kid the keys to a candy store.

With a nod, I sealed the deal. Her smile shrunk in length but somehow grew brighter. Those perfect teeth were no longer visible. Her hands were in the air, and her feet were marching toward me. Her silent celebration grew loud as she wrapped her arms around my neck and pulled me in for a kiss, simultaneously squealing.

Vallei was infectious. I kissed her lips and allowed her smile to transfer, pasting one on my face as well. When she stepped back, hands still in the air as she swayed her hips from one side to the other, I watched her with so much adoration in my eyes and heart.

"Thanks, Cap!" Though she could purchase the entire spot her-damn-self, her gratitude was sincere.

If I wasn't buying the damn plants, she wasn't getting them, and I liked it that way. Vallei had her own bread, but she wanted to use mine. That's how it was supposed to be. I'd flip my pockets inside out before I allowed her to touch a dime in her account.

Providing and protecting had been instilled in me long ago, and it didn't rest simply because a person could provide for or protect themselves. That shit remained intact under all circumstances — *for Pops, Chem, Malachi, Aeir, Makai, Glacier, Milo, Nature, and for Vallei.*

"Anything, Pretty."

"Good choice," Tanter, who happened to own the cool little spot fresh off the highway, confirmed.

It was ducked off but still on the service road on the side of the express. The trees she claimed to have begun growing the day she got the keys to the building were her idea of seclusion. She'd had the right one, if you asked me. It also created a less brutal habitat for the things she loved growing in months that could claim their lives.

"She's beautiful," Vallei sang as she grabbed the one she had been looking at and tucked it under her arm.

There was no more room in the basket.

"Well, this feels like the sign for us to leave." She chuckled with a shake of her head.

"Hardly," I responded. "If we need three more carts, then we'll grab 'em. We're not ready until you're ready."

"I'm ready." She yawned.

I led her toward the register where Tanter was waiting. Instead of stopping to allow her to scan the barcodes on the plants, I reached into my pocket and removed the fifteen hundred dollars I'd separated from the rest of my wad and laid it on the counter.

"Goodnight."

With a slight stutter from the utter shock she suffered, Tanter was slow to respond. "Uh, I, uh... Well, th-thank you. Goo-goodnight, now."

Softly, Vallei added, "Goodnight."

I packed each plant safely in the truck using the wrap that was provided. Once they were squared away, I helped Vallei climb up. When I reached over to grab her seatbelt, she placed a hand on mine. Though words didn't emerge, I knew there was something to be said. There was something on her mind, something she needed to get off her chest.

"What's up, Pretty?"

"Thank you."

I nodded. "My pleasure."

"I know." Sighing, she laid her head on the seat.

"Your studio would be the perfect place for all your new creatures," I suggested, plugging the belt into the slim compartment designed for it.

"Or your home."

She turned to face me, waiting for a rebuttal. I didn't have one. And telling her anything other than yes was too hard of a battle. It simply wasn't within my mental capacity.

"Anything, Pretty."

That smile tugged at her lips as she wrapped her arms around her body, rubbing her arms to bring herself comfort. She was no stranger to self-soothing. With closed eyes, she embraced her limbs, making my stomach knot. I moved closer, unbuckling the seatbelt I'd just secured. I scooted both hands underneath her bottom and scooped her out of the passenger seat. Her arms wrapped around my neck. Her head lowered, right under my chin. Her legs, they found their way around my waist.

I held her closely. Tightly. Quilting her with comfort. Whatever she was reminded of that made her fight to stay in the moment a few seconds ago, I needed her to forget. It wasn't a time to let anything steal the joy it hadn't created.

"Should you ever need comfort, Vallei, look no further," I whispered in her ear.

Her silence was disheartening. I looped my fingers around her hair and pulled her back until I could see that face of hers. Even with glossy eyes and a single tear on her cheek, she was flawless.

"You hear me?"

Because it was all she could muster, she lifted her head up and then let it fall repeatedly. She was delicate to the touch. I allowed her to lay her head on my shoulder a little while longer. I wasn't sure when I'd begun twisting my body from one side to another, but I didn't realize it was happening until Vallei's lips were on mine, and she was saying things I wanted to hear.

"Take me home, please. I'm ready to lay in your arms."

I complied without hesitation. Once we were both inside the truck and ready for the road, I hiked up the slow jams on the stereo and hit the highway. Vallei was hanging on by a thread. Exhaustion had her on her third yawn. Darkness sheeted the sky.

As her grip around my hand began to loosen, my eyes fell upon her. Like a baby, she'd drifted into a peaceful sleep. I contemplated riding until the sun rose, and we both made the best of wherever we landed, but I knew that running from our reality to become one wasn't the solution. Time was.

Between her and the road, I found peace. I lifted the back of her hand and placed it to my lips. She smelled as sweet as she was. Love had dealt her a fucked-up deck, but it didn't mean she wasn't deserving of it in its purest form. Strongly and wholeheartedly, I felt that it was my obligation. And I'd oblige.

With so much paper on the line, my trigger finger was

itching. But a trail of blood was the last thing I wanted to leave when my legacy was something far more fitting. My family had put up their hard-earned cash to secure my spot and help me get it off the ground, and the nigga that was willing to get down and dirty with me was in the joint. For once, that felt like a blessing because, without a doubt, I'd have my Glock to that nigga's dome until his signature was secured.

You've grown. I tried reminding myself.

And I had. But some shit was engraved in my character. In my head. In my heart. Some shit, it wasn't any shaking, no matter how hard I tried. I just prayed I could remain patient, remain steadfast while setting some shit in motion that would free Pretty and all the paper she'd worked her ass off to save.

One person crossed my mind. Two, honestly, but one stemmed from the other. I quickly unlocked my phone, using my knee to steer the wheel. Through my contacts, I searched for the name of the person who would have some answers for me, surely. If not tonight, then soon.

"Well, what a pleasure! I'm almost afraid to ask why I'm finally getting a call from someone who claims to love me as much as I love myself. How bad is it?"

"Royce." I tittered, kissing the skin of my teeth. "Hello to you as well."

"Don't try to sweet talk me, Mercer. You talk to Roulette all the time. I don't know how to feel about that."

"Roulette brings me business."

"So, is that the key to your heart?"

"The reason I'm calling is."

"What's her name?" She sighed. I could hear her plopping down as she began typing away.

"For you to look her up before we even end the call?" I chuckled.

"I'm going to do that anyway, so spill. And tell me what's the matter. You sound stressed."

"I don't." Calling her bluff was easy. It was simple. Royce was as nosey as they came, which was why she was in the right profession. Her inquisitive personality didn't blossom suddenly. I recall the few times they spent hours at Pop's house to give their parents a break.

She was always building cases and searching for evidence around the house to make the case she'd built solid. For hours at a time, she would interview Pops, piecing together his life story and trying to figure out how she could take care of the void our parents' deaths had left in our home.

"Ok, maybe I lied, but still... spill."

"Vallei Novelles. Po—"

"Grammy-winning, songwriting, poetry-writing, album-opening, violinist? Shut up, Mercer. Is that who you're seeing?"

"How do you know her?"

"The only people who wouldn't are those living under a rock."

"Is that supposed to be an insult?"

"If that's how you took it."

"Yeah, aight. I'm still big bro, Royce."

"Anyway, she's married."

"Unmarry her."

"Huh?"

"That's the task on my hands, to unmarry her."

"Is it abuse?" she whispered as if she was suddenly in the presence of someone else.

"She's unhappy, Royce. I want her in my bed when I lay down every night. As long as she's married, that can't happen. So, unmarry her. That's the task."

"I find it hard to believe a husband is stopping you fro—"

"Thirty-six million is. It has nothing to do with that nigga."

Her silence was fueled by the rapid pecking of computer keys. I let her continue whatever she was doing, not speaking again until she did.

"Thirty-six point two million dollars, to be exact." She gasped. "Everything she touches goes platinum. And the investment. Wow. She doesn't spend a dime of her earnings. Well, not a full one. She spends less than one percent of her earnings yearly. She doesn't even own a—"

"Vehicle."

"No. Only a bike. She purchased it off her credit card three years ago."

"And you know all of this how?"

"Don't act like you didn't call me for a reason, Mercer. You gave me a name and knew exactly what I'd do with it. Now, Phillip Tremble. Her husband."

"Um hm."

"He's paying rent at an apartment complex just south of their home. Thirteen minutes away. She pays the mortgage, which is incredibly low because she's a first-time homebuyer who went through a program. So, this isn't their rent that swallows his monthly earnings. His account will be in the negative within six months if he continues this way. In February, it looks like he went on vacation. He wen—"

"I don't give a fuck what that nigga been doing. Vallei is my only concern."

"Hush. I'm just thinking out loud and seeing what I'm working with."

"Well, call me and let me know what you're working with once it's something I can work with. I can't send something that belongs to me back to its lawful owner too many times. That shit ain't in me."

"I know. Just hold tight, and I will make sure this works out in your favor. You have to give me a bit of time. From what I can see, the men from his family's firm have never lost a divorce case in their history of practice. Their number one client is men who either refuse to pay up, want to pay less, or want half of what their wives have."

"And that ain't an option."

"I know."

"Hit me up when you have something for me."

"Of course."

Royce was the first to end the call. I sat my phone down on the armrest and brought Vallei's hand to my lip again. This time, she stirred in her sleep. I watched her find comfort against my arm, using it as a pillow underneath her head.

Sleep well, Pretty.

SIX

Anxiety had me fidgeting with the fabric of my skirt. Though nothing was particularly wrong, nothing felt right, either. Fifteen days had passed since I'd last seen Mercer's handsome face, kissed his lips, or heard his voice. I was losing the hearing in my left eye. And with my right eye, I couldn't smell a thing.

Hives appeared each time I thought of his dark skin and perfectly groomed facial hairs. I hadn't seen my smooth brown skin in two weeks. Withdrawals weighed heavy on my heart. His absence was one that I'd never grow fond of. The tiny, fine bumps on my arms were proof.

There wasn't a day that went by that I didn't want to reach out, show up at his restaurant to keep him company or stretch out in his large bed. There was too much room on the mattress for him to sleep alone. It was built for companionship, and so was I.

As I gnawed on my lower lip, I stared down at my cell, contemplating my next move. Another day without a peep from Mercer was too much to ask of me. Listening to the men of Phillip's family cackle down the hall was all the motivation I needed. Not only had I grown tired of the sound of their voices, but I knew, for a fact, that they all knew of his infidelity.

"What's got your panties in a bunch, Vallei? You've hardly said three words, and I've been talking to you for the last ten minutes."

"Sorry, Penelope. I j—I have a lot on my mind."

"Hopefully, it's nothing to do with that peanut-head brother of mine. Girl, I keep telling you to drop his ass and find you somebody better. He is not the one, sis. Love that man, but he isn't."

She'd been saying it from the start. In the beginning, I assumed it was the little sister-big brother rivalry that had her wishing for better for me. However, as she got older, her stance never changed, and our marriage began to take blow after blow. I understood that sibling rivalry had little to do with her warnings. Womanhood, that's what she was most true to when delivering the advice she had been giving for years.

Unlike the rest of the Trembles, Penelope and I got along well. She was the little sister I'd never had growing up. I'd helped her choose her dress for prom, saw her walk across the stage to graduate high school and college, we'd taken road trips together, and she'd toured with me for three months when my last poetry album was released. Every week, we covered four cities.

By the end of the tour, we'd been to thirty-six cities across several states. The next album would require more time on the road and more cities to tackle. And though I'd enjoyed my time with Penelope, there was only one person I wanted by my side when I hit the road this time.

"How about we move this party up to the bedroom, where it's less..." She paused. "commotion. The fellas are obnoxious."

"Penelope, I feel like I'm the only one indulging. You've handed me two drinks since they went into the cigar chamber."

"Okay, and when you come up to my room, we can continue filling you with drinks. I'm trying to watch my figure. Plus, I need you a bit tipsy for what I'm about to tell you."

"Hmmm. Does it have anything to do with that cute little boyfriend of yours?" I asked, finally ready to listen to whatever was on her mind.

"It has everything to do with him. Now, come on. Grab that bottle. I have the rest."

She gathered everything she'd need to create a personal bar for us upstairs in her bedroom. It was big enough for an actual bar, but she wasn't much of a drinker. Not even her youth could convince her other-wise. She contributed her reservations to the men in her family who clung to the bottle every chance they got.

We took the spiraling staircase up to her bedroom where she closed and locked the door behind us. I lay across the plush throw, ready to hear whatever was about to come from her lips. Now that we were alone, I could pinpoint the fear in her almond eyes. She pressed her back against the door and breathed deeply as tears fought their way down her face.

"Awwww. Penelope. What's the matter?"

I stood, finding my way over to her, until she halted me with a hand in the air.

"Please. I'm fine. I... I have something to tell you. I ju —I know how you feel about these things and before I tell anyone... I don't even know for sure, Vallei."

"What is it? Is everything okay? Is your mother alright? Your father?"

"Yes. Yes. They're all fine."

"Then what is it?"

"It's about me."

"What about you? Has he hurt you?"

"No."

"Then wha—"

"I think I'm pregnant."

She knocked the wind out of my chest. I held a hand there, making sure my heart didn't fall out. It felt like it had. I was breathless, gasping for air that just didn't seem to come to me. My eyes fluttered, flashes of black alerting me that I was opening and closing them. Seconds passed,

I wasn't sure how many before I could see straight, and the small, invisible bugs stopped floating around. It wasn't until then that I could speak again.

"I, uh... How do you know?"

Pushing past my personal feelings, I aimed to support Penelope in any way she needed me to at the moment. That was more important than the parts of me that were broken and couldn't be fixed.

"I don't. I took a test earlier today and haven't been in my bathroom since. It's on the counter, underneath the towel. Can you have a l—"

"Yes. Yes. Of course. Do you want to look with me?"

"No. Ju-just tell me what it says."

"Okay. Give me a second."

I tossed the remainder of the mixed cocktail she'd made as she laid the ingredients on the desk near her window. Once it was emptied, I passed the glass to her.

"Another one?" she asked, eager to calm my raging heart.

"No, babe. I'm fine."

Slowly, I made my way into the bathroom, where a black towel was sprawled out on the counter. I lifted it, finding a pregnancy test underneath. Squinting, I read the small screen that displayed her results. Surely enough, Penelope was expecting.

My arms went around my body as I stared at the test, imagining it was mine. Even if only for a few seconds, as I squeezed my body tightly, I enjoyed the good news. Shuffling in the room quickly reminded me that this wasn't my reality. It was my sister-in-law's. And more than I had wanted to since I left his home fifteen days ago, I wanted to call him. The yearning was so thick in my belly that everything I'd consumed threatened to spill.

"So," she called out. "What does it say?"

With the test in my hand, I peeked around the corner. I wasn't sure where I'd mustered the smile, but I managed one.

"That you're going to be a wonderful mom," I told her, handing her the test to see for herself.

Briefly, she observed it just as I had before: her brows crinkled, and her mouth slacked.

"We weren't trying. It sor... it just happened."

We weren't trying. The words broke my heart into a thousand pieces. I'd tried for years and years, never finding a positive pregnancy test on my counter. A new couple that was not focused on parenthood had magically gotten pregnant with no effort involved. It was unfair, but it was life. I'd learned to accept it long ago and roll with the punches.

"I-I'm sorry. I didn't mean to sa—"

"It's fine. It's fine."

"But are you?" she asked, stopping to have a good look at me.

With a shrug, I tilted my head, trying to be okay and not so deep in my feelings, but it was hard. Admitting was easier than lying, so I went with the truth. It was always the solution in my head.

"No," I admitted with a smile, shaking my head.

"I understand if you need a minute."

"This isn't my moment, Penelope. It doesn't matter if

I'm okay. This moment is about you. It's about me supporting you. Congratulations."

"It's not fair if I don't acknowledge you and your feelings in the process. We're a team, Vallei. That's how that works. We have months to talk baby and pregnancy. But right now, you matter most. So, tell me, what will make you feel better right now?"

It didn't take me very long to answer the question. A response was at the tip of my tongue; it had been all night.

"I need to make a call."

"A call?"

"Yes. One that your brother or no one else can know about."

"Hmmm. So, Vallei does have secrets." She laughed.

"No. I'm still the most boring girl in the world, but this has to stay between me and you."

"So does this pregnancy," she warned.

"Okay. I promise." I ran my index and thumb across my lips as if I was zipping them.

"Okay. I promise, too."

I wasted no time going through my text messages to find the number that I'd hovered over a hundred times before. Still, I hadn't saved it on my phone, too afraid that a contact would make this all real. Him real. My feelings real. And my troubles real.

Mercer's phone started ringing, deeming me silent as if I hadn't known I'd placed a call. I grew anxious, waiting for an answer, waiting to hear his voice on the other line. By the third ring, I felt nauseous, as if I'd puke at any second. By the fifth one, I couldn't bear the wait any longer. I ended the call and stuffed my phone in the pocket of my skirt. Because it was a cargo skirt with over-sized pockets, the phone fit perfectly.

"Woah. Are you going to give up that easily?"

"I shouldn't have called."

"Vallei. Don't be so hard on yourself."

"Seriously, I shouldn't have. I have no right to disturb his peace. He's made it clear that we can—we shouldn't be involved. I just keep wishing I was with him, near him, in his presence every waking hour of the day."

"Okay, and I thought I had some news. Let me sit down for this. Keep talking. I'm listening."

"I don't want to make this about me."

"Too late. Now, spill."

"His name is Mercer. Mercer Domino."

"Domino? You snagged a Domino? Shut up! That youngest one, Milo, I wanted that man like I wanted a shiny new car for my college graduation. He wouldn't take the bait. Luckily, he didn't, or I wouldn't have met Danny."

"I love Danny for you."

"Me, too."

"That's all that truly matters."

"Not what they say," she emphasized, rolling her eyes, referring to the men below us who were still laughing and choking off cigar smoke occasionally.

"No. Danny is good for you. Your father had his mind set on you marrying a lawyer. It doesn't matter who you date. He probably won't approve."

"And if he doesn't approve, then neither of the others will."

"Exactly. So, do what feels right in your heart as long as it's not causing you mental, physical, or emotional harm."

"Danny is the sweetest, Vallei. He'd never."

"I know."

"But back to Mercer. I've seen him before. He was the chef fo—Oh my God! Did you meet him there?"

"No. I met him at our home, actually, while your brother was away."

"Good. Moved right on over for something better."

"He stayed the night," I confessed, my cheeks flushing red.

"Shut up! You're lying."

"I wish I were. The dinner was the second time I saw him. He didn't know I was married. Our home is full of artwork, but there are no personal pictures. Our only wedding pictures are in a photo album in the China cabinet I thrifted."

"The one I loved so much and want to have when I buy a home soon. Me and Danny are looking."

"Good for you. But yes, that one. He used to own our home. He left something in the backyard, buried. Something really important that he needed. It took him two days to find it. He built me an entire garden and creative studio for the inconvenience."

"A man!" she cheered. "Phillip could never!"

"Hush." I quieted her with a finger to my lips.

"Sorry. Tell me more. I love a good love story."

"Nobody's in love yet, Penelope."

"Babe, have you seen your face since you've been talking about this man? I've never seen you talk about my brother this way or look, so, eh, what's the word? So... content and so blissful while doing so."

"Blissful?"

"Yes. Like there's glitter floating around that head of yours every time you think of him."

"Hearts," I corrected.

Bursting into laughter, she nodded. "Hearts will do."

"I don't know that I love Mercer, but there are feelings there. A craving so deep that it aches to think of him. Every part of me desires a different part of him. Every second. Every minute. Every hour. Every day. I feel so unbalanced as if I'm stumbling and I just can't catch my footing. It's been hell since we last seen each other. I hate living this way."

"Then don't. Leave that man, Vallei. I love my brother, but he is not it. Maybe for a woman that will give him the same energy he gives. But that's not who you are. And, you... you love with your entire heart, not just a little piece. Phillip is a great guy, but he's a shitty partner."

"He wasn't always like this."

"Maybe not always like he is now, but he's always had his ways."

"I know."

"I'm happy for you, Penelope. Despite anything else I'm feeling right now, I am."

"I know. And this will be ours. This is our baby."

"You're saying that now, but when I'm trying to keep the baby for three weeks at a time, I doubt it'll be the case."

"Three hours. Let's just start with three hours."

"That'll suffice, *for now*."

"Good."

A knock on the door startled us both. As Penelope hid the pregnancy test in her bra, I headed toward the door to unlock it. I wasn't surprised to find my husband behind it with his hands in his pocket.

"You ready to head home?"

I nodded as I watched his eyes roam my body. Secretly, I longed to find the same admiration in his eyes that I saw in Mercer's when he combed over me. But there was nothing but an emptiness that wished to be filled by something else or someone else. When he turned to head down the stairs, I peeped my head back into the room and said my goodbyes.

"See you later, girlfriend."

"I'll call you sometime next week. Don't be like—" she stopped to zip her lips. "Pick up for me because I don't give up easily."

"I knooooow."

"Love ya."

"Love ya back."

I followed Phillip out of his family home and to his truck where we both got inside. The drinks that I'd been influenced to have alone, the positive pregnancy test, and the fact that the one person I wanted to sort my feelings out with hadn't answered the phone left me deep in my feelings.

Experiencing new lows right beside the man who was supposed to be the highlight of my life was more revealing than almost any other moment had been since I'd decided to take my heart into my own hands. The clarity was real. It was crippling. It was humbling.

The vibration on my leg reminded me of where I'd shoved my phone in an effort to bury the disappointment of an unanswered call. My heart hammered against my chest as I dug into the pocket to retrieve my phone.

As I'd suspected, the unsaved number that I'd learned almost every digit sat at the top of my screen. Instead of a regular call, it was a FaceTime call coming through. Without the heart to silence it or ignore the call, I simply laid it on my lap and hiked the stereo up a bit more to drown out the vibrations. They stopped, but only momentarily.

It seemed as if Mercer didn't give up so easily either because it was his number looping the screen when I flipped it over again. I peered in Phillip's direction, realizing that I didn't plan to keep Mercer waiting or let the call ring out this time.

More than I wanted peace in my chaotic marriage, I wanted to hear his voice. More than I wanted to keep my husband from worrying about my dealings, I wanted to talk. And more than I wanted my husband to take me to our home, I wanted him to drop me off at Mercer's.

That's how profound my connection to this man was. And I felt not even a bit of shame. If anything, I was justified. At least, that's what I told myself when I slid my finger across the screen to answer the call. Because it was a regular one this time, concealing his identity was still possible.

"Hello?"

My heart galloped in my chest as I waited for his baritone to soothe every ache I had, heal every wound that had been created since his absence, and make sense of the patience I was trying to practice until everything in my world was squared away.

"Pretty." He called my name, filling me to capacity.

"Cap," I whispered.

"Where are you? What's the matter?"

Without revealing anything, Mercer understood that something was wrong.

"I'll be fine." I whimpered, watching my fingers tap against my leg.

"That's not what I asked." The low growl in his tone let me know that I'd better start talking, or there would be consequences. "I'm coming to get you, Pretty. I'm on my way."

"Cap."

"I'm on my way."

"Please don't."

"You sound like you're near the point of tears. Staying home while you deal with your shit alone isn't an option. I wasn't asking you. I was telling you. I'm on my way."

"I'll come to you," I mumbled into the phone, cutting my eyes toward Phillip.

"Then come on. You have forty-five minutes before I come knocking, Vallei."

He ended the call without another word. I immediately opened the Clock app on my phone and set a timer for forty-five minutes. I then tracked the distance between my home and his.

According to Google, it was a thirty-four-minute bike ride. Phillip and I were approximately six minutes from home. As soon as the wheels stopped spinning, I needed to be on my way to Mercer's. I'd have three to five minutes to spare within that timeframe before he dotted his front door in search of me.

Phillip kept his eyes between the road and his phone, entertaining someone through texts. I observed the constant responses and the urgency in his smile without saying a word. Clarity continued to show up for me in ways that made everything going on in my marriage tolerable. Because I knew the ending was near, what Phillip was involved with concerned me none, as long it didn't affect my health or wealth.

Slowly, I climbed out of the truck once we'd reached our destination. I needed to change the slingbacks I wore for the sneakers that were at my front door. Baffled, Phillip stopped in his tracks, wondering why I was putting on the only sneakers I slipped into when it was time to ride my bike.

"A bike ride?" he asked.

"Yes."

"At this hour?"

"It's only eight, Phillip."

"And dark out."

"I have a lot on my mind. I need the fresh air. I need to feel it on my face, in my hair, in my lungs. I feel like I'm suffocating."

"Whatever you say, Vallei. Be sure to take your house key and the can of mase hanging near the coats in case you encounter any problems. I'll probably be asleep by the time you make it back in. I'm exhausted."

Unsure exactly how my night would unfold, I simply nodded. Telling him I'd see him later was possibly a lie, so I wouldn't go that route. I remained silent. It felt most natural and relevant.

I contemplated changing into something a bit more comfortable but quickly changed my mind. The clock was ticking, and running upstairs would put me behind by a few minutes. I made my way to the garage and got onto my bike, making sure it would still be a comfortable ride. The stretch that the long, cotton material of my skirt gave was exactly what I needed.

My journey started as soon as the garage door was down. As the wind tapped against my skin, my liberation was set in stone. Coming to terms with the fact that my feelings were the result of a failed marriage was so much easier as the memories came in one after the other. There were so many happy times between Phillip and I.

Until the doctor explained my diagnosis, every day had been a breeze in our marriage. As if a switch was flipped that day, nothing had been the same since. Any sane woman would've walked out of the door a long time ago, possibly the minute she noticed her husband was disgusted with her incompetence and lack of ability to reproduce.

However, it was likely they didn't have so much to lose. I'd lost enough in love. I refused to give Phillip any more of me than he'd already taken. In my opinion, he already had enough.

Tears stained my cheeks, but I wiped them away as quickly as they came. The pain was absent. It was my newfound freedom that had my emotions bubbling over. The breezy bike ride was symbolic of just that, making me tear up as I entertained my thoughts with the idea of divorce.

Mercer · Vallei

I arrived at Mercer's home to find him waiting at the door. A chance to ring the doorbell was a chance I never got because the door swung open as I stepped onto the large porch that ran the length of the front of his home. With open arms, he waited for me.

Quietly, I walked right into his warm embrace. In his arms was a place I was honored to call home. It wasn't a dwelling that I'd decorated with the prettiest pieces and limited-edition artwork. It was a person. It was Mercer.

His presence reminded me that I'd been a nomad for the better half of my life. From the moment I left my parents' home, I'd needed a place of my own with characteristics that didn't include numerous walls and doors.

It was a heart, a mind, arms, legs, and a smile that completed my home. And they all belonged to the man pulling me inside his residence, unclothing me as I took one step after the other. No words were exchanged, yet silent orders were given and taken. Without a single piece of cloth on my body, I started for the stairs but was quickly swept off my feet and into the air.

He knew his home well. His eyes never left me as he made it up the stairs, into his bedroom, and to his bathroom, where the sound of water running in the tub that was in the center of the large space could be heard. Soft, beautiful sounds surrounded us.

"Thanks, Cap."

Clearing my throat, I waited for him to leave me lonely. It never happened. He never left my side. And when I finally came to the realization, I was able to relax. My eyes adjusted to the low lights, surrendering to the mood that had been set for me.

Mercer reached over and stopped the water from running. The plain white shirt that he wore shouldn't have done for his body what it was doing. The warm water added a few degrees to my heightening temperature. Mercer was responsible for the rest.

"Tell me what's wrong so that I can make it right," he demanded, sitting next to the tub.

As he exposed my eyes to a brand-new corner of the bathroom, I was rendered speechless. A brand new, shiny violin leaned against a stand not too far from where we were.

Dear God, who is this man, and did you mean him for

my good? I questioned, staring at the instrument. It was perfect. My fingers began itching at the thought of its touch and the beautiful sounds it would make as I strung it, releasing everything that was keeping me bound.

"Pretty."

"Hm?"

His voice was as comforting as my art. Poetry and composing music, for so long, had been my sole source of contentment for years. But since Mercer, things had changed. It wasn't my pen and paper I wanted to run to. It was him.

"Tell me what's wrong so that I can make it right."

"A violin?"

My nostrils flared with emotion as my chest caved.

"Do you like it?" He looked back at the brown beauty.

I nodded. "Yes."

"Good. It's been here for a week now. I didn't think you'd have the chance to see it so soon."

"Cap," I began, shifting my eyes toward him. "It's been the hardest two weeks of my life, going on as if you don't exist. You never existed. And I haven't been experiencing parts of you that are memorable. I've missed you every day so much it hurts."

"Me, too." He sighed, taking my hand and pressing it against his chest.

I could feel the beat of his heart. It matched mine.

"But I could never pretend that you don't exist. Because you're right here, even when you're not around."

"God, I wish this could all be over."

"Tell me what's wrong," he requested. "I won't repeat myself again, Pretty."

"A close friend of mine, we found out she's pregnant."

Nodding, he grabbed the bottle of body wash and the towel that was at the edge of the tub. He soaped it up and signaled for me to lean forward. It wasn't until my entire top half was coated in bubbles and I'd stood on my feet that he began speaking again.

"Your heart will never not hurt at the mention of pregnancies, births, and children. It saddens me greatly, Pretty. I am part of a very fruitful family. Children are born yearly, sometimes more than one.

"Our union wasn't on accident. And there's no way I'll ever be forced to believe that God would place you in our midst to make you suffer one pregnancy after the other. One birth after the other. I won't believe that. That isn't your story. Neither is it mine.

"When all of this shit is over, and the dust settles, we're going to get another opinion. Another one if that one isn't in our favor. I believe that you are capable of natural conception and childbirth. I've already spoken to God about it. Trust me, Pretty, that man has never let me down."

"You sound so confident."

"Because I am. There's nothing more that we need to discuss. When the time is right, it will happen."

"Okay."

His words reminded me of my mother's. She, too, refused to settle with my diagnosis. However, I was a realist, and after years of trying, I was forced to side with the facts.

"Infertility cost me my marriage." I scoffed, still trying to place my feelings.

"Infertility exposed the fragility, flaws, and bruised ego of the nigga you chose to marry. It didn't cost you shit."

"Merc—"

"Don't ever blame yourself for what a nigga does and doesn't do. Because one thing I know for sure, if he can and really want to, then he will. For a woman I truly love, I'd go find a fucking baby if that's what she wanted, if that's what I wanted. The doctor could tell you right now today that you're dying of cancer and have only a year to live.

"I'd make it my business to make sure you live the fullest, most memorable year of your existence so that you can think about me during your transition. And you're not fearful because you know without a doubt we'll do it all again next lifetime. When you love someone, you do that. No matter the circumstances.

"Loving a partner with conditions is pointless. Either I'm all in, or I'm not in at all. It's simple, Vallei. So, don't piss me off by blaming a failed marriage on your inability to produce children for a nigga. Got me ready to go beat his ass right now." Mercer huffed, turning the dial for the water. With contorted features, he began rinsing the soap from my body. I felt inclined to apologize. Making him upset was never my goal.

"I'm sorry."

"Don't tell me you're sorry, Pretty. You've done nothing wrong. But please understand you're talking to a man whose father went and rescued the love of his life from a mental institution only for her to take his life and hers. We don't do conditions, Vallei.

"My parents are testaments that things don't ruin marriages, people do. Get that through your skull, baby. And let that be the last time we discuss what was when it comes to you and that nigga. Don't even think of that shit in my presence."

"I don't," I replied honestly. "I just... I don't know where that came from."

"Leave it there next time, Pretty."

"Are you upset?"

Losing his composure seemed to be impossible, but it felt like I'd ruffled a few feathers.

"Not even a little. My only priority is you tonight. That ain't changed and will not change. Have you eaten?"

"Yes."

"Step out for me."

I followed instructions, stepping onto the rug and stretching my arms wide. Mercer wrapped the towel around my body and guided me toward the bedroom. Once inside, he used a second towel to dry parts of me that were still wet.

His large hands ran the length of my body with cool cream that smelled like vanilla and honey. The combination was heavenly, and so were his fingers against my skin. Like a well-oiled machine, I lay in waiting as he pulled the covers he'd pushed back over my body after he was finished. Naked, I experienced a slight chill as they warmed.

"Lay with me," I begged, tucking the cover underneath my chin.

"Under one condition," he explained, leaning in to kiss the worry lines across my forehead.

"Anything, Captain."

His smile warmed me to the core. The low chuckle that stumbled from his frame gave me butterflies. Fine wasn't a full enough word to explain the ungodly, unfair beauty of this man.

He was beyond anything I'd ever dreamt of. He was beyond my wildest imagination. He was beyond earthly. He belonged wherever the angels were, wherever God kept His most holy, sacred creatures.

He was beyond the land and seas that he'd created for us common folk. He was mythical. He was magical.

"You stealing my shit, Pretty?"

His smile had superpowers. It could heal the deepest wounds. Made me feel as if I could get through anything, get over anything, get around anything. It was the sign I needed. The sign that made me feel invincible.

"Only because I mean it."

"Share your art with me."

"Hm?" His request blindsided me.

"That's the condition," he explained to me. "Share your art with me."

"Cap, I—"

"I don't like to beg, Vallei. In fact, I think it's beneath me, but I'm willing if that's what it takes."

"I just... I've never shared unfinished pieces with anyone. I've never shared anything that hasn't been recorded or mixed and mastered. I've nev—"

"Had anyone ask, either," he spoke, quickly realizing that was the actual truth and what had me hung up, unable to progress through the moment. "I'm asking, Pretty."

I extended my arms, needing to feel his all around me. His mind and his heart were both undoing parts of me that exposed inconsistencies and insecurities that I was unaware of, and it was triggering. But running wasn't an option.

Mercer quickly scooped me into his arms, confirming what I already knew was true in his world.

"You're alright."

"My vulnerability has only ever existed in my art. That's my refuge."

"Not anymore."

"I feel s-so exposed," I admitted, confessing my awareness of the hollow parts of me that he carved a little more of each time he opened his mouth.

"I want you bare or not at all."

I pulled back, a painful smile tugging at my lips.

"Hand me the violin, Captain."

"Say less."

The excitement that raised his cheekbones at the news that I was ready to unleash my fears, my pain, my stress, my inner thoughts, my dark parts, and everything else that belonged to me in the comfort of his bedroom made my head light and my heart heavy. Nevertheless, I accepted the instrument he handed me, understanding that it was *anything for Captain. Anything. Everything.*

"This has just come to me," I expounded.

Words began to align with my heart, demanding they see the light of day. Demanding they meet the man responsible. Demanding they touch him in the same places he was touching me, without his hands, feet, fingers, and toes.

"I'm listening, Pretty."

I strung the violin, prematurely tuning it, knowing that I was ready to use it regardless. I'd figure out the logistics later.

"Thanks." My cheeks peaked, displaying the pleasure I experienced, knowing that my audience of one held the man who was slowly etching his name on parts of me that were unseen and seemingly undiscovered.

"The name."

"Anything."

A subtle nod gave me the courage to begin, placing any reservations on the back burner.

The grass never seemed greener on the opposite side.
The flowers weren't that much brighter.
It was the allurement of imperfection that piqued my interest and fueled my curiosity.

*In a world where perfection is a source of power, I
wanted to reign supreme elsewhere.
I'm the furthest from perfect.
So it was just the place for me.
I'm here now.
Amongst things, amongst a person just as flawed,
you see.
Hoping we can continue to coexist.
Hoping we can just be.
Because it's anything when it comes to him.
And it's anything when it comes to me.*

SEVEN

Mercer

Though I took one step at a time, my heart was far beyond my feet. It was already in the room I was headed toward, in front of the person my eyes and limbs were feigning for. A full day at the restaurant made my drive home much sweeter, knowing that I wouldn't be entering an empty space another evening. The knowledge of her presence turned my trip to the house into my journey home. My walk through the foyer was even different.

Finally making it into the bedroom where the sleeping beauty continued resting, I contemplated waking her or letting her sleep a bit longer. All day, she'd been in and out. I made her promise to let her body do exactly what it needed to, even if that meant sleeping the entire day away. She'd obliged. But now, I was trying to keep myself from being the contradiction of my own demands.

She's so fucking perfect for me. Her hair was no longer wild and free. It was plaited in long braids that had been piled into a ponytail when she'd come to me. Now, they were sprawled out on the cover.

Little trinkets dangled from a lot of the strands. Jewels. Crystals. Butterflies. Gold rings. A bunch of shit that I would imagine looked a mess in anyone's hair but somehow enhanced her beauty. *Her mystic. Her art. Her face. Her features.*

Instead of disturbing her, I made a temporary resting spot in the chair near my bed. Upon sitting in it, I found myself struggling to acclimate to the distance. It was my most difficult task of the day.

Of the week.

Possibly of the month.

Even harder than keeping my truck home and not in front of the residence she shared with her husband. Because I didn't give a fuck about shit they had going on. Pretty belonged to me. That wasn't up for debate.

I slid the chair across the floor until I was right next to the bed. The frame became a footstool. Twenty-four stemmed roses fell against my jeans. I'd handpicked each and every one of them myself, hoping that they made Pretty feel a bit better about the night she'd experienced and the pain of being told she couldn't bear children plagued her with.

The lack of physical touch she'd revealed to me made it hard for me to keep my hands off her. However, I managed because another shot of that shit between her legs would have me calling off all bets. I was a patient man, but there were a few things I wasn't in control of. My unsettling, uncompromising hunger for Vallei was one. She had me by the fucking balls.

"Cap?" Slowly, she stirred.

I could feel the drumming of my heart against my chest as I sat up, placing the roses near her face. She was almost dangling from the side of the bed. Slob ran down her cheek. There was no doubt in my mind that she was resting well. Her serotonin was having its way in my home, which was exactly how it was supposed to be.

"I'm here, Pretty."

"What time is it?"

"Almost six."

"I've slept all day."

Her eyes finally opened.

"That's okay."

"Flowers? What's the occasion?" she asked, sitting up.

"One isn't needed for you to enjoy staring at roses, Pretty."

She paused, momentarily, before nodding. Helping her unlearn unhealthy tactics that had her settling for less than I was capable of giving her would be a joy of mine.

"Thank you."

"Anything, Vallei."

She pulled the roses into her arms and buried her face inside, making the decision to bring her along with me instead of encouraging her to return home so much simpler.

"Get dressed. We have somewhere to be in an hour."

"Get dressed." She tittered. "My clothes are sweaty from my bike ride unless you've cleaned them. My necessities are all home. I can't—"

"Stop running that little mouth of yours and trust that my requests aren't made unless I know you can fall through with it. Either because I can make it happen myself or because I've provided you with everything you need to see them to fruition."

"I don't follow." She sighed with slumped shoulders.

"Have you forgotten your growing wardrobe through that door?"

I pointed, hoping to jog her memory. When her mouth fell open, I knew she followed.

"Anything, Pretty. Get that through that skull of yours, baby."

"I will. I promise," she assured me.

"In the meantime, come shower with me. And keep your hands to yourself."

"Are you fucking serious?" She scoffed, not believing the demands I'd made. "As if that's possible."

"It is."

"Then, I'm not joining you."

She said that shit like I gave a damn, as if my rules weren't law in this bitch. I reached over and picked her and them roses up off the bed. Her body bounced as I headed toward the bathroom where we'd be showering. I'd waited all fucking day for this moment. Not seeing it through wasn't an option.

"Mercer!"

"Keep that shit to yourself unless I'm digging you out, Pretty. And I'm not digging you out right now."

"We have to compromise," she pleaded.

"Put the flowers on the counter."

I lowered her to her feet. She landed as softly as I wanted her living. Hardships were part of her past. From the moment I met her moving forward, I'd been making plans to soften every area of her life.

And they were plans that would not fall short. They were plans that would blossom more and more over time. Plans that would solidify her world and mine.

"Are you even listening to me?" She pouted, pursing her lips and folding her arms across her chest.

"I'm always... always listening to you, Vallei. But right now, you not saying shit."

"Compromise," she repeated.

Giving it a second thought, I massaged my beard with my fingers. It didn't take long for me to fall in line.

Anything, Pretty.

A gasp fell from her body as I lifted her in the air, smelling her arousal as I did so.

"Dinner is in an hour, but I guess I could manage an appetizer."

Her words fell upon deaf ears as I licked her sweetest spot. She wanted a compromise. This was it. My face planted in her pussy was all Pretty would get out of me. It was all I had if I wanted my medication to continue its job.

Mercer · Vallei

I didn't care how many months had passed, dinner still didn't feel quite right without Makai. His absence was becoming the bane of my existence. I wanted him home, and I didn't mean whenever that nigga felt like coming. I wanted him home now.

"Malachi, Aeir... This is Vallei. Vallei, Malachi, and his wife, Aeir."

"Nice to meet both of you."

I watched Aeir pull Vallei in for a hug, though her hand was outstretched. I hadn't expected anything else from my brother's wife. Her welcoming spirit was as genuine as her love was. She nurtured relationships like no one I'd ever met. One with Vallei seemed to be in the works, and I was far from opposed.

We continued around the table, stopping near a standing Milo, who was cradling his youngest in his arms. Our palms slapped one another. Careful not to smoosh the little one, I patted his back and greeted him warmly.

As the baby of the group, he deserved all the love that was reserved for him. He'd suffered a greater loss when we loss our parents. He'd had less time with them than us all. And nothing either of us did or said would recover that time.

"Milo... Nature... This is V—"

"Fleur Novelles," Nature rushed out.

Her pretty brown eyes widened as she reached out and pulled Vallei in for a hug. Her body rocked from one side to the other rapidly.

"What are the odds?" She huffed. "Oh God, you're even prettier in person!"

"I agree," I exclaimed. *That's why her name is Pretty*.

"I love you so much! Well, your work, of course. My husband is about tired of hearing your voice in—"

"That's her?" Milo asked, pointing in Vallei's direction. "The one that won't shu—"

"Aye," I warned.

"If you knew how many times I've heard that soothing ass, deep ass, beautiful ass voice, you'd understand. What's even worse is I like the shit."

"I feel ya, my nigga." I agreed. Vallei had a gift.

"That's why I want her to shut the hell up. Got a nigga feeling all types of ways."

I nodded again.

"Is it even okay for us to like shit like that?"

I shrugged. "I don't even know, man. Hard not to."

"Exactly. Nevertheless, welcome to the family. Milo."

"Vallei."

"I already did that for you two," I reminded them.

"Doesn't hurt to do it twice." Milo shrugged.

"Give me the baby. It's time for a good nap," Nature suggested.

Taking a peek at Vallei, I searched for any signs of discomfort. All I found was joy. Joy that she was unable to contain. She rubbed the sides of her folded arms, bursting from the seams, almost wanting to say something.

"Let her help, Nature," I spoke up, extracting the words she couldn't.

Immediately, her eyes found mine. With her head tilted rightward, she mouthed words I recognized.

Thank you, Cap.

With a hand to my chest, I tapped twice and nodded. Nature wasted no time transferring the baby from her hands to Vallei's, who was quickly overwhelmed and overcome with love at once. She secured the package and looked to Nature for instructions.

"Down this hallway."

Glacier's voice turned both Milo's and my heads. Smiles tugged at our lips as we watched her wobble into the dining room. With twin girls growing in her womb, it made getting around a lot more complicated.

"Remind me to get her a driver when she's in Berkeley." I nudged Milo.

"She won't go the full length of the pregnancy."

"I doubt it, too. As long as our girls are healthy and strong, I don't give a damn."

"Think we need to strap her ass to a seat so she can birth them here?"

"Nah. But we do need to get a plan in motion. She's alright with having them here. We'll have to drive her back when she's ready, though."

"I don't mind," Milo claimed.

"Me either."

Filling in for Makai during his absence was as hard as it was rewarding. After embracing Malachi and Aeir, Milo was her next stop. Then, I was her final destination. Pops had opened the door for her.

"Mercer!" she greeted, leaning forward to embrace me.

"What's up? How you feeling?"

"Tired." she breathed. "Very tired. Is the food ready?"

"Yeah. We prepared it at the restaurant, and Pops brought it home."

"Good, because we're starved."

Vallei was at my side, again, smiling lovingly at a baffled Glacier.

"I'm Glacier."

"Nice to meet you. I'm—"

"I know who you are," she insisted. "It's... You're even prettier than th—"

"That's the same thing I said," Nature interrupted.

"Gosh." Glacier laughed. "I don't know why I expected anything else. Your work is just as beautiful."

"How far along are you?" Pretty inquired.

Her inquisitiveness was disheartening but interesting at once. I wondered if she was deepening the knife in her heart or healing the wound it left. Either way, I was comforted by the smile on her face. It was genuine. Whether from pure curiosity or happiness, I was content with it.

"Not far enough," Glacier admitted.

"Past your due date?"

"No. I have another three months or so."

"Oh wow."

"Twins," I explained, knowing exactly what Vallei was thinking.

"Yes." Glacier chuckled. "If this was one kid, I'd be concerned. But it's two."

"Congratulations." Pretty cackled.

"Alright, y'all 'bout ready to eat? This woman said my grandbabies are hungry!" Pops yelled over everyone.

"We're ready," Milo called out.

"Good, because I didn't care one way or the other. I was feeding them babies. Come on, Glacier. Let me fix your plate."

"I got it, Pops."

He nodded, waving for me to go ahead. Already knowing that she wanted a little of everything, I grabbed a glass plate and began lifting the lids of the dishes that sat on the warmers.

From the sidelines, I watched Vallei connect with every woman in our circle, effortlessly. I wasn't sure if witnessing her enjoy the food I'd made again or sharing unfiltered laughs with the ladies was my favorite part of the night. My heart was full.

Every so often, I felt her hand against my thigh underneath the table. Craving physical touch to be re-centered as an introvert was a habit I quickly picked up on of hers. I marked it in the Book of Vallei that I'd begun the moment I saw her pretty face.

Pages were rapidly filling. Each chance I got, I'd study my content to strategize and plan a future full of happiness for the main character of my book. The only character in my book.

An hour, thirty-two minutes, and thirteen seconds after grace was said, we began clearing out to return to our respectable home. Though I knew it was the best thing to do, I didn't want to return Vallei to hers. I didn't respect shit about that motherfucker but her.

"Your family." She chuckled, leaning into my arm as we walked, hand-in-hand, toward my car. "It's beautiful."

"Appreciate that, Pretty."

"I really enjoyed myself. I can't remember the last time my family gathered and had a really good time. After my grandfather's death, I think we just drifted apart. Any time my mom tries to get us all together, there are more excuses than plans to attend, so she always ends up canceling long before the day.

"It saddens me, sometimes, to even think about, but tonight really reminded me that there was a time I laughed as much, hugged as much, smiled as much, and just communicated with humans. Feels like my violin and my notebook are my best friends most days. Mal would kill me if she heard me say that, but it's true.

"Other than that, it's all business in my world. It's almost always all business, which is why I like album mode most. I can breathe and focus on crafting content I can have to myself for a little while."

I listened as she shared her thoughts. It was pleasant

hearing what was happening in that head of hers. I'd been wondering all night.

"I don't want to go home," she admitted as I buckled her seatbelt.

"Don't say shit like that, Pretty."

"What? I'm serious, Cap."

"Don't say it, 'cause I won't take your ass."

"Then don't."

"A few nights of paradise and a lifetime of pain, Pretty. That's what you're asking for, but I can't give it to you and have you regretting this very moment every time you check your bank statement."

I bit the inside of my lip, drawing blood. Violence was always the answer for me and the niggas that shared the same blood, but it wasn't in my best interest right now. Every time I closed my eyes, I saw my Glock to that nigga's dome, but it was a risk I wasn't willing to take.

I have a brother in the slammer right now. I hadn't been out too long. I couldn't break my people's heart a third time by going back. Not when patience, something I practiced well, was the better solution.

With sad eyes, she stared back at me. "You're always right. Some moments, I want you more than the money."

"And others, you're thinking with your heart right here and not the mimicked beat of it down here," I told her, pointing to her chest and then her pussy.

"Can you blame me?"

Dick. That's what she wanted. It was why she was willing to sacrifice at least eighteen million dollars. We weren't teenagers. Neither were we young, dumb adults.

Both over thirty, our aged maturity was enough for me to deny her of such a disgusting fate. So, I wouldn't, but a solution was working its way around the emptiness in my head. I kissed her lips and slammed her door, leaving the question unanswered.

Silently, I steered us toward my home. Vallei listened to the music that was on shuffle, mixing the station I'd created especially for her. R&B was amongst the few genres that were in rotation. With her lids sealed, she didn't notice we'd made it to my home until my truck was parked, and I hopped out.

"What are we do—"

"Shut up, Pretty."

I needed her silence more than my next breath. Otherwise, I'd make sense of the situation and take her ass right home where she needed to be.

She'd already unbuckled the seatbelt by the time I made it to her. I helped her down and led her into the house with the truck still running. We wouldn't be very long. With pent-up frustrations on both of our ends, I wasn't counting on an extensive stay.

"Mercer. Please. Expla—"

"Pull all that shit down. And please, shut the fuck up, baby."

Obliging, she freed her bottom half, exposing parts of her that I wanted in my mouth, on my dick, and sliding across my face. Sending her home un-fucked was something I simply couldn't manage. I needed her too exhausted and too fucking high off this dick to even pay that nigga any mind. I needed her to have her fix, one that would hold her over until the next time I slid in her guts.

"Hold them ankles, Pretty."

"Caaaaaaap—" she moaned, and I'd barely even touched her.

My fingertip brushed against the dark parts of her pussy that buried that pink, pretty shit that drove a nigga wild.

"Arch that back. Put that pussy in the air."

"Please."

"Don't make me say that shit twice."

I entered her realm with two fingers, moist from the cream I'd swiped from her drippings.

"Ooooooh God."

"That's exactly who we both need."

With those last words, I replaced my fingers with my tool, digging in her shit with ease. She was so fucking wet. Always wet. Too fucking wet. Shit was ridiculous and needed to be studied.

"And you better not fall, Pretty, or we running this shit back until you get it together."

In and out of her, I stroked. The sound of her appreciation made it hard to hear anything else. I stirred in her shit, making sure to rearrange her insides in ways that only I could repair.

"Mercerrrr, I'm cumming."

"I see," I confessed, watching her pussy spit out the prettiest filth I'd ever witnessed.

On the tips of her toes, as her legs began to weaken, she stumbled forward.

"Pretty," I called out.

Quickly, she reclaimed her balance on unsteady legs. Her pussy contracted around my dick, extracting my semen from my sack. With each stroke that followed, I risked letting off in that shit. And hadn't I wanted to bury my dick in her mouth, I would've. But I had other plans.

I pulled out of her reluctantly, hating the freedom immediately. Cold air after a warm, cozy stay was treacherous. I fell to my knees and lapped up the remnants of her gratification.

"Merrrrr," she dragged, surely ready to fall on her face.

"Pretty," I warned.

She straightened up, ankles still resting against her palms. I stood up, stroking my dick as I rounded her, loving her form. She was flawless. *She was mine.*

"On your knees."

I watched her scramble before plopping onto the floor, happy to fulfill the request. With a fist full of braids, I slid my dick into her mouth. It wasn't until my veins disappeared and I tapped the back of her throat that I stopped and pulled all the way out to give her a second to breathe.

She'd need all the oxygen she could get because once I reentered her warmth, I wasn't coming out until vomit was on my floor or my cum was sliding down her throat. Those were the only options.

"Open up for him."

Slowly, I eased back in. I watched from above as her eyes began to water. Saliva lubricated my shaft, coating it

just like her pussy had. Both holes were wet. My preference. My type of shit.

Tapping against the back of her throat made her
stomach cave. The threat of vomit that was shown with
each stroke was pure motivation as I became lost in her
world. Slob ran down her chin, landing on her chest and
titties.

I had the right mind to stick my dick between them
and fuck them, too, but her mouth was too promising. I
was stuck. Couldn't escape. Not even for a second.

"Urgh!" Vallei gagged with a face full of tears.

"That's it, baby."

I fucked her face. Slowly, intensely.

"URGH."

"You look so fucking pretty."

It was hard keeping my shit together when she was
being such a good, good girl and looking so damn pretty
doing so. I clenched the cheeks of my ass, feeling my nut
reach the tip of my dick. My toes curled so rapidly that
they popped.

"Fuck. That's it, Pretty. Suck this motherfuc—shit!"

My grip around her hair tightened as my body
bounced involuntarily.

"FUCK."

With every bit of strength I could muster, I removed
myself until I could see the head of my dick. Semen shot
up on the roof of her mouth, all over her gums, and finally
on her tongue.

"Fu—"

I closed my eyes, desperate to calm my racing heart.

"Swallow it, Pretty. Quit playing with it."

I opened my eyes to see Vallei push the mouth full of cum down her throat. Savoring it was useless. There was more to come. I'd give her a lifetime supply when this all blew over.

"I need to wash up."

"Put your clothes back on. We're leaving."

"Cap."

"You're not washing shit off, Pretty. I said we're securing your bag. I never said I wouldn't let that nigga know what time it is."

EIGHT

I entered my home, reeking of Mercer's greatness. The clearing of Phillip's voice upon entering was frightening and unexpected. I turned to find him in an unusual spot. The sitting room near the door was one that didn't see much of him.

"Phillip," I greeted him, taking off for the stairs. The shower was my first stop.

"You left home around eight o'clock last night. That's the longest bike ride I've ever heard of, Vallei."

His observation halted my stride. Because I was still extremely elevated from the last few minutes of my time with Mercer. I struggled to match his energy. I cared little about his feelings at the moment. I felt good. It was possibly all that mattered to me. I was unsure, which was why I stayed to hear more.

"You're not even wearing your biking sneakers."

I'm not. Mercer got me these. I looked down, tilting my right foot to get a good look at the Chanel loafers.

"Please, Phillip. Can you say what you have to say, or let me continue up the stairs? I'm ready for bed."

"Say what I have to say?" He tittered. "When did we start talking to each other like that?"

"When di—" I scoffed. "When did we stop talking to each other? Phillip, you haven't heard anything I've said to you in three years. Suddenly, you're listening. Suddenly, you notice me. Well, please understand that I've noticed you so long ago. Noticed the late nights. Noticed the long absences. Noticed the employees with lingering touches and longing eyes. I have not once bothered you with my observations. I've given you peace and privacy. Please give me the same."

"Are you seeing someone else?" With hands in his pocket, he stepped closer, asking.

Seeing? I was insulted. *I'm in love with this man, Phillip. I'm in love with him.*

As the words begged to be liberated, I remained silent, staring at my husband. The pain in his eyes mirrored the pain I saw in mine for three whole years. Now that it no longer existed in mine, it had been transferred to his. As painful as it was to witness, I didn't have enough fucks to give. That had been me, and he hadn't saved me from my hell. Saving him was not in my plans, either.

"Are you, Phillip?"

I stepped closer, waiting for an answer.

"Don't answer that because we both know the truth, right? The better question is, how many? How long? Those are the questions we're at at this point. Because we know the answer to the first one. You're in love. I can see it all over your fucking face, just like I see the disappointment each time you walk through that door. What you fail to realize is I'm not begging you to be here. There was a time that I would've, but my God, has that time passed."

"Vallei—"

"I'm going upstairs to the bed I sleep in alone and have been for months. You, you're going to let me and not bother me anymore for the rest of the night. We're going to act like this conversation never happened and carry on like we've been carrying on, Phillip."

Nodding, he allowed his guilt to silence him.

"I'm sorr—"

"Phillip. Let's just act like this conversation never happened."

I marched up the stairs, refusing to wait for a reply. Because if I waited a second longer, I'd be right back out of the door and off to a place where I felt welcomed, wanted, loved, and utterly admired. I would've gone back to him. *Back home.*

Heading to the bathroom to soak for hours in the garden tub excited me. I peeled my clothes off one piece at a time, recalling moments in Mercer's foyer. Satisfaction crossed my features. Standing in the mirror, I examined my aching hips and waist. Mercer's handprint had left marks.

The darker red indentions made my vagina ache as the thumping below began. How I was still craving his stroke after he'd performed with precision less than thirty minutes ago was baffling. I squeezed my muscles, hoping to feel him inside of me again soon. It's where he belonged. *I was home*.

Closing my eyes, I embraced everything I felt for once. A smile ripped my lips apart as his handsome face came into full view. His words, as demanding as they were, heightened my sensitivity. They made his stroke feel so much better, whether he was between my top or lower set of lips.

"My God, Mercer," I whispered as I opened my eyes and made my way toward the tub.

If I didn't get inside soon, I'd be touching myself in places where he'd left his stench with promises to return. I started the water and watched it collide with the bottom of the tub, wishing it was me. That feeling of Mercer's tongue against my clit made me squirm against the cold ceramic.

Damn it.

I caved, climbing inside and placing my feet on the edge of the tub. I slid up until my butt was against the front of it. Water connected with my most sensitive spot. Lightly, it hammered against it as it flowed down.

My neck rolled as I closed my eyes, waiting for

Mercer to appear behind my lids. He wasn't long. Per usual, he hated keeping me waiting.

Anything, Pretty.

His words rocked my body. My top teeth sunk into my bottom lip. Mercer's tongue circled my clit before latching onto it. Once he locked his focus, nothing more mattered. His plan to devour me worked in both of our favor. I began to buckle. My body tried folding itself in two as my orgasm knotted my stomach and strained my muscles.

"Ahhhh." I breathed out, hardly able to contain myself. "Mer-Mercer."

Sensitive to the touch, I slid from under the water in one swift motion.

"Mercer." I cried out breathlessly.

"You called me?"

Phillip's presence was startling. With crinkled brows, I tried catching a break in my respiratory cycle. It was happening rapidly, and I wanted it to slow down. My heart, too. It slammed against my chest with each beat.

"Vallei?"

"No." I coughed, holding a hand to my chest.

"I'm hearing shit." Shaking his head, he headed out of the door again.

"Lock the door behind you," I called out to him.

Suddenly, I felt naked. Exposed. *Disgusted.* More than my clothes had been stripped in the few seconds Phillip was in my presence. It wasn't until he'd made it out of the door that I was able to rest my head against the back of the tub and breathe deeply.

A smile tugged at my lips, eventually forcing a snigger. Then, there were two. Before I could contain myself, I was chuckling with tears running from my eyes.

You have to behave, Pretty. Mercer's voice made me nod. He was right.

Mercer Vallei

My wrinkled skin accepted the butter and oil that I slathered it with fresh out of the tub. I'd stayed inside for two hours, readjusting the water's temperature each time it was too cold to bear. The spark of creativity might've been part of the reason I unstopped the drain and allowed the water to flow out as well.

The need to touch the very floor that Mercer had made possible so that I could feel closer to him was fueling my fire. After making sure I was properly moisturized, I pushed my soiled clothes down the chute and replaced them with the baggiest sweats I could find in my closet, a cropped tank, and a flannel.

I gathered a few blankets, my notebook, my phone, and my violin before heading downstairs. Phillip had left the sitting room and migrated into the living room where he was watching television. I continued toward the studio that I'd hardly stepped foot inside since it had been built.

A few pieces had been moved in, but nothing worth gloating about. A rug. Two small tables. A bean bag. And a hammock. Other than that, it was empty. I didn't give a damn. It's where I wanted to be tonight. It's where I needed to be.

As I walked the path that led to the door, the smell of rain tickled the hairs of my nose. There was something special, something beautiful about the way rain announced itself before its arrival. Its courtesy was wondrous.

I dialed the digits that matched the day I'd met Mercer. He'd made it the code to enter the studio. The man was intentional, and there wasn't a damn thing I could do about it. Getting with his program was seemingly the only option, and I wasn't complaining.

As I stepped inside, low lights that cast warmth over the room that I could hardly explain welcomed me. Relief met me at the threshold. I began freeing my arms of all the things I'd collected.

The blankets went into the hammock. The violin went beside it. My gadgets were laid on the small table next to it. Carefully, I climbed into the hammock with my violin in tow. The slouched posture wasn't great for playing, but having it next to me was enough encouragement to encourage my creativity.

I continued the battle and inconvenience of what came most naturally to me over the last two months. Ignoring the longing for a connection between Mercer and me was much like running shards of glass across the skin by way of clothing, hoping to undress at the end of the night unscathed. It was diabolical. It was delusion. But I surrendered to the narrative, closed my eyes, and waited for the words to appear.

Share your art with me. His voice lulled every inch of me.

I relaxed against the threads of the hammock, expecting my word bank to begin overflowing. However, nothing surmounted. Nothing but visions of his pleasant smile and eyes, both in my direction and showing their appreciation for my presence.

I picked up my cell and unlocked the screen. At this point, anything would suffice. I scrolled my phone to find the single picture I'd taken of Mercer as he slept beside me. A trip to the kitchen to grab water in the wee hours had blessed me with the most precious piece of content. A perfect memory.

His dark skin blended against the dark sheets on his bed. They were black, just like him. Unable to help myself, I shared the image with the man himself. With baited breaths, I waited for the gray bubbles to appear. They never did. My pleasantries were replaced with anxiousness as I exited the practically empty thread and released the breath I'd been holding. As I did, my phone vibrated against my skin.

The unsaved number was calling. I answered almost immediately, afraid he'd change his mind, hang up, or I'd miss the call. Neither felt like realities I wanted to face. Not when I was missing him bad. Missing him all over.

"Hello, Captain."

"I'm offended by your lack of exhaustion. Should I return and give you something to fall asle—"

"I am incredibly exhausted." I yawned. "I fell asleep twice in the tub. I guess those naps powered me up a bit.

Nevertheless, I'm laying down and there's one thing on my mind."

"Yeah?" He yawned, too. It was hilarious, the way they traveled.

"Well, two, but one doesn't matter all that much."

I pulled the cover up toward my chin, getting more comfortable.

"Everything matters, Pretty. So, let's start with that one."

"Buying furniture for the studio. Tonight is my first night here."

"I can sleep later. I have a partner with a furniture spot. He'll open the doors withou—"

"It's late, Cap. I want to rest, and I want you to do the same."

"Then why are you on my line?" He chuckled. It was the sweetest sound.

"Because I needed to hear your voice before I went to sleep."

"Hm. What's the other thing on your mind, Pretty?"

"You."

Silence twiddled the line. I could hear my heart as it raced, beating harder each second we remained soundless.

"I'm on my way," he spoke finally.

"Cap."

"What?"

"Stay home." I sighed, realizing I'd provoked this behavior. Had I left him alone and never sent the message, then we'd both be on our way to sleep.

"Pre—"

"Stay home."

His grunt was a sign that he was capable of following orders, though he preferred giving them instead.

"And talk to me. Tell me something... something you haven't told anyone else."

Needing to feel that his world was as inclusive as I dreamt it to be, I wanted his secrets. I wanted his fears. I wanted his pleasures. I wanted everything.

"I'm no closed book, Pretty. There are a few men who share the same blood as me and who know anything there is to know about me. My apologies, but the only thing they are unaware of, I've already shared."

"Your diagnoses."

"Yes."

"Will you tell them?"

"Therapy."

"Hm?"

"That's the only thing they're not privy to."

"But it still deals with your... Cap, I don't want to call it an illness. I find it hard to associate you with that word. You're perfect to me in every way."

"That's the term. Mental illness. Bipolar disorder. However you chop and screw it, the fact remains even if you think I'm perfect, Pretty. I'm not. I can promise you that shit."

"How are you? Mentally?"

The pause left my chest hiked as I held my breath in anticipation of his response.

"Hello?"

"I'm here."

"I asked a question," I reminded him.

"I know, baby. I'm just trying to process my thoughts."

"Is it hard?"

"Honesty, no. But it's not always simple, either. Which is why I'm having a hard time placing my words and thoughts and all that shit."

"Has no one ever as—"

"Never," he rushed out. "So thank you. Let me get that out before we even continue."

"Don't thank me, Cap. I'm just following my heart's orders."

"Following your heart's orders, huh?"

"Yes. Now, answer me. Please."

"Aside from structured parts of my day, of my word, you know... stable bits and pieces, I find myself confused. Brain fuzz is a symptom I've always struggled with. After being diagnosed, it made all the sense.

"Because I'm an adult now, with so many moving parts in my life, it's always present. But when it comes to the people, places, and things that appear most often, I'm good."

"What about me?" I wondered aloud. "What about me, Cap?"

"Vallei."

"Tell me."

Afraid that his words would hurt, I braced for impact. Mercer was quickly claiming parts of me that had been deadened or simply unavailable because they were supposed to belong to the man I'd vowed to love for life.

But with honesty, I could admit that there wasn't anything Phillip could say to me that would destroy me, like disheartening words from Mercer. Phillip's words meant nothing. His, they meant everything. They could cut me like broken glass, heal me like a medicated bandage, or fuel me like oil in a car's tank.

"Though your physical presence isn't a stable structure in my life, your heart's presence is never not around. I feel you the entire sixty seconds of a minute. I feel you the entire sixty minutes in an hour.

"I feel you the entire twenty-four hours of the day. I feel you every day of the week. I feel you every day of the month. There's nothing fuzzy about our connection, my feelings toward you, or where you fit in my future.

"That's how I know you were meant to be here, part of my world. Because, from the moment I saw you, Pretty, you fit. Like a routine, you fit. Like family, you fit. The shit I feel for you could have everything to do with that. Not sure, but I'm not complaining."

"What do you feel for me?"

I wiped the tears from my eyes, trying my hardest not to alert Mercer of my emotional state.

"We should sleep now."

"Tell me."

"Where will any of this get us, Pretty? Besides fighting to make the shit we dream tonight a reality like we already are."

"I don't care." I cried, releasing the most gratifying

tears I'd ever cried. They were rooted in so many great things. "I don't care. Tell me."

"You belong to someone else, Vallei."

"I belong to you!" I forced out, taking offense to his statement. "And you to me. Avoiding the feelings that make that real, makes us real, will not make any of it unreal."

"I didn't say it would. I have no doubt in my mind that it won't. I'm just trying to find out the point in breaking hearts the way you want me to break yours tonight."

"You wouldn't."

"Not intentionally. Never. But telling you how I feel will. Because when you get off this phone, you'll feel pain so deep that you'll want to see a medic. Your heart won't stop hurting. Your head won't stop replaying my words. They'll be looped, swelling your heart each time they repeat themselves.

"You'll eventually decide that you'd rather have the life I can provide for you than the one you're living and flee your dwelling. And all the waiting you've been doing will be in vain. All the preparations I've been making will be in vain. 'Cause you'll make a split decision, and then I'll have to watch you regret it each day I wake up to that pretty face.

"It'll etch away at you, at our connection, at our world, and eventually destroy everything we've built. Listen to me when I tell you that my feelings don't matter right now. Making you mine, with no restrictions or connections to anyone else, that's all that matters right now, Pretty.

"I'm choosing to be proactive and avoid what could be the dismantling of something so beautiful, so necessary. Let me. Please let me, baby."

Words failed me. For every one of them I couldn't muster, another tear fell from my eyes. I used the blanket to catch them because clearing my face was pointless. I rolled my tongue around my mouth, filling the void he'd created growing bigger. I was only proving his point. I knew it, but I couldn't find the strength to care.

"I don't want to," I admitted. Still a blubbering mess, I knew that it was all I could make out.

"Stop crying, Vallei. Don't force my hand. Don't force me to come wipe them tears from your face myself."

I knew, without a doubt, that he would. I also knew deep within that he didn't want to. His maturity level was commendable. Because I wanted to cry like a baby on his lap while he lied to me and told me everything was all right. It wasn't.

I was stuck between a rock and a hard place. Things I'd busted my ass to have were on the line. I refused to give them up, and I refused to put Mercer's livelihood at risk, either. However, my pussy and my heart were on the same path.

He was the destination. The quicker I understood I'd make it to him, regardless, the better we'd both be. But I was struggling.

"Tell me the things you feel for me," I pled, unable to move on until he confirmed I wasn't alone in my pool of emotions. Not until he confirmed I wasn't the only one with my heart on my sleeve.

"You're a glutton for torture, Pretty."

"It makes for good artistry." The confession was no surprise to either of us.

The sound of the numbers on the keypad startled me. The idea that Phillip was punching them created a disturbance in my head that I wasn't prepared for. I tried climbing out of the hammock but was unsuccessful.

When the door opened, I quieted, knowing that only one person had access other than me. I peeped over the fabric that I was drowning in to find Mercer's phone to his ear. Only a few feet away from me, I watched as he drew the device closer to his lips.

"I love you, too, Vallei."

His words made my features turn upward. My heart shattered a hundred times.

"Wh-what are you doing here?"

"I couldn't bear the thought of your heart breaking in my absence. That belongs to me. It's my responsibility."

"Mercer." I cried into the line as if he wasn't standing a few feet away. He said only a few more words. I almost missed each one. My heart's drumming was loud, alarming even.

"And I came to wipe them tears, Pretty, and let you know that shit gone be aight."

The line died as his feet began to move. In his hand was a white handkerchief that he placed against my face.

"I need you to listen to me, Vallei."

I nodded, looking up at him, waiting for whatever was about to fall from his lips.

"I'm a nigga that gets shit done. One that will move mountains. Dry seas. Calm storms. Start riots if that's what it takes to make sure shit goes my way. It's the only thing I've ever done. This is the first situation where my hands are tied. And this motherfucker, right here, ain't making it no better for me." He pointed to his chest.

"Accepting my need to have patience is fucking with me up here." He pointed to his head.

"My trigger finger is itching. I don't want to stop applying pressure to that motherfucker until that man in there is lifeless. Divorce would be instant. You'd be mine, wholly, instantly. But what does that solve, for real? I'd be forced to lie down his whole fucking family. And I don't mind. Not at all.

"But I'd never rest another day in my life, and neither would you. Everything would be over. Your career would suffer. Your freedom would be in jeopardy. And ultimately, you'd hate me. I can't have that on my dome. So, I need you to chill, Pretty. Because when you call, I'm coming.

"When you cry, I'm dropping everything to see 'bout you. When you need me, I'm there. When you miss me, I will cross the ocean to get to you. I'm invested; heart, dick, and dome. I need you to understand that. You have control of me.

"All because of this motherfucker right here." He laid a finger on his chest again. "Do you understand me?"

I nodded.

"Work with me, baby. Let me work this shit out."

I understood everything falling from his lips, but my heart wasn't hearing anything coming from them.

"Come 'er," he demanded, pulling me from the hammock into his arms. "Let me make you feel better, Pretty."

My threads were torn as he hurriedly freed my pussy. Before I could digest what was happening, his dick was inside of me, making everything in my world right again. He pressed my body against the wall, bringing my eyes near his as he stared into my soul.

"I love you."

His embrace was unraveling. I was ready to vomit at the mouth, but I couldn't. He felt too good to me. Savoring him was more important than telling him all the things I felt.

"I love you, Pretty. Don't ever wonder."

"Stay."

"Don't ask that of me because I will."

"I-I'm sorrrry."

I clung to him, burying my face into the crook of his neck as my orgasm mounted. In his arms was where I stayed until his semen filled me. And just as quickly as he'd come, he'd gone, but not before I fell asleep against his chest in the hammock that kept our bodies pressed against each other.

On the table just a few feet away, he'd left enough money for me to furnish a new home, claiming it was for the studio. Though I didn't need the funds, he forced me to take them. More than the money, I was satisfied with the fact that he hadn't just heard me while we were on the line. He'd listened.

I hated the thought of waking in the morning without him by my side. If it hadn't been clear to me before, I now knew the lengths Mercer would go for me. I promised myself to never abuse his generosity, his love, his heart.

I loved it too much. Somehow, someway, I felt as if I loved him too much. Waiting our turn to love freely was something I'd have to subscribe to. It wasn't ideal, but it was required.

Mercer Vallei

Mal dragging me out of the house shouldn't have surprised me any. Yet, as I sat next to her in the pedicure chair, I was still wondering why my baggy sweats had been replaced with something more appropriate for the late spring weather in Berkeley.

Clinging to my violin or my bed sheets would've sufficed. They both sounded like the perfect day and had been the closest to one since the last time I'd encountered the man who brightened my days.

My post-Mercer era was one that I wasn't fond of. Eighteen days without him in my line of vision should've been against every law known to man. Though depression wasn't my official diagnosis, it felt so close to it.

No calls.

No texts.

No voicemails.

Nothing.

Wondering if he'd forgotten about me, about our love triggered me in ways I didn't know were possible. As my thoughts drove me back to the depths of my existence, I silenced a call from my mother, deciding I'd call her back at a later hour.

He must remember us. The thought soothed me all over.

"Hey!"

Mal snapped a finger as she called out to me. The softness of her tone wasn't one that I witnessed often. It let me know that she was holding a sacred space for me and wasn't pretending as if my feelings weren't valid. She understood I wasn't in pain, but every day was painful.

"Tell me what's going on up there."

"The same thing that has been over the twelve million phone calls we've shared."

"Fair enough. But tell me anyway. I want to see your face when you tell me you're sick to the stomach following the absence of a man who is not your husband that has been dicking you down like he is. You know the man I'm referring to, right?

"The one that has you ready to pull every braid out of your head and hold your ass in the air, hoping he smells your arousal miles and miles away 'cause your cat in heat. The man that will have your ticket to heaven revoked, though you're a literal angel.

"Tell me about that, right here, in my face. Forget

FaceTime. And I don't mind an ugly cry to really bring some theatrics in this production. I want the works."

A smile stretched my face. Giggles made my body expand and shrink over and over. And that magical feeling that one described as laughter reminded me that it had been a while since we'd encountered one another.

"Seriously?"

"Umm hmm. Got my little sweet ass juice they call a mixed drink to enjoy the show. I want poetry. I want song. I want all the things. My money's worth, to be accurate. That gel pedicure is not cheap."

"You invited me out, Mal. Pretty much kidnapped me."

"And the only way you'll meet your freedom again is to tell everything. So, get to talking."

"I promise there's absolutely nothing new."

"Vallei. That feels untrue." She pressed with a tilted head.

"Alright. Alright."

I nodded, preparing to tell her something I hadn't already. There wasn't much. But there was a slightly significant detail I'd left out of our conversations intentionally.

"I miss him more today than I did yesterday. I don't know, Mal. I don't know how much longer I can go on without showing up at his doorstep."

"What's stopping you? I think he'd like that."

"I shouldn't. That's what's stopping me. He's working, Mal."

"How do you know?"

"Because twice a week, I take a bus ride downtown. I've told myself it's to clear my head, but that's untrue. It's because his restaurant is on the route. I always feel so close to him in those moments.

"They're the only time I feel alive other than when I'm writing or discussing the details of my upcoming project with my team. They're the only time I feel like my presence is justified. Like, it's okay for me to be there. Even though we're forbidden."

"Have you seen him? Has he seen you?"

"I doubt that he has. But I feel him each and every time. The fluttering in my stomach, the racing of my heart... it all tells me that he's near. And for now, that's enough for me. It has to be."

"For how long, though?"

Sighing, I shrugged. "Until it's not. I'll cross that bridge when I get to it. Right now, it gets me over the hump and into the next week."

"Good."

"Ah. I feel insane. I probably sound like it, too."

"You don't. You sound like a woman in love, one who has experienced something wilder than her big, colorful dreams. I'm just waiting for the bridal party and wedding. This will be the one. I can feel it."

Smirking, I waited until she finished dancing in her seat to shoot her vision down.

"That's not what I want, Mal."

"What isn't?" She calmed down. Her mouth slacked as she waited for me to clarify.

A fresh stream of oxygen left me as I gripped the back of my neck with my hand.

"Marriage. A wedding. Any of it. I just... I just want to be deeply, wholly, completely in love without the law needing to make it *real*. That's not my reality, I don't think. At least not right now. No time soon, honestly."

"So, if you were given the chance, you wouldn't marry this man?"

"Probably not. And it's not because he wouldn't make the perfect husband. It's simply because I'm not interested in being a wife. Not anymore. Him being my partner in life doesn't mean we have to do anything more than love one another and create the safest space to be exactly who we are.

"Nothing more is needed. Not a ring. Not a wedding. My vow to Mercer won't need a minister present to make it official, you know? My vow to love him every day once this is over won't require a wedding dress or a bridal party.

"It'll only require my commitment to continue vowing when times are good and bad. Where and when or what I'm wearing when I exercise or acknowledge that commitment doesn't matter."

Nodding, Mal settled with my explanation.

"Sorry for ruining your plans."

"You haven't. Not at all. As long as you're happy, then so am I. Doesn't quite matter what that happiness looks like as long as it's safe, healthy, and beneficial to your overall well-being."

"Thanks, babe."
"Always."

NINE

"Lord, I'm trying, but this matter is beyond me at this stage. I'm going to need more than therapy to stay away from that nigga's wife. In no way, shape, form, or fashion do I want to. And I've never been into doing things I don't want to do.

"Especially when I'm feeling like this. My heart says she belongs to me. You feel me? She's so pretty and so perfect. You showed your ass when you made that one.

"I'm forever thankful. Grateful. Man, I love that woman. I'm missing her something awful, and you're the only nigga that can stop me from pulling up to her crib and picking her up tonight. I'm tired of sleeping alone.

"I want her in my bed. This sh—man, everything is taking so long. Legal this, legal that. My bullets can solve all them problems. But it—"

"Nigga, are you praying?"

"He's the only nigga who can keep me out of Vallei's box tonight. Unless you trying to suit up, then go take your piss."

"Nigga, my suit stay ready. Just tell me when and where. I'm sliding every time. No questions asked."

"Good, because you might need it if the Lord isn't quick to answer this prayer."

"Man, I don't even want to know what it is."

I nodded because I wasn't willing to go into detail anyway. My focus was elsewhere.

"You're a better man than me, Mercer. I'd burn all that shit down, including the house, with him in that motherfucker. That law firm would have holes in every window the contractor put in that bitch."

"The type of time I really want to be on, but growth is a beautiful thing."

"Thirty-six million is," he corrected.

"Yes. Yes, it is, my nigga. Got to make sure she keeps her paper."

"That's priority. The paper is always priority."

"Always."

Momentarily, my pacing halted. Staring back at Lawe, I nodded. He stepped past me and into the bathroom. It was where I'd just come from.

Before I stepped foot outside of his home and made my way to the house, I had to talk to the man upstairs. I wouldn't be responsible for my actions tonight if I didn't. My internal navigation was leading me in Vallei's direction. I could feel the gravitational pull.

When my bearings were gathered, I made my way back to the living room where the fellas were, including the new additions to the family. Luca, Laike, and Keanu were in town. It was a rare but beautiful occasion.

They'd loaded their plane and made the stop on the way to a sunny paradise for their family vacation. The wives and children were all at one of the many properties Lawe and Laike shared ownership of. Tomorrow, they'd be in the wind again.

But tonight, we were tossing back drinks, counting our blessings, and talking shit. Knowing that every single one of them was going to the crib to lay up in something warm and wet as fuck left me with a lot of feelings and Vallei at the top of my dome.

Though there were options, and Jas had made it clear on numerous occasions that her pussy was available whenever, wherever, there was only one person I wanted to slide into the rest of my days. The time on my phone uncovered a detail about her that I knew to be true without total confirmation.

1:48:02am.

She's asleep.

Internally and externally, I smiled, hoping she was resting well.

"I'm 'bout to get on up out of here," I announced,

slapping Ledge's hand and pulling him in for a hug. It was always good to see the brother of reason after too much time with Lawe.

"Drive safe, nigga."

"Of course."

Around the room, I said my goodbyes and embraced every person among us. There was nothing like family, extended or not. We were black men, continuing to thrive in a system that was built to destroy us. Each meeting was monumental. I took none of them for granted, whether for a few hours or a few days.

The humid May weather stuck to my skin the second I stepped out of the door. I hopped inside my truck and shifted the gear immediately. My engine had been started before my prayer began with the simple push of a button.

Home. I warned. *Go home.*

Lucky Daye's "F***n' Sound" boomed through the sound system, blurring my thoughts and my visions. Lost in a world of my own, I cruised the neighborhood we were all blessed enough to own homes in. Some of us more than one.

Upon arrival at my destination, I drew blood from my bottom lip. A steady eye on the bedroom upstairs with the low, golden glow warmed me inside out. A woman who deserved nothing but royalty was resting there. And though I hated to disturb her, my mission to make it home wouldn't be complete.

The start of my drive had begun with my dwelling in mind, but there was no place like home. There was no place like her. Not even the house I paid a mortgage on could compare. It was simply walls, shelter from the rain. Vallei, though. She was home.

I dialed her line. I contemplated hanging up and letting her rest because I knew she needed it. However, ending the call was a battle I quickly lost when I heard the first ring. By the third, her voice was serenading my heart.

"Hello." She groaned sleepily.

Unable to respond because I was busy having my fill of her, replaying the one word over in my head, I remained silent.

"Captain."

She petitioned for my attention. She had it. All of it.

"Come outside, Pretty. I can't fathom another night without you in my bed."

Her silence was telling. The light came on in the bedroom just as I heard her footsteps in the background.

"Pretty."

"Anything, Cap."

She ended the call, leaving me to wait and watch through the window as her shadow moved slowly around the room. Within three minutes, it disappeared and was replaced with darkness. Seconds later, Vallei appeared at her front door.

Waiting for her to reach me felt like a matter of life or death. I climbed my lanky ass out of the truck and walked around to the passenger side where I rested on the hood of the car with my arms stretched. She walked right into them, where she belonged.

"God," she whispered, running her nose along my skin. "I've missed you."

Grabbing her neck, I lowered my mouth onto hers. She opened to receive me, reminding me that the decision had already been made for me at the top of my night. The only place I could've ended was in her presence. And that shit was glorious.

"I've missed you more," I admitted against her soft, juicy lips.

"I'm recording now. I have a session at eight."

"I'll make sure you're there, Pretty."

"Thank you. I'm ready to go home."

"Say less."

I strapped her in seconds later. After settling beside her, I began the short journey to my house. Her fingers separated mine. I relaxed them against hers and brought the backside up to my lips for a kiss. It didn't matter that our time together was limited. Whenever we made it back to each other, our distance had made our hearts fonder.

My hard dick and hard head were trouble for me, but sometimes I couldn't deny their genius. Watching Vallei tiptoe up my stairs after we'd made it in had me thanking them both. The liquor that had me horny enough to wake Pretty up from her sleep had worn off, seemingly.

Or maybe it was the fact that Vallei's presence overpowered it, leaving me more inebriated than I'd care to admit. It was a different intoxication, though. One that made me want nothing more than to slide under the covers and let her push her ass up against me so we could both fall asleep.

Entering her wasn't on my priority list at the moment. She'd be fucked, thoroughly before leaving my presence, but it wouldn't be right now. I had five hours to fall into her pussy. For now, I wanted her body against mine and a little rest.

"What?" She yawned, turning the covers back after removing her clothes.

It had been far too long since I'd gotten a glimpse of her unclothed body. Every inch of it was flawless.

"Nothing."

I pulled back the covers on the side that I frequented most. We both climbed in. Vallei was making it difficult to keep my man down. Her naked ass was not what I imagined pressed against me when I snatched her ass across the bed.

Nevertheless, I complained none and closed my eyes to catch some sleep. Within seconds, I was out. The way Pretty calmed me should've been unlawful.

Mercer · Vallei

"I didn't like her much," Kleu sassed, smacking her lips and rolling her neck as she pushed the profile to the side.

"You didn't like anyone, it seems." Sighing, I removed the profile from my stack, too. We all had the same papers, in the same order, as we went through the list of candidates we'd interviewed for employment at *The M.*

"Well, put better people in front of me, and maybe I'll change my mind. It's a no on her, too. Baby couldn't remember the mock order to save her life. There's no point in that cute face if there's only air upstairs. We're looking for proficient, polished employees. Not pretty ones. I understand wanting to snag a high roller, but she won't be doing that here. We might lose him as a client if the pretty waitress can't even remember he said no scallops on his dish because he's allergic."

Though she was blowing me with her logic, I wouldn't disagree or deny her. She knew what she was talking about, and she'd made this damn place hers without my permission. If she didn't want them on payroll, then they wouldn't be.

"So, another round of interviews, it seems."

"Umm hm. I'm going through the applications this time. I can pick the people we call to come interview myself."

"I can help."

"I'm saying this with as much love as I can muster, Aeir. I promise it's from a place of love."

"Then don't say it," I warned, knowing where this was going.

Aeir believed in chances. She was a sweetheart. She wasn't confrontational. She was the complete opposite of Kleu. She'd feel the need to take a chance on almost anyone who filled out an application, which was why I hadn't let her go through them, to begin with.

Kleu was too hard on everyone, which was why I hadn't bothered letting her go through them either. Now, it seemed I had no choice. She'd try to fight me if I refused. And I'd hate to have to shoot Lawe behind, putting his woman in a headlock to calm her ass down.

"Say it, please. Maybe it's something I can work on," Aeir demanded.

"No. Don't. It's what makes you, you and why I love you, honey."

"Then, it's good, right?" She squinted, unsure if she was asking the right question.

"Yeah," I assured her.

"You're too soft," Kleu blurted. "You'll feel it necessary to pick the majority of these folks just to give them a place of employment, and that isn't enough for The M. We want the best of the best."

I tuned the women out as a text came through my phone. Seeing Pretty pop up on my screen with disheveled braids and my sheets wadded around her as she slept peacefully, missing her fucking studio session, awakened my heart. Six days had passed since she was last there, which had been six restless nights for me.

Not only because she was elsewhere but because the opening of my spot was getting closer. June twentieth was the date. We were in May and only had the kitchen staff secured. Busboys, waitresses, hostesses, valet, and concierge were still on the list of positions to hire for.

Kleu's claims to be the client concierge weren't taken seriously initially, but her attention to detail and ability to please top spenders without batting an eye had me thinking long and hard about scratching it off the list. Getting the big bucks rolling in was a specialty of hers.

That was her lane, and I was tempted to put her in it per her request. Roulette had made it abundantly clear that she was sending her highest spenders. Kleu sealing their fate as long-term, returning clients sounded like a plan. She was well-rounded and had a mouth on her that could convince niggas to do anything she wanted them to.

Hi.

What's good, baby?

Nothing. Just letting you know I'm headed out.

Alright. Let me know when you touch down.

I'll be going on stage shortly after. I can't make a promise.

Let me know when you touch down, Pretty.

Okay.

What are you doing? she texted again.

Finalizing the employee roster.

Oh. Good. I won't keep you.

I'm trying to be a kept nigga, baby. You can keep me if you want me.

I toyed with her, watching the gray bubbles appear as soon as the message was delivered.

I do. That's not even a question.

I'm nervous. A little, she admitted.

Why?

I never perform when in album mode. My mind is always occupied. I prefer silence so I

can hear myself think over long periods of time. Months.

Don't go.

I have to, Captain. Doc is looking forward to me opening his ceremony. I can't let him down. I told him I would. The contracts were signed a year ago. I have to fall through on my promise. All I have is my word. I try to keep it.

I feel you. You're going to rock that mic, Pretty. And when you're done, Ima let you rock mine.

Really? she asked with a smiley face following.

Whenever you make it back and have a chance to catch your breath, I got you.

It was too fucking hard to ignore the shit I felt for Vallei. I needed a good night's rest, and only a few hours with her would help me achieve that shit. So, a mid-day session with my dick down her throat before returning her to her doorstep sounded much better than another few days or weeks without her.

Why am I looking forward to that more than my performance?

The way she sucked dick, I knew exactly why she was looking forward to it. My dick in her mouth was like a violin in her hands or a pen pressed against her finger-tips. It was pure art when she rolled her neck and ran my balls through her fingers.

"Hello!"

You got this. Hit me up when you get to where you're going. I'll be waiting.

I love you.

I love you, too, Pretty.

I didn't put my phone down until I was ready, despite Kleu's frustration. The chuckling that followed as I matched her gaze pissed her off even more.

"Lawe makes a lot of questionable decisions, but that nigga had it right when he made you one of them."

"Cause without hesitation, one can always bet on Black," she exclaimed.

"Factual." I couldn't disagree. The fucking girl was always right.

"Now, back to these applicants that suck."

"Cut him some slack, Kleu. He tried."

"Not hard enough."

"Aight. You got it. Handle that shit. You know what you're doing. I trust you." I surrendered, closing the folder in front of me.

"Finally, a Domino with some sense!" she yelled as I exited the room I felt like she was holding me hostage in. "Talking about you trust me. Boy, this is my shit. Haven't you taken notice?"

"How did you even become a part of this?" I tossed over my shoulder, knowing I'd strike a nerve.

"Real shit, Mercer, get the fuck out of my office before I change all the locks on this building, and have you wondering how you can be a part of this. Don't make me call my man because he'll do it. We both know that."

"No one is afraid of your nigga, Kleu. I taught that nigga how to cock and shoot his hammer. I'll teach him how it feels to be disarmed and shot in the leg with his own shit so that he can think about the mistake he made every time it rains."

"Well, you wouldn't know because you'd be nine feet under not even a week after you make that decision."

"Nine?" I chuckled, turning to face her from the hallway.

"Nine, nigga. Six ain't enough for that big ass ego of yours," she explained, slamming the door in my face.

"And that's not your office. That's mine."

"Read the sign on the door!"

Sure enough, she'd taped her name over mine, concealing the true identity of the room. I didn't bother tearing it down because it would go back up. I focused my attention elsewhere, wondering which of the rooms we'd be clearing out to get her and Aeir an office so they could stay out of mine.

"They both need to get a fucking job." I grunted with a shake of my head.

This is their job. The voice of reasoning sounded off in my head.

My ringing phone rescued me from the hell the women in my life were trying to keep me in.

"Yeah," I answered, waiting for Milo to come through the line.

"Still going missing, huh?"

"Quit clocking my location, Milo."

"When did we begin keeping secrets?" he inquired.

"When we became grown-ass men that don't tell each other everything."

"I can't name anything this consistent in my life that I

haven't shared with either of you. We don't rock like that. Never have."

He was right. But opening up about a disorder that claimed the lives of our parents wasn't as simple as the other shit.

"Milo, little bro, I don't know what to tell you, man."

"The truth. I'm a lot of things, Mercer, but stupid isn't one. I have crossed out almost every scenario but two. One makes my stomach turn and gets me up at weird hours of the night. So, talk to me. Let me rest, my nigga."

"What is your gut telling you, Milo?"

"That you're either at chemo once a week or you're seeing a therapist."

"I don't have cancer," I stated, leaning against the wall.

Continuing to leave out the little detail about my mental health was eating away at him. He didn't deserve that type of unnecessary stress. I felt like shit for making him.

"I ha—" I stopped to breathe. "Moms shared her special gift with me."

Silence echoed loudly in my ear. The news hit him just as it had me. Speechless, he continued to listen.

"My bad, bro. Just dealing with this shit one day at a time. Therapy is something that keeps the fuzziness from building in my brain. Keeps me talking. Keeps me aware of my feelings. I thought the shit was pointless when I began, but it's not. It's keeping me together. That and the shit they got me o—"

"Who? Who got you on?"

"My doctor."

"Your doctor." He choked. Aside from the anger in his voice, there was hurt. Deep, organically rooted hurt that was justified. "I'm a fucking doctor, bro."

"I know. I ju—"

"You just shit, Mercer! Dude, what the fuck are you saying to me right now? You know... you know how I feel about this. How I've been combing through our profiles year after year, trying to figure out where that was deposited and you gave me nothing.

"I've been ready to fight this fight with whoever from day one. I've been on standby. Why wouldn't you tell me? Why would you do that to me? Huh?"

Hearing his voice crack left cracks in my chest. Again, he was right.

"I'm not trying to be selfish. I'm not trying to disregard your feelings but fuck that. You've spent your whole life making sure we were straight. Whole life, Mercer. Who the fuck making sure you straight? Huh? Don't rob me of that opportunity. You have no right. I've dedicated my life to this shit. I'll drop it all and dedicate the rest of this motherfucker to you if that's what needs to be done."

"I can't let you do that, Milo. I'm sorry I didn't tell you earlier. You're right. Your feelings are valid. You have every right to be upset."

"Upset? Nigga, my chest hurting. I'm not upset about shit."

Rubbing my hand through my beard, I nodded in understanding.

"Alright. I take full responsibility for that."

"But fuck how I'm feeling right now. How are you feeling? Talk to me, man."

"Don't do that."

"Don't do what? Badge and credentials aside, you're my fucking brother. Ima do it and I'ma do it again."

"That's part of the reason I kept quiet. I didn't want anything between us to change."

"And it won't. This ain't the first time I've checked in with you and it won't be the last. So, how you feeling, nigga?"

Sighing, I released a load of air. Again, Milo was right. Checking on our mental state was nothing new. We all had moments that made him question if we had been given our mother's special gift. There was no need for him to question it anymore. I'd made his job a little easier.

"I'm good."

"What medications are you on, and who is your physician?"

"I'll send you the medication when I get to my truck."

"The physician."

"Why?"

"So I can go crack that motherfucker upside the head."

Chuckling, I shook my head. "Nah. That won't be necessary."

"I know because we're transferring you to my off—"

"Milo."

"I don't want to hear that shit, Mercer. They don't give a fuck about you. Most of them. I will make sure that you're taking the right medications and receiving the best care. It's the least I can do to return the favor."

"What favor?"

"Brotherhood, nigga."

The line died immediately after. The clearing of a throat pulled my line of vision in the opposite direction. Kleu stood with folded arms and hiked eyebrows.

"I don't want to talk about it," I admitted, running a hand over my face.

"You don't have to. This changes nothing. I deal with one of you fools on a daily. Your crazy can't beat his crazy. I'm sure of that. Shit, tell Milo he might need to check Lawe's head next."

"He should've started with that nigga," I agreed.

Kleu made her way down the hallway, widening her arms.

"What?"

"Mercer, don't play with me. I'm a tough girl. I don't give these out often, so you better take it."

I opened my arms and brought her closer, accepting the hug she was offering. It was exactly what I needed at the moment. I wouldn't tell her that and blow her head up any bigger than it was, but I was grateful for her timing.

When everything around me quieted, and my pill made its way down my throat, Vallei crossed my mind. I had a hard time believing she ever left. Just scooted over a bit to allow me to handle business before centering herself again. I exited the final menu options I'd chosen for Glacier's shower to open our messages to make sure she hadn't sent a message I'd missed when clearing the palette of beverage choices the truck brought through.

Noticing the lack of notifications for her, I tapped the button to initiate a call myself. Like a lost dog trying to find its way home, I waited for my owner to pick up the line. When the ringing ceased, and her voice replaced it, that silly ass smile pulled my cheeks further apart. My legs involuntarily began rocking back and forth underneath the wheel.

"Cap," she called out to me.

"Didn't I tell you to call me when you touched down, Pretty?"

"I was about to dial your number."

"Let me see you," I demanded, tapping the camera icon to put a video call through.

"Give me a second," she told me, her nervous energy stiffening my muscles.

Her background noise quieted almost instantly.

"I'm alone now."

"I didn't care if you weren't, Vallei. When I call, pick up."

"Cap."

Gnawing, I nodded my head, knowing that I needed to chill the fuck out. A walking contradiction she was making me. With every conversation, stroke of her pussy, and text message exchanged, I was becoming more territorial. The shit we had going on wouldn't last too much longer. Royce wrapping shit up was the news I needed to hear sooner than later.

"I wish I was sorry, Vallei."

"I know. Call back."

I tapped the button again. This time, her face appeared. She was stunning. Gold, shimmery shit sat in the inner corners of her eyes. More jewels were added to her hair. Her lips were covered with a brown combination of the sorts.

I noticed every fucking thing about her, including the new bracelet and thin chain I'd sent to the studio the day she actually made it. They were accompanied by red roses that she thanked me for later.

"I like that chain."

"It's so dainty and so pretty."

"Just like you."

"What's inside of it? Let me see."

As if I didn't know already, I waited for her to open it and display the image she'd taken of me as I slept after a night with her. She closed the locket and revealed the diamonds that concealed it again.

"That's a good look."

"It is. I'm in love with it. And the man that gave it to me. He's the sweetest."

"Is that right?"

"Yes. And I wish he were here right now."

Her words had me feeling a way.

"Yeah?"

"Yes. I miss him."

She pouted, making me forget about the fitted dress she wore under the big-ass knitted sweater she wore with boots that had platforms and were almost a mile high. Everything she put together was random, but that shit was just right for her.

Because I couldn't stand to see that look on her face or know that she missed me as much as I was missing her, I ended the call abruptly. I couldn't stomach it. Couldn't stomach the distance or the separation at the moment. I started the engine of my truck, ready to hit the highway.

She was two hours away. I'd be there in one and a half. I checked her Instagram for the exact location, making sure I was headed in the right direction. Her face on my screen stopped the music that I'd hiked momentarily.

I ignored the call and turned that shit up a little more, bobbing my head to the beat as some nigga rapped about the exact situation I'd found myself in with Vallei.

TEN

With clammy palms, I stepped off the stage with Phillip's help. His commitment to appear to be heading a perfect marriage was commendable. He never missed a performance unless I was touring. He was at every event I was invited to. My calendar was synced with his personal calendar, which alerted him whenever my assistant added a new, important travel-related date.

Applauses continued to ring out even as I made my way out of the venue. I was in search of two things: a quiet place and some privacy to place a call. Mercer's abrupt ending to our call was heavy on my heart. I couldn't fathom getting through the day without hearing his voice again, to know that he was okay and things between us were well.

"Would you like to grab something to eat? They have an entire b—"

"No. I don't have an appetite. Still trying to stomach the performance and the crowd's energy."

And the way he ended our call.

"So, to the room?"

"Yes, to decompress."

We turned one corner after the other, not stopping until we reached the side of the lobby where the elevators were. Seeing the gold doors allowed me to catch hold of my breath. The post-performance jitters began to wear off.

I pressed the button to fetch the elevator just as Phillip's phone began ringing. I watched out of the corner of my eye as he silenced the call. It began ringing again almost immediately after.

As the elevator doors slid open slowly, I heard him kiss the skin of his teeth. A familiar scent garnered my attention. Long, never-ending limbs appeared behind the gold doors. The face of the man that had my heart in a chokehold made my heart throb, the one in my chest and my pussy. Their beats were in sync.

Gasping, I searched for the slightest bit of air. Anything would suffice. Mercer had stolen what I had left. The smirk on his face was agonizingly beautiful. The unsettling feeling that I always had after a performance disappeared. I couldn't hear a thing. I grew incoherent with each passing second. Everything around me stopped moving.

A single head tilt summoned my presence. It wasn't until my body was next to his and I was staring back at my husband, who'd finally taken that call, that I realized I'd even begun walking in his direction. The way my body responded to his demands and his desires without hesitation was frightening and astounding at the same time.

"Yo-you came."

"Anything, Pretty."

"What will I tell him?" I asked, staring at Phillip as he paced the floor, going back and forth with whoever he'd taken the call from.

"You can go tell that nigga I'm about to take you to my room and fuck you on every single surface and eat that shit until you're climbing the walls until the sun rises, or you can let that nigga figure that shit out himself."

The elevator doors closed, sealing my fate and making the decision for me. Finally alone, Mercer wasted little time wrapping his fingers around my neck and pulling me closer. His tongue was down my throat and his free hand was gripping the middle of my butt, filling his hand with a piece of both cheeks.

"Ummmm."

I leaned into him, enjoying his warmth. He made every moment better. This one was no exception.

"Hi."

When he finally cut me loose, I got lost in those dark eyes and bushy brows.

"Hello, Pretty."

"Wh—"

"Don't ask me that shit, baby. You know the drill. If I even feel like you need me, I'm pulling up. Now that that's been established, don't insult me with that question again. Aight?"

I nodded, hoping like hell I wasn't salivating at the mouth. The energy he exuded was so hard to recover from. Dizzy in the head, I watched him wet the lips that I'd lubricate with my juices as the night grew older.

"When you look at me, it makes me want to do things to you that you won't be so quick to admit to your homegirls."

"Ca-Cap."

His long arm reached the control board, pulling the lever that prompted an emergency stop. His eyes never left mine as he stepped forward, cornering me on the right side of the elevator.

"Turn around for me," he requested.

I knew better than to have him ask twice. I turned around, allowing him to comb over my body with his eyes as a breath hiked into my chest. His hands roamed my sensitivity, creating small bumps on my shoulders and backside.

Cold air brushed against my cheeks, confirming the exposure of my entire butt. The thong I wore was pointless. It covered the meat of my perfectly bald v, but nothing more.

"Grip that rail."

My manicured nails grabbed hold of the silver rail, bending my body slowly.

"Pretty, arch that back before you piss me the fuck off, baby."

A moan crept from my lips as the words left his. Knowing exactly what was next, I spread my legs, giving him the view he was anticipating. The black thong appeared from my crack with his influence and a bit of fishing on his end. I fought for a glimpse of what was transpiring behind me.

"Turn back around."

Spit flew from his mouth just before I complied. My stomach caved, knowing exactly where it had gone.

"Meeeeeerrrrcer."

He entered me without warning, sticking his dick down my canal until he reached the pit of it.

"Fuck. Shit way too... fuckin' good."

He pulled out of me almost instantly. I whipped my neck around, ready to demand he reenter until I witnessed the defeat on his face. He stuffed himself back in his pants and fondled with the control board. The elevator began moving instantly.

"How much water have you had today, Vallei?"

"Two... three bottles."

His question threw me completely off guard.

"Pull your dress down. There's Gatorade in the mini-fridge. When you get inside, I need you to kill the entire bottle. You'll need to stay hydrated."

"I don't understand."

I pulled my dress down, covering my lady parts.

"You don't need to understand. You need to listen."

The doors opened. I immediately realized I'd visited the same floor before my performance. It's where I got dressed and prepared for my set. It was where Phillip and I shared a room with double beds.

I took Mercer's extended hand and followed him to the very end of the hall. He entered the space with the tap of a key. I hardly had a foot in the door before a Gatorade was shoved in my hands.

"Drink."

I followed his orders while watching him remove the black collar shirt he wore. One by one, he unfastened the buttons in front of me, making sure I was complying. Satisfied with my actions, he made his way through the suite with incredible views and grabbed a black bag from a black Louis Vuitton duffle.

The first item removed was a set of cuffs, completely taking me by surprise. I choked on the liquid I'd been sipping. Patting my chest, I tried to gather my bearings. Mercer paused momentarily, making sure that I wasn't coughing up an actual lung. I nodded to let him know that I was okay, though I was struggling to catch my breath.

Next was a blindfold.

Then, nipple clip.

Kegel balls.

A small vibrator.

And a rod that extended when he stretched it. On each end was a set of ankle cuffs.

My eyes bloomed, astounded by the neatly arranged gadgets Mercer had presented.

"Ca—"

"Finish your drink, Pretty."

I chugged more, hoping it would last longer than it should because I was unsure of what was in store for me. By the way Mercer undressed, leaving on nothing but his briefs, and commencing to stare at me with fire in his eyes, I assumed it was those things that he mentioned me not wanting to admit to my friends. When the bottle was empty, I stood, wondering what was next. Mercer didn't leave me confused for long.

"Come 'er."

Without haste, I made my way toward him. I stopped beside the bed, where he began stripping me of my clothes. Unlike him, I was left naked. Bare. Vulnerable. *Aroused.*

"Do you remember your safe word, Pretty?"

Nodding, I confirmed.

"Good. If ever the pleasure or the pain becomes insufferable, reel me back in. Understood?"

I nodded again.

"On the bed."

Gently, I sat on the bed, my eyes running over the objects beside me.

"Focus on me, Pretty. Not what's next to you."

I nodded.

"Your safe word?" He asked, picking up the rod with ankle cuffs.

"Domino."

"Good."

It was his second time asking me about it, so I assumed at some point during the night, it would be important. While I was leery, I was anticipating that moment just as much.

"Middle of the bed."

I complied without a word exchanged. From the center of the bed, I watched as he kneeled, cuffing my right ankle. My left was next. He leaned in and clamped both nipples, simultaneously.

"Cap!" I yelped in pain. My vagina began to salivate from the pressure of the pinching. Immediately, I needed him inside of me.

"Please."

"Quiet, Pretty."

My chest heaved as he moved on to the cuffs. One by one, he bound my wrists. With a rope that appeared out of thin air, it seemed, he interlocked the cuffs and secured them to the bed. Blindfolds covered my eyes, sealing my fate.

"Mercer," whimpering, I fought to maintain my composure and decrease my level of sensitivity.

My sexual urges increased. My desire to be plowed like dirt intensified. And, when his tongue swiped across my clit, my reflexes quickened. I felt my body bounce from the bed, searching for his lips, searching for him. I desperately needed more.

"Caaaaaaaaap."

He heard my thoughts, offering me more of his lethal oral satisfaction. Simultaneously, he slid a ball up my ass.

One.

Two.

Three.

Four.

The entire strand was lodged inside of me. Naturally, I squeezed.

"My God!"

He sucked my clit into his mouth, circling his tongue slowly. The pleasure was agonizing. It was way too good. He was way too good. And, then, suddenly, he was gone.

"Mer–"

"I'm here, Vallei."

From a distance, I heard his voice. He was near, but still too far away. When his body heat warmed my nipples to a crisp, I was able to mark his location. The pressure that surrounded them increased, causing the most pleasurable pain they'd ever felt.

"I'm going to cum," I announced, loudly, wondering just what kind of sick individual climbed to their mountain's top simply from nipple exertion.

My throbbing center tingled. My stomach deflated. All the air drained from my lungs as I struggled to catch my breath.

"Ummmmm. Mercer. Oh my G– Ummm."

I struggled to gain my composure. Every touch. Every movement. Every feeling. It was all to the tenth power. And, I was drowning in my own pleasure, my own inclination. Breathlessly, I tried preparing for the descent, but Mercer had no intentions of letting me down. He removed one clamp, and replaced it with his tongue. Then his teeth.

"Ahhhhhh," I groaned, overwhelmed with his presence.

His fingers dipped into my honey, curving upward and finding that spot that made me twitch. He raked his teeth over my pebbles. Sucking and biting, concomitantly, he extracted cream from my center. I could feel the bed beneath me soak as ejaculation sprouted from me.

"That's it, Pretty. Make that pussy talk to me."

Mercer emptied me until I was dry. Tears ran down my face, wetting the blindfold. I tried closing my legs to reduce the sensation but was quickly reminded that it was impossible.

"Don't do that," Mercer warned.

"Please."

"Please, what?"

"Put it inside of me," I begged, needing to feel him deeply rooted.

"That's not how this works," he explained.

"Mercer."

"Taste him, then I'll consider your request, Pretty."

Before I could answer, his dick was down my throat. I nearly vomited. I could hear his gruntled despair as he pulled out of my mouth.

"That's what I like to see."

He gave me little time to gather myself before he was back in my mouth, fucking it as he did my pussy. And, to admit I was climbing that mountain again, hearing his barbaric growls, was shameful.

"Fuck."

He ejected himself at once. I questioned where he'd disappeared for a split second before he revealed his location.

"Caaaaaap!"

He'd slid into home base, right where I wanted him. Right where I needed him. Right where he was supposed to be.

Mercer · Vallei

The vibrating of my phone woke me from my slumber. Sunlight shined through the curtains, making my eyes burn when attempting to open them. I closed them almost instantly, feeling around the bed for my phone.

"Hello?"

"Morning, Vallei."

Mercer's voice on the line was baffling. I patted the space beside me to find it empty.

"Where'd you go?"

"Got some business to handle in the city."

"I miss you already."

"I know. I miss you, too, Pretty. I'm on the highway thinking, I'm 'bout ready to take you on a date."

"A date?"

"Yes."

"Seriously?" I sat up in bed, running my hand through my braids.

"Yes. You've been in the studio busting your ass. I've been handling business myself. A night with you sounds like the perfect remedy for my exhaustion."

"It does. Soooo, I guess the question is when?"

"The end of the week. I'm pulling up. Wherever you are, it doesn't matter."

"Where are we going?"

"You ask too many questions, baby."

"Just curious."

"I know. Get ya ass up and get back to Berkeley. You feel too far, already."

"Okay. I'm getting up now. I guess I'll call you when I get back."

"Yeah. Do that."

"Okay.'

"And Pretty?" He stopped me from ending the call.

"Yes."

"Thanks for last night."

My jaws ached as a smile nearly split my lips. Flashes of our adventure made my stomach knot.

"I should be thanking you."

"Shit goes both ways. Hit me up when you touch down."

"I will."

I pulled the covers over my head as I fell back onto the pillow. My feet lifted from the threads and began fighting for space underneath.

"Ahhhhh!" I squealed, quickly determining I was completely and utterly obsessed with the man who had turned me every way but loose well into the morning hours.

How he was even up and active was a mystery to me. Whatever he had in his system, I needed in mine, too. Because, other than floating from my night, I was in shambles. A mess. And I wanted nothing more than to lie in bed until the sun fell and rose again.

Getting myself together took a bit longer than expected. When I stepped out of the room, I didn't feel any more prepared than I had when I opened my eyes. I massaged my wrists while trekking down the hallway, remembering the restraints that kept them bound and heightened my anxiety. Because our room was only a few doors down, I struggled to believe Phillip and the other hotel guests didn't hear my pleas throughout the night,

Disheveled with a pussy that was dismantled, I walked into the hotel room I shared with Phillip. The quietness made me check my phone. The screen was blank. It had gone dead. Sighing, I began searching for the power cord.

Stranded in Perry was not how I'd planned my morning, but if Phillip had picked up and left once he discovered I wouldn't return or because he heard my destruction throughout the night, I couldn't say I blamed him. Just as I plugged my phone up next to the bed, I noticed my husband's bag was still in the corner where he'd left it.

My curiosity grew the longer I stared at it. It hadn't moved a single inch. Phillip hadn't touched it. The door of our hotel room crept open while I tried to make sense of it all.

"Vallei," he greeted nervously.

"Phillip," I acknowledged him.

We both grew silent, but our eyes never left one another's. Phillip was the first to falter. Dropping his head, he began pacing the floor.

"I'm sorry."

"I'm listening."

Folding my arms, I waited for him to do something I would never even consider. Exposing my hand was completely out of the question.

"I needed to clear my head. Get some fresh air. I got some crazy news last night that had me feeling a way. I began drinking at the bar, and that's all I remember, Vallei. I woke up on a couch that wasn't the one I remembered from our room."

"And with a woman that wasn't me."

"I didn't say all—"

"But that's what happened, right?"

He nodded, scratching his head.

"Did it happen to be a stranger, or was it the person that desperately needed to get through to you last night?"

"Baby, come on, now."

"Answer the question, Phillip."

Suddenly, he didn't have any more words. Scoffing, I shook my head from one side to the other. I rolled my tongue around my mouth. Phillip's absence kept me from explaining mine. His infidelity had worked in my favor once again.

"Why don't you just save yourself the misery and be with her, Phillip? Any woman that's foolish enough to drive hours to come fuck you with your wife in the same hotel should be the woman you spend your days with. Not me."

"Vallei. You're talking reckless."

"Or truthfully, right?"

"You're suggesting divorce as if that's even an option. I made a promise to love you to the end of my life, and that's what I'm going to do."

Finding his explanation hilarious, I sniggered.

"Love me? Phillip, that ship sailed so long ago."

"And I'm fighting to reel it back in. I'm trying. I'm trying. I'm trying."

"Did you start this morning? After your night?"

"Baby." He sucked his teeth.

"Love isn't something you have to force, Phillip. It's the most natural thing to ever exist. It's automatic. It doesn't need much influence. You won't have to try and try and try. It'll just happen. It stopped happening for us years ago. From the moment the doctor told us I couldn't conceive, you've given me your ass to kiss. And for a very long time, Phillip, I kissed it. But I'm tired.

"Because, unlike you, I really tried and tried and tried to get the man that I loved to see that I was still worthy of his love, despite my lack of reproduction capabilities. For three years, I've watched you change. I've watched you grow bitter. I remember the day I realized you'd begin hating to step foot in our home.

"I think it took eight months to get over that discovery. I've watched you mourn the end of an affair and begin a new one. I've slept in our bed alone countless nights, waiting for you to decide when you were coming back home. On so many occasions, I thought you wouldn't. While it's been said that absence makes the heart grow fonder, it's a lie.

"Your absence pushed me further and further away from you until I began growing comfortable with it. At this point, I pray that you'll decide to stay away from home. I've fallen in love with the quietness. The silence. The stillness. The person I become. The routine I fall into.

"The freedom. The idea that I can survive without you because there was once a time I didn't know if I could. I've fallen for it all. And I've come to the conclusion that it's not me that lacks anything.

"And it's not my fault that our marriage is crumbling. It's you, Phillip. You're the issue. Not me. I've done nothing but love you in spite of, but goddamnit, I'm tired."

"Vallei, I promise I under—"

"You don't get to talk, Phillip," I silenced him calmly. "You had three years to talk, yet you ignored me and my feelings. This time, it's me that will ignore your feelings and not give a damn about the guilt that might come as a result. I'd like it very much if you didn't say another word to me. All I want is to get back home so I can prepare for whatever happens next in this fucked up arrangement we call a marriage."

I wasted no time grabbing the rolling suitcase I'd brought along and filling it with my things. Phillip respected my wishes, remaining silent as he waited for me to prepare for the road.

When I was ready, he took my belongings downstairs. The sadness that plagued every feature of his face meant little to nothing to me. I was ready to leave, not only Perry but the marriage as well. I'd replaced my clothes with baggy sweats and a hoodie that I'd cut the sleeves and bottom half of.

On my feet, I opted for fuzzy slippers. I pulled a hat over my head and drew the strings of the hoodie closer to conceal my identity. Encountering anyone on my way to the truck was not an idea I was fond of.

I avoided every eye that looked in my direction once I touched the lobby. The truck was pulled up, waiting at the valet. I slid into the passenger seat and was instantly reminded of the night I'd had. Mercer had pleasured me to the point of pain. I could still feel him *and* the instruments he'd probed my pussy with.

The dreadful drive began with the music low and Phillip's brows wrinkled. There was something to be said, and he was itching to let it out. I didn't bother hiking the volume because I knew it would come down, eventually. When he cleared his throat seconds later, I nodded, having called it. I knew Phillip well. He was so predictable.

"Divorce isn't in your best interest, Vallei. This, we both know."

I remained silent, refusing to exude my energy. It was pointless.

"My family won't let me walk away empty-handed. They—"

"You, Phillip. You mean you," I corrected him, never taking my eyes off my phone as I opened my message threads.

"Will require half of everything you've acquired in our marriage, including our home. Alimony will be part of the equation."

I nodded, confirming I'd already known everything he was running down.

"Without me and my influence, none of this would be possible, so it's only right that half of it—"

"Please, Phillip. I have a headache. You're expressing your intentions to rob your wife of things that you had no hand in creating. Whether you were at my side or not, love, God knew the hour and day he'd create avenues and opportunities for me beyond my wildest dreams. So, please. Spare me. Have your way, Phillip. At this point, it's not worth my sanity."

Nausea hit me like a sack of bricks as the words stopped flowing.

"We can fix this, Vallei. This is us we're talking about. I've fucked up, aight. I'll admit that, but there's no woman in the world I've ever loved the way I love you. I just lost myself a little after learning we could never have children."

"And instead of considering how I felt or the sickness and death part of our vows, you sought comfort elsewhere. Phillip, just be quiet. Please. My head is throbbing, and every word you speak is making my stomach turn."

Disgust was at the top of my list of feelings. I was repulsed. Puke threatened to spill at any moment. I reclined my seat and lifted my phone so that I could see my screen better. Mal was the first message I tapped on.

I can't stay any longer.

What's the matter? What happened? Can you call me? Her text came through one after the other. I read them as one.

My heart and my head are beyond the point of return.

This man makes my soul itch. I'm unsettled by his presence. He disturbs my spirit. My nervous system is in shambles when he's near. I deserve to be freed from this torture. I'll figure out the rest when I'm out of the situation and able to think clearly.

Call me!

I will once I'm home. Or once I'm gone. I can't imagine another night in misery.

She didn't respond. She didn't need to.

Hey. Mercer was heavy on my heart.

What's up, baby?

Headed home.

Everything good?

The way he knew without me ever having to say that something was wrong was proof that souls could tie and persons were specially made for certain people. Mercer was mine.

It will be.

Talk to me, Pretty.

I want out, Captain.

I waited for a response, but no bubbles appeared.

Mercer.

Nothing more needs to be said, baby.

What are you doing?

Pulling up at the restaurant. About to get my hands busy. I'll see you later.

Okay.

My mother's thread was the next I opened. I tried finding the words to share, but I had none. Instead, I closed my eyes and tried to stop the spinning going on in my head.

"I love you, Vallei. No matter what you might think or what my actions say, I love you."

Shut up, Phillip. My inner thoughts remained locked inside my head as I followed the voice of reasoning that appeared.

Breathe, Pretty. They were words he'd recited over and over throughout the night.

Take your time. Feel it. Slow, baby. Let it build. Just like that. Coaching me through my orgasms while refusing to let me climb to my peak too soon or feel too much at once was menace behavior. Mercer's sexual nature was becoming one of my favorite attributes.

His need to explore, his desire to please, and his knowledge of the female body were a deadly combination that I wanted in my world until my dying day. With no teeth and a CPAP machine in old age, I still wanted his dick down my throat and his fingers on my scalp.

Hearing his voice stopped the waves of nausea that came rolling in with a vengeance. I found a pocket of comfort and used it to lead me into a deep slumber.

I didn't open my eyes until I heard Phillip making his exit. The familiar surroundings made it clear we'd made it home. I grabbed the small bits that I'd carried to the truck with me and climbed out shortly after. When I made it to the door, he was already there waiting for my bags.

I unlocked the door and hurried inside, needing to empty my bladder and start my bathwater. I managed both within seconds of making it to the top stair. Lavender scented the space. My slippers trekked across the floor, preparing all the things I'd need for a long, relaxing soak after an eventful night.

The anxiety that I was waiting for to appear, knowing that by the time I came to terms with the fact that my marriage was officially over, my necessary items would be packed in my suitcase, and I'd be on my way out of the door, never showed. I lowered my naked, bruised frame into the water and was greeted with a perfect temperature.

Just as soon as I grabbed the tray with neatly rolled herbs, a thunderous knock on the door stopped me in my tracks. My eyes cut toward the door of the bathroom, but I knew the knock had come from the one downstairs. The doorbell sounded shortly after. More pounding followed.

The combination continued as I jumped from the tub, assuming Phillip hadn't heard a peep. Because he was downstairs, I found it hard to believe. As I got the robe around my body and tied it at my waist, a startling revelation nearly brought me to my knees.

Mercer.

ELEVEN

Mercer

3:32:54pm.

It was the time I'd calculated almost to a science. Because Vallei wasn't getting out of the whip or on her way inside the house, I imagined I was a few minutes late. My nostrils flared at the thought of her entering a space that no longer served her with a motherfucker that didn't deserve her.

I hopped out of my ride and stalked to the front door. Upon arrival, I beat my knuckles against it. I used the same hand to tap against the doorbell.

Again.

Again.

Again.

And again.

My fingers beat against the door a second time. Only when I was satisfied with the announcement of my arrival did I step back and wait for the door to open. I was hoping Pretty came waltzing through the crib to meet me at the door, but I didn't give a fuck if it wasn't. Tiptoeing around a nigga that I could split in two wasn't exactly my definition of a decent hour.

He could either shut the fuck up and watch Pretty leave with a nigga that meant her well, or he could shut the fuck up and watch Pretty leave with a nigga that meant her well. The third option was for him to watch her walk away with a pistol shoved in his mouth if he couldn't shut the fuck up. It was simple.

When the door stretched, and the geeky ass nigga appeared, I released a short breath. Simultaneously, I removed my piece from my waist and held it at my side. Confusingly, he looked at me, wanting to know what the hell I was doing at his home.

"Uh... Hello. Chef, right?"

He extended a hand that I ignored.

"Where's Vallei?"

"My wife?" He scoffed, dropping his hand.

Chuckling, I nodded. "Yeah. Her."

"I'm sorry. I don't understand. How do you know Vallei and what is it that you want with her?"

"To take her back to the crib and fuck her until she feels better until she forgets all the time she wasted waiting for a nigga who was never meant for her to get his shit together. Then, I want to cook her dinner, feed her, and then fuck her some more. You know, shit that you don't have the privilege of doing."

His chest swelled as he snatched the glasses off his big ass nose. I couldn't help but find him comical. He made it almost impossible to keep a straight face.

"I put money in your pocket, introduce you to my wife, and you go behind my back and sleep with—"

"We hardly do any sleeping, Square."

"You're fucking kidding me right now?"

His skin reddened as spit flew from his mouth. He stepped forward, but the tip of my gun backed his ass right up.

"Make another step, and you'll be changing a shit bag for the rest of your life. I do not get down like that. I will shoot the shit out of you and take your bit—wife while you bleed out on your doorstep."

He wasted no time stepping his ass back, knowing what was best for him.

"Your wife has been thoroughly fucked over the last four months, and as a man that can't get his head out of his ass long enough to notice... it's too late, homie.

"Cause once I stepped into her life and did things to her body that you don't have the bandwidth to, right in that bed of yours and on that table you have your meals on, she had no choice but to fall.

"Shit, it was her only option. I'm her only option. You might have introduced me to your wife, but I already knew her. Knew how good that thang between her legs is. How deep. How tight. How wet. How sweet. And how it has a habit of biting back. I already knew her, Square. Knew what made her cream.

"Knew what made her cum. Knew every inch of her body. Knew how bad her internal struggle was without ever knowing you existed. Because the truth is, she's a good girl. One of the angels on earth who should walk around with a Halo hovering over her.

"But you're too blinded by your own ego to see that glow on her. I noticed it the second I came in contact with her. At that very moment, your time was up. I'm sorry it's taken me so long to get with you about that. I was trying to mind my manners, but fuck that. And fuck you."

The door widened as I ended my statement. I'd heard Pretty making her way down the stairs seconds earlier. When she appeared at his side, a smile replaced the smug on my face.

"You ready?" I asked, crossing my hands one over the other in a failed attempt to conceal my weapon. Frightening Vallei wasn't in my intentions.

"Yes. I ju... I need to get dressed."

"You can leave all this shit, Pretty. I'll replace it all."

"I know." She sighed. "But there are a few things that are irreplaceable, Cap."

"Say less."

I pushed forward, stepping up and into their home. Square stepped his ass back.

"What are y... What are you doing?" he asked.

"Shut the fuck up," I demanded, walking through the foyer that I knew well.

"I won't be long," Vallei explained.

"Get your shit, baby. I'll be right here waiting."

Because thirst was making my throat too dry to bear, the kitchen was my destination. I grabbed a bottle of water from the fridge and made myself comfortable on the couch in the sitting room, where Square watched me from the doorway.

"You're going to reg—"

"Shut up, nigga. I promise I'm not going to say that shit again."

With a tilt of his head and a nod, he quieted. Vallei was down the stairs within minutes, toting an overnight bag. I stood, immediately rushing to her side to claim it. It looked fairly heavy. Before stepping out, I leaned my head to the right to get a better look at the face of a nigga who'd just lost his woman. His soul had left his body already. Only a shell of him was left.

"Check this shit out," I started, placing a thumb on my nose. "If you try any slick shit in her absence, I'm on your ass. If you try to file for divorce in her absence, I'm on your ass. If you touch her accounts in her absence, I'm on your ass.

"If you dial her line, I'm on your ass. If you even think about her too much, I'm on your ass. Hear me very fucking clearly when I say that there is no such thing as a crazy ex when I'm in the picture. I'm the only crazy one in this shit.

"And my crazy ain't the kind of crazy you want to test because I have no limits. I have no reservations. I do know how to stop once I start, so don't get me started, nigga."

With that, I ushered Vallei out of the door with a hand on the small of her back. She remained quiet until we were both alone and in the comfort of my truck. She rested her head against my shoulder, pulled my shirt toward her face, and released sounds I'd only heard in the wilderness, in nature, or behind the wall when niggas got news about their people on the outside, not seeing another day on God's green earth.

She wept like a woman who had lost everything. She wept like an exhausted mother. She wept like a lost child. She wept like a patient in pain. She wept like she'd been waiting for this day all her life.

And each time another sound exited her mouth, a deep, agonizing pain slowly moved across my chest. I didn't budge, letting her have the moment she needed. I rubbed her back, making sure she understood I was there and wasn't going any fucking where.

"Thank you." She whimpered.

"Anything, Pretty."

"I lo-love you so much."

She was a blubbering mess. I pulled her onto my lap and wrapped her arms around my neck.

"Hug me, Pretty."

Her grip was loose, letting me know she was still in

the thick of her emotions. I caressed her back, easing her into a better space.

"Tighter, baby."

She succeeded.

"Tighter."

"I love you." She cried.

"I love you, too, Pretty. It's gone be aight. We good. You good. Stop crying. You're breaking my heart."

I lifted her limp body from my chest. She nodded as I cleared her pretty face of the tears.

"When I told you I'd see you later, I meant that. When I told you nothing more needed to be said, I meant that. When you need me, I'll always be there, Vallei. I don't care where you are or who I have to go through to get to you. I'm coming. Always."

"I know."

"Good." I kissed her forehead and then her swollen lips. Baby was catching hell. Feelings all over the place.

When she finally got herself together long enough to sit up straight, she climbed back into the passenger seat. She reclined it back as far as it would go and shrunk her entire body into a ball.

I reached over her and pulled the seatbelt over her body. It wasn't bring your girl to work day, but that's exactly where we were headed. She could cry in my chest all day if she needed to. Whatever she needed... it didn't matter to me.

Mercer · Vallei

I walked in the back door with Vallei in tow. Kleu was already waiting in my office, ready to make me regret returning. I could tell by the look on her face, she was displeased with something I'd done or an issue she'd bumped into.

"Well, M—oh. Shit."

"Not right now, Kleu."

"I'm not thinking about you anymore," she divulged. "I'm more concerned with this damsel in distress. Who do I need to beat up, babe? I fight niggas, too. Well, my man does. But still."

"Vallei, Kleu. Kleu, Vallei. My... I don't even know what she is," I criticized. "She's good people, though."

"Whatever is going on is nothing a little food and conversation can't fix. You hungry?"

"Yes."

"Alright. You heard her, Mercer. Get in the kitchen and cook the lady some food."

Worried that Vallei would be easily overwhelmed, I gestured toward the door with my head. Kleu picked up on it, finding her way out of the door while still talking to Vallei.

"Anything in particular you want? I'm going to call in reinforcement. Hang tight and dry those pretty eyes, baby. The day will get better. You hear me?"

"Yes." Vallei sighed.

"If this nigga did something to you, just blink, and I promise I'll call my dude up here to check his big ass."

"No. He did nothing but save me from a marriage that I was drowning in."

"Oh, honey. Yes. Dry those tears quickly. We don't cry over men. Men cry over us. Before you leave here, we're going to make sure you feel much better."

"Thanks." She smiled.

The sadness was all in her tone, movements, and eyes. My baby was hurting, and I hated it. I didn't doubt at all that the hurt stemmed from time wasted and hope given. No woman wanted to leave a marriage she'd volunteered her heart for. It was meant to be forever. Square had little to do with the actual pain she felt.

In the hallway, Kleu followed me toward the kitchen. When I thought we were far enough, I stopped and pulled her closer so that I didn't risk Vallei hearing me.

"She's fragile, Kleu. And easily overwhelmed. Take it easy on her."

"You went and stole somebody's wife, Mercer? What the hell?"

"Shit, in my defense, if that nigga was at the house when I came through to get my paper, his wife wouldn't have been taken."

She looked me up and down as if she didn't believe a word I was saying.

"Okay. Maybe you're right. She was as good as mine from the moment I saw her. I wouldn't have given a fuck whether she was married or not."

"That sounds more like it." She nodded.

"But real shit, she's lightweight. She's in touch with her emotions, and she doesn't hide them. She wears them on her sleeve. She's a p—"

"Poet. I know who she is, Mercer. And I'm a woman, too. Just because I don't wear my emotions on my sleeves doesn't mean I don't have them. I know how to handle her, and I know exactly what she needs. Community is all. With that, you can get through whatever."

"You and Aeir drive me crazy enough, man. Don't call them folks up here."

"Too late. I'm already texting them, and everybody said they could use a meal, so cook plenty, Chef."

Anything, Pretty. The words echoed in my head. If putting up with the women of the family was a small price to pay, then I didn't mind. As I combed over my hair with my hand, I made my way to the kitchen, anticipating a long-ass night.

I began prepping for an alfredo-based pasta, pan-seared steak, and a delicious caramel cookie dessert that would be topped with hand-rolled ice cream. It was a simple enough meal that would serve the ladies well as they chatted about whatever the fuck they needed to chat about. The thought of being surrounded by women led me to Royce's contact. I needed an update on the progress she'd made.

"Hello, Mercer."

"Damn, the phone didn't even ring."

"I felt you about to call. Probably because I was plan-ning to call you in a few, anyway. Nevertheless, we're here."

"What you got for me? I need some good news because I'm 'bout ready to blow this nigga a new asshole."

"That won't be necessary. You'd only leave me with a bigger mess to clean. Please, spare me the headache and calls from that brother of yours. My God."

Chuckling, I agreed silently. Chem was well-calculated and cautious until it came down to the people he loved. Then, all bets were off. He'd show up on any block, ready to make believers out of motherfuckers, no matter what their credentials were.

"Anyway, I had the papers drawn up. I figured having him served isn't an option."

"Serving that nigga myself."

"Figured. Now, the signature security, I'm still combing through Roulette's files, videos, and logs. I'll need a little more time to complete the workup. It's a lot."

"Is it enough for what I'm trying to do?"

"Yes. But I want to make sure there is absolutely no way any of them can wiggle their way out of this."

"Bet."

"But I just have to ask, Mercer. How is she? Staying put has to be hard right now."

"I went got her."

Royce sighed. I pictured her shaking her head.

"You knew I would."

"I did, but I was holding onto hope. You know, at least until we had everything."

"Nah. She said she was ready to roll. So, she's here with me now."

"Oh, wow. You meant today?"

"Not even two hours ago."

"Oh."

"She's here now. I'm about to start dinner for her and the rest of the ladies."

"Like who?"

"Like whoever. If you trying to swing by, then bring your ass on."

"How do you know I'm in town? I'm in Clarke."

"You're lying through your front teeth."

"How do you know?"

"Because you're combing through Roulette's shit. That's how."

"See, this is exactly why I want her back in the city where she belongs. Now you know my whereabouts."

"Man, come through. I want you to meet her. And I know your greedy ass hungry."

"Um hmm. Roulette and I were heading to dinner at seven."

"Head on over here. I'll make sure I'm done by seven."

"Sounds like a plan."

I ended the call without another word. As I did, I felt Vallei's arms around my waist. She rested her head on my back and released hot air from her body.

"How are you feeling?"

"Better."

"Kleu has invited t—"

"It's fine, Cap. I'm fine. I will be, at least. And I'm looking forward to their company."

"Really?"

"There's something about when Black women unite. We can move mountains. We're no strangers to solutions. It's the most beautiful, unfiltered experience ever, witnessing Black women laugh loudly and step fully into who we are as we dine, sip, and converse. We heal one another. As much as I like my quiet, I love our energy. Right now, it's what I need to push through this moment."

I turned around, pulling her into my chest.

"I love you, Pretty."

"I know," she responded. "That's why I love you back."

"Sit here and keep me company before they steal you away. They're stingy as fuck with each other. I can't fight all of them at once."

Sniggering, she held her hands up and waited for me to lift her onto the counter.

"Make enough for Mal. She's coming, too."

"I didn't doubt that for a second. The way she pulled up to a nigga's crib, I like her."

"She will fight a bear for me."

"I bet she'd win, too."

"I'd be afraid for the bear, not for her."

A comfortable silence fell between us. I connected my phone to the sound system and placed the playlist she'd shared with all her favorite love songs on repeat. Having her in my most sacred space, liberated and ready to explore the rest of life with me, made me feel shit that I didn't know I could.

She felt so right in my world. I knew she belonged. And each day, I'd work to keep her happy and her head high.

I'll give you the time of your life
Just wait til we can go outside

The words resonated with me as I watched her from afar, eyes trained on me as well. A smile pressed our lips together. The love filled the gap between us. It was so big and so beautiful, just like the woman I shared it with.

TWELVE

It wasn't the sun in my eyes that awakened me from my intoxicated slumber. It was Mercer and his ungodly tool. He buried it inside of me as he buried his head between my breasts before taking the right one into his mouth.

Wadded sheets pressed against my palms. Not until my orgasm had subsided did I release them. And it wasn't until Mercer's semen had filled me to the brim that he released me. Breathlessly, we both struggled to find comfort.

Dewy skin made the room feel hotter than it was. And at this point, physical touch wasn't the solution.

Mercer rolled onto his side of the bed to interfere with the transfer of body heat. Both of our temperatures were elevated.

Minutes passed before either of us could speak. My mouth was dry, and my head was pounding. I'd talked until my jaws were sore. Laughed until my throat went hoarse. And smiled a million times. In addition to Kleu, Aeir, Nature, Royce, Roulette, and Mal, we were joined by Malachi, Milo, Lawe, and Aeir's best friend, who was in town on a nursing assignment.

I enjoyed every second of their company. Mercer's time in the kitchen paid off well. Every plate was empty by the time we began to clean. I had no doubt about the success of his restaurant. He knew what he was doing in the kitchen.

And if I had anything to say about it, then the entire Berkeley would be making their way downtown to check him out. This was one of those times that I fully intended to use my influence to make sure his dreams come true.

"Good morning."

"Good morning."

Rolling over, I propped my head up to see my man a bit better. Waking up to him had never felt better.

"I know that look, Pretty. What's on your mind?"

"You haven't asked me to be your date to the grand opening."

He tittered with a shake of his head. We'd discussed details of the grand opening all night. His family had, at least. I simply gave my opinion when asked.

"You for real right now?"

"Um hmm."

"Baby."

"Neither have you asked me to be your girlfriend."

"Vallei."

"I mean it. I'm not playing."

"I see. But I thought you understood you would be by my side that night. Where else would you be?"

"But I want to be your date."

"You will be."

"Not if you don't ask," I reminded him, pursing my lips.

He slid up in the bed. As he sat up, he trained his eyes on mine. "I imagine I have to court you before I make you my woman, so asking that question is pointless."

"Right. Right." I nodded.

"But at the same time, baby, I've been all up in that shit, so do we take a step back or—"

"Wait. No."

"Pretty, you gave that shit up before the first date!" He clowned. "And I thought you were a saint."

"Shut up, Cap. I did not. We can consider dinner that night the first date."

"The dinner you never got to eat because I had your legs spread on that fucking table."

His reminders made me sink deeper into the bed, pulling the covers over my head.

"You're getting off-topic. I need you to focus, Captain. Focus."

He snatched them from my head.

"And I would consider dinner with your family the second date. And we—" I paused, trying to think of another answer.

"We what?" He waited, impatiently.

"I'm trying to think. Wait."

"Don't strain your brain trying to think of shit that never happened, but I'll give you those first two."

"Fine."

"But that all changes today."

"Last night was like a date. A big family date."

"True."

"And dinner at your house that night Mal stopped by."

"Okay, True."

"And to my defense, anyone seeing us out would've ended terribly for me."

"Aight. Aight."

"See, give us some credit. We do more than find our way to bed."

"Yeah, aight." He laughed. "It doesn't matter, though. I'm taking you on a date tonight. And I'm not sliding in you when I get to the crib, so don't ask."

"What about before we get here?" I questioned.

"Be my date to the grand opening," he deflected.

"Under one condition."

"Anything, Pretty."

"Clear thirty minutes of the night for me to perform a set."

He remained silent, considering what I'd just said.

"You fucking with me or what?"

"No. I'm not. I want this to be the best night of your life. I know that it'll be a packed house without me, but I can bring some people in, too, Cap. You've done so much for me. Let me repay you in some way."

"I don't need repayment, Vallei. I told you I'm not keeping score. Never have. Everything I did and will continue to do is because I want to, not because I need anything in return. Being you, being in my world, that's all you ever have to do for me. Exist. That's it, baby. I'm overcompensated. Having you near is the best reward."

His words quieted me for a while, but I still felt strongly about my presence and wanted to perform for the entertainment of those who were in attendance.

"Okay, but I still want to."

"Then you can. I won't say no. Shit, can't say no. But it's, by no means, repayment."

"No." I shook my head.

"As long as you understand that, then we good."

"I do."

"Aight. Now, get up so we can shower. If I'm taking you on a date, I figure I should make sure you prepared to put that shit on tonight."

"Are you threatening me with a good time, Captain?"

"If a shopping spree is a good time, then yeah."

"Ahhhhh!" Squealing, I kicked my legs under the cover.

He left me there, shaking his head as if he was growing sick of my antics already. If so, then he needed to get it together because he had a lifetime to put up with me. I was his problem now, and I took pride in that.

Mercer · Vallei

The dress I wore clung to my body, suffocating my nervous system. It happened to be the prettiest olive green. The cotton fabric was soft and stretchy. I wore Christian Dior pumps that matched a new bag that Mercer forced me to love during our time at the store.

The guest room had become my dressing room. My clothes hung from the closet, and the three pieces I'd tried in front of the mirror were sprawled across the bed. I was following Mercer's orders and making his house my home for the time I was here, figuring out what was next for me.

It was the fourth option that sold me. I didn't want to take it off when it was time to shower and begin preparing for my night out with Mercer. Now that body butter was slathered over my skin and the bits of makeup I used to enhance my features was set, the dress was here to stay.

"Knock. Knock."

Hearing Mercer's sultry tone began the waterworks below. I cringed, knowing I'd just gotten out of the shower and had already ruined my panties. I spun on my heels to find him fully dressed, olive covered him from head to toe.

"Mind getting this for me?"

He extended his arm to show me his unbuttoned right sleeve.

"Of course."

I fought the effects of his cologne. Between that and his dark skin in the button-down and olive slacks had me dizzy in the head. He obliterated the distance between us within a second. I swallowed as he approached, praying I had the stretch to get through the night without stripping this man down to nothing.

I accepted his hand into mine. His touch was still so magical. Four and a half months later and the same spark lit my soul on fire. Nothing had changed but the intensity. Having the ability to love him freely and out loud made our connection so much more rewarding.

"You look stunning," he complimented, disarming the silence we shared.

"Thank you, Cap. I was thinking the same things."

"Appreciate it."

I managed to get the button fastened in time to look up and see the adornment in his dark eyes. Rolling my eyes, I stepped back.

"What?"

"I can't admire what's mine?" He chuckled, fisting his palm.

His gaze was mesmerizing.

"Well, the jury is still out on that. You haven't quite put in your offer yet."

"Stop fucking playing with me, Pretty."

His hand went around my neck as he pulled me forward. He leaned down until we were eye to eye. Nose to nose. Lips hugging one another. I shuddered. It was a shame, the hold Captain had me in. When he was around, I was never well. I was always a sniff or kiss away from buckling knees and breathless fainting.

"You ready?"

Because I was unable to speak, I nodded.

"Come on."

Hand in hand, we exited the room, descended the stairs, and headed out of the door. He helped me into the truck, buckling my seatbelt before making his way around the truck to do the same.

Our palms rejoined as he settled. It wasn't until he kissed the back of my hand that I noticed his right wasn't empty. It contained a single red rose. Where he'd gotten it had me just as confused as he did most times. He was a man of resources. It was fascinating to watch.

"Where'd this come from?" I chuckled.

"The nursery we visited," he informed me, deeming me silent.

"Baby! How?"

"Yesterday, I called and had Tanter express a couple of roses by mail."

"A few?"

Shrugging, he signaled toward the backseat. My eyes bloomed just as they had before she snipped them. A fresh, insanely large bouquet of roses filled the middle of the backseat.

"How many, Cap?"

"A hundred."

"Oh God, they're beautiful. I feel like it's a special occasion. These are gorgeous."

"You are the occasion, Pretty. You should wake up to them every day, and I'ma make sure you do from this day forward."

"Will this ever end?" I asked, voicing my fears.

I wanted to stay in the new lover's phase for a lifetime. It was the best phase of the relationship cycle. Excitedly, you woke up daily, happy to be with the person who made your heart smile.

"Not on my end. I can't speak for you, baby, but this isn't seasonal. This is a lifestyle, one that you're welcome to reap the benefits of until you decide that this is not where you want to be."

"I wouldn't want to be anywhere else."

"Then don't worry about shit changing because it won't. The day that I can't love you properly, I'll leave. I'm a grown-ass man who can use his words. Before I break you down or break your spirit, I will break my own heart and walk away. I pray that day never comes, but we're human, and life is unpredictable. But if I have anything to say about it, I'm here until they shovel the dirt over me."

"Sometimes I feel like I'm in a dream, and I keep wondering when I'll wake up."

"This ain't a dream. This is us."

I flipped our hands around. This time, I kissed the back of his, getting a smile from those kissable lips.

"Where are we going?"

Before I was too caught up in my emotions, I changed the subject.

"Wherever we're going. Just sit back and look pretty."

He hiked the volume on the stereo to drown out anything else I was ready to ask. Sniggering, I did as I'd been told. Twenty minutes later, we were pulling up to a fixture that resembled an abandoned building.

Hadn't it been Mercer at the wheel, I would've been trying to get the hell out of dodge. But if he was leading, I was following. Even if it was to the pits of hell. His influence on me was incredibly shameful, but I harbored no shame.

I held his hand as we journeyed the short distance to the door where a man who measured over six feet and was pushing four hundred pounds opened the door. Curiously, I watched him and Mercer slap palms and then pull one another in for a brotherly embrace.

"Ya room is waiting on you," he assured Mercer.

"Bet. Bet."

Through the doors, down a hallway, and into a dimly lit room, Mercer led me. I was so stunned by the interior beauty that I remained silent until I was seated with an apron around my neck.

"I never expected this." Gesturing around the room, I expressed my satisfaction with the speakeasy. It was concealed perfectly.

"What is this place?"

"The Boys' Club - Roulette."

"Roulette?" My eyes blossomed. "As in Roulette?"

"Yes. There's Rouge, her main spot, and then there's The Boy's Club. A private club for men."

"I'm not a man."

"No shit, Pretty. I needed a place outside of my work-space for the date I had in mind."

"So, we won't get the full Boys' Club experience? That's no fair."

"Yeah?"

"I mean, we're here. Why not?"

"Sounds like a fucking plan to me, but first, I must make good on my word."

"Our date?" I smiled.

With a nod, he confirmed, tapping buttons on the iPad that was on the table I was seated at.

Is you up right now?

What you on right now?

Is you drunk right now?

But you know I got a man.

I don't care right now.

Pull your hair now.

I'm tryna beat it right now.

But you know I got a man.

I don't give a fuck.

The lyrics Chris Brown began singing along with a female lead had my brows racing for my hairline. Shortly after the initial shock wore off, I began bobbing my head and body to the beat. Mercer's head tilt lifted me from my seat. I gravitated toward his magnetic pull, still moving my body to the beat.

He grabbed my hand once I was in arm's reach, spinning me around until my butt was pressed against his hard. Slowly, I leaned forward until my hand fell from his. I grabbed my knees and ground my body against his. The song changed as I dipped lower and then swayed my way back up.

How I'm 'posed to miss you every night
How you left me standing in the rain
How you gone forget about all the things we did

I was unsure who was singing, but the voice was lovely, and the words were hitting me right where they needed to. Mercer pulled me upward, wrapping his hand around my neck as our bodies rocked from side to side in sync.

"Thoughts in the positions I can see you in. Introduce you to some ghetto romance," he sang in my ear.

My nipples hardened to the point of pain, begging to be freed from the fabric of my dress.

"Handcuff keys in the dresser; we can leave 'em there. You know it don't make no difference, I can leave it in."

Together, we rode out the beat until the song ended. Before another played, Mercer freed me. The lust in his eyes matched the thirst in mine.

"Let's wash up, baby. I'm about to teach you how to make that pasta you were raving about yesterday from scratch."

"From scratch?"

"Down to the noodles. You ready?"

"Yes," I exclaimed excitedly.

He led me to the sink to wash my hands, and we

immediately got to work. Our first task was making the dough. While I gathered and measured the ingredients on the card he'd given me, he busied himself in the fridge.

FLOUR
EGG
OLIVE OIL
SALT
JUICE FROM SPINACH (FOR COLOR)

The recipe he'd written by hand was the cutest. I then realized it was my first time seeing his handwriting.

"Here."

I accepted the glass of wine that he handed me. It was red and sweet to the taste. Mercer, on the other hand, had a brown liquid in his cup that he swirled before tossing a swig back.

"Grab that bowl." He pointed at the silver dish next to me. "This is what we'll use for mixing."

With Mercer's assistance, I made a buttery, soft, non-sticky dough. Together, we kneaded and strung it to make the perfect spaghetti noodles. Next, we molded bow ties. Penne noodles proved to be a bit difficult. Shells were a perfect balance between challenging and exciting.

"Babe. That's way too long," I declared, watching Mercer hand roll the dough that was left over.

"It's the perfect size, Pretty."

I watched him begin to slice it strategically, leaving me to wonder if the smaller pieces were long enough. Instead of continuing to drill the man who prepared dishes for a living, I busied myself with the transfer of the noodles from the table to the counter where we'd begin the next phase of the lesson.

Though Mercer would be teaching me how to make a creamy alfredo from scratch, it wasn't the sauce we'd coat our pasta in. Instead, I opted for a tomato-based sauce that would pair well with the scallions, shrimp, and chicken that we'd top it with.

Track after track, the music selection seemed to improve. It felt impossible with each song being so well-executed, but I found myself retracting my thoughts when the next beat dropped.

THIRTEEN

Vallei

Once the noodles were squared away, I met Mercer at the counter, where he was cleaning his hands with the rag hanging from his apron. His wide hand squeezed my cheeks as he pulled me in for a hug. I wrapped my hands around his neck, simultaneously noticing just how much we were communicating our feelings with our limbs.

His legs opened to welcome me between them. I stepped forward, solidifying our connection. The neatly arranged noodles caught my attention.

Chuckling, I asked, "Cap, what have yo—Mercer?"

Will you be mine, Pretty?

Words formed from the fresh pasta noodles left me in shambles, trying to process it while also trying to keep my heart from falling out of my chest. The warm tears that touched my cheeks upon blinking let me know that I wasn't in a dream.

This wasn't my imagination. I was real. He was real. We were real.

His thumb barely served its purpose. Slightly smearing the thick tears across my face. My brows folded inward. Pain was evident in my chest. The moment felt so perfect that I was mourning its lost before it ended.

"Baby." Words were a challenge.

"Don't cry, Pretty. This for you, because I knew you were the first time I laid eyes on you."

"Thank you," I whispered.

"You wanted a nigga to ask, so answer me. Don't keep me waiting."

Nodding, I answered his question. I melted into him again. As if he knew just what I needed, he squeezed me tightly. Immediately after, Mercer ran his hands up and down my body.

"I love you, Vallei. If there's nothing else you're certain of in this world, you can be certain I'll never stop."

"I love you, too."

"Nah, look at me, Pretty."

He held both sides of my face once I was standing straight. I met his demands, gazing into those alluring rounds of his.

"It's not just that I love you. That's putting this shit mildly. I'm in love with you. I'm indebted to you. I'm invested in you. I'm interested in you, your dreams, your wants, your needs, your hurt, your pain, your happiness, your well-being, your health, your ever... your everything.

"And with every second, I'm increasingly in awe of the woman you are, the strength that you have, and all that you've achieved while remaining truest to who you are. You're a fucking gem, baby. Nothing or no one can make me believe anything differently. I see you—up here and in here."

He pointed to my head and then my chest before kissing my lips.

"Your soul is pure. Your heart is gold. Your intentions are good. Don't ever change that, Pretty."

His arms were around me, again rocking me from one side to the other. My face flushed with embarrassment as hunger pains roared, vibrating between us. The music concealed the sound, but there was no denying the movement.

"I'm hungry," I announced as if it was a surprise.

"I see, baby. Let me feed you."

"Please."

We separated reluctantly. Instead of warming the counter and watching him do what he loved most, I was in on the action. Heavy whipping cream, the most beautiful array of seasonings, blended sundried tomatoes, garlic paste, mushrooms, a spoonful of chipotle peppers in adobo sauce, baby spinach, and cup full of four cheeses made the perfect sauce for the noodles that boiled quicker than any store-bought pasta I'd ever cooked.

Chilled wine continued flowing as we sat down to

eat. I'd smiled a million and twenty-six times since I'd awakened. Mercer pulling his chair up until our knees touched under the table curved my lips up into another one. I dug into my food, immediately falling in love with the combustion of flavors. The slight spice was the perfect addition to cut the boldness of the tomato sauce we'd made in the blender.

"Ummmmmmm."

I had another fork full. And then another. After the third one, I realized Mercer had barely touched his.

"Are you not hungry?"

"Habit." He shrugged. "After cooking, I hardly care to eat much of the meal. I'll have more. Feeding you is my priority right now. I want you to clean your plate, Pretty."

His deepened tone and the altering of his position made me swallow the food that was floating around my mouth. Instead of the wine, I opted for water to quench my sudden thirst.

Yes, Captain.

The words were on the tip of my tongue. The atmosphere shifted completely. The broken promises Mercer had made all day about not finding our way to bed, clinging to each other as we reached our climaxes, was apparent.

"Tell me, Vallei."

He stroked his beard, staring daggers at me.

"Anything, Cap," I surrendered, naturally submitting to a man that was worthy of my submission.

"Your wildest fantasy?"

Choking off the water I was steadily chugging to keep

cool, I failed to gain my composure. I wasn't at all expecting the question that had come from his lips.

"Wi-wildest fantasy?"

"You heard me, Pretty."

I nodded, confirming his observation. "Well, uh, I—"

"Speak up, Vallei. Now is not the time for you to whimper. There will be a time, but this isn't it. Tell me."

Thoughts raced through my head. He was tapping into aspirations of mine that I assumed was reserved for small nooks in my brain to live out their days and die with me.

"I asked a question."

"To be observed," I mumbled.

"Hm?"

"To... to be observed."

"You want someone to watch you get fucked?" He clarified with a tilt of his head and a sly smirk on his face.

Fearful of what was on his mind, I wanted to take it back. However, there was no turning back with Mercer.

"Yes." I moaned unintentionally. The visions had me clenching my pussy muscles and closing my eyes.

"Finish your food, Pretty."

What he planned to do with that piece of information piqued my anxiety. I opened my eyes and stuffed another fork full of pasta. Another. And another. And another. Slowly, I consumed my entire meal under Mercer's watchful eye. His plate was half full when he stood and began cleaning the table.

Silently, we exited the private room we'd been in. I was still in possession of my wine glass as we made our way into another room. This one was slightly bigger, dark, and carpeted. Music sheeted the silence. A pole was stationed in the center of the room. Two seemingly comfortable love seats sat a mere two feet from each other with a table between them.

Another iPad, just like the one from the other space, stole Mercer's attention. He began pecking away as I took note of the details of the room. Vintage, possibly thrifted, gold frames filled the empty walls that were covered in the prettiest floral wallpaper. The pastel flowers were the perfect pop of colors on the navy background.

A dark wood table with two chairs beneath it sat to the far right of the room. It concluded the furniture collection inside. The minimalistic concept matched well with the walls, which were the true statements. One was full of different-sized mirrors. Another was hand-painted with dark swirls that almost matched the dark paint they were drawn on top of.

"Right here," Mercer demanded, patting his lap.

I hadn't noticed he'd taken a seat. I wasted no time lowering my body onto his.

"Relax."

Small, fine bumps raised my skin. Involuntary body spasms forced unpredictable, subtle twitches. Mercer paid close attention to detail. Close attention to me. As small as the movement was, he didn't miss it.

"I have questions."

"I have answers," he replied.

"What are we doing in here?"

As the words left my mouth, the music changed. Low,

warm light spilled into the room, announcing another presence. Mile-high heels and laced lingerie hardly covered the treasured parts of the deep brown skin that belonged to a literal beauty queen.

With stunning features and an even more stunning frame, she claimed my vision without a word spoken. Upon reaching the stage, she grabbed the lone pole. Slowly, she rotated, eyes meeting mine each time she rounded it.

"Cap."

Mouth agape, I decided that one more question wouldn't hurt, especially since he hadn't answered the first.

"Stand up, Pretty."

"What's happening? What are we do—Cap."

He pulled my dress over my head. My breasts fell slightly. The fact that they'd managed their perkiness after so many years was still baffling, but I wasn't complaining. Neither was Mercer because he used his tongue to greet my pebbled nipples one by one.

"The Boy's Club is where fantasies meet reality."

Momentarily, he stopped talking and loosened his bottoms. When they fell to the ground, displaying his veiny tool that had been hidden beneath his briefs, I swallowed the lump in my throat.

"You want to indulge, then let's fucking indulge, Pretty.

By the hand, he grabbed me, pulling me toward the table on the right side of the room. I wasn't quite sure what would transpire next, but Mercer being a part of the plan was enough to have me all in, ready to face anything. Everything.

Putting on a brave face, I gained control of my features, making sure they all mirrored the adoration for the man and the moment he was creating for me. The space he held for me was heartening. He'd made me the center of his world in the four months I'd been present. Obliging and meeting his every command was only a way to show a fraction of the ways I wanted to satisfy Mercer.

"Hands." He groaned in my ear, cupping my ass with his right hand.

I placed both of mine on the table.

"Arch that fucking back, Pretty. Please don't play with me. I have time tonight."

Knowing that even if he didn't, he'd make time, I stretched my hands out and grabbed the other side of the table to perfect my arch. My stomach touched the cold surface, making me flinch slightly.

"That's it, baby."

His fingers trailed my skin, starting at my shoulders and ending at my waist. The black thong that shied away, hiding between my cheeks, fell to the floor. Anticipation filled me. I didn't know what I was waiting for, but I knew, without a doubt, that I'd love it. That was my only option with Cap, or he'd continue until he struck gold. Displeasure wasn't part of his program.

"There are mirrors. Plenty," he began.

I nodded, digesting each word from his mouth.

"Keep your eyes open, Pretty. If you close them, we stop, and we go home. You have two jobs tonight. One is to make sure her eyes never leave you. The other is to cum for me. Understood?"

"Yeeees."

Clenching my walls, I steadied my line of vision. Orbs stalked me as the dancer continued gyrating her hips and rubbing the lace that covered her vagina. Mercer spread my legs by scooting both my feet over with one of his.

My lower set of lips was next. He spread them apart and filled the space between them with a tongue. On his knees, he probed my pussy with his tongue. Efforts to flee failed as my climb on top of the table was halted with a hand to my ankle.

In cursive, Mercer inscribed his name across my flesh. His trip to my asshole wasn't anticipated, but I appreciated every second. He didn't stay long. My clit became his main objective. The feel of his tongue pressed against it was heavenly.

Intoxicated far beyond any legal limit, my lids grew heavier with each stroke of his tongue. It wasn't until they halted that I realized my eyes were closing. Worry lines creased my forehead as I watched Mercer stand to his feet behind me.

Fuck.

"You 'bout to piss me off, Pretty." He growled lowly.

"I'm sorrrrrry. Meeer—"

He entered me without warning. Effortlessly, Mercer filled me to the brim. I could still feel the engravement of his name across my center. The evidence his tongue left behind increased my sensitivity.

The first orgasm was swift, impactful, and enough to nearly knock me unconscious. The idea of Mercer ending our night early encouraged me to stay awake with my eyes trained on the third person in the room. Her beauty was enough to send me into oblivion.

"Your shit so good."

Mercer's praise stuck to me like glue.

"I love you."

"As you should," he boasted, never missing a stroke. "Pussy just pathetic." Though he'd murmured, I still made out every word.

His hands moved from my waist to my shoulders, trapping me so that I couldn't save my cervix from his tool. Each time his tip met it, I wanted to explode. Not because he'd reached my floor, but because at that moment, the thickest vein on his dick rubbed against my g-spot as his balls smacked my clit.

The holy trinity nearly brought me to my knees each and every time. I fell victim to their viciousness while my second orgasm threatened me with a memorable time. Lazy lids made it hard to focus on anything but the intensity of the moment. His skill. His stroke. *Him.*

"Keep your fucking eyes open." He grunted, twirling my ponytail around his hand and pulling my head up. "Do you want to go home, Pretty?"

"Nooo."

The sound of our skin smacking as he buried himself inside of me, over and over, was slowly dismantling me. It was the most barbaric, yet sweetest sound I've ever heard.

With each stroke, our connection was deepened. Our souls tied tighter. Our love intensified.

Even in the next lifetime, I wanted Mercer as my own. He was too fucking addictive. It didn't matter how, but I would make it my business to find him time and time again.

Straight ahead, I watched as the talented dancer slid her lace to the side. Her middle and index fingers circled her clit before dipping into her special sauce.

"Merrrrrrcer."

I tightened around him as waves crashed against me. He cared nothing about my ascent. He continued knocking my pussy into a new stratosphere.

"Merceeeeer!"

WHAP.

WHAP.

WHAP.

WHAP.

"Oh God!"

Everything tingled. From my scalp down to the soles of my feet. I stiffened, having no choice but to surrender to the orgasm that completely consumed my midsection.

Mercer · Vallei

I didn't remember walking to the truck. I didn't remember the drive to Mercer's home. I didn't remember taking the stairs. I didn't remember undressing. I didn't remember climbing in bed. I didn't remember falling asleep.

"Cap?"

Darkness surrounded me, but my heart helped me identify my location instantly. His bed was as familiar to me as his arms. I swiped a hand across the empty side of the bed, releasing a sigh as the void he left crept in.

I slid my legs from underneath the cover and sat at the edge of the bed to gather myself. Remnants of Mercer made Kegels pleasurable. On wobbly legs, I stood on my feet and stretched my body. The oversized shirt I wore had Mercer's scent all over it, making it hard to consider another minute without him in sight.

I took the stairs in search of him. The kitchen was my first stop. He wasn't there. I grabbed a bottle of water from the fridge, ready to continue my search. It didn't last very long. I found him in the den, stretched out on the sectional that was perfect for the men of the Domino family. They were long men. A standard couch would only piss them off and numb their legs in the process.

I walked inside to find his eyes trained on me. He'd known I was near before I knew I'd discover him inside. Tired eyes matched mine. We were one and the same at the moment. He patted the space on the couch in front of him, beckoning for me. I wasted no time gliding across the floor to join him.

He removed the large pillows from the back of the couch to make more room. The throw blanket at the end of the couch was sprawled across my body the second it touched the cushions. Comfort encouraged the release of a deep, lengthy breath.

I was exactly where I wanted and needed to be. Mercer's embrace had healing powers. So did his dick, and I'd had my fair share of it tonight. Thoughts of not having access to his embrace or the tool between his legs on nights that I spent alone saddened me. It was possibly too far in the future to worry about, but that didn't stop the pain from soaring through me.

"What's the matter, Pretty?"

"Nothing."

"Don't lie to me." He kissed my forehead.

"I ju... I can't help but think about the nights that coming downstairs to lay comfortably in your arms is not this simple. I'm going to miss this. Miss you."

"Vallei, I don't follow. When will there be a time when that's the case?"

"When I have my own place," I reminded him. It was a conversation we'd poked around but hadn't fully invested our energy or words in.

"I don't think it's necessary, but I understand your immediate need for independence."

His stance remained. He wanted me in his home, but I knew that our relationship's health was banking on the time I needed to spend alone. As much as I loved Mercer and was falling deeper for him each day, ignoring the long years I'd spent in a marriage with a man that I still cared for to some degree would only cause cracks in our foundation.

Suffocating in Mercer's love was grand, but using it

as a blanket to suffocate the feelings I harbored for my failed marriage would prove to be lethal to my emotional health. It wasn't a step I was willing to take. With him, I craved a healthy kind of love, one that would withstand the test of time and bounce back from any blow that threatened its existence. I wanted a love that was immeasurable, one that was invincible.

"It's not my independence that I'm trying to exercise, Cap."

"Then what is it, Pretty?"

"My healing. When I said I didn't need saving, I meant it in some ways, not all. Time alone will allow me to begin to truly grow from this all."

His silence made me slightly nervous. I wanted to know what he was thinking, what he was feeling.

"Say something."

"Anything, Vallei. You know this already. I mean that shit."

"But do you understand? Do you understand why I need time to fix me?"

"I do."

"And if I decided that I want to retain a private residence, would you understand that, too?"

"Whether you're in my home or your own, my love for you won't change. Haven't our time taught you anything?"

"Yes."

"Clear your head. Don't beat around the bush with me. Tell me what you want. Tell me what you need. I'll meet you in the middle."

"My desires to one day be a wife again don't exist."

He nodded. "Okay."

"I've lived with a man for years and years. The idea of having my own space, having my own home, fills me with joy."

"Is that why you had the creative studio built?"

"Unfortunately, I didn't create anything but more memories with you in it, and that's good enough for me. It gave me a sense of freedom, though, the few times I visited."

"Good. Means it served its purpose."

"Cap, I don't want to feel like I'm bringing the trauma from my marriage into your home and piling it up on us. I can't do that to you, to us. So, before I take steps forward, I need to sit here and really feel everything the moment is offering, good or bad."

"I'm here, Vallei. For every phase. You don't have to explain why, when, and how you're trying to get your shit together. Just tell me how I can help. You need me to build a fucking house next to mine? Cop you a condo? Go put that nigga out of your crib? What's up?"

"I don't want to breathe that air another day of my life. When he leaves, I'd like to rent it out."

"Alright, then, that's what we'll do. But what do you want right now?"

"Somewhere cozy. Somewhere surrounded by nature. Somewhere for me to spend the next few months getting my head on straight."

"I'm on it."

"Cap, I already know a place," I admitted.

"Yeah?"

"My mother inherited it from my grandfather. She cleans it monthly but never stays. I don't want to be there forever. It won't be my official residence. But it's a start."

"I'll figure out the rest during your stay. How far away is it?"

"Approximately forty-five minutes. Is that too far?"

"Were three hours too far?"

I was instantly reminded of the measures he'd taken. His offense was justified. He'd proven himself too many times for me to ask such crazy questions.

"I was thinking... Maybe a month. Or three. Or six."

"However long you need, Pretty. I'm here."

"Friday through Sunday at your home?"

"A middle I can meet you at."

"Thank you, Cap."

"No need for all that. Just take your ass to sleep and shut up. I'm tired."

I snuggled up against him. My eyes closed involuntarily. He was my peace bringer.

FOURTEEN

Three weeks later...

Saturday mornings had become my favorite. It marked the first morning of a visit from Vallei. Waking up with her soft hair against my skin was delightful. This time, though, she'd stolen my heart a day earlier. Friday was here, marking the official grand opening of The M. Vallei laid, sprawled across my bed, with her hair covering half the pillow.

Though she wasn't one hundred percent, she was elated to join me for the night's activities. Nonstop, she'd been running through her set. It was only thirty minutes, but she wanted it to be perfect. The remainder of the guest list was quickly filled out after she announced her presence. My baby had the magic touch and refused to let her people down.

"Pretty," I whispered in her ear.

"Five more minutes," she whined.

Placing a hand on her forehead, I checked for a fever. She was cool to the touch, as she had been since she'd begun complaining the previous day.

"It's been five minutes five times, Vallei."

Chuckling, she pulled the covers over her head. "Really?"

"Yes. Here. I made you some broccoli cheddar soup and a little cocktail that'll get you together."

"What's inside?"

"All the things to boost your energy and get rid of your diarrhea."

"Cap!" she hissed.

"Well, it is what you have."

"It's not. And I told you not to worry. This is a girl thing. It's nothing new."

"I've been on your line for five months, baby. It's brand fucking new because I've never seen you down and out."

"Because my incompetent ovaries decide when they want to cooperate and bring on the flood. PMSing and period symptoms, however, is a girl thing."

Nodding in understanding, I sat the tray over her. "I get it. Sit up and eat this."

She slid up and leaned against the headboard. My baby was a mess. A pretty one, nonetheless.

"Are you excited about tonight?"

"Yeah. Got some loose ends to tie up."

"That means you're leaving me, huh?"

"It does, but I'll be back in about an hour to get you."

"I have to start getting dressed now?"

"No. Not until I get back. We're not leaving out immediately."

"Okay."

"Eat, Pretty. And drink all of that."

"I will. I promise."

I leaned forward, tittering as I watched her lean back further.

"Fuck are you doing?"

"My breath is mad right now. Please, Captain."

"Girl, give me a kiss. I don't give a fuck. It can't be any worse than you've been smelling in the bathroom since you got here."

"O my God. See, I should've stayed home. I knew it."

"I would've just come and got your ass like I did."

"I'm going to use the bathrooms downstairs from now on. And don't try to come in talking to me, either."

"Why not? That's the best conversational pit to ever exist."

"And shower? And shave? And just get on my nerves in general."

"Fuck you, Pretty, with all due respect."

I tapped her lips and stood on my feet.

"That might just help bring it on down," she suggested.

"Say less. Get ready to arch that back and toot that motherfucker in the air before our night ends."

"Yes, Captain."

"I'll be right back. All of that shit better be gone."

"Yes, Captain."

I exited the bedroom while searching my contacts. Royce's line began ringing as I hit the third step. She was on the line by the time I made it to the final one.

"Good morning."

"Headed there now. Your people ready?"

"Yes. We were waiting for your call."

"Bet. Be there in about ten, fifteen."

"See you in a bit."

I ended the call as I slid into my whip. Within twelve minutes, I was in front of the home that I'd visited a little too often in the past, violating a nigga's space as if he didn't exist. Because, to me, he didn't. He'd got caught slipping. It was just my luck.

Now, I was blessed with a woman who had a heart as pretty as her mind and a soul as beautiful as her face. He considered her a problem, and I was a problem solver. Taking her up off his hands was a pleasure of mine.

"Good morning," the constable greeted me.

Because I'd rather taste shit than kick shit with any member of the law, I shifted my attention toward Royce.

"The file," I requested.

She handed me a folder much thicker than I'd been anticipating. Swiftly, I swiped through the pages, finding photo after photo, along with logs, services, and employees they'd come in contact with. Over the years, the entire Tremble family had spent over two million dollars with Roulette to make their fantasies their reality.

The smoking gun we'd been waiting for was in my hand. The memory card that was in a Ziplock bag and stapled to the back was footage of their comings and goings. The footage matched each date on the files, solidifying each piece of evidence.

Wanting to get back to Vallei, I marched toward the door with Royce and the other nigga behind me. A swift pound on the door and a few doorbell dings later, and Phillip was standing before us. His facial hair nearly covered his whole fucking face. He reeked of liquor and funk. I'd bet my last dollar he hadn't seen the shower more than twice in the three weeks that Pretty had been gone. Instead of waiting for permission, I barged in. Once inside, I realized I'd rather stand on the porch. The house smelled almost as bad as him. Evidence of his drunken depression was all over the place.

"What is it that you could possi—"

"Shut the fuck up, nigga. I thought we went over this shit last time?"

I turned to the constable, urging him to handle his business.

"Serve this nigga so you can roll."

He shuffled his feet and pushed forward to hand him the papers in his hand.

"Phillip Tremble, you're being served by Vallei

Novelles. Here you'll find divorce documents that you're encouraged to sign and s—"

"The door is that way."

His job had been done. His time with us had ended. He made his way out of the door without another word.

"You share that man's blood, for real." Royce sighed.

"So do you. So, please make your point clear."

"Asshole."

Getting down to business, I handed him the file in the entryway, piling it right on top of the papers he'd been served.

"You might want to open that shit first."

He took my piece of advice. His eyes widened as he began flipping through the file.

"Inside is every single detail about the Trembles' visits to Rouge and The Boy's Club. Every time you got your dick sucked. Every time you titty fucked. Every time you slid into some pussy that didn't belong to your wives.

"Every time you brought a dance. Every time you participated in an orgy. Every time you batted an eye at a woman. Every drink you consumed. Every recreational drug you indulged in. It's all there. Everything. And for a law firm full of corrupt motherfuckers with squeaky-clean backgrounds, I doubt this will go over well.

"Loss of clients. New court proceedings from the ex-spouses of the people the law firm served because now your actions and logic are questionable. You can kiss those new clients goodbye. No one will want to work with your family after such a big, dirty scandal.

"The women they love won't want to be associated

with their asses no more, either. They'll be representing each other. I'll make sure it's the only cases they ever see again. I will make sure the practice falls. It'll be my life's mission, and it won't take me long at all.

"A few clicks. The internet is a wild place. And the woman standing beside me doesn't bullshit."

"I don't," Royce agreed.

"So, before this gets ugly, I need you to put your signature on that paper, my nigga. And forget Vallei ever existed."

"Ho-how'd you ge—"

"None of that matters. Sign them fucking papers."

Royce stepped forward with a pen.

"In this case, the proceedings will be speedy. The documents confirm you agree to the divorce itself, as well as giving Vallei the right to retain all her assets. There are several clauses to ensure the satisfaction of this matter without the chance of disrupting her, speaking of her publicly or privately, or attempting to obtain any amount of money that she's worked for since the day your marriage was considered lawful.

"You'll find a full NDA on the final page as well as a tally of your funds. I need you to sign off on them both, agreeing to walk out of the marriage exactly how you entered it and keeping quiet while doing so," Royce explained to him. "We don't mind you reading through it all. I have all day."

"No you don't and neither do I. Sign that shit so I can roll."

"This shit is unreal."

"Sign the fucking papers."

He took the pen from Royce and began scribbling his name on each line that needed a signature. Royce collected the stapled pack with a smile. She was victorious again. The girl was lethal and good at what she did. Anything you put in front of her, she could handle. That's why she'd been appointed her position and played it well.

I didn't hesitate to hit the door. I had what I'd come for. There was no need to stay. The condition of the house made it hard to do so anyway.

"I need you up out this bitch in a week. When I pull up Friday, let there be no traces of your existence." I yelled over my shoulder on the way out.

The disgust in his tone stopped me in my tracks. "She's useless." He scoffed. "She can't even give you a child."

With a nod and a tilted head, I contemplated knocking every tooth out of that nigga's mouth, but I quickly realized it wasn't worth it. Without a doubt, he'd have them people at my door. It was grand opening night. Shit was bigger than him and this moment.

"She couldn't give you a child, Square. Her womb recognized real. My junior got her ass hugging the toilet and complaining of fatigue right now. I'll be sure to send you an invitation to the baby shower, my nigga. And when you get there, sit your bitch ass down and shut the fuck up. See that fumble up front and in person."

I left him with something to chew on and walked Royce to her ride. Though victorious, she had some shit festering in that forehead of hers. When she pressed her back against the door instead of allowing me to open it, I prepared for the bullshit. I turned to face the house we'd just left, removing my Glock from my waistline and letting it rest by my side. If we weren't leaving yet, I needed to make sure we were both safe and my eyes were trained for any signs of danger.

"What?"

"My junior got her ass hugging the toilet?"

"You heard every word out of my mouth, Royce."

"I did, but you haven't mentioned... It doesn't even matter. Has it been confirmed?"

"Nah."

"Why not?"

"Because she's scared. Motherfuckers tell you, you can't carry a child for so long that you begin to believe them. It'll take a miracle to convince Pretty she's pregnant, but I'm no fool. She keeps hollering about her period. That motherfucker not coming, Royce."

"So, where do you go from here? How do you bring it to her? Do you wait until her belly swells, or do you push for her to visit Nature's office?"

"Nah, that wouldn't be a good idea. Neither of them. I picked up a test this morning while I was at the store. Wanted to get this shit over with before I had her piss on it. When I get that confirmation, I don't want nothing else to fuck up that moment. Not thoughts of her situation. Not that nigga. Not that marriage. Nothing."

"Understood. Well, congratulations!"

"Appreciate it."

"Give me a hug!"

She extended her arms and got them knocked down immediately.

"I don't underestimate niggas. Turning my back is not an option right now. Hug me tonight. I'll see your ass at the opening."

"I'll be there."

Mercer Vallei

Gripping the wheel, I took a second to consider all the moving parts of my life. Everything made different parts of my heart rejoice. Vallei's presence was the epitome of happiness. She brought so much peace. She kept my head on straight.

Therapy was still going strong. Popping my daily pills had become easier and less daunting with Milo's name on the prescription. It had taken a full week to adjust to the change in medications, but I felt better, lighter, and less convicted of the hell of a disorder that claimed the most important people in our world.

The opening of The M filled me with pride. The years I spent behind the wall, I was loaded with books that were written by chefs, restaurant owners, and bakers. I used the skills I was learning to make better meals in the slammer. Eventually, I was being paid commissary to make the best of the bullshit we were limited to inside, in addition to working in the kitchen where I enhanced every meal that was served.

Opening a restaurant with all the knowledge I'd consumed in jail felt like shit was coming full circle. Hadn't I sat my ass down for all those years, I wouldn't have gained an interest in becoming a chef. I'd still be in the kitchen, and I'd still be whipping over a hot stove, but it wouldn't be dinner for the wealthy. It would be for the junkies that came knocking as soon as their eyes opened in the morning.

Going legit was a gift that I knew would keep giving. I was thankful that my brothers believed in me enough to take a chance that I wasn't willing to take alone. That million would still be buried and Vallei wouldn't be in my bed waiting on me to return if they hadn't. I owed them niggas for life.

Even the thought of the possibility of a little one growing in Vallei's womb had me excited. I'd prayed too many times for God not to hear that particular portion of my pleas. Confirmation wasn't needed. God was a miracle worker and in the blessing business. We were on the brink of our miracle child. Vallei hadn't had a period since March. Though they were irregular, it only made sense.

There was only one thing weighing on my heart. Only one aspect of my life that I wasn't satisfied with. Makai's absence was ringing loudly in my head. I missed him night and day. There was no sugarcoating the shit or ignoring that ache in my chest. He was supposed to join us, side by side, tonight. He wouldn't be here, though, and that cut me deep.

I entered my home fifteen minutes after starting my engine. I'd taken an additional two minutes in the driveway, living in the moment. Holding space for everything in my world. When I took the stairs, I wasn't empty-handed. It was time to confirm the next step in our relationship and the rapid changes to our future.

Having a child at forty felt like perfect timing. Vallei was a multi-platinum poet who craved motherhood. I happened to be a chef who was in demand and opening a restaurant that would gain success over the next year.

We had an entire village of women and men ready to support us in any and every way possible. I'd met Vallei's mother when I helped her move into their family's cabin in the mountains. It was as cozy as she'd described. She had fallen in love with it for a reason.

She and her pops barely spoke, but there was no beef. When the time was right, I'd meet him, too. She was locked in with my people. The only person she hadn't met was Makai, but that introduction would come soon enough.

"Pretty!"

She'd fallen asleep again.

Stirring, she groaned. "It's been an hour already?"

"Nah, but I need you to do something for me."

"Hm?"

I tossed the pregnancy test onto the bed. It landed on her chest, right underneath her chin.

"Cap, that could've hit me in the face," she whined.

"Up, baby."

"What do you want me to do?"

Yawning, she sat up, feeling around the bed for the box. When she discovered it, she began shaking her head from one side to the other.

"Piss on that for me, Pretty. Confirm what I already know."

"Mercer. I'm no... I'm not taking that."

She pushed the test away.

"Vallei."

She continued shaking her head, sliding down in bed, and pulling the covers over her head. The whimpers she released shattered my heart. That fear was draining. It was crippling. It was overpowering. And it was on Vallei's ass. I sat on the side of the bed and wrapped my arms around her, respecting wishes she hadn't voiced by leaving her under the covers.

"Baby."

"I'm not going to give myself false hope, Mercer. I can't crush my spirit like that. I can't break my heart that way. I can't have children. We know it."

"You can't deny what's happening to your body, either. This is not a period, Vallei."

"It could be."

"Please, take the test."

"I can't."

"You can. I'm right here to help. This doesn't have to go beyond this room. You and me, we're the only ones who have to know the results."

"What if it's positive?" She blubbered.

"How would you feel?"

"I don't want to hope for something that I know is medically impossible."

"Baby, doctors don't have the last word. God does. That's the only doctor I truly trust besides my brother. Miracles happen every day. Why is it so hard to believe that you're worthy of one? We're worthy of one?"

"If you've gone through what I have, then maybe you'd understand."

"But I haven't. So, meet me in the middle, Vallei. I meet you there every single time. Take the test."

Feeling her body begin to stretch, dismantling the ball she'd crouched into, I lifted up to allow her to come from under the cover. Her face was drenched in tears. Worry crinkled her face and glossed her eyes.

"I'm scared."

"No matter what it says, it doesn't change what I feel for you or how I feel about you. Having a child is something we both want, but it's not necessary to live a full, fulfilling life. I'm happy either way, Pretty, as long as you're by my side."

"Can you come into the bathroom with me?"

"Yes. Of course. All I need is your piss. I can handle the rest. I got you."

I pulled her into my arms and out of the bed. With the pregnancy test in my hands, I carried her into the bathroom where I rested her on the toilet. She was wearing a tee without panties beneath, another sign that she didn't believe her period was coming.

Vallei was cautious. I was almost certain she wouldn't

be lying in my bed without at least a layer of protection between her and the sheets. Instead of addressing it, I focused my attention on the instructions on the box.

"Here. We're just going to put it in here instead of trying to perfect your aim," I explained, holding up the cup I used to gargle with morning and night. "And stick it in there."

"Okay."

As I continued going over the instructions, Vallei filled about a quarter of the cup and used the toilet bowl for the rest. I dipped the stick, put the cap on it, and flipped it over to begin the three-minute wait. Vallei had no interest in staying, afraid she'd only be heartbroken in return. When she tried walking past to get back in bed, I snatched her back.

"If death comes for me tonight, girl. I want you to know that I love you."

I pulled her into my chest and began rocking from side to side while singing in her ear. She wrapped her arms around my neck and pressed her face against mine. The track continued to flow, and so did my words. I felt each one of them deep in my chest.

"Messin' around with you is gone get me life. But when I look into your eyes. Man, you're worth that sacrifice."

I kissed her cheek. She responded by squeezing me tighter.

"If this is the kind of love that my mom used to warn me about," I harped, feeling a surging pain in my chest. I missed that lady more than I let on, especially during moments like this one. Having a mother to turn to, question, and bug the shit out of would've been wonderful.

"I'm in trouble. I'm in real big trouble."

To my surprise, Pretty didn't leave me hanging. When Mary's part came on, she joined in.

"So cold, sometimes I feel like I'm a prisoner. I think I'm trapped here for a while."

"Okay, Pretty. Okay."

"And every breath I fight to take. It gets hard as these four walls."

Word for word, we sang to one another until the song ended. And when our performance was done, Vallei was visibly better. I decided to do the honors. Flipping the stick over, I read the single word that popped up in the small window. Everything around me blurred, including Vallei's pretty, tearful face.

FIFTEEN

Magic Under the Mud

Dig
Don't you ever stop
Shovel and shove.
Hasn't anyone told you? there's magic under
the mud
A sea of treasure
Much too beautiful to be exposed
To visit this exhibition
You've got to dig a hole

An array of colors
Bold and bold
Everlasting ethic like the miners,
They're still digging for gold
Down here, we don't require the Sun's light to look
this good
Haven't you heard?
There's magic under this here mud
Tucked deep within the darkness is where we
shine
It's the shade
It's the coolness
It's the secrecy
That keeps our structure blemish-free
And our beauty refined
We don't bother
Neither do we bite
Though we're thankful for the day,
Our finest hours are dark like the night
Fair warning...
Don't bother with gloves,
Somebody should've told you by now,
There's magic under the mud

Applause rang out, forcing my eyes open. The first set of orbs I found belonged to the man who had shoveled until he found my magic. A smile curved my lips upward, exposing every tooth possible. The M was packed to the brim, everyone here to see the man of the hour. The man of my world.

"Thank you for digging that day. Congratulations, my love. Wishing you all the success."

I lifted my glass of water in the air as he lifted his drink.

"I love you."

"I love you."

I ended my set and made my way through the space to connect with the man that I loved physically, mentally, emotionally, and spiritually. The man who had made me a true believer. The man who had given me a gift that I had never expected but was happy to have.

"You look ravishing, Fleur," Mercer teased, calling me by my pseudonym.

He placed a hand on my stomach as he welcomed me in for a hug.

"How you feeling, Momma?" he whispered in my ear.

"I'm better," I admitted. "But hungry."

"Come on. I have your food waiting underneath the lamp."

"Cap, you don't have to leave. I can manage it on my own."

"Don't insult me, Pretty. Come on."

I followed his lead, eventually ending up in the kitchen where there was pure chaos. But amongst it all, there was a slightly familiar face. One that I felt like I knew or should've known but didn't. It reminded me of the one that I kissed often and sought for comfort. Yet, it didn't belong to Malachi or Milo.

"Makai?" I whispered, trying to place a name to the face.

"That's gray hair in his beard, baby. That's not glistening water. His name is Chemistry. Keep your eyes open, he won't be long. Blink and you'll miss him."

"I have no intention of leaving so soon, Mercer."

The depth of his voice was soul-rocking. It was deep. Yet, soft at once. Just like Mercer, he commanded my attention.

"Has hell frozen?" Mercer asked, stepping forward to embrace the man that shared his features.

"Fuck you, nigga. Congratulations."

"Appreciate you."

I watched from afar but somehow felt included in the moment, nonetheless.

"Vallei, Chem. Chem, Vallei."

Just as the introduction ended, a woman as beautiful as the man she stepped up beside appeared from behind the double doors that led to the offices.

"Nice to meet you."

"You got the wife outside," Mercer tittered. "Yeah. Hell done definitely frozen over."

"Vallei, this is my wife, Egypt. Egypt, this is Vallei."

"Your dress is gorgeous," she proclaimed, extending a hand.

"So are you."

Chocolate skin peeked from parts of her that her dress didn't cover. She was dipped in gold jewelry, resembling a queen who'd stepped off her throne momentarily to address the common people. I wasn't sure who she was, but her presence was unsettling in the best ways.

As if I was speaking to royalty. As if I was to bow and kiss the back of her hand. Maybe it was her aura, or maybe it was the Black hospitality that I'd watched my mother greet other Black women with my entire life.

"Mercer." She nodded.

"Egypt."

Her arms went around him as the seriousness of her tone and facial features softened, ending in a heart-warming smile.

"It's been so long."

"For good reasoning," he exclaimed.

"Ha-ha." Her forced laugh made me chuckle, though I was unsure of the inside joke.

"We won't keep you," Chem told Mercer. "We're headed to the suite upstairs to watch the festivities from afar."

"But not indulge."

Nodding, Chem confirmed.

"One love, man."

"One love," he replied as he took off.

"Did your mother have the same kid five times?" I asked as soon as we were alone again. Aside from the kitchen madness, of course.

"I don't see it."

"Because you're one of them."

I followed behind Mercer as he deepened our distance in the kitchen. We reached the lights where he retrieved my plate. The steps were the next task to tackle. I made the journey up and into the suite he'd reserved for my friends, family, and a few people from my team that made the performance possible.

Carry, June, Brandon, and Fatima all stood around, clutching their bags. It was obvious their time with me had come to an end. Their bellies were full, and they were preparing to leave.

"There she goes!" June shouted when I stepped through the door.

"You did great, honey!"

"I can see now that this album is about to be off the chain."

"It'll be my best body of work," I expressed. "Thank you all for coming. I'm aware that it's late, and you need to get home."

"Yes, but I'll talk to you first thing Monday morning. I have a few ideas," Carry assured me.

"Okay. See you guys later."

I searched for Mal, but she was nowhere to be found. I would bet my last dollar that she was on the prowl, searching for her forever. Everyone Mercer had introduced me to who wasn't attached to someone seemed like a candidate for my friend, so I hoped she found exactly what she was looking for.

"Hey. That was so good, baby," my mother exclaimed, opening her arms while rushing toward me.

"Thanks."

"Is Dad comfortable?"

"Yes. He's around here somewhere. The man never gets out of the house. I'm happy you invited him."

"I'm happy he's enjoying himself."

I watched from afar as Mercer placed my plate on the table in the middle of the small suite. When he took a seat, I sighed in defeat.

"Mom, give me a second."

I stalked toward him, sitting on the couch next to him, when I finally made it.

"Baby, you have an entire restaurant full of people here for you. Sitting down to watch me eat isn't necessary."

"But it's what I want to do, Pretty. The people can wait. Here. Start with some water. You must be thirsty."

Knowing I wouldn't win the war, I allowed him to uncap the water and place it on my lips. I gulped until I was satisfied and my throat was no longer scratchy. As soon as he lowered it, I noticed the one person of the Tremble descent I connected with effortlessly. Her tiny, round belly made me smile.

"Penelope," I called out.

She whipped her head toward me, cheeks high in the air.

"Vallei!"

She rested her feet and her legs, having a seat on the sofa across from the one we were perched on.

"Mercer, this is Penelope. Penelope, this is Mercer."

"Nice to finally meet the man who snatched my girl up and showed her what life is truly about."

"Same. Same."

Mercer wasn't a man of many words in public spaces, but the fact that he managed a few at a time for the people I loved just as he did the people he loved was only one of the reasons I couldn't get enough of him.

"Baby. I'm serious. You don't have to wait. I'll come down when I'm done. Okay?"

Reluctantly, Mercer stood and made his way out of the door. I knew he didn't want to, but I'd nag him until he returned to post. Downstairs, in the main dining area, where he could mix and mingle.

"He doesn't really like people, huh?"

"No," I divulged to Penelope.

"Figures. And you're trying to put the man out. He's hiding."

"I know, but he promised me he wouldn't."

"He wants to be by your side. You bring him comfort."

"Which is why I'm about to clean my plate and get back to him."

"Ahhhhh! My girl is in love."

"Deeply."

"I know that's right, babe. It's so rewarding. I want every woman to experience this."

"Speaking of every woman, I have a few to introduce you to. Some I just met tonight, but the rest I know well. They're all very good people."

"Which is all that matters, not the amount of time you've known them."

Her words stuck with me as I began digging into my food. She was right. Time wasn't a measurement of love.

It was simply... time. I loved Mercer more than I'd loved any man before him, yet we'd spent the least amount of time together.

Our connection, our goodness, was more mature than the length of our relationship. More mature than what was expected from two people who'd only known one another for less than half a year.

By the time I finished my food, Penelope had disappeared. I didn't bother searching for her upon realizing Mercer wasn't at his post. I began combing the entire building for him.

"Hey, have you seen Mercer?" Malachi was the first person I asked.

"I haven't."

I continued, being sure to revisit the kitchen. It was the area he'd frequented since the night began to make sure that everything was going according to plan. He wasn't there, either.

"Have you seen Mercer?" Kleu was the next person I asked.

Per usual, she had answers for me.

"He was taking a moment in his office. He's probably in the restroom now. That's where he was headed."

"Thank you."

"Of course."

I rounded three corners, dodging everyone who cared to stop and talk. There wasn't a single person in the building that I cared about having a conversation with more than my man at the moment. Everyone else and everything else could wait. I made it to the stretch that led to both restrooms, where I halted immediately.

The heart that Mercer had begun mending, the one that he'd nursed back to health, stopped beating. My brows rushed to the center of my forehead as pain ripped through me. Everything around me faded to black. Unable to move, I stood on weak legs. The wall beside me caught my palm and helped me maintain my balance.

The brown-skinned woman with long, flowing tresses who stood in front of Mercer with both of his hands inside of hers didn't match the description of anyone in his immediate circle. Watching her comfort him in his time of need, during his despair, was repulsive. Vomit swelled my throat, threatening to spill.

However, I'd much rather ruin my custom-designed black gown than allow either of them to see me in my distressed state. I summoned the strength and stood tall, demanding my knees to gain the strength necessary to get me out of dodge.

Just as I turned to leave, her arms went around him, pulling him in for a hug. I picked up the bottom of my dress as hot tears crashed against my cheeks. Finding Mal was my next task because staying any longer was not an option for me.

"Vallei!" The sound of his voice boomed through the hallway.

This time, it didn't stop me in my tracks. It didn't make me lose interest in everything else around me. It wasn't the voice of reasoning. It was the reason for the pain. More soared through me, making my escape a bit harder than necessary.

I felt the weight of it all on my shoulders. Before I could round the corner completely, I felt a hand on my wrist. A second later, my body was against the wall, with Mercer staring into my teary eyes.

"Why are you crying, Pretty?"

I couldn't manage words, not as fast as I wanted to. But when they finally came to the surface, I pushed them out as best I could. I hated the way my voice sounded when I opened my mouth. The pain was evident. The vulnerability was evident.

"I don't want to talk about it."

"Tears running down your face, Vallei, and you're ignoring me when I call your name. We're going to talk about it. We're not sweeping shit under the rug. And we're not fighting about shit. Not when we can handle it like adults right here, right now.

"You're not allowed to bury your pain in this relationship, Pretty. Get that through your skull. Open your mouth and tell me what's the matter? Tell me what's wrong so I can right that shit."

Pretending it never happened was the way I coped in my marriage. It was a survival tactic. Knowing that it was prohibited in the relationship I was building with Mercer forced me to address my feelings and face them head-on. Not as time progressed, but at the moment, I felt them.

Because I mattered. My thoughts mattered. My love mattered. Though this was new to me, it made me feel empowered instead of like a helpless, vulnerable lump on a log.

"Talk to me."

"Who is she?"

The question that would haunt me for months in my marriage came out so effortlessly. And without a doubt, I was certain I'd receive an answer. The man before me was eager to respond. He simply wanted me to confront my feelings so that I'd begin adapting and allowing him space to help me unlearn behavior that had kept my heart somewhat intact over the last few years.

"Listen," he began, licking his lips for emphasis. "We're not beefing about a woman. Ever. Not today, not tomorrow, not next week, not next month. No woman who isn't family is worth those tears you're crying or making you upset.

"They don't mean enough to me. I'll cut them out of my life in an instant if they make you uncomfortable. That's no problem, Pretty. I'm not sure how much I have to say, but I don't mind saying that shit until I'm blue in the face.

"If that gives you the security you need. Because that's all that matters. Any-fucking-thing, Pretty. Anything. Any-fucking-thing. You hear me?"

I nodded, afraid that if I spoke, my emotions would topple over, and I'd become a blubbering mess.

"Don't run away from shit when it comes to us. Face it. Face me. Tell me how you're feeling. Tell me what's going on in your head. Tell me how your heart is feeling and how fucked up I got you because I won't hesitate to tell you. Her name is Ainsleigh. She's the woman responsible for my therapy sessions. Aside from you, she's the woman that is keeping my head on straight. I skipped my session this morning so that she could come here tonight. I figured I'd need the additional support—mentally. That's what that was. And that's why she's still standing over there, to make sure I'm alright. There's nothing more. Don't wait for me to break your heart, Pretty, because it won't happen. I'm for you, always and in all ways."

"I'm sorry."

"Don't be. I should've informed you. I should've done a better job. This is my fault. I won't let you take the blame. It's on me."

"Can you hug me?" I caved, needing to feel his love surrounding me.

"Yes. I can do whatever you need me to, Vallei."

Before wrapping his arms around me, he wiped my face clean of tears.

"Stop all this fucking crying. You're alright. I'm alright. We're good. If you ever feel like we're not, just tell me. Don't run from nothing. Step. Because I'ma step 'bout you, Pretty. No questions asked. I expect the same."

"I love you." I cried into the jacket of his sleeve. "And I can't stop crying."

"Because your emotions are all over the place."

"I'm pregnant."

Still in shock, I repeated the words I'd been repeating since discovering it.

"As a motherfucker. Hormones raging and shit."

"I'm sorry."

"Don't apologize. Stop doing that and pull yourself together. I have someone I want you to meet."

"She probably thinks I'm crazy."

"Frankly, I don't give a fuck what she thinks about you. Nobody else, either."

"Cap."

"I'm for real, Pretty. But I'd have you know she thinks the world of you because I do. You've been a hot topic in our sessions for the last three and a half months. You've made her job a lot easier. Trust me, she knows you're not crazy. You're just in love."

He took my hand and led me toward the woman I assumed meant my relationship no good.

"Ainsleigh, this is Vallei. Vallei, this is Ainsleigh, my therapist."

Extending a hand, she greeted me with her pleasant perfume and sultry tone.

"Good to finally meet the woman who's made my weekly sessions a lot easier. Please tell me where to start sending the checks."

Chuckling, I willed my tears away. She was beautiful. "Keep it. I think I can manage."

"Well, at least you could join us for a session. I've been trying to convince Mr. Domino of this for a while, but he refuses."

"I don't want to intrude on hi—"

"I didn't think you'd want to come," Mercer admitted.

"I don't mind. Not at all. If you're comfortable."

"I'm good with it, Pretty."

"I'll set something up. We can see how it goes. Couple's therapy is a specialty of mine. I'd love to have you both in my office at least once."

"Okay. Whenever you're ready for me, he'll let me know."

"Sure thing. Let me get back to my table. I bumped into this man, losing his head on my way out of the restroom. I hope no one has stolen my chair."

"They're all assigned. You're good," Mercer informed her.

"Good. Good. See you soon, Mr. Domino. Nice to meet you, Vallei."

She waltzed off, headed to her chair. Mercer's arms wrapped around me. His palms pressed against my belly as he whispered in my ear, "Vallei's having a baby."

BEFORE YOU GO...

The *epilogue* is next, but before you go...

This concludes the Berkeley Bred series, one that consists of four books that take you on a journey with each brother of the Domino clan as they discover love —some for the first time and some all over again.

I enjoyed writing this series because it was heavy from book one and focused on a few things that my lighthearted, airy love stories just don't.

Grief — the ugliest, most difficult kind
Imperfection — the kind that makes you worth loving, still
Heartache — the kind that lingers for life and lots of it
Loss — my God, these men lost a lot
Mental illness — because it is REAL and it is worth exploring

Representation — all kinds... all kinds
Infidelity — the good kind, if there's a such thing
Struggle — poverty was real for the Dominoes.
Privilege wasn't given, they had to create it for themselves
and they've done well.

WHAT ABOUT CHEM?

I know you're curious about Chem. More details on what
happens with Chem are here. Keep your eyes open.
What I have in store for you 2024, no heart or Kindle can
prepare for.

With God's generosity, we'll have a good year.

G

***P.S. Grab your ticket to Me & My Romance
Friends if you'd like to see me in Dallas, TX
this year. Tickets are sold on
meandmyromancefriends.com***

EPILOGUE

Four months later...

I removed the headphones from my ear, silencing Vallei's voice. The unreleased version of her album had been on rotation since she'd sent it to me two weeks ago. My nightly cleans while alone had become my favorite part of the night. There were a few finishing touches to put on the album, but it would be out in the new year.

She was waiting for the birth of our son, Malachi, so touring wasn't an issue. She was also waiting for his birth so she could include him on the album. His cries of discomfort after being pulled from his mother's womb and into a different world was the album ending she craved. I couldn't wait until that moment came.

We didn't have very long. We discovered Vallei was three months along at Nature's office. Pretty was now seven months into the pregnancy and handling it like a champ. It was a blessing seeing her wobble around the house Friday through Monday. We maintained our schedules and would until the baby was born.

She'd then reside in the second wing of my home being built for her stay. A sky bridge connected the two dwellings. It was the perfect compromise for her desire for independence while still maintaining a safe distance so that I wasn't far in the event of an emergency or she simply needed me near.

At my desk, I scanned the menu for the upcoming corporate event we were hosting, mid-day. The success of *The M* was rapid and steadily growing. Reservations were booked for the next three and a half months. Cancellations were rarely made.

The only chance the public had to get in without a reservation was our huge bar area. There were high-top tables and a lengthy bar top to sit at. However, the experience was mediocre in comparison to the guest dining in the main suite on the first floor and the private suites on the second floor.

Satisfied with everything Pops had listed, I began packing my shit up to leave. Kleu and Aeir were both tackling the private event together. Vallei and I were scheduled for a doctor's visit. As if she'd known I was thinking of her, a message from her appeared.

Dill pickle chips.

Homemade vanilla ice cream.

Hot puffs.

Peach drink.

Her lists were always random, but she always got exactly what she wanted. She found joy in my late nights closing down the restaurant. Catering to her cravings was much simpler.

However, she understood that if I wasn't already out, I would get out if she needed me to. I'd driven the forty-five-minute drive to bring her sour gummies in the middle of the night. I'd do that shit again without an issue.

Anything, Pretty.

I love you. Waiting up.

I love you, too.

That last line was a lie she told often without the intention. I took that as my sign to get my ass out of the door. She wouldn't be able to wait up too long. And if she didn't get to indulge in at least one of her cravings, she'd be crying when morning came because it was possible they would have changed. Sleep was near for her. I could feel it.

I locked up and was on the road within minutes of receiving the text. It wasn't until I got closer to the neighborhood that I stopped at a gas station. The bell dinged over my head upon entrance. I scanned the aisles for her current cravings, making sure to get the brands she favorited. I grabbed a few extras just in case she wanted to revisit some of the snacks she'd devoured the previous week.

"Is that all?" the cashier questioned as she began to scan the items.

"Hopefully, shit. You never know with pregnant women."

"I wonder week after week why you're loading up on snacks. That explains it all." She cackled.

The dinging of the bell caught both of our attention. In walked a very familiar face, one I hadn't gotten even a glimpse of since the day I left with signed divorce papers. Within seven days, he'd vacated the property.

I had it scrubbed clean and removed traces of Vallei's existence in the home before putting it on the market for rental. It didn't take long for a couple to snatch it off the market and sign a two-year lease to secure the rental rate.

"Let me call you back."

Phillip quickly ended the call he was on. His direction changed, and he began heading in my direction instead of toward the aisles.

"Don't step to me, nigga, or it'll be the last fucking step you make," I warned.

"I come in peace, man."

"It's the only way you can come, my nigga."

"I don't have a problem. I don't. I ju—"

"I got a problem solver, so I'm not worried if you do."

"I just wanted to congratulate you and—you know."

I noticed he was still abiding by the restrictions of the

divorce that had been finalized. Speaking Vallei's name in public was forbidden.

"Yeah."

"You opened my eyes to a lot of shit, man. And as fucked up as it was, I just want to tell you thanks. Thanks for opening my eyes so that I could finally get my shit together."

I wasn't sure what response the nigga was itching for, but I didn't have a pep talk or words of encouragement on my dome.

"I don't give a fuck what I helped you do. I hope you die a slow, painful death soon. That's what you deserve for the damage you've done to her heart. Fucking up so that I could luck up was the best thing you've done your whole life, Square.

"Make this the last time you stop me and try to converse. Next time, I'm decking you in your shit. You don't deserve to speak to me in any fashion. When you see me, walk the other way, nigga."

I placed two twenties on the counter and grabbed Vallei's shit.

"God, that guy is always mad," Phillip murmured, but I heard every word.

"'Cause niggas like you are a waste of space," I said over my shoulder as I made my way out of the door.

I wanted that nigga's blood on my hands, but breaking Vallei's heart wasn't an option. Knowing that I'd broken my promises and risked my freedom with a child on the way would crush her.

Nigga, you growing soft, I joked as I slid in my whip.

Love will do that to you. I reasoned.

"Use your head." Malachi's voice invaded my thoughts. He'd made it clear that he wasn't on board with my desire to end that man's life.

"Focus. Don't let it depart." Chem backed his logic.

It was times like these that I wished Makai was home. Instead of trying to talk some sense into me, he'd be asking me when, where, and how I wanted to get the job done.

Bring your ass home, nigga. I thought, pulling into my driveway.

Stepping into the house to the smell of vanilla, brown sugar, and caramel let me know that Vallei had been creating, again, with candles lit all around her. The personal recording studio was possibly the best addition to my home. Creating in comfort opened up so many avenues for her artistry.

With everything I'd gotten from the store, I headed up the stairs and into the bedroom. As expected, my Pretty was fast asleep. The body pillow that she used for a more comfortable sleep was sandwiched between her legs and under her head. She was draped in her favorite attire. One of my shirts and a pair of my briefs.

I slid into bed behind her and pressed my body against hers to let her know that I was here, now. She stirred, grabbing my hand and placing it on her belly. Movement from inside made me smile. My entire world was in my hands.

"I love you, Pretty."
"I love you, Cap."

The end

For additional content featuring Mercer and Vallei, click here.

HUFFINGTON NEWS

Join over 8,000 honorary Huffington residents for monthly broadcasts delivered right to their preferred devices.

Broadcasts include but aren't limited to:

- A beautiful monthly newsletter detailing everything happening in Huffington
- Extensive snippets of upcoming projects (sneak peeks)
- Release day reminders that include links (to remove the guest work from searching for books on Amazon/Ghuffington.com)
- First to hear about surprise releases
- Exclusive discounts + offers for Huffington residents
- A monthly wrap-up detailing everything that has happened in Huffington since the release of the Huffington Newsletter

Ready to become a resident?

Click here.
[https://huffingtonnews.ck.page/4693a79283]

MORE FROM GREY HUFFINGTON

Find the entire collection of Grey Huffington titles below. Titles in the catalog are available in eBook (amazon.com, + ghuffington.com), paperback (ghuffington.com), or audiobook (audible + ghuffington.com) formats.

Syx + the City
Syx + the City 2
Syx Thirty Seven
Syxth Giving
Syx Whole Weeks

Wile + Reckless
Wilde + Relentless
Wilde + Restless

Mr. Intentional
Unearth Me

The Sweetest Revenge
The Sweetest Redemption

Half + Half
The Emancipation of Emoree

Sleigh
Sleigh Squared

The Gifted
Memo
Give her Love. Give her Flowers.

Unbreak Me
Uncover Me

As we Learn
As we Love

Just Wanna Mean the Most to You
Sensitivity
10,000 Hours
Darke Hearts
muse.

Softly
Peace + Quiet
Press Rewind
Jagged Edges
My Person

The Realm of Riot Thimble
Whose Love Story is it Anyway?
Unhand Me

Home*
Blues*
31st*
Now That We're Here.*

Then Let's Fuck About It*
Giving Thanks

A Month of Sundays Ep 1
A Month of Sundays Ep 2
A Month of Sundays Ep 3
Dinner at Ever + Luca's
Saylah
The Mayor's Ball
Elm

THE EISENBERG EFFECT
Luca
Lyric
Ever*
Laike
Baisleigh*
Liam

THE DOMINO EFFECT
Ledge

Halo*
Lawe
Kleuless*

BERKELEY BRED
Malachi
Anna*
Milo
Makai
Glacier*
Mercer
Vallei*

THE GREY LIST
Chemistry "The Chemist"
Egypt
Rather "The Therapist"

\-\-

* signifies the publication is available EXCLUSIVELY
on ghuffington.com.

\-\-

Prefer Audiobooks?

Did you know **there's a library FULL of
audiobooks on ghuffington.com** for the lovers
who listen?

We're building so you can continue to listen to the books you've been hearing good things about. There are currently over 17 audiobooks waiting for you to indulge.

In addition to our audiobook library, we have an audiobook club for those who care to save 40-50% off their audiobooks. **Heard is not mandatory to shop audiobooks but we do recommend taking a look at the perks.**

Audiobooks Available (**exclusively on GHuffington.com**)

Chemistry
Egypt
Ever
Baisleigh
Halo
Kleuless
Anna
Glacier
Vallei (coming soon)
Muse.
Elm.
Sensitivity
The Realm of Riot Thimble
Whose Love Story is it Anyway?
Unhand Me

www.ingramcontent.com/pod-product-compliance
Lightning Source LLC
Chambersburg PA
CBHW011148310726
48973CB00010B/2817

9781964560076